POOR FOLK
THE GAMBLER

FYODOR DOSTOYEVSKY

POOR FOLK
THE GAMBLER

TRANSLATED BY

C. J. HOGARTH

GYAN

Published by

Gyan Publishing House
5, Ansari Road
Daryaganj, New Delhi-110002
Phone: 011-47034999, 9811692060
E-mail: books@gyanbooks.com

Distribution Network
gyanbooks.com
India, USA, Canada, UK, Australia

ISBN: 978-81-212-7819-5 (PB)
First Published, 1915

2nd Impression 2024

Printed at: Gyan Press, Delhi.

POOR FOLK THE GAMBLER
Author: FYODOR DOSTOYEVSKY, TRANSLATOR: C. J. HOGARTH

EVERYMAN, I will go with thee,

and be thy guide,

In thy most need to go by thy side

FYODOR DOSTOYEVSKY

Poor Folk
The Gambler

TRANSLATED BY

C. J. HOGARTH

INTRODUCTION BY

NIKOLAY ANDREYEV, PH.D., M.A.

Lecturer in Slavonic Studies in the University of Cambridge

DENT : LONDON

EVERYMAN'S LIBRARY

DUTTON : NEW YORK

INTRODUCTION

In 1877 Dostoyevsky recorded in his *Diary of a Writer* the circumstances in which he first obtained recognition from the literary celebrities of his day. 'With all my being I felt that this was a solemn moment, a turning point from which there could be no return, something quite new was beginning, something beyond anything I had ever imagined, even in my most fervid dreams. . . . It was the most wonderful moment of my whole life. When I was a convict I remembered it, it gave me courage. Even now I still remember it with profound emotion.'

This 'most wonderful moment' had occurred when Dostoyevsky realized that his talents had been recognized by the leading critic of the period—Vissarion Belinsky. What had led up to this momentous recognition? Dostoyevsky had written his first story, *Poor Folk*. He revised it radically four times. After the last revision in May 1845 he wrote to his brother: 'I took it into my head to alter it yet again. . . . It is now almost twice as good.' A friend, Grigorovich, a writer with whom he was sharing rooms, advised Dostoyevsky to show the manuscript to a publisher—the poet Nekrassov. Nekrassov and Grigorovich started to read the manuscript and became so enthusiastic that they read the whole novel aloud to each other without a break. At four o'clock in the morning, almost weeping with excitement, they burst in on the author to congratulate him. Nekrassov passed on the manuscript to Belinsky, with the words: 'A new Gogol has been born!' Belinsky, we are told, replied dampingly: 'If we're to believe you, new Gogols are always springing up overnight like mushrooms.' When, however, Belinsky had read *Poor Folk* and Dostoyevsky was subsequently introduced to him, the young author was met by a torrent of excited praise and exhortation ending with the words: 'Because you are an artist truth is revealed to you: you have the gift of perceiving the truth—a gift you must treasure. Be true to your vocation and become a great writer.'

But what is so remarkable about the rather slight story, told in letter form, which constitutes *Poor Folk*? What qualities awoke such enthusiasm and gave rise to such accurate prognostications of greatness in highly qualified circles even before it had been published?

Dostoyevsky himself, in the beautiful lyrical article entitled 'Petersburg Dreams in Poetry and Prose', tells of the genesis of this first book. He recalls how as a very young man, having given up his brief military career as an engineer, he was feeling his way towards some form of literary activity (which he originally envisaged in the sphere of drama and in the spirit of Schiller). One 'wintry January evening', when he was walking along the banks of the River Neva, it suddenly came over him that 'the whole world' was 'like some improbable, magical fantasy, like a dream'. The 'ardent imaginings' in which he had previously indulged, the world of romantic heroes, Don Carlos and Posa, faded before a very different 'dream'. 'And a different kind of story began to take shape: dark corners, the heart of a minor official, honest and disinterested, moral and loyal to his superiors, and, together with him, a young girl, ill-treated and sad; and my heart was deeply torn by their story.' This, according to Dostoyevsky, was the origin of the plot of *Poor Folk*. The plot itself, in the opinion of most literary historians, was an immense event in the development of Russian prose. Dostoyevsky had introduced—in the words of the nineteenth-century critic N. N. Strakhov—'a bold and decisive amendment to Gogol', who had been up till then the idol of literary Russia. The 'amendment' consisted in introducing living people into Gogol's world of masks, marionettes, ruthless irony and grotesque. For this experiment, Dostoyevsky selected Gogol's *Overcoat*. In this brilliant short story the great satirist made his hero a caricature of a civil servant—dull, crushed by life, without a word to say for himself—who has to make the most drastic sacrifices in order to be able to buy a new overcoat and, when this is almost immediately stolen from him, dies of grief. In *Poor Folk* Dostoyevsky's hero, Makar Dievushkin, is also a little man—an insignificant, unhappy civil servant: but his dreams are centred not on such symbols of material felicity as the possession of a new winter coat but on his unselfish, inspiring and unrequited love for the girl Varen'ka.[1] Dievushkin reads Gogol's *Overcoat* and reacts with indignation to Gogol's 'libel' on the human race, somewhat naïvely considering that the elements of caricature are applicable directly to himself: 'And why should anyone write such a thing? What's the use of it? Why, it's a malicious book, Varen'ka; it is simply not true to life, because it just couldn't be that a civil servant like that should ever have existed. No, I shall put in a complaint, Varen'ka, I shall put in a formal complaint.' Dostoyevsky's hero admires another story—Pushkin's *The Station-master*.[2] Here, in the character of Pushkin's hero, he sees the reflection of his 'own heart'. There is much in common between the situation in which Dievushkin finds himself and that of the father in Pushkin's story. Both are trying to 'save' a beloved young girl from a seducer. Both are 'thrust aside'. The father takes to drink and dies. Dostoyevsky's hero plunges into 'debauch' and the inference is that he, too, will hardly survive for long his separation from Varen'ka.

The young Dostoyevsky, using Dievushkin as his mouthpiece, appeared as the protagonist of the Pushkin tradition in his attitude to living people. This attitude is an intrinsic part of the natural pathos not only of Dostoyevsky's work but of all Russian nineteenth- and twentieth-century literature with its profound humanity and its heedful compassion towards 'the injured and the insulted'. Against this factual background, Dostoyevsky's famous statement, 'We have all come out from under Gogol's *Overcoat*,' takes on a different meaning from that so frequently and superficially ascribed to it. It is not only the acknowledgment of a debt, but also the

[1] Barbara in C. J. Hogarth's translation.

[2] This story is brilliantly translated by Natalie Duddington and published in Everyman's Library, No. 898.

declaration of Russian literature's emancipation from the 'soullessness' of Gogol and of his school of which the novel *Poor Folk* is the literary refutation.

Multiple quotations could be given to illustrate the underlying polemic with Gogol which runs through Dostoyevsky's story. Perhaps, however, the symbolism inherent in the names which Gogol and Dostoyevsky gave their heroes is in itself sufficient evidence: Gogol's civil servant is called Bashmachkin, a contemptuous derivative of shoe suggesting something whose natural function is to be trodden on, whereas Dostoyevsky's is Makar Dievushkin. The Christian name Makar is associated in a Russian proverb with a man beset by misfortunes; the surname Dievushkin, on the other hand, is associated with tenderness of soul—the folk-lore 'dusha-devitsa' or 'soul-maiden'—and creates the impression that its bearer must have the sensitive and loving soul of a young girl.

Literary historians also point out—with some justification—that Dostoyevsky at the time of writing *Poor Folk* was influenced by the French sociological novel, perhaps particularly by Balzac, whose work he was translating into Russian. Dostoyevsky's novel is of course much more than a pamphlet directed against Gogol; it is also a deliberately tendentious sociological novel which touches on many very actual problems treated in other Russian works of the period, a revival of the sentimental manner, justified by the personality of the hero, a rebuttal of romantic prejudice (the substitution of a simple middle-aged man and his love for the glamour of 'exceptional individuals'), a realistic essay in the depiction of details of everyday life and an affirmation of the absolute value of every human personality.

It was the combination of all these features which so impressed Dostoyevsky's contemporaries when they first read *Poor Folk* in manuscript and which ensured the novel's popularity with later generations.

Poor Folk may be considered as a kind of literary manifesto based on a deliberate struggle for the acceptance of certain literary conventions in Russian prose.

The Gambler is a very different proposition. It is almost an extract from Dostoyevsky's own biography, the bitter fruit of experience retold in the form of a story of two conflicting passions—love and gambling.

On 18th September 1863 Dostoyevsky wrote from Rome to his friend, the critic N. N. Strakhov: 'The plan of my story is getting along quite well, as far as I can judge. . . . The hero is a Russian living abroad. . . . All his vital juices, strength, vigour and boldness have gone into roulette. He's a gambler—but not an ordinary gambler. . . . He is a poet in his own way, but the thing is that he is ashamed of this poetry [gambling] because he is profoundly aware of its ignobility, even though the love of risk sets him up in his own eyes. The whole story is the account of how, for the third year running, he plays at roulette from gaming-house to gaming-house.'

Dostoyevsky emphasizes: 'If *The House of the Dead* captured the attention of the public as a description of convicts, whom no one had described *graphically* before *The House of the Dead*, then this story is bound to attract attention as a graphic and very detailed description of the game of roulette. I think that it may turn out to be quite a good piece of work. After all, *The House of the Dead* was interesting. And I shall endeavour to make this description of a kind of hell, of a scene like that of the "convicts' bath-house" into a real picture.'

At the same time Dostoyevsky wanted to describe 'the contemporary state of the Russian abroad' who, because he 'has no reason for existence in Russia', wastes his strength on pointless passions.

The first draft of the novel was made then and there 'on scraps of paper'. But the book was actually written in October 1866 when, in the course of a month, the writer dictated the whole novel. (The young lady who took the dictation was Anna Grigor'evna Snitkina, who became Dostoyevsky's second wife in February of the following year.)

Dostoyevsky's biographers have now established quite definitely that the heroine of *The Gambler*, the proud and imperious beauty Polina, is in many ways a picture of

Appolinaria Suslova, who served to a greater or lesser degree as the prototype of all Dostoyevsky's 'infernal heroines'.

Suslova was a young authoress, a convinced advocate of emancipation for women, and a contributor to Dostoyevsky's journal *Time*. Dostoyevsky fell in love with her and she became his mistress, probably in 1861, but Suslova was bored by his passion and, in 1863, left for Paris; Dostoyevsky followed her but, on the way, in Wiesbaden, he yielded for the first time to the obsession with roulette which was to prove his most ruinous pastime. On 26th August he arrived in Paris, where he learnt that Suslova had become enamoured of a medical student who had already abandoned her. Dostoyevsky took on the role of platonic friend and comforter and they set out together on a two months' journey through Europe in a turgid atmosphere of suppressed passion and desperate gambling fever. Dostoyevsky met Suslova once again in Wiesbaden in 1865, but his 'fatal passion' for her continued to haunt him for many years—even after his second marriage.

Suslova's diary and Dostoyevsky's letters of this period confirm the authenticity of many details which appear in *The Gambler*. The autobiographical element is very marked, and in this, perhaps, lies the chief interest of the work. There are, however, other significant features in the structure of the novel. The story is made up of rather superficial intrigues, not very profound but effectively sensational, which combine to expose the emptiness of the life of 'Russians abroad' and thus lend the novel a certain socio-historical interest. Dostoyevsky also lavishes much attention on the characterization of 'the national traits' of his personages. It may be that certain features of Dostoyevsky the journalist, the author of the more chauvinistic pages of *The Diary of a Writer*, are already in evidence in these malevolent portraits of the French, whom the narrator detests, and of the Germans and Poles, whom he despises. Only the Englishman Mr Astley finds favour in his eyes, and it seems therefore natural that he should be chosen to reveal 'the secret' that Polina, in her heart of hearts, loves and has always loved the 'Gambler'. The Russians themselves, however, do not escape sharp criticism and reproach. 'Russians are endowed with too great a profusion and variety of talents,' muses the hero—and in the meantime Russian ability founders uselessly in a morass of vain passions.

Various motifs are interwoven in *The Gambler* but the central theme of the novel is the irreconcilability of the hero's two passionate obsessions, love and gambling. His inability to resist the fascination of the gaming tables in order to devote himself whole-heartedly to the tragically complicated affairs of the proud and demanding Polina arouses in her that 'love-hatred' which Dostoyevsky was to depict with ever deepening psychological insight as the dominating emotion of the 'infernal' heroines of his later novels.

NIKOLAY ANDREYEV.

1962.

SELECT BIBLIOGRAPHY

COLLECTED WORKS. *The Novels of Dostoevsky*, translated by Constance Garnett, 12 vols., 1912–20.

SEPARATE WORKS (titles in English; dates of first Russian editions). *Poor Folk*, 1846 (trans. L. Milman, 1894); *The Double*, 1846; *The Family Friend*, 1859; *Memoirs from the House of the Dead*, 1861–2 (trans. H. S. Edwards, 1888; Jessie Coulson, 1956); *Summer Impressions*, 1863 (trans. K. Fitzlyon); *Letters from the Underworld*, 1864; *Crime and Punishment*, 1866 (trans. D. Magarshack, 1951; A. Kropotkin, 1953, Jessie Coulson, 1953); *The Gambler*, 1866; *The Idiot*, 1868 (trans. F. Whishaw, 1887; D. Magarshack, 1955); *The Eternal Husband*, 1870; *The Possessed*, 1871–2 (trans. Constance Garnett, 1931); *The Raw Youth*, 1875; *An Author's Diary*, 1876–7 (trans. B. Brasol, 1949); *The Brothers Karamazov*, 1879–80.

The three suppressed chapters of *The Possessed* were published (in translation by S. S. Koteliansky and Virginia Woolf) as *Stavrogin's Confession*, 1922.

LETTERS. *Letters of F. M. Dostoevsky to his Family and Friends*, trans. Ethel Colbourne Mayne, 1914, 1917, 1961, with an Introduction by A. Yarmolinsky; *New Dostoevsky Letters*, trans. S. S. Koteliansky, 1929; *Letters of Dostoevsky to his Wife*, trans. E. Hill and D. Mudie, 1930.

BIOGRAPHY AND CRITICISM. J. A. T. Lloyd, *A Great Russian Realist*, 1912; E. A. Soloviev, *Dostoyevsky: his Life and Literary Activity*, 1916; J. Lavrin, *Dostoyevsky and his Creation*, 1920; A. Dostoyevskaya, *Feodor*

Dostoyevsky: a Study, 1921; J. Middleton Murry, *Feodor Dostoyevsky*, 1923; Hermann Hesse, *In Sight of Chaos*, 1923; A. Gide, *Dostoyevsky*, 1925; A. J. Meier-Graefe, *Dostoyevsky, the Man and his Work*, 1928; E. H. Carr, *Dostoyevsky, 1821–1881*, 1931; N. A. Berdyaev, *Dostoyevsky, an Interpretation*, 1934; A. Yarmolinsky, *Dostoyevsky: a Life*, 1934; G. Abraham, *Dostoyevsky*, 1936; Z. Maurina, *A Prophet of the Soul*, 1940; E. J. Simmons, *Dostoyevsky*, 1940; I. Roe, *The Breath of Corruption. An Interpretation of Dostoyevsky*, 1946; H. Troyat, *The Firebrand*, 1946; S. Freud, *Dostoyevsky and Parricide*, 1947; S. Mackiewicz, *Dostoyevsky*, 1947; J. C. Powys, *Dostoyevsky*, 1947; L. A. Zander, *Dostoyevsky*, 1948; R. Curle, *Characters of Dostoyevsky*, 1950; C. M. Woodhouse, *Dostoievsky. A Biography*, 1951; V. Ivanov, *Freedom and the Tragic Life. A Study in Dostoyevsky*, 1952; C. E. Passage, *Dostoyevsky the Adaptor*, 1954; M. Slonim, *Three Loves of Dostoyevsky*, 1957; V. Seduro, *Dostoyevski in Russian Literary Criticism*, 1957; R. E. Matlaw, *The Brothers Karamazov. Novelistic Technique*, 1957; R. L. Jackson, *Dostoyevsky's Underground Man in Russian Literature*, 1958; G. Steiner, *Dostoyevsky or Tolstoy*, 1959; R. Payne, *Dostoyevsky, a Human Portrait*, 1961; P. D. Westbrook, *The Greatness of Man: an Essay on Dostoyevsky and Whitman*, 1961; D. Magarshack, *Dostoyevsky: A Life*, 1962; R. L. Jackson, *Dostoyevsky's Quest for Form*, 1966.

SEE ALSO: K. Waliszewski, *A History of Russian Literature*, 1897; A. Brückner, *A Literary History of Russia*, 1908; Maurice Baring, *Landmarks in Russian Literature*, 1910; E.-M. de Vogüé, *The Russian Novel*, 1913; P. Kropotkin, *Russian Literature, Ideals and Realities*, 1916; Maurice Baring, *An Outline of Russian Literature*, 1929; Ivar Spectar, *The Golden Age of Russian Literature*, 1943; J. Lavrin, *An Introduction to the Russian Novel*, 1945; R. Hare, *Russian Literature from Pushkin to the Present Day*, 1947; D. S. Mirsky, *A History of Russian Literature*, 1949; M. Slonim, *The Epic of Russian Literature*, 1950; V. Zenkovsky, *A History of Russian Philosophy*, 1953; V. Zenkovsky, *Russian Thinkers and Europe*, 1953; M. Slonim, *An Outline of Russian Literature*, 1958.

BIBLIOGRAPHICAL SURVEY. H. Muchnic, 'Dostoyevsky's English Reputation, 1881–1936,' in *Smith College Studies in Modern Languages*, xx, 3/4, 1938.

CONTENTS

POOR FOLK

April 8th.

MY DEAREST BARBARA ALEXIEVNA,—How happy I was last night—how immeasurably, how impossibly happy! That was because for once in your life you had relented so far as to obey my wishes. At about eight o'clock I awoke from sleep (you know, my beloved one, that I always like to sleep for a short hour after my work is done)—I awoke, I say, and, lighting a candle, prepared my paper to write, and trimmed my pen. Then suddenly, for some reason or another, I raised my eyes—and felt my very heart leap within me! For you had understood what I wanted, you had understood what my heart was craving for. Yes, I perceived that a corner of the curtain in your window had been looped up and fastened to the cornice as I had suggested should be done; and it seemed to me that your dear face was glimmering at the window, and that you were looking at me from out of the darkness of your room, and that you were thinking of me. Yet how vexed I felt that I could not distinguish your sweet face clearly! For there was a time when you and I could see one another without any difficulty at all. Ah me, but old age is not always a blessing, my beloved one! At this very moment everything is standing awry to my eyes, for a man needs only to work late overnight in his writing of something or other for, in the morning, his eyes to be red, and the tears to be gushing from them in a way that makes him ashamed to be seen before strangers. However, I was able to picture to myself your beaming smile, my angel—your kind, bright smile; and in my heart there lurked just such a feeling as on the occasion when I first kissed you, my little Barbara. Do you remember that, my darling? Yet somehow you seemed to be threatening me with your tiny finger. Was it so, little wanton? You must write and tell me about it in your next letter.

But what think you of the plan of the curtain, Barbara? It is a charming one, is it not? No matter whether I be at work, or about to retire to rest, or just awaking from sleep, it enables me to know that *you* are thinking of me, and remembering me—that *you* are both well and happy. Then when you lower the curtain it means that it is time that I, Makar Alexievitch, should go to bed; and when again you raise the curtain it means that you are saying to me, "Good morning," and asking me how I am, and whether I have slept well. "As for myself," adds the curtain, "I am altogether in good health and spirits, glory be to God!" Yes, my heart's delight, you see how easy a plan it was to devise, and how much writing it will save us! It is a clever plan, is it not? And it was my own invention, too! Am I not cunning in such matters, Barbara Alexievna?

Well, next let me tell you, dearest, that last night I slept better and more soundly than I had ever hoped to do, and that I am the more delighted at the fact in that, as you know, I had just settled into a new lodging—a circumstance only too apt to keep one from sleeping! This morning, too, I arose (joyous and full of love) at cockcrow. How good seemed everything at that hour, my darling! When I opened my window I could see the sun shining, and hear the birds singing, and smell the air laden with scents of spring. In short, all nature was awaking to life again. Everything was in consonance with my mood; everything seemed fair and spring-like. Moreover, I had a fancy that I should fare well to-day. But my whole thoughts were bent upon you. "Surely," thought I, "we mortals who dwell in pain and sorrow might with reason envy the birds of heaven which know not either!" And my other thoughts were similar to these. In short, I gave myself up to fantastic comparisons. A little book which I have says the same kind of thing in a variety of ways. For instance, it says that one may have many, many fancies, my Barbara—that as soon as the spring comes one's thoughts become uniformly pleasant and sportive and witty, for the reason that, at that season, the mind inclines readily to tenderness, and the world takes on a more roseate hue. From that little book of mine I have culled the following passage, and written it down for you to see. In particular does the author express a longing similar to my own where he writes:

> "Why am I not a bird free to seek its quest?"

And he has written much else, God bless him!

But tell me, my love—where did you go for your walk this morning? Even before I had started for the office you had taken flight from your room, and passed through the courtyard—yes, looking as vernal-like as a bird in spring. What rapture it gave me to see you! Ah, little Barbara, little Barbara, you must never give way to grief, for tears are of no avail, nor sorrow. I know this well—I know it of my own experience. So do you rest quietly until you have a little regained your health. But how is our good Thedora? What a kind heart she has! You write that she is now living with you, and that you are satisfied with what she does. True, you say that she is inclined to grumble, but do not mind that, Barbara. God bless her, for she is an excellent soul!

But what sort of an abode have *I* lighted upon, Barbara Alexievna? What sort of a tenement, do you think, is this? Formerly, as you know, I used to live in absolute stillness—so much so that if a fly took wing it could plainly be heard buzzing. Here, however, all is turmoil and shouting and clatter. The *plan* of the tenement you know already. Imagine a long corridor, quite dark, and by no means clean. To the right a dead wall, and to the left a row of doors stretching as far as the line of rooms extends. These rooms are tenanted by different people—by one, by two, or by three lodgers as the case may be, but in this arrangement there is no sort of system, and the place is a perfect Noah's Ark. Most of the lodgers are respectable, educated, and even bookish people. In particular they include a tchinovnik (one of the literary staff in some government department), who is so well-read that he can expound Homer or any other author—in fact, *anything*, such a man of talent is he! Also, there are a couple of officers (for ever playing cards), a midshipman, and an English tutor. But, to amuse you, dearest, let me describe these people more categorically in my next letter, and tell you in detail about their lives. As for our landlady, she is a dirty little old woman who always walks about in a dressing-gown and slippers, and never ceases to shout at Theresa. I myself live in the kitchen—or, rather, in a small room which forms part of the kitchen. The latter is a very large, bright, clean, cheerful apartment with three windows in it, and a partition-wall which, running outwards from the front wall, makes a sort of little den, a sort of extra room, for myself. Everything in this den is comfortable and convenient, and I have, as I say, a window to myself. So much for a description of my dwelling-place. Do not think, dearest, that in all this there is any hidden intention. The fact that I live in the kitchen merely means that I live behind the partition wall in that apartment—that I live quite alone, and spend my time in a quiet fashion compounded of trifles. For furniture I have provided myself with a bed, a table, a chest of drawers, and two small chairs. Also, I have suspended an ikon. True, better rooms *may* exist in the world than this—much better rooms; yet *comfort* is the chief thing. In fact I have made all my arrangements for comfort's sake alone; so do not for a moment imagine that I had any other end in view. And since your window happens to be just opposite to mine; and since the courtyard between us is narrow, and I can see you as you pass,—why, the result is that this miserable wretch will be able to live at once more happily and with less outlay. The dearest room in this house costs, with board, thirty-five roubles—more than my purse could well afford; whereas *my* room costs only twenty-four, though formerly I used to pay thirty, and so had to deny myself many things (I could drink tea but seldom, and *never* could indulge in tea and sugar as I do now). But, somehow, I do not like having to go without tea, for every one else here is respectable, and the fact makes me ashamed. After all, one drinks tea largely to please one's fellow men, Barbara, and to give oneself tone and an air of gentility (though, of myself, I care little about such things, for I am not a man of the finicking sort).

Yet think you that, when all things needful—boots and the rest—have been paid for, much will remain? Yet I ought not to grumble at my salary,—I am quite satisfied with it; it is sufficient. It has sufficed me now for some years, and, in addition, I receive certain gratuities.

Well, good-bye, my darling. I have bought you two little pots of geraniums—quite cheap little pots, too—as a present. Perhaps you would also like some mignonette? Mignonette it shall be if only you will write to inform me of everything in detail. Also, do not misunderstand the fact that I have taken this room, my dearest. Convenience and nothing else, has made me do so. The snugness of the place has caught my fancy. Also, I shall be able to save money here, and to hoard it against the future. Already I have saved a little money as a beginning. Nor must you despise me because I am such an insignificant old fellow that a fly could break me with its wing. True, I am not a swash-buckler; but perhaps there may also abide in me the spirit which should pertain to every man who is at once resigned and sure of himself. Good-bye, then, again, my angel. I have now covered close upon a whole two sheets of notepaper, though I ought long ago to have been starting for the office. I kiss your hands, and remain ever your devoted slave, your faithful friend,

MAKAR DIEVUSHKIN.

P.S.—One thing I beg of you above all things—and that is, that you will answer this letter as *fully* as possible. With the letter I send you a packet of bon-bons. Eat them for your health's sake, nor, for the love of God, feel any uneasiness about me. Once more, dearest one, good-bye.

April 8th.

MY BELOVED MAKAR ALEXIEVITCH,—Do you know, I must quarrel with you. Yes, good Makar Alexievitch, I really *cannot* accept your presents, for I know what they must have cost you—I know to what privations and self-denial they must have led. How many times have I not told you that I stand in need of *nothing*, of absolutely *nothing*, as well as that I shall never be in a position to recompense you for all the kindly acts with which you have loaded me? Why, for instance, have you sent me geraniums? A little sprig of balsam would not have mattered so much: but geraniums! Only have I to let fall an unguarded word—for example, about geraniums—and at once you buy me some! How much they must have cost you! Yet what a charm there is in them, with their flaming petals! Wherever did you get these beautiful plants? I have set them in my window as the most conspicuous place possible, while on the floor I have placed a bench for my other flowers to stand on (since you are good enough to enrich me with such presents). Unfortunately, Thedora, who, with her sweeping and polishing, makes a perfect sanctuary of my room, is not over-pleased at the arrangement. But why have you sent me also bon-bons? Your letter tells me that something special is on foot with you, for I find in it so much about paradise and spring and sweet odours and the songs of birds. Surely, thought I to myself when I received it, this is as good as poetry! Indeed, verses are the only thing that your letter lacks, Makar Alexievitch. And what tender feelings I can read in it—what roseate-coloured fancies! To the curtain, however, I had never given a thought. The fact is that when I moved the flower-pots it *looped itself* up. There now!

Ah, Makar Alexievitch, you neither speak of nor give any account of what you have spent upon me. You hope thereby to deceive me, to make it seem as though the cost always falls upon you alone, and that there is nothing to conceal. Yet I *know* that for my sake you deny yourself necessaries. For instance, what has made you go and take the room which you have done, where you will be worried and disturbed, and where you have neither elbow-space nor comfort—you who love solitude, and never like to have any one near you? To judge from your salary, I should think that you might well live in greater ease than *that*. Also, Thedora tells me that your circumstances used to be much more affluent than they are at present. Do you wish, then, to persuade me that your whole existence has been passed in loneliness and want and gloom, with never a cheering word to help you, nor a seat in a friend's chimney-corner? Ah, kind comrade, how my heart aches for you! But do not overtask your health, Makar Alexievitch. For instance, you say that your eyes are over-weak for you to go on writing in your office by candle-light. Then why do so? I am sure that your official superiors do not need to be convinced of your diligence!

Once more I implore you not to waste so much money upon me. I know how much you love me, but I also know that you are not rich. . . . This morning I too rose in good spirits. Thedora had long been at work, and it was time that I too should bestir myself. Indeed, I was yearning to do so, so I went out for some silk, and then sat down to my labours. All the morning I felt light-hearted and cheerful. Yet now my thoughts are once more dark and sad—once more my heart is ready to sink.

Ah, what is going to become of me? What will be my fate? To have to be so uncertain as to the future, to have to be unable to foretell what is going to happen, distresses me deeply. Even to look back at the past is horrible, for it contains sorrow that breaks my very heart at the thought of it. Yes, a whole century in tears could I spend because of the wicked people who have wrecked my life!

But dusk is coming on, and I must set to work again. Much else should I have liked to write to you, but time is lacking, and I must hasten. Of course, to write this letter is a pleasure enough, and could never be wearisome; but why do you not come to see me in person? Why do you not, Makar Alexievitch? You live so close to me, and at least *some* of your time is your own. I pray you, come. I have just seen Theresa. She was looking so ill, and I felt so sorry for her, that I gave her twenty kopecks. I am almost falling asleep. Write to me, in fullest detail, both concerning your mode of life, and concerning the people who live with you, and concerning how you fare with them. I should so like to know! Yes, you *must* write again. To-night I have purposely looped the curtain up. Go to bed early, for, last night, I saw your candle burning until nearly midnight. Good-bye! I am now feeling sad and weary. Ah that I should have to spend such days as this one has been. Again good-bye.—Your friend,

BARBARA DOBROSELOVA.

April 8th.

MY DEAREST BARBARA ALEXIEVNA,—To think that a day like this should have fallen to my miserable lot! Surely you are making fun of an old man? . . . However, it was my own fault—my own fault entirely. One ought not to grow old holding a lock of Cupid's hair in one's hand. Naturally one is misunderstood. . . . Yet man is sometimes a very strange being. By all the Saints, he will talk of doing things, yet leave them undone, and remain looking the kind of fool from whom may the Lord preserve us! . . . Nay, I am not angry, my beloved; I am only vexed to think that I should have written to you in such stupid, flowery phraseology. To-day I went hopping and skipping to the office, for my heart was under your influence, and my soul was keeping holiday, as it were. Yes, everything seemed to be going well with me. Then I betook myself to my work. But with what result? I gazed around at the old familiar objects, at the old familiar grey and gloomy objects. They looked just the same as before. Yet *were* those the same inkstains, the same tables and chairs, that I had hitherto known? Yes, they *were* the same, exactly the same: so why should I have gone off riding on Pegasus back? Whence had that mood arisen? It had arisen from the fact that a certain sun had beamed upon me, and turned the sky to blue. But why so? Why is it, sometimes, that sweet odours seem to be blowing through a courtyard where nothing of the sort can be? They must be born of my foolish fancy, for a man may stray so far into sentiment as to forget his immediate surroundings, and to give way to the superfluity of fond ardour with which his heart is charged. On the other hand, as I walked home from the office at nightfall my feet seemed to lag, and my head to be aching. Also, a cold wind seemed to be blowing down my back (enraptured with the spring, I had gone out clad only in a thin overcoat). Yet you have misunderstood my sentiments, dearest. They are altogether different to what you suppose. It is a purely paternal feeling that I have for you. I stand towards you in the position of a relative who is bound to watch over your lonely orphanhood. This I say in all sincerity, and with a single purpose, as any kinsman might do. For, after all, I *am* a distant kinsman of yours—the seventh drop of water in the pudding, as the proverb has it—yet still a kinsman, and at the present time your nearest relative and protector, seeing that where you had the right to look for help and protection you found only treachery and insult. As for poetry, I may say that I consider it unbecoming for a man of my years to devote his faculties to the making of verses. Poetry is rubbish. Even boys at school ought to be whipped for writing it.

Why do you write thus about "comfort" and "peace" and the rest? I am not a fastidious man, nor one who requires much. Never in my life have I been so comfortable as now. Why, then, should I complain in my old age? I have enough to eat, I am well dressed and booted. Also, I have my diversions. You see, I am not of noble blood. My father himself was not a gentleman; he and his family had to live even more plainly than I do. Nor am I a milksop. Nevertheless, to speak frankly, I do not like my present abode so much as I used to like my old one. Somehow the latter seemed more cosy, dearest. Of course, this room *is* a good one enough; in fact, in *some* respects it is the more cheerful and interesting of the two. I have nothing to say against it—no. Yet I miss the room that used to be so familiar to me. Old lodgers like myself soon grow as attached to our chattels as to a kinsman. My old room was such a snug little place! True, its walls resembled those of any other room—I am not speaking of that: the point is that the recollection of them seems to haunt my mind with sadness. Curious that recollections should be so mournful! Even what in that room used to vex me and inconvenience me now looms in a purified light, and figures in my imagination as a thing to be desired. We used to live there so quietly—I and an old landlady who is now dead! How my heart aches to remember her, for she was a good woman, and never overcharged for her rooms. Her whole time was spent in making patchwork quilts with knitting-needles that were an arshin[1] long. Oftentimes we shared the same candle and board. Also she had a granddaughter, Masha—a girl who was then a mere baby, but must now be a girl of thirteen. This little piece of mischief, how she used to make us laugh the day long! We lived together, a happy family of three. Often of a long winter's evening we would first have tea at the big round table, and then betake ourselves to our work; the while that, to amuse the child and to keep her out of mischief, the old lady would set herself to tell stories. What stories they were!—though stories less suitable for a child than for a grown-up, educated person. My word! Why, I myself have sat listening to them, as I smoked my pipe, until I have forgotten about work altogether. And then, as the story grew grimmer, the little child, our little bag of mischief, would grow thoughtful in proportion, and clasp her rosy cheeks in her tiny hands, and, hiding her face, press closer to the old landlady. Ah, how I loved to see her at those moments! As one gazed at her one would fail to notice how the candle was flickering, or how the storm was swishing the snow about the courtyard. Yes, that was a goodly life, my Barbara, and we lived it for nearly twenty years. . . . How my tongue does carry me away! Maybe the subject does not interest you, and I myself find it a not over-easy subject to recall—especially at the present time. Darkness is falling, and Theresa is busying herself with something or another. My head and my back are aching, and even my thoughts seem to be in pain, so strangely do they occur. Yes, my heart is sad to-day, Barbara. . . . What is it you have written to me? "Why do you not come *in person* to see me?" Dear one, what would people say? I

[1] An ell.

should have but to cross the courtyard for people to begin noticing us, and asking themselves questions. Gossip and scandal would arise, and there would be read into the affair quite another meaning than the real one. No, little angel, it were better that I should see you to-morrow at Vespers. That will be the better plan, and less hurtful to us both. Nor must you chide me, beloved, because I have written you a letter like this (reading it through, I see it to be all odds and ends); for I am an old man now, dear Barbara, and an uneducated one. Little learning had I in my youth, and things refuse to fix themselves in my brain when I try to learn them anew. No, I am not skilled in letter-writing, Barbara, and, without being told so, or any one laughing at me for it, I know that, whenever I try to describe anything with more than ordinary distinctness, I fall into the mistake of talking sheer rubbish. . . . I saw you at your window to-day—yes, I saw you as you were drawing down the blind! Good-bye, good-bye, little Barbara, and may God keep you! Good-bye, my own Barbara Alexievna!—Your sincere friend,

MAKAR DIEVUSHKIN.

P.S.—Do not think that I could write to you in a *satirical* vein, for I am too old to show my teeth to no purpose, and people would laugh at me, and quote our Russian proverb, "Who diggeth a pit for another one, the same shall fall into it himself."

April 9th.

MY DEAREST MAKAR ALEXIEVITCH,—Are not you, my friend and benefactor, just a little ashamed to repine and give way to such despondency? And surely you are not offended with me? Ah! Though often thoughtless in my speech, I never should have imagined that you would take my words as a jest at your expense. Rest assured that *never* should I make sport of your years or of your character. Only my own levity is at fault; still more, the fact that I am so weary of life.

What will such a feeling not engender? To tell you the truth, I had supposed that *you* were jesting in your letter; wherefore my heart was feeling heavy at the thought that you could feel so displeased with me. Kind comrade and helper, you will be doing me an injustice if for a single moment you ever suspect that I am lacking in feeling or in gratitude towards you. My heart, believe me, is able to appraise at its true worth all that you have done for me by protecting me from my enemies, and from hatred and persecution. Never shall I cease to pray to God for you: and should my prayers ever reach Him and be received of Heaven, then assuredly fortune will smile upon you!

To-day I am not well. By turns I shiver and flush with heat, and Thedora is greatly disturbed about me. . . . Do not scruple to come and see me, Makar Alexievitch. How can it concern other people what you do? You and I are well enough acquainted with each other, and one's own affairs are one's own affairs. Good-bye, Makar Alexievitch, for I have come to the end of all I had to say, and am feeling too unwell to write more. Again I beg of you not to be angry with me, but to rest assured of my constant respect and attachment.—Your humble, devoted servant,

BARBARA DOBROSELOVA.

April 12th.

DEAREST MISTRESS BARBARA ALEXIEVNA,—I pray you, my beloved, to tell me what ails you. Every one of your letters fills me with alarm. On the other hand, in every letter I urge you to be more careful of yourself, and to wrap up yourself warmly, and to avoid going out in bad weather, and to be in all things prudent. Yet you go and disobey me! Ah, little angel, you are a perfect child! I know well that you are as weak as a blade of grass, and that, no matter what wind blows upon you, you are ready to fade. But you *must* be careful of yourself, dearest; you *must* look after yourself better; you *must* avoid all risks, lest you plunge your friends into desolation and despair.

Dearest, you also express a wish to learn the details of my daily life and surroundings. That wish I hasten to satisfy. Let me begin at the beginning, since, by doing so, I shall explain things more systematically. In the first place, on entering this house, one passes into a very bare hall, and thence along a passage to a mean staircase. The reception-room, however, is bright, clean, and spacious, and is lined with redwood and metal-work. But the scullery you would not care to see; it is greasy, dirty, and odoriferous, while the stairs are in rags, and the walls so covered with filth that the hand sticks fast wherever it touches them. Also, on each landing there is a medley of boxes, chairs, and dilapidated wardrobes; while the windows have had most of their panes shattered, and everywhere stand washtubs filled with dirt, litter, eggshells, and fish-bladders. The smell is abominable. In short, the house is not a nice one.

As to the disposition of the rooms, I have described it to you already. True, they are convenient enough, yet every one of them has an *atmosphere*. I do not mean that they smell badly so much as that each of them seems to contain something which gives forth a rank, sickly-sweet odour. At first the impression is an unpleasant one, but a couple of minutes will suffice to dissipate it, for the reason that *everything* here smells—people's clothes, hands, and everything else—and one grows accustomed to the rankness. Canaries, however, soon die in this house. A naval officer here has just bought his fifth. Birds cannot live long in such an air. Every morning, when fish or beef is being cooked, and washing and scrubbing are in progress, the house is filled with steam. Always, too, the kitchen is full of linen hanging out to dry; and since my room adjoins that apartment, the smell from the clothes causes me not a little annoyance. However, one can grow used to anything.

From earliest dawn the house is astir as its inmates rise, walk about, and stamp their feet. That is to say, every one who has to go to work then gets out of bed. First of all, tea is partaken of. Most of the tea-urns belong to the landlady; and since there are not over many of them, we have to wait our turn. Anyone who fails so to do will find his teapot emptied and put away. On the first occasion that was what happened to myself. Well, is there anything else to tell you? Already I have made the acquaintance of the company here. The naval officer took the initiative in calling upon me, and his frankness was such that he told me all about his father, his mother, his sister (who is married to a lawyer of Tula), and the town of Kronstadt. Also, he promised me his patronage, and asked me to come and take tea with him. I kept the appointment in a room where card-playing is continually in progress; and, after tea had been drunk, efforts were made to induce me to gamble. Whether or no my refusal seemed to the company ridiculous I cannot say, but at all events my companions played the whole evening, and were playing when I left. The dust and smoke in the room made my eyes ache. I declined, as I say, to play cards, and was therefore requested to discourse on philosophy; after which no one spoke to me at all—a result which I did not regret. In fact, I have no intention of going there again, since every one is for gambling, and for nothing but gambling. Even the literary tchinovnik gives such parties in his room—though, in his case, everything is done delicately and with a certain refinement, so that the thing has something of a retiring and innocent air.

In passing, I may tell you that our landlady is *not* a nice woman. In fact, she is a regular beldame. You have seen her once, so what do you think of her? She is as lanky as a plucked chicken in consumption, and, with Phaldoni (her servant), constitutes the entire staff of the establishment. Whether or not Phaldoni has any other name I do not know, but at least he answers to this one, and every one calls him by it. A red-haired, swine-jowled, snub-nosed, crooked lout, he is for ever wrangling with Theresa, until the pair nearly come to blows. In short, life is not over pleasant in this place. Never at any time is the household wholly at rest, for always there are people sitting up to play cards. Sometimes, too, certain things are done of which it would be shameful for me to speak. In particular, hardened though I am, it astonishes me that men *with families* should care to live in this Sodom. For example, there is a family of poor folk who have rented of the landlady a room which does not adjoin the other rooms, but is set apart in a corner by itself. Yet what quiet people they are! Not a sound is to be heard from them. The father—he is called Goshkov—is a little grey-headed tchinovnik who, seven years ago, was dismissed the public service, and now walks about in a coat so dirty and ragged that it hurts one to see it. Indeed, it is a worse coat even than mine! Also, he is so thin and frail (at times I meet him in the corridor) that his knees quake under him, his hands and head are tremulous with some disease (God only knows what!), and he so fears and distrusts everybody that he always walks alone. Reserved though I myself am, he is even worse. As for his family, it consists of a wife and three children. The eldest of the latter—a boy—is as frail as his father, while the mother—a woman who, formerly, must have been good looking, and still has a striking aspect in spite of her pallor—goes about in the sorriest of rags. Also I have heard that they are in debt to our landlady, as well as that she is not over kind to them. Moreover I have heard that Gorshkov lost his post through some unpleasantness or other—through a legal suit or process of which I could not exactly tell you the nature. Yes, they certainly *are* poor—O, my God, how poor! At the same time, never a sound comes from their room. It is as though not a soul were living in it. Never does one hear even the children—which is an unusual thing, seeing that children are ever ready to sport and play, and if they fail to do so it is a bad sign. One evening when I chanced to be passing the door of their room, and all was quiet in the house, I heard through the door a sob, and then a whisper, and then another sob, as though somebody within were weeping, and with such subdued bitterness that it tore my heart to hear the sound. In fact, the thought of these poor people never left me all night, and quite prevented me from sleeping.

Well, good-bye, my little Barbara, my little friend beyond price. I have described to you everything to the best of my ability. All to-day you have been in my thoughts; all to-day my heart has been yearning for you.

I happen to know, dearest one, that you lack a warm cloak. To me too these St. Petersburg springs, with their winds and their snow showers, spell death. Good heavens, how the breezes bite one! Do not be angry, beloved, that I should write like this. Style I have not. Would that I had! I write just what wanders into my brain, in the hope that I may cheer you up a little. Of course, had I had a good education, things might have been different; but, as things were, I could not have one. Never did I learn even to do simple sums!—Your faithful and unchangeable friend,

MAKAR DIEVUSHKIN.

April 25th.

MY DEAREST MAKAR ALEXIEVITCH,—To-day I met my cousin Sasha. To see her going to wrack and ruin shocked me terribly. Moreover, it has reached me, through a side wind, that she has been making inquiry for me, and dogging my footsteps, under the pretext that she wishes to pardon me, to forget the past, and to renew our acquaintance. Well, among other things she told me that, whereas you are not a kinsman of mine, she is my nearest relative; that you have no right whatever to enter into family relations with us; and that it is wrong and shameful for me to be living upon your earnings and charity. Also, she said that I must have forgotten all that she did for me, though thereby she saved both myself and my mother from starvation, and gave us food and drink; that for two and a half years we caused her great loss; and, above all things, that she excused us what we owed her. Even my poor mother she did not spare. Would that she, my dead parent, could know how I am being treated! But God knows all about it. . . . Also, Anna declared that it was solely through my own fault that my fortunes declined after she had bettered them; that she is in no way responsible for what then happened; and that I have but myself to blame for having been either unable or unwilling to defend my honour. Great God! *Who*, then, has been at fault? According to Anna, Hospodin[1]

[1] Mr.

Bwikov was only right when he declined to marry a woman who—— But need I say it? It is cruel to hear such lies as hers. What is to become of me I do not know. I tremble and sob and weep. Indeed, even to write this letter has cost me two hours. At least it might have been thought that Anna would have confessed *her* share in the past. Yet see what she says! . . . For the love of God do not be anxious about me, my friend, my only benefactor. Thedora is over apt to exaggerate matters. I am not *really* ill. I have merely caught a little cold. I caught it last night while I was walking to Bolkovo, to hear Mass sung for my mother. Ah, mother, my poor mother! Could you but rise from the grave and learn what is being done to your daughter!

B. D.

May 20th.

MY DEAREST LITTLE BARBARA,—I am sending you a few grapes, which are good for a convalescent person, and strongly recommended by doctors for the allayment of fever. Also, you were saying the other day that you would like some roses; wherefore I now send you a bunch. Are you at all able to eat, my darling?—for that is the chief point which ought to be seen to. Let us thank God that the past and all its unhappiness are gone! Yes, let us give thanks to Heaven for that much! As for books, I cannot get hold of any, except for a book which, written in excellent style, is, I believe, to be had here. At all events people keep praising it very much, and I have begged the loan of it for myself. Should you too like to read it? In this respect, indeed, I feel nervous, for the reason that it is so difficult to divine what your taste in books may be, despite my knowledge of your character. Probably you would like poetry—the poetry of sentiment and of love making? Well, I will send you a book of *my own* poems. Already I have copied out part of the manuscript.

Everything with me is going well; so pray do not be anxious on my account, beloved. What Thedora told you about me was sheer rubbish. Tell her from me that she has not been speaking the truth. Yes, do not fail to give this mischief-maker my message. It is not the case that I have gone and sold a new uniform. Why should I do so, seeing that I have forty roubles of salary still to come to me? Do not be uneasy, my darling. Thedora is a vindictive woman—merely a vindictive woman. We shall yet see better days. Only do you get well, my angel—only do you get well, for the love of God, lest you grieve an old man. Also, who told you that I was looking thin? Slanders again—nothing but slanders! I am as healthy as could be, and have grown so fat that I am ashamed to be so sleek of paunch. Would that *you* were equally healthy! . . . Now good-bye, my angel. I kiss every one of your tiny fingers, and remain ever your constant friend,

MAKAR DIEVUSHKIN.

P.S.—But what is this, dearest one, that you have written to me? Why do you place me upon such a pedestal? Moreover, how could I come and visit you frequently? How, I repeat? Of course, I *might* avail myself of the cover of night; but, alas! the season of the year is what it is, and includes no night time to speak of. In fact, although, throughout your illness and delirium, I scarcely left your side for a moment, I cannot think how I contrived to do the many things that I did. Later, I ceased to visit you at all, for the reason that people were beginning to notice things, and to ask me questions. Yet, even so, a scandal has arisen. Theresa I trust thoroughly, for she is not a talkative woman; but consider how it will be when the truth comes out in its entirety! What *then* will folk not say and think? Nevertheless, be of good cheer, my beloved, and regain your health. When you have done so we will contrive to arrange a *rendezvous* out of doors.

June 1st.

MY BELOVED MAKAR ALEXIEVITCH,—So eager am I to do something that will please and divert you in return for your care, for your ceaseless efforts on my behalf—in short, for your love for me—that I have decided to beguile a leisure hour for you by delving into my locker, and extracting thence the manuscript which I send you herewith. I began it during the happier period of my life, and have continued it at intervals since. So often have you asked me about my former existence—about my mother, about Pokrovski, about my sojourn with Anna Thedorovna, about my more recent misfortunes; so often have you expressed an earnest desire to read the manuscript in which (God knows why) I have recorded certain incidents of my life, that I feel no doubt but that the sending of it will give you sincere pleasure. Yet somehow I feel depressed when I read it, for I seem now to have grown twice as old as I was when I penned its concluding lines. Ah, Makar Alexievitch, how weary I am—how this insomnia tortures me! Convalescence is indeed a hard thing to bear!

B. D.

I

Up to the age of fourteen, when my father died, my childhood was the happiest period of my life. It began very far away from here—in the depths of the province of Tula, where my father filled the position of steward on the vast estates of the Prince P——. Our house was situated in one of the Prince's villages, and we lived a quiet, obscure, but happy life. A gay little child was I—my one idea being ceaselessly to run about the fields and the woods and the garden. No one ever gave me a thought, for my father was always occupied with business affairs, and my mother with her housekeeping. Nor did any one ever give me any lessons—a circumstance for which I was not sorry. At earliest dawn I would hie me to a pond or a copse, or to a hay or a harvest field, where the sun could warm me, and I could roam wherever I liked, and scratch my hands with bushes, and tear my clothes in pieces. For this I used to get blamed afterwards, but I did not care.

Had it befallen me never to quit that village—had it befallen me to remain for ever in that spot—I should always have been happy; but fate ordained that I should leave my birthplace even before my girlhood had come to an end. In short, I was only twelve years old when we removed to St. Petersburg. Ah! how it hurts me to recall the mournful gatherings before our departure, and to recall how bitterly I wept when the time came for us to say farewell to all that I had held so dear! I remember throwing myself upon my father's neck, and beseeching him with tears to stay in the country a little longer; but he bid me be silent, and my mother, adding her tears to mine, explained that business matters compelled us to go. As a matter of fact, old Prince P—— had just died, and his heirs had dismissed my father from his post; whereupon, since he had a little money privately invested in St. Petersburg, he bethought him that his personal presence in the capital was necessary for the due management of his affairs. It was my mother who told me this. Consequently we settled here in St. Petersburg, and did not again move until my father died.

How difficult I found it to grow accustomed to my new life! At the time of our removal to St. Petersburg it was autumn—a season when, in the country, the weather is clear and keen and bright, all agricultural labour has come to an end, the great sheaves of corn are safely garnered in the byre, and the birds are flying hither and thither in clamorous flocks. Yes, at that season the country is joyous and fair, but here in St. Petersburg, at the time when we reached the city, we encountered nothing but rain, bitter autumn frosts, dull skies, ugliness, and crowds of strangers who looked hostile, discontented, and disposed to take offence. However, we managed to settle down—though I remember that in our new home there was much noise and confusion as we set the establishment in order. After this my father was seldom at home, and my mother had few spare moments; wherefore I found myself forgotten.

The first morning after our arrival, when I awoke from sleep, how sad I felt! I could see that our windows looked out upon a drab space of wall, and that the street below was littered with filth. Passers-by were few, and as they walked they kept muffling themselves up against the cold.

Then there ensued days when dullness and depression reigned supreme. Scarcely a relative or an acquaintance did we possess in St. Petersburg, and even Anna Thedorovna and my father had come to loggerheads with one another, owing to the fact that he owed her money. In fact, our only visitors were business callers, and as a rule these came but to wrangle, to argue, and to raise a disturbance. Such visits would make my father look very discontented, and seem out of temper. For hours and hours he would pace the room with a frown on his face and a brooding silence on his lips. Even my mother did not dare address him at these times, while, for my own part, I used to sit reading quietly and humbly in a corner—not venturing to make a movement of any sort.

Three months after our arrival in St. Petersburg I was sent to a boarding-school. Here I found myself thrown among strange people; here everything was grim and uninviting, with teachers continually shouting at me, and my fellow-pupils for ever holding me up to derision, and myself constantly feeling awkward and uncouth. How strict, how exacting was the system! Appointed hours for everything, a common table, ever-insistent teachers! These things simply worried and tortured me. Never from the first could I sleep, but used to weep many a chill, weary night away. In the evenings every one would have to repeat or to learn her lessons. As I crouched over a dialogue or a vocabulary, without daring even to stir, how my thoughts would turn to the chimney-corner at home, to my father, to my mother, to my old nurse, to the tales which the latter had been used to tell! How sad it all was! The memory of the merest trifle at home would please me, and I would think and think how nice things used to be at home. Once more I would be sitting in our little parlour at tea with my parents—in the familiar little parlour where everything was snug and warm! How ardently, how convulsively I would seem to be embracing my mother! Thus I would ponder, until at length tears of sorrow would softly gush forth and choke my bosom, and drive the lessons out of my head. For

I never could master the tasks of the morrow; no matter how much my mistress and fellow-pupils might gird at me, no matter how much I might repeat my lessons over and over to myself, knowledge never came with the morning. Consequently I used to be ordered the kneeling punishment, and given only one meal in the day. How dull and dispirited I used to feel! From the first my fellow-pupils used to tease and deride and mock me whenever I was saying my lessons. Also, they used to pinch me as we were on our way to dinner or tea, and to make groundless complaints of me to the head mistress. On the other hand, how heavenly it seemed when, on Saturday evening, my old nurse arrived to fetch me! How I would embrace the old woman in transports of joy! After dressing me, and wrapping me up, she would find that she could scarcely keep pace with me on the way home, so full was I of chatter and tales about one thing and another. Then, when I had arrived home merry and lighthearted, how fervently I would embrace my parents, as though I had not seen them for ten years. Such a fussing would there be—such a talking and a telling of tales! To every one I would run with a greeting, and laugh, and giggle, and scamper about, and skip for very joy. True, my father and I used to have grave conversations about lessons and teachers and the French language and grammar; yet we were all very happy and contented together. Even now it thrills me to think of those moments. For my father's sake I tried hard to learn my lessons, for I could see that he was spending his last kopeck upon me, and himself subsisting God knows how. Every day he grew more morose and discontented and irritable; every day his character kept changing for the worse. He had suffered an influx of debts, nor were his business affairs prospering. As for my mother, she was afraid even to say a word, or to weep aloud, for fear of still further angering him. Gradually she sickened, grew thinner and thinner, and became taken with a painful cough. Whenever I reached home from school I would find every one low-spirited, and my mother shedding silent tears, and my father raging. Bickering and high words would arise, during which my father was wont to declare that, though he no longer derived the smallest pleasure or relaxation from life, and had spent his last coin upon my education, I had not yet mastered the French language. In short, everything began to go wrong, to turn to unhappiness: and for that circumstance my father took vengeance upon myself and my mother. How he could treat my poor mother so I cannot understand. It used to rend my heart to see her, so hollow were her cheeks becoming, so sunken her eyes, so hectic her face. But it was chiefly around myself that the disputes raged. Though beginning only with some trifle, they would soon go on to God knows what. Frequently even I myself did not know to what they related. Anything and everything would enter into them, for my father would say that I was an utter dunce at the French language; that the head mistress of my school was a stupid, common sort of women who cared nothing for morals; that he (my father) had not yet succeeded in obtaining another post; that Lamonde's Grammar was a wretched book —even a worse one than Zapolski's; that a great deal of money had been squandered upon me; that it was clear that I was wasting my time in repeating dialogues and vocabularies; that I alone was at fault, and that I must answer for everything. Yet this did not arise from any *want of love* for me on the part of my father, but rather from the fact that he was incapable of putting himself in my own and my mother's place. It came of a defect of character.

All these cares and worries and disappointments tortured my poor father until he became moody and distrustful. Next he began to neglect his health: with the result that, catching a chill, he died, after a short illness, so suddenly and unexpectedly that for a few days we were almost beside ourselves with the shock —my mother, in particular, lying for a while in such a state of torpor that I had fears for her reason. The instant my father was dead creditors seemed to spring up out of the ground, and to assail us *en masse*. Everything that we possessed had to be surrendered to them, including a little house which my father had bought six months after our arrival in St. Petersburg. How matters were finally settled I do not know, but we found ourselves roofless, shelterless, and without a copper. My mother was grievously ill, and of means of subsistence we had none. Before us there loomed only ruin, sheer ruin. At the time I was fourteen years old. Soon afterwards Anna Thedorovna came to see us, saying that she was a lady of property and our relative; and this my mother confirmed—though, true, she added that Anna was only a very *distant* relative. Anna had never taken the least notice of us during my father's lifetime, yet now she entered our presence with tears in her eyes, and an assurance that she meant to better our fortunes. Having condoled with us on our loss and destitute position, she added that my father had been to blame for everything, in that he had lived beyond his means, and taken upon himself more than he was able to perform. Also, she expressed a wish to draw closer to us, and to forget old scores; and when my mother explained that, for her own part, she harboured no resentment against Anna, the latter burst into tears, and, hurrying my mother away to church, then and there ordered Mass to be said for the "dear departed," as she called my father. In this manner she effected a solemn reconciliation with my mother.

Next, after long negotiations and vacillations, coupled with much vivid description of our destitute position, our desolation, and our helplessness, Anna invited us to pay her (as she expressed it) a "return visit." For this my mother duly thanked her, and considered the invitation for a while; after which, seeing that there was nothing else to be done, she informed Anna Thedorovna that she was prepared gratefully to accept her offer. Ah, how I remember the morning when we removed to Vassilievski Island![1] It was a clear, dry, frosty morning in autumn. My mother could not restrain her tears, and I too felt depressed. Nay, my very heart seemed to be breaking under a strange, undefined load of sorrow. How terrible it all seemed! . . .

[1] A quarter of St. Petersburg.

II

At first—that is to say, until my mother and myself grew used to our new abode—we found living at Anna Thedorovna's both strange and disagreeable. The house was her own, and contained five rooms, three of which she shared with my orphaned cousin, Sasha (whom she had brought up from babyhood), a fourth was occupied by my mother and myself, and the fifth was rented of Anna by a poor student named Pokrovski. Although Anna lived in good style—in far better style than might have been expected—her means and her avocation were conjectural. Never was she at rest; never was she not busy with some mysterious something or other. Also, she possessed a wide and varied circle of friends. The stream of callers was perpetual—although God only knows who they were, or what their business was. No sooner did my mother hear the door-bell ring than off she would carry me to our own apartment. This greatly displeased Anna, who used again and again to assure my mother that we were too proud for our station in life. In fact, she would sulk for hours about it. At the time I could not understand these reproaches, and it was not until long afterwards that I learnt—or rather, I guessed—why eventually my mother declared that she could not go on living with Anna. Yes, Anna was a bad woman. Never did she let us alone. As to the exact motive why she had asked us to come and share her house with her I am still in the dark. At first she was not altogether unkind to us, but, later, she revealed to us her real character—as soon, that is to say, as she saw that we were at her mercy, and had nowhere else to go. Yes, in early days she was quite kind to me—even offensively so, but afterwards I had to suffer as much as my mother. Constantly did Anna reproach us; constantly did she remind us of her benefactions, and introduce us to her friends as poor relatives of hers whom, out of goodness of heart and for the love of Christ, she had received into her bosom. At table, also, she would watch every mouthful that we took;

and if our appetite failed, immediately she would begin as before, and reiterate that we were over-dainty, that we must not assume that riches would mean happiness, and that we had better go and live by ourselves. Moreover, she never ceased to inveigh against my father —saying that he had sought to be better than other people, and thereby had brought himself to a bad end; that he had left his wife and daughter destitute; and that, but for the fact that we had happened to meet with a kind and sympathetic Christian soul, God alone knew where we should have laid our heads, save in the street. What did that woman *not* say? To hear her was not so much galling as disgusting. From time to time my mother would burst into tears; her health grew worse from day to day, and her body was becoming sheer skin and bone. All the while, too, we had to work —to work from morning till night, for we had contrived to obtain some employment as occasional sempstresses. This, however, did not please Anna, who used to tell us that there was no room in her house for a modiste's establishment. Yet we had to get clothes to wear, to provide for unforeseen expenses, and to have a little money at our disposal in case we should some day wish to remove elsewhere. Unfortunately the strain undermined my mother's health, and she became gradually weaker. Sickness, like a cankerworm, was gnawing at her life, and dragging her towards the tomb. Well could I see what she was enduring, what she was suffering. Yes, it all lay open to my eyes.

Day succeeded day, and each day was like the last one. We lived a life as quiet as though we had been in the country. Anna herself grew quieter in proportion as she came to realise the extent of her power over us. In nothing did we dare to thwart her. From her portion of the house our apartment was divided by a corridor, while next to us (as mentioned above) dwelt a certain Pokrovski, who was engaged in teaching Sasha the French and German languages, as well as history and geography —" all the sciences," as Anna used to say. In return for these services he received free board and lodging. As for Sasha, she was a clever, but rude and uncouth, girl of thirteen. On one occasion Anna remarked to my mother that it might be as well if I also were to take some lessons, seeing that my education had been neglected at school; and, my mother joyfully assenting, I joined Sasha for a year in studying under this Pokrovski.

The latter was a poor—a very poor—young man whose health would not permit of his undertaking the regular university course. Indeed, it was only for form's sake that we called him "The Student." He lived in such a quiet, humble, retiring fashion that never a sound reached us from his room. Also, his exterior was peculiar—he moved and walked awkwardly, and uttered his words in such a strange manner that at first I could never look at him without laughing. Sasha was for ever playing tricks upon him—more especially when he was giving us our lessons. But unfortunately, he was of a temperament as excitable as herself. Indeed, he was so irritable that the least trifle would send him into a frenzy, and set him shouting at us, and complaining of our conduct. Sometimes he would even rush away to his room before school hours were over, and sit there for days over his books, of which he had a store that was both rare and valuable. In addition, he acted as teacher at another establishment, and received payment for his services there; and whenever he had received his fees for this extra work he would hasten off and purchase more books.

In time I got to know and like him better, for in reality he was a good, worthy fellow—more so than any of the people with whom we otherwise came in contact. My mother in particular had a great respect for him, and, after herself, he was my best friend. But at first I was just an overgrown hoyden, and joined Sasha in playing the fool. For hours we would devise tricks to anger and distract him, for he looked extremely ridiculous when he was angry, and so diverted us the more (ashamed though I am now to admit it). But once, when we had driven him nearly to tears, I heard him say to himself under his breath, "What cruel children!" and instantly I repented—I began to feel sad and ashamed and sorry for him. I reddened to my ears, and begged him, almost with tears, not to mind us, nor to take offence at our stupid jests. Nevertheless, without finishing the lesson, he closed his book, and departed to his own room. All that day I felt torn with remorse. To think that we two children had forced him, the poor, the unhappy one, to remember his hard lot! And at night I could not sleep for grief and regret. Remorse is said to bring relief to the soul, but it is not so. How far my grief was internally connected with my conceit I do not know, but at least I did not wish him to think me a baby, seeing that I had now reached the age of fifteen years. Therefore, from that day onwards I began to torture my imagination with devising a thousand schemes which should compel Pokrovski to alter his opinion of me. At the same time, being yet shy and reserved by nature, I ended by finding that, in my present position, I could make up my mind to nothing but vague dreams (and such dreams!). However, I ceased to join Sasha in playing the fool, while Pokrovski, for his part, ceased to lose his temper with us so much. Unfortunately this was not enough to satisfy my self-esteem.

At this point I must say a few words about the strangest, the most interesting, the most pitiable human being that I have ever come across. I speak of him now—at this particular point in these memoirs—for the reason that hitherto I had paid him no attention whatever, and began to do so now only because everything connected with Pokrovski had suddenly become of absorbing interest in my eyes.

Sometimes there came to the house a ragged, poorly-dressed, grey-headed, awkward, amorphous—in short, a very strange-looking—little old man. At first glance it might have been thought that he was perpetually ashamed of something—that he had on his conscience something which always made him, as it were, bristle up and then shrink into himself. Such curious starts and grimaces did he indulge in that one was forced to conclude that he was scarcely in his right mind. On arriving he would halt for a while by the window in the hall, as though afraid to enter; until, should any one happen to pass in or out of the door—whether Sasha or myself or one of the servants (to the latter he always resorted the most readily, as being the most nearly akin to his own class)—he would begin to gesticulate and to beckon to that person, and to make various signs. Then, should the person in question nod to him, or call him by name (the recognised token that no other visitor was present, and that he might enter freely), he would open the door gently, give a smile of satisfaction as he rubbed his hands together, and proceed on tiptoe to young Pokrovski's room. This old fellow was none other than Pokrovski's father.

Later I came to know his story in detail. Formerly a civil servant, he had possessed no additional means, and so had occupied a very low and insignificant position in the service. Then, after his first wife (mother of the younger Pokrovski) had died, the widower bethought him of marrying a second time, and took to himself a tradesman's daughter, who soon assumed the reins over everything, and brought the home to rack and ruin, so that the old man was worse off than before. But to the younger Pokrovski fate proved kinder, for a landowner named Bwikov, who had formerly known the lad's father and been his benefactor, took the boy under his protection, and sent him to school. Another reason why this Bwikov took an interest in young Pokrovski was that he had known the lad's dead mother, who, while still a serving-maid, had been befriended by Anna Thedorovna, and subsequently married to the elder Pokrovski. At the wedding Bwikov, actuated by his friendship for Anna, conferred upon the young bride a dowry of five thousand roubles; but whither that money had since disappeared I cannot say. It was from Anna's lips that I heard the story, for the student Pokrovski was never prone to talk about his family affairs. His mother was said to have been very good-looking; wherefore it is the more mysterious why she should have made so poor a match. She died when young—only four years after her espousal.

From school the young Pokrovski advanced to a gymnasium,[1] and thence to the University, where Bwikov (who frequently visited the capital) continued

[1] Secondary school.

to accord the youth his protection. Gradually, however, ill-health put an end to the young man's university course; whereupon Bwikov introduced and personally recommended him to Anna Thedorovna, and he came to lodge with her on condition that he taught Sasha whatever might be required of him.

Grief at the harshness of his wife led the elder Pokrovski to plunge into dissipation, and to remain in an almost permanent condition of drunkenness. Constantly his wife beat him, or sent him to sit in the kitchen; with the result that in time he became so inured to blows and neglect that he ceased to complain. Still not greatly advanced in years, he had nevertheless endangered his reason through evil courses—his only sign of decent human feeling being his love for his son. The latter was said to resemble his dead mother as one pea may resemble another. What recollections, therefore, of the kind helpmeet of former days may not have moved the breast of the poor broken old man to this boundless affection for the boy? Of naught else could the father ever speak but of his son, and never did he fail to visit him twice a week. To come oftener he did not dare, for the reason that the younger Pokrovski did not like these visits of his father's. In fact, there can be no doubt that the youth's greatest fault was his lack of filial respect. Yet the father was certainly rather a difficult person to deal with, for, in the first place, he was extremely inquisitive, while, in the second place, his long-winded conversation and questions—questions of the most vapid and senseless order conceivable—always prevented the son from working. Likewise the old man occasionally arrived there drunk. Gradually, however, the son was weaning his parent from his vicious ways and everlasting inquisitiveness, and teaching the old man to look upon him, his son, as an oracle, and never to speak without that son's permission.

On the subject of his Petinka, as he called him, the poor old man could never sufficiently rhapsodise and dilate. Yet when he arrived to see his son he almost invariably had on his face a downcast, timid expression that was probably due to uncertainty concerning the way in which he would be received. For a long time he would hesitate to enter, and if I happened to be there he would question me for twenty minutes or so as to whether his Petinka was in good health, as well as to the sort of mood he was in, whether he was engaged on matters of importance, what precisely he was doing (writing or meditating), and so on. Then, when I had sufficiently encouraged and reassured the old man, he would make up his mind to enter, and quietly and cautiously open the door. Next he would protrude his head through the chink, and if he saw that his son was not angry, but threw him a nod, he would glide noiselessly into the room, take off his scarf, and hang up his hat (the latter perennially in a bad state of repair, full of holes, and with a smashed brim)—the whole being done without a word or a sound of any kind. Next the old man would seat himself warily on a chair, and, never removing his eyes from his son, follow his every movement, as though seeking to gauge Petinka's state of mind. On the other hand, if the son was not in good spirits, the father would make a note of the fact, and at once get up, saying that he had "only called for a minute or two," that, "having been out for a long walk, and happening at the moment to be passing," he had "looked in for a moment's rest." Then silently and humbly the old man would resume his hat and scarf; softly he would open the door, and noiselessly depart with a forced smile on his face—the better to bear the disappointment which was seething in his breast, the better to help him not to show it to his son.

On the other hand, whenever the son received his father civilly the old man would be struck dumb with joy. Satisfaction would beam in his face, in his every gesture, in his every movement. And if the son deigned to engage in conversation with him, the old man always rose a little from his chair, and answered softly, sympathetically, with something like reverence, while strenuously endeavouring to make use of the most *recherché* (that is to say, the most ridiculous) expressions. But, alas! he had not the gift of words. Always he grew confused, and turned red in the face; never did he know what to do with his hands or with himself. Likewise, whenever he had returned an answer of any kind, he would go on repeating the same in a whisper, as though he were seeking to justify what he had just said. And if he happened to have returned a *good* answer he would begin to preen himself, and to straighten his waistcoat, frockcoat, and tie, and to assume an air of conscious dignity. Indeed, on these occasions he would feel so encouraged, he would carry his daring to such a pitch, that, rising softly from his chair, he would approach the bookshelves, take thence a book, and read over to himself some passage or another. All this he would do with an air of feigned indifference and sangfroid, as though he were free *always* to use his son's books, and his son's kindness were no rarity at all. Yet on one occasion I saw the poor old fellow actually turn pale on being told by his son not to touch the books. Abashed and confused, he, in his awkward hurry, replaced the volume wrong side uppermost; whereupon, with a supreme effort to recover himself, he turned it round with a smile and a blush, as though he were at a loss how to view his own misdemeanour. Gradually, as already said, the younger Pokrovski weaned his father from his dissipated ways by giving him a small coin whenever, on three successive occasions, he (the father) arrived sober. Sometimes, also, the younger man would buy the older one shoes, or a tie, or a waistcoat; whereafter the old man would be as proud of his acquisition as a peacock. Not infrequently, also, the old man would step in to visit ourselves, and bring Sasha and myself gingerbread birds or apples, while talking unceasingly of Petinka. Always he would beg of us to pay attention to our lessons, on the plea that Petinka was a good son, an exemplary son, a son who was in twofold measure a man of learning; after which he would wink at us so quizzingly with his left eye, and twist himself about in such amusing fashion, that we were forced to burst out laughing. My mother had a great liking for him, but he detested Anna Thedorovna—although in her presence he would be quieter than water and lowlier than the earth.

Soon after this I ceased to take lessons of Pokrovski. Even now he thought me a child, a raw schoolgirl, as much as he did Sasha; and this hurt me extremely, seeing that I had done so much to expiate my former behaviour. Of my efforts in this direction no notice had been taken, and the fact continued to anger me more and more. Scarcely ever did I address a word to my tutor between school hours, for I simply could not bring myself to do it. If I made the attempt I only grew red and confused, and rushed away to weep in a corner. How it would all have ended I do not know, had not a curious incident helped to bring about a *rapprochement*. One evening, when my mother was sitting in Anna Thedorovna's room, I crept on tiptoe to Pokrovski's apartment, in the belief that he was not at home. Some strange impulse moved me to do so. True, we had lived cheek by jowl with one another; yet never once had I caught a glimpse of his abode. Consequently my heart beat loudly—so loudly, indeed, that it seemed almost to be bursting from my breast. On entering the room I glanced around me with tense interest. The apartment was very poorly furnished, and bore few traces of orderliness. On table and chairs there lay heaps of books; everywhere were books and papers. Then a strange thought entered my head, as well as, with the thought, an unpleasant feeling of irritation. It seemed to me that my friendship, my heart's affection, meant little to him, for *he* was well-educated, whereas *I* was stupid, and had learnt nothing, and had read not a single book. So I stood looking wistfully at the long bookshelves where they groaned under their weight of volumes. I felt filled with grief, disappointment, and a sort of frenzy. I felt that I *must* read those books, and decided to do so—to read them one by one, and with all possible speed. Probably the idea was that, by learning whatsoever *he* knew, I should render myself more worthy of his friendship. So I made a rush towards the bookcase nearest me, and, without stopping further to consider matters, seized hold of the first dusty tome upon which my hands chanced to alight, and, reddening and growing pale by turns, and trembling with fear and excitement, clasped the stolen book to my breast with the intention of reading it by candle light while my mother lay asleep o' nights.

But how vexed I felt when, on returning to our own room, and hastily turning the pages, only an old, battered worm-eaten Latin work greeted my eyes! Without loss of time I retraced my steps. Just when I was about to replace the book I heard a noise in the corridor outside, and the sound of footsteps approaching. Fumblingly I hastened to complete what I was about, but the tiresome book had become so tightly wedged into its row that, on being pulled out, it caused its fellows to close up too compactly to leave any place for their comrade. To insert the book was beyond my strength; yet still I kept pushing and pushing at the row. At last the rusty nail which supported the shelf (the thing seemed to have been waiting on purpose for that moment!) broke off short; with the result that the shelf descended with a crash, and the books piled themselves in a heap on the floor! Then the door of the room opened, and Pokrovski entered!

I must here remark that he never could bear to have his possessions tampered with. Woe to the person, in particular, who touched his books! Judge, therefore, of my horror when books small and great, books of every possible shape and size and thickness, came tumbling from the shelf, and flew and sprang over the table, and under the chairs, and about the whole room. I would have turned and fled, but it was too late. "All is over!" thought I. "All is over! I am ruined, I am undone! Here have I been playing the fool like a ten-year-old child! What a stupid girl I am! The monstrous fool!"

Indeed, Pokrovski was very angry. "What? Have you not done enough?" he cried. "Are you not ashamed to be for ever indulging in such pranks? Are you *never* going to grow sensible?" With that he darted forward to pick up the books, while I bent down to help him.

"You need not, you need not!" he went on. "You would have done far better not to have entered without an invitation."

Next, a little mollified by my humble demeanour, he resumed in his usual tutorial tone—the tone which he had adopted in his new-found rôle of preceptor:

"When are you going to grow steadier and more thoughtful? Consider yourself for a moment. You are no longer a child, a little girl, but a maiden of fifteen."

Then, with a desire (probably) to satisfy himself that I was no longer a being of tender years, he threw me a glance—but straightway reddened to his very ears. This I could not understand, but stood gazing at him in astonishment. Presently he straightened himself a little, approached me with a sort of confused expression, and haltingly said something—probably it was an apology for not having before perceived that I was now a grown-up young person. But the next moment I understood. What I did I hardly know, save that, in my dismay and confusion, I blushed even more hotly than he had done and, covering my face with my hands, rushed from the room.

What to do with myself for shame I could not think. The one thought in my head was that he had surprised me in his room. For three whole days I found myself unable to raise my eyes to his, but blushed always to the point of weeping. The strangest and most confused of thoughts kept entering my brain. One of them—the most extravagant—was that I should dearly like to go to Pokrovski, and to explain to him the situation, and to make full confession, and to tell him everything without concealment, and to assure him that I had not acted foolishly as a minx, but honestly and of set purpose. In fact, I *did* make up my mind to take this course, but lacked the necessary courage to do it. If I had done so what a figure I should have cut! Even now I am ashamed to think of it.

A few days later my mother suddenly fell dangerously ill. For two days past she had not left her bed, while during the third night of her illness she became seized with fever and delirium. I also had not closed my eyes during the previous night, but now waited upon my mother, sat by her bed, brought her drink at intervals, and gave her medicine at duly appointed hours. The next night I suffered terribly. Every now and then sleep would cause me to nod, and objects grow dim before my eyes. Also, my head was turning dizzy, and I could have fainted for very weariness. Yet always my mother's feeble moans recalled me to myself as I started, momentarily awoke, and then again felt drowsiness overcoming me. What torture it was! I do not know, I cannot clearly remember, but I think that, during a moment when wakefulness was thus contending with slumber, a strange dream, a horrible vision, visited my overwrought brain, and I awoke in terror. The room was nearly in darkness, for the candle was flickering, and throwing stray beams of light which suddenly illuminated the room, danced for a moment on the walls, and then disappeared. Somehow I felt afraid—a sort of horror had come upon me—my imagination had been over-excited by the evil dream which I had experienced, and a feeling of oppression was crushing my heart. . . . I leapt from the chair, and involuntarily uttered a cry—a cry wrung from me by the terrible, torturing sensation that was upon me. Presently the door opened, and Pokrovski entered.

I remember that I was in his arms when I recovered my senses. Carefully seating me on a bench, he handed me a glass of water, and then asked me a few questions—though how I answered them I do not know. "You yourself are ill," he said as he took my hand. "You yourself are *very* ill. You are feverish, and I can see that you are knocking yourself up through your neglect of your own health. Take a little rest. Lie down and go to sleep. Yes, lie down, lie down," he continued without giving me time to protest. Indeed, fatigue had so exhausted my strength that my eyes were closing from very weakness. So I lay down on the bench with the intention of sleeping for half an hour only; but I slept till morning. Pokrovski then awoke me, saying that it was time for me to go and give my mother her medicine.

When the next evening, about eight o'clock, I had rested a little and was preparing to spend the night in a chair beside my mother (fixedly meaning *not* to go to sleep this time), Pokrovski suddenly knocked at the door. I opened it, and he informed me that, since, possibly, I might find the time wearisome, he had brought me a few books to read. I accepted the books, but do not, even now, know what books they were, nor whether I looked into them, despite the fact that I never closed my eyes the whole night long. The truth was that a strange feeling of excitement was preventing me from sleeping, and I could not rest long in any one spot, but had to keep rising from my chair, and walking about the room. Throughout my whole being there seemed to be diffused a kind of elation—of elation at Pokrovski's attentions, at the thought that he was anxious and uneasy about me. Until dawn I pondered and dreamed; and though, I felt sure, Pokrovski would not again visit us that night, I gave myself up to fancies concerning what he might do the following evening.

That evening, when every one else in the house had retired to rest, Pokrovski opened his door, and opened a conversation from the threshold of his room. Although, at this distance of time, I cannot remember a word of what we said to one another, I remember that I blushed, grew confused, felt vexed with myself, and awaited with impatience the end of the conversation—although I myself had been longing for the meeting to take place, and had spent the day in dreaming of it, and devising a string of suitable questions and replies. Yes, that evening saw the first strand in our friendship knitted; and each subsequent night of my mother's illness we spent several hours together. Little by little I overcame his reserve, but found that each of these conversations left me filled with a sense of vexation at myself. At the same time, I could see with secret joy and a sense of proud elation that I was leading him to forget his tiresome books. At last the conversation turned jestingly upon the upsetting of the shelf. The moment was a peculiar one, for it came upon me just when I was in the right mood for self-revelation and candour. In my ardour, my curious phase of exaltation, I found myself led to make a full confession of the fact that I had become wishful to learn, to *know*, something.

since I had felt hurt at being taken for a chit, a mere baby. . . . I repeat that that night I was in a very strange frame of mind. My heart was inclined to be tender, and there were tears standing in my eyes. Nothing did I conceal as I told him about my friendship for him, about my desire to love him, about my scheme for living in sympathy with him, and comforting him, and making his life easier. In return he threw me a look of confusion mingled with astonishment, and said nothing. Then suddenly I began to feel terribly pained and disappointed, for I conceived that he had failed to understand me, or even that he might be laughing at me. Bursting into tears like a child, I sobbed, and could not stop myself, for I had fallen into a kind of fit; whereupon he seized my hand, kissed it, and clasped it to his breast —saying various things, meanwhile, to comfort me, for he was labouring under a strong emotion. Exactly what he said I do not remember—I merely wept and laughed by turns, and blushed, and found myself unable to speak a word for joy. Yet, for all my agitation, I noticed that about him there still lingered an air of constraint and uneasiness. Evidently he was lost in wonder at my enthusiasm and raptures—at my curiously ardent, unexpected, consuming friendship. It may be that at first he was amazed, but that afterwards he accepted my devotion and words of invitation and expressions of interest with the same simple frankness as I had offered them, and responded to them with an interest, a friendliness, a devotion equal to my own, even as a friend or a brother would do. How happy, how warm was the feeling in my heart! Nothing had I concealed or repressed. No, I had bared all to his sight, and each day would see him draw nearer to me.

Truly I could not say what we did not talk about during those painful, yet rapturous, hours when, by the trembling light of a lamp, and almost at the very bedside of my poor sick mother, we kept midnight tryst. Whatsoever first came into our heads we spoke of—whatsoever came riven from our hearts, whatsoever seemed to call for utterance, found voice. And almost always we were happy. What a grievous, yet joyous, period it was—a period grievous and joyous at the same time! To this day it both hurts and delights me to recall it. Joyous or bitter though it was, its memories are yet painful. At least they seem so to me, though a certain sweetness assuaged the pain. So whenever I am feeling heartsick and oppressed and jaded and sad those memories return to freshen and revive me, even as drops of evening dew return to freshen and revive, after a sultry day, the poor faded flower which has long been drooping in the noontide heat.

My mother grew better, but still I continued to spend the nights on a chair by her bedside. Often, too, Pokrovski would give me books. At first I read them merely so as to avoid going to sleep, but afterwards I examined them with more attention, and subsequently with actual avidity, for they opened up to me a new, an unexpected, an unknown, an unfamiliar world. New thoughts, added to new impressions, would come pouring into my heart in a rich flood; and the more emotion, the more pain and labour, it cost me to assimilate these new impressions, the dearer did they become to me, and the more gratefully did they stir my soul to its very depths. Crowding into my heart without giving it time even to breathe, they would cause my whole being to become lost in a wondrous chaos. Yet this spiritual ferment was not sufficiently strong wholly to undo me. For that I was too fanciful, and the fact saved me.

With the passing of my mother's illness the midnight meetings and long conversations between myself and Pokrovski came to an end. Only occasionally did we exchange a few words with one another—words, for the most part, that were of little purport or substance, yet words to which it delighted me to apportion their several meanings, their peculiar secret values. My life had now become full: I was happy—I was quietly, restfully happy. Thus did several weeks elapse. . . .

One day the elder Pokrovski came to see us, and chattered in a brisk, cheerful, garrulous sort of way. He laughed, launched out into witticisms, and, finally, resolved the riddle of his transports by informing us that in a week's time it would be his Petinka's birthday, when, in honour of the occasion, he (the father) meant to don a new jacket (as well as new shoes which his wife was going to buy for him), and to come and pay a visit to his son. In short, the old man was perfectly happy, and gossiped about whatsoever first entered his head.

My lover's birthday! Thenceforward I could not rest by night or day. Whatever might happen, it was my fixed intention to remind Pokrovski of our friendship by giving him a present. But what sort of present? Finally I decided to give him books. I knew that he had long wanted to possess a complete set of Pushkin's works, in the latest edition; so I decided to buy Pushkin. My private fund consisted of thirty roubles, earned by handiwork, and designed eventually to procure me a new dress; but at once I dispatched our cook, old Matrena, to ascertain the price of such an edition. Horrors! The price of the eleven volumes, added to extra outlay upon the binding, would amount to at least *sixty* roubles! Where was the money to come from? I thought and thought, yet could not decide. I did not like to resort to my mother. Of course she would help me, but in that case every one in the house would become aware of my gift, and the gift itself would assume the guise of a recompense—of payment for Pokrovski's labours on my behalf during the past year; whereas I wished to present the gift *alone*, and without the knowledge of any one. For the trouble that he had taken with me I wished to be his perpetual debtor—to make him no payment at all save my friendship. At length I thought of a way out of the difficulty.

I knew that of the hucksters in the Gostinni Dvor one could sometimes buy a book—even one that had been little used and was almost entirely new—for a half of its price, provided that one haggled sufficiently over it; wherefore I determined to repair thither. It so happened that, next day, both Anna Thedorovna and ourselves were in want of sundry articles; and since my mother was unwell and Anna lazy, the execution of the commissions devolved upon me, and I set forth with Matrena.

Luckily I soon chanced upon a set of Pushkin, handsomely bound, and set myself to bargain for it. At first more was demanded than would have been asked of me in a shop; but afterwards—though not without a great deal of trouble on my part, and several feints at departing—I induced the dealer to lower his price, and to limit his demands to ten roubles in silver. How I rejoiced that I had engaged in this bargaining! Poor Matrena could not imagine what had come to me, nor why I so desired to buy books. But, oh horror of horrors! as soon as ever the dealer caught sight of my capital of thirty roubles in notes, he refused to let the Pushkin go for less than the sum he had first named; and though, in answer to my prayers and protestations, he eventually yielded a little, he did so only to the tune of two-and-a-half roubles more than I possessed, while swearing that he was making the concession for my sake alone, since I was "a sweet young lady," and that he would have done so for no one else in the world. To think that only two-and-a-half roubles should still be wanting! I could have wept with vexation. Suddenly an unlooked-for circumstance occurred to help me in my distress.

Not far away, near another table that was heaped with books, I perceived the elder Pokrovski, and a crowd of four or five hucksters plaguing him nearly out of his senses. Each of these fellows was proffering the old man his own particular wares; and while there was nothing that they did not submit for his approval, there was nothing that he wished to buy. The poor old fellow had the air of a man who is receiving a thrashing. What to make of what he was being offered him he did not know. Approaching him, I inquired what he happened to be doing there; whereat the old man was delighted, since he liked me (it may be) no less than he did Petinka.

"I am buying some books, Barbara Alexievna," said he, "I am buying them for my Petinka. It will be his birthday soon, and since he likes books I thought I would get him some."

The old man always expressed himself in a very roundabout sort of fashion, and on the present occasion he was doubly, terribly confused. Of no matter what book he asked the price, it was sure to be one, two, or three roubles. The larger books he could not afford at all; he could only look at them wistfully, fumble their leaves with his finger, turn over the volumes in his hands, and then replace them. "No, no, that is too dear," he would mutter under his breath. "I must go and try somewhere else." Then again he would fall to examining copy-books, collections of poems, and almanacs of the cheaper order.

"Why should you buy things like those?" I asked him. "They are such rubbish!"

"No, no!" he replied. "See what nice books they are! Yes, they *are* nice books!" Yet these last words he uttered so lingeringly that I could see he was ready to weep with vexation at finding the better sorts of books so expensive. Already a little tear was trickling down his pale cheeks and red nose. I inquired whether he had much money on him; whereupon the poor old fellow pulled out his entire stock, wrapped in a piece of dirty newspaper, and consisting of a few small silver coins, with twenty kopecks in copper. At once I seized the lot, and, dragging him off to my huckster, said: "Look here. These eleven volumes of Pushkin are priced at thirty-two-and-a-half roubles, and I have only thirty roubles. Let us add to them these two-and-a-half roubles of yours, and buy the books together, and make them our joint gift." The old man was overjoyed, and pulled out his money *en masse;* whereupon the huckster loaded him with our common library. Stuffing it into his pockets, as well as filling both arms with it, he departed homewards with his prize, after giving me his word to bring me the books privately on the morrow.

Next day the old man came to see his son, and sat with him, as usual, for about an hour; after which he visited ourselves, wearing on his face the most comical, the most mysterious expression conceivable. Smiling broadly with satisfaction at the thought that he was the possessor of a secret, he informed me that he had stealthily brought the books to our rooms, and hidden them in a corner of the kitchen, under Matrena's care. Next, by a natural transition, the conversation passed to the coming fête-day; whereupon the old man proceeded to hold forth extensively on the subject of gifts. The further he delved into his thesis, and the more he expounded it, the clearer could I see that on his mind there was something which he could not, dared not, divulge. So I waited and kept silence. The mysterious exaltation, the repressed satisfaction which I had hitherto discerned in his antics and grimaces and left-eyed winks gradually disappeared, and he began to grow momentarily more anxious and uneasy. At length he could contain himself no longer.

"Listen, Barbara Alexievna," he said timidly. "Listen to what I have got to say to you. When his birthday is come, do you take *ten* of the books, and give them to him yourself—that is, *for* yourself, as being *your* share of the gift. Then *I* will take the eleventh book, and give it to him *my*self, as being *my* gift. If we do that, *you* will have a present for him and *I* shall have one—both of us alike."

"Why do you not want us to present our gifts together, Zachar Petrovitch?" I asked him.

"Oh, very well," he replied. "Very well, Barbara Alexievna. Only—only, I thought that——"

The old man broke off in confusion, while his face flushed with the exertion of thus expressing himself. For a moment or two he sat glued to his seat.

"You see," he went on, "I play the fool too much. I am for ever playing the fool, and cannot help myself, though I know that it is wrong to do so. At home it is often cold, and sometimes there are other troubles as well, and it all makes me depressed. Well, whenever that happens, I indulge a little, and occasionally drink too much. Now, Petinka does *not* like that; he loses his temper about it, Barbara Alexievna, and scolds me, and reads me lectures. So I want by my gift to show him that I am mending my ways, and beginning to conduct myself better. For a long time past I have been saving up to buy him a book—yes, for a long time past I have been saving up for it, since it is seldom that I have any money, unless Petinka happens to give me some. He knows that, and, consequently, as soon as ever he perceives the use to which I have put his money, he will understand that it is for his sake alone that I have acted."

My heart ached for the old man. Seeing him looking at me with such anxiety, I made up my mind without delay.

"I tell you what," I said. "Do *you* give him *all* the books."

"*All?*" he ejaculated. "*All* the books?"

"Yes, all of them."

"As my own gift?"

"Yes, as your own gift."

"As my gift alone?"

"Yes, as your gift alone."

Surely I had spoken clearly enough, yet the old man seemed hardly to understand me.

"Well," said he after reflection, "that certainly would be splendid—certainly it would be *most* splendid. But what about yourself, Barbara Alexievna?"

"Oh, I shall give your son nothing."

"What?" he cried in dismay. "Are you going to give Petinka nothing—do you *wish* to give him nothing?" So put about was the old fellow with what I had said that he seemed almost ready to renounce his own proposal if only I would give his son something. What a kind heart he had! I hastened to assure him that I should certainly have a gift of some sort ready, since my one wish was to avoid spoiling his pleasure.

"Provided that your son is pleased," I added, "and that *you* are pleased, *I* shall be equally pleased, for in my secret heart I shall feel as though *I* had presented the gift."

This fully reassured the old man. He stopped with us another couple of hours, yet could not sit still for a moment, but kept jumping up from his seat, laughing, cracking jokes with Sasha, bestowing stealthy kisses upon myself, pinching my hands, and making silent grimaces at Anna Thedorovna. At length she turned him out of the house. In short, his transports of joy exceeded anything that I had yet beheld.

On the festal day he arrived exactly at eleven o'clock, direct from Mass. He was dressed in a carefully mended frockcoat, a new waistcoat, and a pair of new shoes, while in his arms he carried our pile of books. Next we all sat down to coffee (the day being Sunday) in Anna Thedorovna's parlour. The old man led off the meal by saying that Pushkin was a magnificent poet. Thereafter, with a return to shamefacedness and confusion, he passed suddenly to the statement that a man ought to conduct himself properly; that, should he not do so, it might be taken as a sign that he was in some way over-indulging himself; and that evil tendencies of this sort led to the man's ruin and degradation. Then the orator sketched for our benefit some terrible instances of such incontinence, and concluded by informing us that for some time past he had been mending his own ways, and conducting himself in exemplary fashion, for the reason that he had perceived the justice of his son's precepts, and had laid them to heart so well that he, the father, had really changed for the better: in proof whereof, he now begged to present to the said son some books for which he had long been setting aside his savings.

As I listened to the old man I could not help laughing and crying in a breath. Certainly he knew how to lie when the occasion required! The books were transferred to his son's room, and ranged upon a shelf, where Pokrovski at once guessed the truth about them. Then the old man was invited to dinner, and we all spent a merry day together at cards and forfeits. Sasha was full of life, and I rivalled her, while Pokrovski paid me numerous attentions, and kept seeking an occasion to speak to me alone. But to allow this to happen I refused. Yes, taken all in all, it was the happiest day that I had known for four years.

But now only grievous, painful memories come to my recollection, for I must enter upon the story of my darker experiences. It may be that that is why my pen begins to move more slowly, and seems as though it were going altogether to refuse to write. The same reason may account for my having undertaken so lovingly and enthusiastically a recounting of even the smallest details of my younger, happier days. But alas! those days did not last long, and were succeeded by a period of black sorrow which will close only God knows when!

My misfortunes began with the illness and death of Pokrovski, who was taken worse two months after what I have last recorded in these memoirs. During those two months he worked hard to procure himself a livelihood, since hitherto he had had no assured position. Like all consumptives, he never—not even up to his last moment—altogether abandoned the hope of being able to enjoy a long life. A post as tutor fell in his way, but he had never liked the profession; while for him to become a civil servant was out of the question, owing to his weak state of health. Moreover, in the latter capacity he would have had to have waited a long time for his first instalment of salary. Again, he always looked at the darker side of things, for his character was gradually being warped, and his health undermined, by his illness, though he never noticed it. Then autumn came on, and daily he went out to business—that is to say, to apply for and to canvass for posts—clad only in a light jacket; with the result that, after repeated soakings with rain, he had to take to his bed, and never again left it. He died in mid-autumn, at the close of the month of October.

Throughout his illness I scarcely ever left his room, but waited on him hand and foot. Often he could not sleep for several nights at a time. Often, too, he was unconscious, or else in a delirium; and at such times he would talk of all sorts of things—of his work, of his books, of his father, of myself. At such times I learnt much which I had not hitherto known or divined about his affairs. During the early part of his illness every one in the house looked askance at me, and Anna Thedorovna would nod her head in a meaning manner; but I always looked them straight in the face, and gradually they ceased to take any notice of my concern for Pokrovski. At all events my mother ceased to trouble her head about it.

Sometimes Pokrovski would know who I was, but not often, for more usually he was unconscious. Sometimes, too, he would talk all night with some unknown person, in dim, mysterious language that caused his gasping voice to echo hoarsely through the narrow room as through a sepulchre: and at such times I found the situation a strange one. Especially during his last night was he lightheaded, for then he was in terrible agony, and kept rambling in his speech until my soul was torn with pity. Every one in the house was alarmed, and Anna Thedorovna fell to praying that God might soon take him. When the doctor had been summoned the verdict was that the patient would die with the morning.

That night the elder Pokrovski spent in the corridor, at the door of his son's room. Though given a mattress to lie upon, he spent his time in running in and out of the apartment. So broken with grief was he that he presented a dreadful spectacle, and appeared to have lost both perception and feeling. His head trembled with agony, and his body quivered from head to foot as at times he murmured to himself something which he appeared to be debating. Every moment I expected to see him go out of his mind. Just before dawn he succumbed to the stress of mental agony, and fell asleep on his mattress like a man who has been beaten; but by eight o'clock the son was at the point of death, and I ran to wake the father. The dying man was quite conscious, and bid us all farewell. Somehow I could not weep, though my heart seemed to be breaking.

The last moments were the most harassing and heartbreaking of all. For some time past Pokrovski had been asking for something with his failing tongue, but I had been unable to distinguish his words. Yet my heart had been bursting with grief. Then for an hour he had lain quieter, except that he had looked sadly in my direction, and striven to make some sign with his death-cold hands. At last he again essayed his piteous request in a hoarse, deep voice, but the words issued in so many inarticulate sounds, and once more I failed to divine his meaning. By turns I brought each member of the household to his bedside, and gave him something to drink, but he only shook his head sorrowfully. Finally I understood what it was he wanted. He was asking me to draw aside the curtain from the window, and to open the casements. Probably he wished to take his last look at the daylight and the sun and all God's world. I pulled back the curtain, but the opening day was as dull and mournful-looking as though it had been the fast-flickering life of the poor invalid. Of sunshine there was none. Clouds overlaid the sky as with a shroud of mist, and everything looked sad, rainy, and threatening under a fine drizzle which was beating against the window-panes, and streaking their dull, dark surfaces with runlets of cold, dirty moisture. Only a scanty modicum of daylight entered to war with the trembling rays of the ikon lamp. The dying man threw me a wistful look, and nodded. The next moment he had passed away.

The funeral was arranged for by Anna Thedorovna. A plain coffin was bought, and a broken-down hearse hired; while, as security for this outlay, she seized the dead man's books and other articles. Nevertheless the old man disputed the books with her, and, raising an uproar, carried off as many of them as he could—stuffing his pockets full, and even filling his hat. Indeed, he spent the next three days with them thus, and refused to let them leave his sight even when it was time for him to go to church. Throughout he acted like a man bereft of sense and memory. With quaint assiduity he busied himself about the bier—now straightening the candlestick on the dead man's breast, now snuffing and lighting the other candles. Clearly his thoughts were powerless to remain long fixed on any subject. Neither my mother nor Anna Thedorovna were present at the requiem, for the former was ill and the latter was at loggerheads with the old man. Only myself and the father were there. During the service a sort of panic, a sort of premonition of the future, came over me, and I could hardly hold myself upright. At length the coffin had received its burden and was screwed down; after which the bearers placed it upon a bier, and set out. I accompanied the cortège only to the end of the street. Here the driver broke into a trot, and the old man started to run behind the hearse—sobbing loudly, but with the motion of his running ever and anon causing the sobs to quaver and become broken off. Next he lost his hat, the poor old fellow, yet would not stop to pick it up, even though the rain was beating upon his head, and a wind was rising and the sleet kept stinging and lashing his face. It seemed as though he were impervious to the cruel elements as he ran from one side of the hearse to the other—the skirts of his old greatcoat flapping about him like a pair of wings. From every pocket of the garment protruded books, while in his arms he carried a specially large volume, which he hugged closely to his breast. The passers-by uncovered their heads and crossed themselves as the cortège passed, and some of them, having done so, remained staring in amazement at the poor old man. Every now and then a book would slip from one of his pockets, and fall into the mud; whereupon somebody, stopping him, would direct his attention to his loss, and he would stop, pick up the book, and again set off in pursuit of the hearse. At the corner of the street he was joined by a ragged old woman; until at length the hearse turned a corner, and became hidden from my eyes. Then I went home, and threw myself, in a transport of grief, upon my mother's breast—clasping her in my arms, kissing her amid a storm of sobs and tears, and clinging to her form as though in my embraces I were holding my last friend on earth, that I might preserve her from death. Yet already death was standing over her. . . .

June 11th.

How I thank you for our walk to the Islands yesterday, Makar Alexievitch! How fresh and pleasant, how full of verdure, was everything! And I had not seen anything green for such a long time!—During my illness I used to think that I should never get better, that I was certainly going to die. Judge, then, how I felt yesterday! True, I may have seemed to you a little sad, and you must not be angry with me for that. Happy and light-hearted though I was, there were moments, even at the height of my felicity, when, for some unknown reason, depression came sweeping over my soul. I kept weeping about trifles, yet could not say why I was grieved. The truth is that I am unwell—so much so, that I look at everything from the gloomy point of view. The pale, clear sky, the setting sun, the evening stillness—ah, somehow I felt disposed to grieve and feel hurt at these things; my heart seemed to be over-charged, and to be calling for tears to relieve it. But why should I write this to you? It is difficult for my heart to express itself; still more difficult for it to forego self-expression. Yet possibly you may understand me. Tears and laughter! . . . How good you are, Makar Alexievitch! Yesterday you looked into my eyes as though you could read in them all that I was feeling—as though you were rejoicing at my happiness. Whether it were a group of shrubs or an alley-way or a vista of water that we were passing, you would halt before me, and stand gazing at my face as though you were showing me possessions of your own. It told me how kind is your nature, and I love you for it. To-day I am again unwell, for yesterday I wetted my feet, and took a chill. Thedora also is unwell; both of us are ailing. Do not forget me. Come and see me as often as you can.—Your own,

BARBARA ALEXIEVNA.

June 12th.

MY DEAREST BARBARA ALEXIEVNA,—I had supposed that you meant to describe our doings of the other day in verse; yet from you there has arrived only a single sheet of writing. Nevertheless, I must say that, little though you have put into your letter, that little is expressed with rare beauty and grace. Nature, your descriptions of rural scenes, your analysis of your own feelings,—the whole is beautifully written. Alas, *I* have no such talent! Though I may fill a score of pages, nothing comes of it—I might as well never have put pen to paper. Yes, this I know of experience.

You say, my darling, that I am kind and good, that I could not harm my fellow-men, that I have power to comprehend the goodness of God (as expressed in nature's handiwork), and so on. It may all be so, my dearest one —it may all be exactly as you say. Indeed, I think that you are right. But if so, the reason is that when one reads such a letter as you have just sent me one's heart involuntarily softens, and affords entrance to thoughts of a graver and weightier order. Listen, my darling; I have something to tell you, my beloved one.

I will begin from the time when I was seventeen years old and first entered the service—though I shall soon have completed my thirtieth year of official activity. I may say that at first I was much pleased with my new uniform; and as I grew older I grew in mind, and fell to studying my fellow-men. Likewise I may say that I lived an upright life—so much so that at last I incurred persecution. This you may not believe, but it is true. To think that men so cruel should exist! For, though, dearest one, I am dull and of no account, I have feelings like every one else. Consequently, would you believe it, Barbara, when I tell you what these cruel fellows did to me? I feel ashamed to tell it you—and all because I was of a quiet, peaceful, good-natured disposition! Things began with " this or that, Makar Alexievitch, is *your* fault." Then it went on to " I need hardly say that the fault is wholly Makar Alexievitch's." Finally it became " *Of course* Makar Alexievitch is to blame." Do you see the sequence of things, my darling? Every mistake was attributed to *me*, until " Makar Alexievitch " became a byword in our department. Also, while making of me a proverb, these fellows could not give me a smile or a civil word. They found fault with my boots, with my uniform, with my hair, with my figure. None of these things were to their taste: everything had to be changed. And so it has been from that day to this. True, I have now grown used to it, for I can grow accustomed to anything (being, as you know, a man of peaceable disposition, like all men of small stature): yet why should these things be? Whom have I harmed? Whom have I ever supplanted? Whom have I ever traduced to his superiors? No, the fault is that more than once I have asked for an increase of salary. But I have never *caballed* for it? No, you would be wrong in thinking so, my dearest one. *How* could I ever have done so? You yourself have had many opportunities of seeing how incapable I am of deceit or chicanery.

Why, then, should this have fallen to my lot? . . . However, since *you* think me worthy of respect, my darling, I do not care, for you are far and away the best person in the world. . . . What do you consider to be the greatest social virtue? In private conversation Evstafi Ivanovitch once told me that the greatest social virtue might be considered to be an ability to get money to spend. Also, my comrades used jestingly (yes, I know only jestingly) to propound the ethical maxim that a man ought never to let himself become a burden upon any one. Well, I am a burden upon no one. It is my own crust of bread that I eat; and though that crust is but a poor one, and sometimes actually a maggoty one, it has at least been *earned*, and therefore is being put to a right and lawful use. What, therefore, ought I to do? I know that I can earn but little by my labours as a copyist; yet even of that little I am proud, for it has entailed *work*, and has wrung sweat from my brow. What harm is there in being a copyist? "He is only an amanuensis," people say of me. But what is there so disgraceful in that? My writing is at least legible, and neat and pleasant to look upon, and his Excellency is satisfied with it. Indeed, I transcribe many important documents. At the same time, I know that my writing lacks *style*; which is why I have never risen in the service. Even to you, my dear one, I write simply and without tricks, but just as a thought may happen to enter my head. Yes, I know all this; but if every one were to become a fine writer, who would there be left to act as copyists? . . . Whatsoever questions I may put to you in my letters, dearest, I pray you to answer them. I am sure that you need me, that I can be of use to you; and, since that is so, I must not allow myself to be distracted by any trifle. Even if I be likened to a rat I do not care, provided that that particular rat be wanted by you, and be of use in the world, and be retained in its position, and receive its reward. But what a rat it is!

Enough of this, dearest one. I ought not to have spoken of it, but I lost my temper. Still, it is pleasant to speak the truth sometimes. Good-bye, my own, my darling, my sweet little comforter! I will come to you soon—yes, I will certainly come to you. Till I do so do not fret yourself. With me I shall be bringing a book. Once more good-bye.—Your heartfelt well-wisher,

MAKAR DIEVUSHKIN.

June 20th.

MY DEAREST MAKAR ALEXIEVITCH,—I am writing to you post-haste—I am hurrying my utmost to get my work finished in time. What do you suppose is the reason for this? It is because an opportunity has occurred for you to make a splendid purchase. Thedora tells me that a retired civil servant of her acquaintance has a uniform to sell—one cut to regulation pattern and in good repair, as well as likely to go very cheap. Now, *do* not tell me that you have not got the money, for I know from your own lips that you *have*. Use that money, I pray you, and do not hoard it. See what terrible garments you walk about in! They are shameful—they are patched all over! In fact you have nothing new whatever. That this is so I know for certain, and I care not *what* you tell me about it. So listen to me for once, and buy this uniform. Do it for *my* sake. Do it to show that you *really* love me.

You have sent me some linen as a gift. But listen to me, Makar Alexievitch. You are simply ruining yourself. Is it a jest that you should spend so much money, such a terrible amount of money, upon me? How you love to play the spendthrift! I tell you that I do not need it, that such expenditure is unnecessary. I know, I am *certain*, that you love me: therefore it is useless to remind me of the fact with gifts. Nor, since I know how much they must have cost you, do I like receiving them. No; put your money to a better use. I beg, I beseech of you to do so. Also, you ask me to send you a continuation of my memoirs—to conclude them. But I know not how I contrived even to write as much of them as I did; and now I have not the strength to write further of my past, nor the desire to give it a single thought. Such recollections are terrible to me. Most difficult of all is it for me to speak of my poor mother, who left her destitute daughter a prey to villains. My heart runs blood whenever I think of it; it is so fresh in my memory that I cannot dismiss it from my thoughts, nor rest for its insistence, although a year has now elapsed since the events took place. But all this you know.

Also, I have told you what Anna Thedorovna is now intending. She accuses me of ingratitude, and denies the accusations made against herself with regard to Monsieur Bwikov. Also, she keeps sending for me, and telling me that I have taken to evil courses, but that if I will return to her, she will smooth over matters with Bwikov, and force him to confess his fault. Also, she says that he desires to give me a dowry. Away with them all! I am quite happy here with you and good Thedora, whose devotion to me reminds me of my old nurse, long since dead. Distant kinsman though you may be, I pray you always to defend my honour. Other people I do not wish to know, and would gladly forget if I could. . . . What are they wanting with me now? Thedora declares it all to be a trick, and says that in time they will leave me alone. God grant it be so! B. D.

June 21st.

My Own, my Darling,—I wish to write to you, yet know not where to begin. Things are as strange as though we were actually living together. Also I would add that never in my life have I passed such happy days as I am spending at present. 'Tis as though God had blessed me with a home and a family of my own! Yes, *you* are my little daughter, beloved. But why mention the four sorry roubles that I sent you? You needed them; I know that from Thedora herself, and it will always be a particular pleasure to me to gratify you in anything. It will always be my one happiness in life. Pray, therefore, leave me that happiness, and do not seek to cross me in it. Things are not as you suppose. I have now reached the sunshine since, in the first place, I am living so close to you as almost to be with you (which is a great consolation to my mind), while, in the second place, a neighbour of mine named Ratazíaev (the retired official who gives the literary parties) has to-day invited me to tea. This evening, therefore, there will be a gathering at which we shall discuss literature! Think of that, my darling! Well, good-bye now. I have written this without any definite aim in my mind, but solely to assure you of my welfare. Through Theresa I have received your message that you need an embroidered cloak to wear, so I will go and purchase one. Yes, to-morrow I mean to purchase that embroidered cloak, and so give myself the pleasure of having satisfied one of your wants. I know where to go for such a garment. For the time being I remain your sincere friend, MAKAR DIEVUSHKIN.

June 22nd.

MY DEAREST BARBARA ALEXIEVNA,—I have to tell you that a sad event has happened in this house—an event to excite one's utmost pity. This morning, about five o'clock, one of Gorshkov's children died of scarlatina, or something of the kind. I have been to pay the parents a visit of condolence, and found them living in the direst poverty and disorder. Nor is that surprising, seeing that the family lives in a single room, with only a screen to divide it for decency's sake. Already the coffin was standing in their midst—a plain but decent shell which had been bought ready-made. The child, they told me, had been a boy of nine, and full of promise. What a pitiful spectacle! Though not weeping, the mother, poor woman, looked broken with grief. After all, to have one burden the less on their shoulders may prove a relief, though there are still two children left —a babe at the breast and a little girl of six. How painful to see these suffering children, and to be unable to help them! The father, clad in an old, dirty frock-coat, was seated on a dilapidated chair. Down his cheeks there were coursing tears—though less through grief than owing to a long-standing affliction of the eyes. He was so thin, too! Always he reddens in the face when he is addressed, and becomes too confused to answer. A little girl, his daughter, was leaning against the coffin—her face looking so worn and thoughtful, poor mite! Do you know, I cannot bear to see a child look thoughtful. On the floor there lay a rag doll, but she was not playing with it as, motionless, she stood there with her finger to her lips. Even a bon-bon which the landlady had given her she was not eating. Is it not all sad, sad, Barbara? MAKAR DIEVUSHKIN.

June 25th.

MY BELOVED MAKAR ALEXIEVITCH,—I return you your book. In my opinion it is a worthless one, and I would rather not have it in my possession. Why do you save up your money to buy such trash? Except in jest, do such books really please you? However, you have now promised to send me something else to read. I will share the cost of it. Now, farewell until we meet again. I have nothing more to say. B. D.

June 26th.

MY DEAR LITTLE BARBARA,—To tell you the truth, I myself have not read the book of which you speak. That is to say, though I began to read it, I soon saw that it was nonsense, and written only to make people laugh. "However," thought I, "it is at least a *cheerful* work, and so may please Barbara." That is why I sent it you.

Rateziaev has now promised to give me something really literary to read; so you shall soon have your book, my darling. He is a man who reflects; he is a clever fellow, as well as himself a writer—such a writer! His pen glides along with ease, and in such a style (even when he is writing the most ordinary, the most insignificant of articles) that I have often remarked upon the fact, both to Phaldoni and to Theresa. Often, too, I go to spend an evening with him. He reads aloud to us until five o'clock in the morning, and we listen to him. It is a revelation of things rather than a reading. It is charming, it is like a bouquet of flowers—there is a bouquet of flowers in every line of each page. Besides, he is such an approachable, courteous, kind-hearted fellow! What am *I* compared with him? Why, nothing, simply nothing! He is a man of reputation, whereas I—well, I do not exist at all. Yet he condescends to my level. At this very moment I am copying out a document for him. But you must not think that he finds any *difficulty* in condescending to me who am only a copyist. No, you must not believe the base gossip that you may hear. I do copying work for him simply in order to please myself, as well as that he may notice me—a thing that always gives me pleasure. I appreciate the delicacy of his position. He is a good, a very good, man, and an unapproachable writer.

What a splendid thing is literature, Barbara—what a splendid thing! This I learnt before I had known Rataziaev even for three days. It strengthens and instructs the heart of man. . . . No matter what there be in the world, you will find it all written down in Rataziaev's works. And so well written down, too! Literature is a sort of picture—a sort of picture or mirror. It connotes at once passion, expression, fine criticism, good learning, and a document. Yes, I have learnt this from Rataziaev himself. I can assure you, Barbara, that if only you could be sitting among us, and listening to the talk (while, with the rest of us, you smoked a pipe), and were to hear those present begin to argue and dispute concerning different matters, you would feel of as little account among them as I do; for I myself figure there only as a blockhead, and feel ashamed, since it takes me a whole evening to think of a single word to interpolate—and even then the word will not come! In a case like that a man regrets that, as the proverb has it, he should have reached man's estate but not man's understanding. . . . What do I do in my spare time? I sleep like a fool, though I would far rather be occupied with something else—say, with eating or writing, since the one is useful to oneself, and the other is beneficial to one's fellows. You should see how much money these fellows contrive to save! How much, for instance, does not Rataziaev lay by? A few days' writing, I am told, can earn him as much as three hundred roubles! Indeed, if a man be a writer of short stories or anything else that is interesting, he can sometimes pocket five hundred roubles, or a thousand, at a time! Think of it, Barbara! Rataziaev has by him a small manuscript of verses, and for it he is asking—what do you think?

seven thousand roubles! Why, one could buy a whole house for that sum! He has even refused five thousand for a manuscript, and on that occasion I reasoned with him, and advised him to accept the five thousand. But it was of no use. "For," said he, "they will soon offer me seven thousand," and kept to his point, for he is a man of some determination.

Suppose, now, that I were to give you an extract from *Passion in Italy* (as another work of his is called). Read this, dearest Barbara, and judge for yourself:

"Vladimir started, for in his veins the lust of passion had welled until it had reached boiling point.

"'Countess,' he cried, 'do you know how terrible is this adoration of mine, how infinite this madness? No! My fancies have not deceived me—I love you ecstatically, diabolically, as a madman might! All the blood that is in your husband's body could never quench the furious, surging rapture that is in my soul! No puny obstacle could thwart the all-destroying, infernal flame which is eating into my exhausted breast! O Zinaida, my Zinaida!'

"'Vladimir!' she whispered, almost beside herself, as she sank upon his bosom.

"'My Zinaida!' cried the enraptured Smileski once more.

"His breath was coming in sharp, broken pants. The lamp of love was burning brightly on the altar of passion, and searing the hearts of the two unfortunate sufferers.

"'Vladimir!' again she whispered in her intoxication, while her bosom heaved, her cheeks glowed, and her eyes flashed fire.

"Thus was a new and dread union consummated.

. . . .

"Half an hour later the aged Count entered his wife's boudoir.

"'How now, my love?' said he. 'Surely it is for some welcome guest beyond the common that you have had the samovar[1] thus prepared?' And he smote her lightly on the cheek."

[1] Tea-urn.

What think you of *that*, Barbara? True, it is a little too outspoken—there can be no doubt of that; yet how grand it is, how splendid! With your permission I will quote you also an extract from Rataziaev's story, *Ermak and Zuleika.*

"'You love me, Zuleika? Say again that you love me, you love me!'

"'I *do* love you, Ermak,' whispered Zuleika.

"'Then by heaven and earth I thank you! By heaven and earth you have made me happy! You have given me all, all that my tortured soul has for immemorial years been seeking! 'Tis for this that you have led me hither, my guiding star—'tis for this that you have conducted me to the Girdle of Stone! To all the world will I now show my Zuleika, and no man, demon or monster of Hell, shall bid me nay! Oh, if men would but understand the mysterious passions of her tender heart, and see the poem which lurks in each of her little tears! Suffer me to dry those tears with my kisses! Suffer me to drink of those heavenly drops, O being who art not of this earth!'

"'Ermak,' said Zuleika, 'the world is cruel, and men are unjust. But *let* them drive us from their midst—*let* them judge us, my beloved Ermak! What has a poor maiden who was reared amid the snows of Siberia to do with their cold, icy, self-sufficient world? Men cannot understand me, my darling, my sweetheart.'

"'Is that so? Then shall the sword of the Cossacks sing and whistle over their heads!' cried Ermak with a furious look in his eyes."

What must Ermak have felt when he learnt that his Zuleika had been murdered, Barbara?—that, taking advantages of the cover of night, the blind old Kouchoum had, in Ermak's absence, broken into the latter's tent, and stabbed his own daughter in mistake for the man who had robbed him of sceptre and crown?

"'Oh that I had a stone whereon to whet my sword!' cried Ermak in the madness of his wrath as he strove to sharpen his steel blade upon the enchanted rock. 'I would have his blood, his blood! I would tear him limb from limb, the villain!'"

Then Ermak, unable to survive the loss of his Zuleika, throws himself into the Irtisch, and the tale comes to an end.

Here, again, is another short extract — this time written in a more comical vein, to make people laugh.

"Do you know Ivan Prokofievitch Zheltopuzh? He is the man who took a piece out of Prokofi Ivanovitch's leg. Ivan's character is one of the rugged order, and therefore one that is rather lacking in virtue. Yet he has a passionate relish for radishes and honey. Once, also, he possessed a friend named Pelagea Antonovna. Do you know Pelagea Antonovna? She is the woman who always puts on her petticoat wrong side outwards."

What humour, Barbara—what purest humour! We rocked with laughter when he read it aloud to us. Yes, that is the kind of man he is. Possibly the passage is a trifle over-frolicsome, but at least it is harmless, and contains no freethought or liberal ideas. In passing, I may say that Rataziaev is not only a supreme writer, but also a man of upright life—which is more than can be said for most writers.

What, do you think, is an idea that sometimes enters my head? In fact, what if I myself were to write something? How if suddenly a book were to make its appearance in the world bearing the title of "The Poetical Works of Makar Dievushkin"? What *then*, my angel? How should you view, should you receive, such an event? I may say of myself that never, after my book had appeared, should I have the hardihood to show my face on the Nevski Prospect; for would it not be too dreadful to hear every one saying, "Here comes the litterateur and poet, Dievushkin—yes, it is Dievushkin himself"? What, in such a case, should I do with my feet (for I may tell you that almost always my shoes are patched, or have just been resoled, and therefore look anything but becoming)? To think that the great writer Dievushkin should walk about in patched footgear! If a duchess or a countess should recognise me, what would she say, poor woman? Perhaps, though, she would not notice my shoes at all, since it may reasonably be supposed that countesses do not greatly occupy themselves with footgear, especially with the footgear of civil service officials (footgear may differ from footgear, it must be remembered). Besides, I should find that the countess had heard all about me, for my friends would have betrayed me to her—Rataziaev among the first of them, seeing that he often goes to visit Countess V., and practically lives at her house. She is said to be a woman of great intellect and wit. An artful dog, that Rataziaev!

But enough of this. I write this sort of thing both to amuse myself and to divert your thoughts. Good-bye now, my angel. This is a long epistle that I am sending you, but the reason is that to-day I feel in good spirits after dining at Rataziaev's. There I came across a novel which I hardly know how to describe to you. Do not think the worse of me on that account, even though I bring you another book instead (for I certainly mean to bring one). The novel in question was one of Paul de Kock's, and not a novel for *you* to read. No, no! Such a work is unfit for your eyes. In fact, it is said to have greatly offended the critics of St. Petersburg. Also, I am sending you a pound of bon-bons—bought specially for yourself. Each time that you eat one, beloved, remember the sender. Only, do not bite the iced ones, but suck them gently, lest they make your teeth ache. Perhaps, too, you like comfits? Well, write and tell me if it is so. Good-bye, good-bye. Christ watch over you, my darling!—Always your faithful friend, MAKAR DIEVUSHKIN.

June 27th.

MY DEAREST MAKAR ALEXIEVITCH,—Thedora tells me that, should I wish, there are some people who will be glad to help me by obtaining me an excellent post as governess in a certain house. What think you, my friend? Shall I go or not? Of course, I should then cease to be a burden to you, and the post appears to be a comfortable one. On the other hand, the idea of entering a strange house appals me. The people in it are landed gentry, and they will begin to ask me questions, and to busy themselves about me. What answers shall I then return? You see, I am now so unused to society—so shy! I like to live in a corner to which I have long grown used. Yes, the place with which one is familiar is always the best. Even if for companion one has but sorrow, that place will still be the best. . . . God alone knows what duties the post will entail. Perhaps I shall merely be required to act as nursemaid; and in any case I hear that the governess there has been changed three times in two years. For God's sake, Makar Alexievitch, advise me whether to go or not. Why do you never come near me now? Do let my eyes have an occasional sight of you. Mass on Sundays is almost the only time when we see one another. How retiring you have become! So also have I, even though, in a way, I am your kinswoman. You must have ceased to love me, Makar Alexievitch. I spend many a weary hour because of it. Sometimes, when dusk is falling, I find myself lonely—oh, so lonely! Thedora has gone out somewhere, and I sit here and think, and think, and think. I remember all the past, its joys and its sorrows. It passes before my eyes in detail, it glimmers at me as out of a mist; and as it does so well known faces appear which seem actually to be present with me in this room! Most frequently of all I see my mother. Ah, the dreams that come to me! I feel that my health is breaking, so weak am I. When this morning I arose sickness took me until I vomited and vomited. Yes, I feel, I know, that death is approaching. Who will bury me when it has come? Who will visit my tomb? Who will sorrow for me? And now it is in a strange place, in the house of a stranger, that I may have to die! Yes, in a corner which I do not know! . . . My God, how sad a thing is life! . . . Why do you send me comfits to eat? Whence do you get the money to buy them? Ah, for God's sake keep the money, keep the money. Thedora has sold a carpet which I have made. She got fifty roubles for it, which is very good—I had expected less. Of the fifty roubles I shall give Thedora three, and with the remainder make myself a plain, warm dress. Also, I am going to make you a waistcoat—to make it myself, and out of good material.

Also, Thedora has brought me a book—*The Stories of Bielkin*—which I will forward you if you would care to read it. Only, do not soil it, nor yet retain it, for it does not belong to me. It is by Pushkin. Two years ago I read these stories with my mother, and it would hurt me to read them again. If you yourself have any books, pray let me have them—so long as they have not been obtained from Rataziaev. Probably he will be giving you one of his own works when he has had one printed. How is it that his compositions please you so much, Makar Alexievitch? I think them *such* rubbish!—Now good-bye. How I have been chattering on! When feeling sad, I always like to talk of something, for it acts upon me like medicine—I begin to feel easier as soon as I have uttered what is preying upon my heart. Good-bye, good-bye, my friend.—Your own B. D.

June 28th.

MY DEAREST BARBARA ALEXIEVNA,—Away with melancholy! Really, beloved, you ought to be ashamed of yourself! How can you allow such thoughts to enter your head? Really and truly you are quite well; really and truly you are, my darling. Why, you are blooming—simply blooming. True, I see a certain touch of pallor in your face, but still you are blooming. A fig for dreams and visions! Yes, for shame, dearest! Drive away those fancies; try to despise them. Why do *I* sleep so well? Why am *I* never ailing? Look at *me*, beloved. I live well, I sleep peacefully, I retain my health, I can ruffle it with my juniors. In fact, it is a pleasure to see me. Come, come, then, sweetheart! Let us have no more of this. I know that that little head of yours is capable of any fancy—that all too easily you take to dreaming and repining; but for my sake cease to do so. Are you to go to these people, you ask me? Never! No, no, again no! How could you think of doing such a thing as taking a journey? I will not allow it—I intend to combat your intention with all my might. I will sell my frockcoat, and walk the streets in my shirt sleeves, rather than let you be in want. But no, Barbara. *I* know you, *I* know you. This is merely a trick, merely a trick. And probably Thedora alone is to blame for it. She appears to be a foolish old woman, and to be able to persuade you to do anything. Do not believe her, my dearest. I am sure that you know what is what as well as *she* does. Eh, sweetheart? She is a stupid, quarrelsome, rubbish-talking old woman who brought her late husband to the grave. Probably she has been plaguing you as much as she did him. No, no, dearest; you must not take this step. What should *I* do then? What would there be left for *me* to do? Pray put the idea out of your head. What is it you lack here? I cannot feel sufficiently overjoyed to be near you, while, for your part, you love me well, and can live your life here as quietly as you wish. Read or sew, whichever you like—or read and do not sew. Only, do not desert me. Try, yourself, to imagine how things would seem after you had gone. Here am I sending you books, and later we will go for a walk. Come, come, then, my Barbara! Summon to your aid your reason, and cease to babble of trifles. As soon as I can I will come and see you, and then you shall tell me the whole story. This will not do, sweetheart; this certainly will not do. Of course I know that I am not an educated man, and have received but a sorry schooling, and have had no inclination for it, and think too much of Rataziaev, if you will; but he is my friend, and therefore I must put in a word or two for him. Yes, he is a splendid writer. Again and again I assert that he writes magnificently. I do not agree with you about his works, and never shall. He writes too ornately, too laconically, with too great a wealth of imagery and imagination. Perhaps you have read him without insight, Barbara? Or perhaps you were out of spirits at the time, or angry with Thedora about something, or worried about some mischance? Ah, but you should read him sympathetically, and, best of all, at a time when you are feeling happy and contented and pleasantly disposed—for instance, when you have a bon-bon or two in your mouth. Yes, that is the way to read Rataziaev. I do not dispute (indeed, who would do so?) that better writers than he exist—even far better; but they are good, and he is good too—they write well, and he writes well. It is chiefly for his own sake that he writes, and he is to be approved for so doing.

Now good-bye, dearest. More I cannot write, for I must hurry away to business. Be of good cheer, and the Lord God watch over you!—Your faithful friend,

MAKAR DIEVUSHKIN.

P.S.—Thank you so much for the book, darling! I will read it through, this volume of Pushkin, and to-night come to you.

MY DEAR MAKAR ALEXIEVITCH,—No, no, my friend; I must not go on living near you. I have been thinking the matter over, and come to the conclusion that I should be doing very wrong to refuse so good a post. I should at least have an assured crust of bread; I might at least set to work to earn my employers' favour, and even try to change my character if required to do so. Of course it is a sad and sorry thing to have to live among strangers, and to be forced to seek their patronage, and to conceal and constrain one's own personality: but God will help me. I must not remain for ever a recluse, for similar chances have come my way before. I remember how, when a little girl at school, I used to go home on Sundays and spend the time in frisking and dancing about. Sometimes my mother would chide me for so doing, but *I* did not care, for my heart was too joyous, and my spirits too buoyant, for that. Yet as the evening of Sunday came on, a sadness as of death would overtake me, for at nine o'clock I had to return to school, where everything was cold and strange and severe—where the governesses, on Mondays, lost their tempers, and nipped my ears, and made me cry. On such occasions I would retire to a corner and weep alone; concealing my tears lest I should be called lazy. Yet it was not because I had to *study* that I used to weep, and in time I grew more used to things, and, after my schooldays were over, shed tears only when I was parting with friends. . . . It is not right for me to live in dependence upon you. The thought tortures me. I tell you this frankly, for the reason that frankness with you has become a habit. Cannot I see that daily, at earliest dawn, Thedora rises to do washing and scrubbing, and remains working at it until late at night, even though her poor old bones must be aching for want of rest? Cannot I also see that *you* are ruining yourself for me, and hoarding your last kopeck that you may spend it on my behalf? You ought not so to act, my friend, even though you write that you would rather sell your all than let me want for anything. I believe in you, my friend—I entirely believe in your good heart; but you say that to me *now* (when, perhaps, you have received some unexpected sum or gratuity) and there is still the future to be thought of. You yourself know that I am always ailing—that I cannot work as you do, glad though I should be of any work if I could get it; so what else is there for me to do? To sit and repine as I watch you and Thedora? But how would that be of any use to you? *Am* I necessary to you, comrade of mine? *Have* I ever done you any good? Though I am bound to you with my whole soul, and love you dearly and strongly and wholeheartedly, a bitter fate has ordained that that love should be all that I have to give—that I should be unable, by creating for you subsistence, to repay you for all your kindness. Do not, therefore, detain me longer, but think the matter out, and give me your opinion on it. In expectation of which I remain your sweetheart, B. D.

July 1st.

Rubbish, rubbish, Barbara!—What you say is sheer rubbish. Stay here, rather, and put such thoughts out of your head. None of what you suppose is true. I can see for myself that it is not. Whatsoever you lack here, you have but to ask me for it. Here you love and are loved, and we might easily be happy and contented together. What could you want more? What have you to do with strangers? You cannot possibly know what strangers are like. I know it, though, and could have told you if you had asked me. There is a stranger whom I know, and whose bread I have eaten. He is a cruel man, Barbara—a man so bad that he would be unworthy of your little heart, and would soon tear it to pieces with his railings and reproaches and black looks. On the other hand, you are safe and well here—you are as safe as though you were sheltered in a nest. Besides, you would, as it were, leave me with my head gone. For what should I have to do when you were gone? What could I, an old man, find to do? Are not you necessary to me? Are not you useful to me? Eh? Surely you do not think that you are not useful? You are of great use to me, Barbara, for you exercise a beneficial influence upon my life. Even at this moment, as I think of you, I feel cheered, for always I can write letters to you, and put into them what I am feeling, and receive from you detailed answers. . . . I have bought you a wardrobe, and also procured you a bonnet; so you see that you have only to give me a commission for it to be executed. . . . No; in what way are you not useful? What should I do if I were deserted in my old age? What would become of me? Perhaps you never thought of that, Barbara—perhaps you never said to yourself, "How could *he* get on without me?" You see, I have grown so accustomed to you. What else would it end in if you were to go away? Why, in my hieing me to the Neva's bank and doing away with myself. Ah, Barbara, darling, I can see that you want me to be taken away to the Volkovo Cemetery in a broken-down old hearse, with some poor outcast of the streets to accompany my coffin as chief mourner, and the grave-diggers to heap my body with clay, and depart and leave me there. How wrong of you, how wrong of you, my beloved! Yes, by heavens, how wrong of you! I am returning you your book, little friend; and if you were to ask of me my opinion of it I should say that never before in my life had I read a book so splendid. I keep wondering how I have hitherto contrived to remain such an owl. For what have I ever done? From what wilds did I spring into existence? I know *nothing*—I know simply *nothing*. My ignorance is complete. Frankly, I am not an educated man, for until now I have read scarcely a single book—only *A Portrait of Man* (a clever enough work in its way), *The Boy who could Play Many Tunes upon Bells*, and *Ivik's Storks*. That is all. But now I have also read *The Station Overseer* in your little volume; and it is wonderful to think that one may live and yet be ignorant of the fact that under one's very nose there may be a book in which one's whole life is described as in a picture. Never should I have guessed that, as soon as ever one begins to read such a book, it sets one on both to remember and to consider and to foretell events. Another reason why I liked this book so much is that, though, in the case of other works (however clever they be), one may read them, yet remember not a word of them (for I am a man naturally dull of comprehension, and unable to read works of any great importance), —although, as I say, one may read such works, one reads such a book as *yours* as easily as though it had been written by oneself, and had taken possession of one's heart, and turned it inside out for inspection, and were describing it in detail as a matter of perfect simplicity. Why, I might almost have written the book myself! Why not, indeed? I can feel just as the people in the book do, and find myself in positions precisely similar to those of, say, the character Samson Virin. In fact, how many good-hearted wretches like Virin are there not walking about amongst us? How easily, too, it is all described! I assure you, my darling, that I almost shed tears when I read that Virin so took to drink as to lose his memory, become morose, and spend whole days over his liquor; as also that he choked with grief and wept bitterly when, rubbing his eyes with his dirty hand, he bethought him of his wandering lamb, his daughter Dunasha! How natural, how natural! You should read the book for yourself. The thing is actually alive. Even *I* can see that; even *I* can realise that it is a picture cut from the very life around me. In it I see our own Theresa (to go no further) and the poor tchinovnik—who is just such a man as this Samson Virin, except for his surname of Gorshkov. The book describes just what might happen to ourselves—to myself in particular. Even a count who lives in the Nevski Prospect or in Naberezhnaia Street might have a similar experience, though he might *appear* to be different, owing to the fact that his life is cast on a higher plane. Yes, just the same things might happen to him—just the same things. . . . Here are you wishing to go away and leave us; yet be careful lest it would not be *I* who had to pay the penalty of your doing so. For you might ruin both yourself and me. For the love of God put away these thoughts from you, my darling, and do not torture me in vain. How could *you*, my poor little unfledged nestling, find yourself food, and defend yourself from misfortune, and ward off the wiles of evil men? Think better of it, Barbara, and pay no more heed to foolish advice and calumny, but read your book again, and read it with attention. It may do you much good.

I have spoken of Rataziaev's *The Station Overseer*. However, the author has told me that the work is old-fashioned, since, nowadays, books are issued with illustrations and embellishments of different sorts (though I could not make out all that he said). Pushkin he adjudges a splendid poet, and one who has done honour to Holy Russia. Read your book again, Barbara, and follow my advice, and make an old man happy. The Lord God Himself will reward you. Yes, He will surely reward you.—Your faithful friend,

MAKAR DIEVUSHKIN.

MY DEAREST MAKAR ALEXIEVITCH,—To-day Thedora came to me with fifteen roubles in silver. How glad was the poor woman when I gave her three of them! I am writing to you in great haste, for I am busy cutting out a waistcoat to send to you—buff, with a pattern of flowers. Also I am sending you a book of stories; some of which I have read myself, particularly one called "The Cloak." . . . You invite me to go to the theatre with you. But will it not cost too much? Of course we might sit in the gallery. It is a long time (indeed I cannot remember when I last did so) since I visited a theatre! Yet I cannot help fearing that such an amusement is beyond our means. Thedora keeps nodding her head, and saying that you have taken to living above your income. I myself divine the same thing by the amount which you have spent upon me. Take care, dear friend, that misfortune does not come of it, for Thedora has also informed me of certain rumours concerning your inability to meet your landlady's bills. In fact, I am very anxious about you. Now, good-bye, for I must hasten away to see about another matter—about the changing of the ribands on my bonnet.

P.S.—Do you know, if we go to the theatre, I think that I shall wear my new hat and black mantilla. Will not that look nice?

July 7th.

MY DEAREST BARBARA ALEXIEVNA,—So much for yesterday! Yes, dearest, we have both been caught playing the fool, for I have become thoroughly bitten with the actress of whom I spoke. Last night I listened to her with all my ears, although, strangely enough, it was practically my first sight of her, seeing that only once before had I been to the theatre. In those days I lived cheek by jowl with a party of five young men—a most noisy crew—and one night I accompanied them, willy-nilly, to the theatre, though I held myself decently aloof from their doings, and only assisted them for company's sake. How those fellows talked to me of this actress! Every night when the theatre was open the entire band of them (they always seemed to possess the requisite money) would betake themselves to that place of entertainment, where they ascended to the gallery, and clapped their hands, and repeatedly recalled the actress in question. In fact, they went simply mad over her. Even after we had returned home they would give me no rest, but would go on talking about her all night, and calling her their Glasha, and declaring themselves to be in love with "the canary-bird of their hearts." My defenceless self, too, they would plague about the woman, for I was as young as they. What a figure I must have cut with them on the fourth tier of the gallery! Yet I never got a sight of more than just a corner of the curtain, but had to content myself with listening. She had a fine, resounding, mellow voice like a nightingale's, and we all of us used to clap our hands loudly, and to shout at the top of our lungs. In short, we came very near to being ejected. On the first occasion I went home walking as in a mist, with a single rouble left in my pocket, and an interval of ten clear days confronting me before next pay-day. Yet, what think you, dearest? The very next day, before going to work, I called at a French perfumer's, and spent my whole remaining capital on some eau-de-Cologne and scented soap! Why I did so I do not know. Nor did I dine at home that day, but kept walking and walking past her windows (she lived in a fourth-storey flat on the Nevski Prospect). At length I returned to my own lodging, but only to rest a short hour before again setting off to the Nevski Prospect and resuming my vigil before her windows. For a month and a half I kept this up—dangling in her train. Sometimes I would hire cabs, and discharge them in view of her abode; until at length I had entirely ruined myself, and got into debt. Then I fell out of love with her—I grew weary of the pursuit. . . . You see, therefore, to what depths an actress can reduce a decent man. In those days I was young. Yes, in those days I was *very* young. M. D.

July 8th.

MY DEAREST BARBARA ALEXIEVNA,—The book which I received from you on the 6th of this month I now hasten to return, while at the same time hastening also to explain matters to you in this accompanying letter. What a misfortune, my beloved, that you should have brought me to such a pass! Our lots in life are apportioned by the Almighty according to our human deserts. To such a one He assigns a life in a general's epaulets or as a privy councillor,—to such a one, I say, He assigns a life of command; whereas to another one He allots only a life of unmurmuring toil and suffering. These things are calculated according to a man's *capacity*. One man may be capable of one thing, and another of another, and their several capacities are ordered by the Lord God himself. I have now been thirty years in the public service, and have fulfilled my duties irreproachably, remained abstemious, and never been detected in any unbecoming behaviour. As a citizen, I may confess —I confess it freely—I have been guilty of certain shortcomings: yet those shortcomings have been combined with certain virtues. I am respected of my superiors, and even his Excellency has had no fault to find with me; and though I have never been shown any special marks of favour, I know that every one finds me at least satisfactory. Also, my writing is sufficiently legible and clear. Neither too rounded nor too fine, it is a running hand, yet always suitable. Of our staff only Ivan Prokofievitch writes a similar hand. Thus have I lived till the grey hairs of my old age; yet I can think of no serious fault committed. Of course, no one is free from *minor* faults. Every one has some of them, and you among the rest, my beloved. But in grave or in audacious offences never have I been detected, nor in infringements of regulations, nor in breaches of the public peace. No, never! This you surely know, even as the author of your book must have known it. Yes, he also must have known it when he sat down to write. I had not expected this of you, my Barbara. I should *never* have expected it.

What? In future I am not to go on living peacefully in my little corner, poor though that corner be—I am not to go on living, as the proverb has it, without muddying the water, or hurting any one, or forgetting the fear of the Lord God and of oneself? I am not to see, forsooth, that no man does me an injury, or breaks into my home—I am not to take care that all shall go well with me, or that I have clothes to wear, or that my shoes do not require mending, or that I be given work to do, or that I possess sufficient meat and drink? Is it nothing that, where the pavement is rotten, I have to walk on tiptoe to save my boots? If I write to you overmuch concerning myself, is it concerning *another* man, rather, that I ought to write—concerning *his* wants, concerning *his* lack of tea to drink (and all the world needs tea)? Has it ever been my custom to pry into other men's mouths, to see what is being put into them? Have I ever been known to offend any one in that respect? No, no, beloved! Why should I desire to insult other folks when they are not molesting *me?* Let me give you an example of what I mean. A man may go on slaving and slaving in the public service, and earn the respect of his superiors (for what it is worth), and then, for no visible reason at all, find himself made a fool of. Of course he *may* break out now and then (I am not now referring only to drunkenness), and (for example) buy himself a new pair of shoes, and take pleasure in seeing his feet looking well and smartly shod. Yes, I myself have known what it is to feel like that (I write this in good faith). Yet I am none the less astonished that Thedor Thedorovitch should neglect what is being said about him, and take no steps to defend himself. True, he is only a subordinate official, and sometimes loves to rate and scold: yet why should he not do so—why should he not indulge in a little vituperation when he feels like it? Suppose it to be *necessary*, for *form's* sake, to scold, and to set every one right, and to shower around abuse (for, between ourselves, Barbara, our friend cannot get on *without* abuse—so much so that every one humours him, and does things behind his back)? Well, since officials differ in rank, and every official demands that he shall be allowed to abuse his fellow officials in proportion to his rank, it follows that the *tone* also of official abuse should become divided into ranks, and thus accord with the natural order of things. All the world is built upon the system that each one of us shall have to yield precedence to some other one, as well as to enjoy a certain power of abusing his fellows. Without such a provision the world could not get on at all, and simple chaos would ensue. Yet I am surprised that our Thedor should continue to overlook insults of the kind that he endures.

Why do I do my official work at all? Why is that necessary? Will my doing of it lead any one who reads it to give me a greatcoat, or to buy me a new pair of shoes? No, Barbara. Men only read the documents, and then require me to write more. Sometimes a man will hide himself away, and not show his face abroad, for the mere reason that, though he has done nothing to be ashamed of, he dreads the gossip and slandering which are everywhere to be encountered. If his civic and family life have to do with literature, everything will be printed and read and laughed over and discussed; until at length he hardly dare show his face in the street at all, seeing that he will have been described by report as recognisable through his gait alone! Then, when he has amended his ways, and grown gentler (even though he still continue to be loaded with official work), he will come to be accounted a virtuous, decent citizen who has deserved well of his comrades, rendered obedience to his superiors, wished no one any evil, preserved the fear of God in his heart, and died lamented. Yet would it not be better, instead of letting the poor fellow die, to give him a cloak while yet he is *alive*—to give it to this same Thedor Thedorovitch (that is to say, to myself)? Yes, 'twere far better if, on hearing the tale of his subordinate's virtues, the chief of the department were to call the deserving man into his office, and then and there to promote him, and to grant him an increase of salary. Thus vice would be punished, virtue would prevail, and the staff of that department would live in peace together. Here we have an example from everyday, commonplace life. How, therefore, could you bring yourself to send me that book, my beloved? It is a badly conceived work, Barbara, and also unreal, for the reason that in creation such a tchinovnik does not exist. No, again I protest against it, little Barbara; again I protest.—Your most humble, devoted servant, M. D.

July 27th.

MY DEAREST MAKAR ALEXIEVITCH,—Your latest conduct and letters had frightened me, and left me thunderstruck and plunged in doubt, until what you have said about Thedor explained the situation. Why despair and go into such frenzies, Makar Alexievitch? Your explanations only partially satisfy me. Perhaps I did wrong to insist upon accepting a good situation when it was offered me, seeing that from my last experience in that way I derived a shock which was anything but a matter for jesting. You say also that your love for me has compelled you to hide yourself in retirement. Now, how much I am indebted to you I realised when you told me that you were spending for my benefit the sum which you are always reported to have laid by at your bankers; but now that I have learnt that you never possessed such a fund, but that, on hearing of my destitute plight, and being moved by it, you decided to spend upon me the whole of your salary—even to forestall it—and when I had fallen ill actually to sell your clothes—when I learnt all this I found myself placed in the harassing position of not knowing how to accept it all, nor what to think of it. Ah, Makar Alexievitch! You ought to have stopped at your first acts of charity—acts inspired by sympathy and the love of kinsfolk, rather than have continued to squander your means upon what was unnecessary. Yes, you have betrayed our friendship, Makar Alexievitch, in that you have not been open with me; and, now that I see that your last coin has been spent upon dresses and bon-bons and excursions and books and visits to the theatre for me, I weep bitter tears for my unpardonable improvidence in having accepted these things without giving so much as a thought to your welfare. Yes, all that you have done to give me pleasure has become converted into a source of grief, and left behind it only useless regret. Of late I have remarked that you were looking depressed; and though I felt fearful that something unfortunate was impending, what has happened would otherwise never have entered my head. To think that your better sense should so play you false, Makar Alexievitch! What will people think of you, and say of you? Who will want to know you? You whom, like every one else, I have valued for your goodness of heart and modesty and good sense—*you*, I say, have now given way to an unpleasant vice of which you seem never before to have been guilty. What were my feelings when Thedora informed me that you had been discovered drunk in the street, and taken home by the police? Why, I felt petrified with astonishment—although, in view of the fact that you had failed me for four days, I had been expecting some such extraordinary occurrence. Also, have you thought what your superiors will say of you when they come to learn the true reason of your absence? You say that every one is laughing at you, that every one has learnt of the bond which exists between us, and that your neighbours habitually refer to me with a sneer. Pay no attention to this, Makar Alexievitch; for the love of God be comforted. Also, the incident between you and the officers has much alarmed me, although I had heard certain rumours concerning it. Pray explain to me what it means. You write, too, that you have been afraid to be open with me, for the reason that your confessions might lose you my friendship. Also, you say that you are in despair at the thought of being unable to help me in my illness, owing to the fact that you have sold everything which might have maintained me, and preserved me in sickness, as well as that you have borrowed as much as it is possible for you to borrow, and are daily experiencing unpleasantness with your landlady. Well, in failing to reveal all this to me you chose the worser course. Now, however, I know all. You have forced me to recognise that I have been the cause of your unhappy plight, as well as that my own conduct has brought upon myself a twofold measure of sorrow. The fact leaves me thunderstruck, Makar Alexievitch. Ah, friend, an infectious disease is indeed a misfortune, for now we poor and miserable folk must perforce keep apart from one another, lest the infection be increased. Yes, I have brought upon you calamities which never before in your humble, solitary life you had experienced. This tortures and exhausts me more than I can tell to think of.

Write to me quite frankly. Tell me how you came to embark upon such a course of conduct. Comfort, oh, comfort me if you can. It is not self-love that prompts me to speak of my own comforting, but my friendship and love for you, which will never fade from my heart. Good-bye. I await your answer with impatience. You have thought but poorly of me, Makar Alexievitch.—Your friend and lover,

BARBARA DOBROSELOVA.

July 28th.

MY PRICELESS BARBARA ALEXIEVNA,—What am I to say to you, now that all is over, and we are gradually returning to our old position? You say that you are anxious as to what will be thought of me. Let me tell you that the dearest thing in life to me is my self-respect; wherefore, in informing you of my misfortunes and misconduct, I would add that none of my superiors know of my doings, nor ever will know of them, and that therefore I still enjoy a measure of respect in that quarter. Only one thing do I fear: I fear gossip. Garrulous though my landlady be, she said but little when, with the aid of your ten roubles, I to-day paid her part of her account; and as for the rest of my companions, they do not matter at all. So long as I have not to borrow money of them I need pay them no attention. To conclude my explanations, let me tell you that I value your respect for me above everything in the world, and have found it my greatest comfort during this temporary distress of mine. Thank God, the first shock of things has abated, now that you have agreed not to look upon me as faithless and an egotist simply because I have deceived you. I wish to hold you to myself, for the reason that I cannot bear to part with you, and love you as my guardian angel. . . . I have now returned to work, and am applying myself diligently to my duties. Also, yesterday Evstafi Ivanovitch exchanged a word or two with me. Yet I will not conceal from you the fact that my debts are crushing me down, and that my wardrobe is in a sorry state. At the same time, these things do not *really* matter, and I would bid you not despair about them. Send me, however, another half-rouble if you can (though that half-rouble will stab me to the heart—stab me with the thought that it is not *I* who am helping *you*, but *you* who are helping *me*). Thedora has done well to get those fifteen roubles for you. At the moment, fool of an old man that I am, I have no hope of acquiring any more money; but as soon as ever I do so I will write to you and let you know all about it. What chiefly worries me is the fear of gossip. Good-bye, little angel. I kiss your hands, and beseech you to regain your health. If this is not a detailed letter, the reason is that I must soon be starting for the office, in order that, by strict application to duty, I may make amends for the past. Further information concerning my doings (as well as concerning that affair with the officers) must be deferred until to-night.—Your affectionate and respectful friend,

MAKAR DIEVUSHKIN.

July 28th.

DEAREST LITTLE BARBARA,—It is *you* who have committed a fault — and one which must weigh heavily upon your conscience. Indeed, your last letter has amazed and confounded me,—so much so that, on once more looking into the recesses of my heart, I perceive that I was perfectly right in what I did. Of course I am not now referring to my debauch (no, indeed!), but to the fact that I love you, and to the fact that it is unwise of me to love you—very unwise. You know not how matters stand, my darling. You know not why I am *bound* to love you. Otherwise you would not say all that you do. Yet I am persuaded that it is your head rather than your heart that is speaking. I am certain that your heart thinks very differently.

What occurred that night between myself and those officers I scarcely know, I scarcely remember. You must bear in mind that for some time past I have been in terrible distress—that for a whole month I have been, so to speak, hanging by a single thread. Indeed, my position has been most pitiable. Though I hid myself from you, my landlady was for ever shouting and railing at me. This would not have mattered a jot — the horrible old woman might have shouted as much as she pleased—had it not been that, in the first place, there was the disgrace of it, and, in the second place, she had somehow learnt of our connection, and kept proclaiming it to the household, until I felt perfectly deafened, and had to stop my ears. The point, however, is that other people did *not* stop their ears, but, on the contrary, pricked them. Indeed, I am at a loss what to do.

Really this wretched rabble has driven me to extremities. It all began with my hearing a strange rumour from Thedora—namely, that an unworthy suitor had been to visit you, and had insulted you with an improper proposal. That he had insulted you deeply I knew from my own feelings, for I felt insulted in an equal degree. Upon that, my angel, I went to pieces, and, losing all self-control, plunged headlong. Bursting into an unspeakable frenzy, I was at once going to call upon this villain of a seducer—though what to do next I knew not, seeing that I was fearful of giving you offence. Ah, what a night of sorrow it was, and what a time of gloom, rain, and sleet! Next, I was for returning home, but found myself unable to stand upon my feet. Then Emelia Ilyitch happened to come by. He also is a tchinovnik—or rather, *was* a tchinovnik, since he was turned out of the service some time ago. What he was doing there at that moment I do not know; I only know that I went with him. . . . Surely it cannot give you pleasure to read of the misfortunes of your friend—of his sorrows, and of the temptations which he experienced? . . . On the evening of the third day Emelia urged me to go and see the officer of whom I have spoken, and whose address I had learnt from our dvornik. More strictly speaking, I had noticed him when, on a previous occasion, he had come to play cards here, and I had followed him home. Of course I now see that I did wrong, but I felt beside myself when I heard them telling him stories about me. Exactly what happened next I cannot remember. I only remember that several other officers were present as well as he. Or it may be that I saw everything double,—God alone knows. Also I cannot exactly remember what I said. I only remember that in my fury I said a great deal. Then they turned me out of the room, and threw me down the staircase—pushed me down it, that is to say. How I got home you know. That is all. Of course, later I blamed myself, and my pride underwent a fall; but no extraneous person except yourself knows of the affair—and in any case it does not matter. Perhaps the affair is as you imagine it to have been, Barbara? One thing I know for certain, and that is that last year one of our lodgers, Aksenti Osipovitch, took a similar liberty with Peter Petrovitch, yet kept the fact secret, an absolute secret. He called him into his room (I happened to be looking through a crack in the partition-wall), and had an explanation with him in the way that a gentleman should—no one except myself being a witness of the scene; whereas in my own case I had no explanation at all. After the scene was over nothing further transpired between Aksenti Osipovitch and Peter Petrovitch, for the reason that the latter was so desirous of getting on in life that he held his tongue. As a result they bow and shake hands whenever they meet. . . . I will not dispute the fact that I have erred most grievously—that I should never dare to dispute, or that I have fallen greatly in my own estimation; but I think I was fated from birth so to do—and one cannot escape fate, my beloved. Here, therefore, is a detailed explanation of my misfortunes and sorrows, written for you to read whenever you may find it convenient. I am far from well, beloved, and have lost all my gaiety of disposition, but I send you this letter as a token of my love, devotion, and respect, O dear lady of my affections.—Your humble servant, MAKAR DIEVUSHKIN.

July 29th.

MY DEAREST MAKAR ALEXIEVITCH,—I have read your two letters, and they make my heart ache. See here, dear friend of mine. You pass over certain things in silence, and write about a *portion* only of your misfortunes. Can it be that the letters are the outcome of a mental disorder? . . . Come and see me, for God's sake. Come to-day, direct from the office, and dine with us as you have done before. As to how you are living now, or as to what settlement you have made with your landlady, I know not, for you write nothing concerning those two points, and seem purposely to have left them unmentioned. Au revoir, my friend. Come to me to-day without fail. You would do better *always* to dine here. Thedora is an excellent cook. Good-bye.—Your own,

BARBARA DOBROSELOVA.

August 1st.

MY DARLING BARBARA ALEXIEVNA,—Thank God that He has sent you a chance of repaying my good with good. I believe in so doing, as well as in the sweetness of your angelic heart. Therefore I will not reproach you. Only I pray you, do not again blame me because in the decline of my life I have played the spendthrift. It was such a sin, was it not?—such a thing to do? And even if you would still have it that the sin was there, remember, little friend, what it costs me to hear such words fall from your lips. Do not be vexed with me for saying this, for my heart is fainting. Poor people are subject to fancies—this is a provision of nature. I myself have had reason to know this. The poor man is exacting. He cannot see God's world as it is, but eyes each passer-by askance, and looks around him uneasily in order that he may listen to every word that is being uttered. May not people be talking of him? How is it that he is so unsightly? What is he feeling at all? What sort of figure is he cutting on the one side or on the other? It is matter of common knowledge, my Barbara, that the poor man ranks lower than a rag, and will never earn the respect of any one. Yes, write about him as you like—let scribblers say what they choose about him: he will ever remain as he was. And why is this? It is because, from his very nature, the poor man has to wear his feelings on his sleeve, so that nothing about him is sacred, and as for his self-respect ——! Well, Emelia told me the other day that once, when he had to collect subscriptions, official sanction was demanded for every single coin, since people thought that it would be no use paying their money to a poor man. Nowadays charity is strangely administered. Perhaps it has always been so. Either folk do not know how to administer it, or they are adepts in the art—one of the two. Perhaps you did not know this, so I beg to tell it you. And how comes it that the poor man knows, is so conscious of, it all? The answer is—by experience. He knows because any day he may see a gentleman enter a restaurant and ask himself, "What shall I have to eat to-day? I will have such and such a dish," while all the time the poor man will have nothing to eat that day but gruel. There are men, too—wretched busybodies—who walk about merely to see if they can find some wretched tchinovnik or broken-down official who has got toes projecting from his boots or his hair uncut! And when they have found such a one they make a report of the circumstance, and their rubbish gets entered on the file. . . . But what does it matter to *you* if my hair lacks the shears? If you will forgive me what may seem to you a piece of rudeness, I declare that the poor man is ashamed of such things with the sensitiveness of a young girl. *You*, for instance, would not care (pray pardon my bluntness) to unrobe yourself before the public eye; and in the same way the poor man does not like to be pried at or questioned concerning his family relations, and so forth. A man of honour and self-respect such as I am finds it pain and grief to have to consort with men who would deprive him of both.

To-day I sat before my colleagues like a bear's cub or a plucked sparrow; so that I fairly burned with shame. Yes, it hurt me terribly, Barbara. Naturally one blushes when one can see one's naked toes projecting through one's boots, and one's buttons hanging by a single thread! As though on purpose, I seemed, on this occasion, to be peculiarly dishevelled. No wonder that my spirits fell. When I was talking on business matters to Stepan Karlovitch he suddenly exclaimed, for no apparent reason, "Ah, poor old Makar Alexievitch!" and then left the rest unfinished. But *I* knew what he had in his mind, and blushed so hotly that even the bald patch on my head grew red. Of course the whole thing is nothing, but it worries me, and leads to anxious thoughts. What *can* these fellows know about me? God send that they know nothing! But I confess that

I suspect, I strongly suspect, one of my colleagues. Let them only betray me! They would betray one's private life for a groat, for they hold nothing sacred.

I have an idea who is at the bottom of it all. It is Rataziaev. Probably he knows some one in our department to whom he has recounted the story with additions. Or perhaps he has spread it abroad in his own department, and thence it has crept and crawled into ours. Every one here knows it, down to the last detail, for I have seen them point at you with their fingers through the window. Oh yes, I have seen them do it. Yesterday, when I stepped across to dine with you, the whole crew were hanging out of the window to watch me, and the landlady exclaimed that the devil was in young people, and called you certain unbecoming names. But this is as nothing compared with Rataziaev's foul intention to place us in his books, and to describe us in a satire. He himself has declared that he is going to do so, and other people say the same. In fact, I know not what to think, nor what to decide. It is no use concealing the fact that you and I have sinned against the Lord God. . . . You were going to send me a book of some sort, to divert my mind. Were you not, dearest? What book, though, could now divert me? Only such books as have never existed on earth. Novels are rubbish, and written for fools and the idle. Believe me, dearest, I know it through long experience. Even should they vaunt Shakespeare to you, *I* tell you that Shakespeare is rubbish, and proper only for lampoons.—Your own,

MAKAR DIEVUSHKIN.

August 2nd.

MY DEAREST MAKAR ALEXIEVITCH,—Do not disquiet yourself. God will grant that all shall turn out well. Thedora has obtained a quantity of work, both for me and herself, and we are setting about it with a will. Perhaps it will put us straight again. Thedora suspects my late misfortunes to be connected with Anna Thedorovna; but I do not care—I feel extraordinarily cheerful to-day. So you are thinking of borrowing more money? If so, may God preserve you, for you will assuredly be ruined when the time comes for repayment! You had far better come and live with us here for a little while. Yes, come and take up your abode here, and pay no attention whatever to what your landlady says. As for the rest of your enemies and ill-wishers, I am certain that it is with vain imaginings that you are vexing yourself. . . . In passing, let me tell you that your style differs greatly from letter to letter. Good-bye until we meet again. I await your coming with impatience.—Your own, B. D.

August 3rd.

MY ANGEL, BARBARA ALEXIEVNA,—I hasten to inform you, O light of my life, that my hopes are rising again. But, little daughter of mine—do you really mean it when you say that I am to indulge in no more borrowings? Why, I could not do without them. Things would go badly with us both if I did so. You are ailing. Consequently I tell you roundly that I *must* borrow, and that I must continue to do so.

Also, I may tell you that my seat in the office is now next to that of a certain Emelia Ivanovitch. He is not the Emelia whom *you* know, but a man who, like myself, is a privy councillor, as well as represents, with myself, the senior and oldest official in our department. Likewise he is a good, disinterested soul, and one that is not over-talkative, though a true bear in appearance and demeanour. Industrious, and possessed of a handwriting purely English, his caligraphy is, it must be confessed, even worse than my own. Yes, he is a good soul. At the same time, we have never been intimate with one another. We have done no more than exchange greetings on meeting or parting, borrow one another's penknife if we needed one, and, in short, observe such bare civilities as convention demands. Well, to-day he said to me, "Makar Alexievitch, what makes you look so thoughtful?" and inasmuch as I could see that he wished me well, I told him all: or, rather, I did not tell him *everything*, for that I do to no man (I have not the heart to do it); I told him just a few scattered details concerning my financial straits. "Then you ought to borrow," said he. "You ought to obtain a loan of Peter Petrovitch, who does a little in that way. I myself once borrowed some money of him, and he charged me fair and light interest." Well, Barbara, my heart leapt within me at these words. I kept thinking and thinking, "If only God would put it into the mind of Peter Petrovitch to be my benefactor by advancing me a loan!" I calculated that with its aid I might both repay my landlady and assist yourself and get rid of my surroundings (where I can hardly sit down to table without the rascals making jokes about me). Sometimes his Excellency passes our desk in the office. He glances at me, and cannot but perceive how poorly I am dressed. Now, neatness and cleanliness are two of his strongest points. Even though he says nothing, I feel ready to die with shame when he approaches. Well, hardening my heart, and putting my diffidence into my ragged pocket, I approached Peter Petrovitch, and halted before him more dead than alive. Yet I was hopeful, and though, as it turned out, he was busily engaged in talking to Thedosei Ivanovitch, I walked up to him from behind, and plucked at his sleeve. He looked away from me, but I recited my speech about thirty roubles, et cetera, et cetera, of which, at first, he failed to catch the meaning. Even when I had explained matters to him more fully, he only burst out laughing, and said nothing. Again I addressed to him my request; whereupon, asking me what security I could give, he again buried himself in his papers, and went on writing without deigning me even a second glance. Dismay seized me. "Peter Petrovitch," I said, "I can offer you no security," but to this I added an explanation that some salary would, in time, be due to me, which I would make over to him, and account the loan my first debt. At that moment some one called him away, and I had to wait a little. On returning he began to mend his pen as though he had not even noticed that I was there. But I was for myself this time. "Peter Petrovitch," I continued, "cannot you do *anything?*" Still he maintained silence, and seemed not to have heard me. I waited and waited. At length I determined to make a final attempt, and plucked him by the sleeve. He muttered something, and, his pen mended, set about his writing. There was nothing for me to do but to depart. He and the rest of them are worthy fellows, dearest,—that I do not doubt; but they are also proud, very proud. What have *I* to do with them? Yet I thought I would write and tell you all about it. Meanwhile Emelia Ivanovitch had been encouraging me with nods and smiles. He is a good soul, and has promised to recommend me to a friend of his who lives in Viborskaia Street and lends money. Emelia declares that this friend will certainly lend me a little; so to-morrow, beloved, I am going to call upon the gentleman in question. . . . What do *you* think about it? It would be a pity not to obtain a loan. My landlady is on the point of turning me out of doors, and has refused to allow me any more board. Also, my boots are wearing through, and have lost every button—and I do not possess another pair! Could any one in a government office display greater shabbiness? It is dreadful, my Barbara—it is simply dreadful!

MAKAR DIEVUSHKIN.

August 4th.

MY BELOVED MAKAR ALEXIEVITCH,—For God's sake borrow some money as soon as you can. I would not ask this help of you were it not for the situation in which I am placed. Thedora and myself cannot remain any longer in our present lodgings, for we have been subjected to great unpleasantness, and you cannot imagine my state of agitation and dismay. The reason is that this morning we received a visit from an elderly—almost an old—man whose breast was studded with orders. Greatly surprised, I asked him what he wanted (for at the moment Thedora had gone out shopping); whereupon he began to question me as to my mode of life and occupation, and then, without waiting for an answer, informed me that he was uncle to the officer of whom you have spoken; that he was very angry with his nephew for the way in which the latter had behaved, especially with regard to his slandering of me right and left; and that he, the uncle, was ready to protect me from the young spendthrift's insolence. Also he advised me to have nothing to say to young fellows of that stamp, and added that he sympathised with me as though he were my own father, and would gladly help me in any way he could. At this I blushed in some confusion, but did not greatly hasten to thank him. Next he took me forcibly by the hand, and, tapping my cheek, said that I was very good-looking, and that he greatly liked the dimples in my face (God only knows what he meant!). Finally he tried to kiss me, on the plea that he was an old man, the brute! At this moment Thedora returned; whereupon, in some confusion, he repeated that he felt a great respect for my modesty and virtue, and that he much wished to become acquainted with me; after which he took Thedora aside, and tried, on some pretext or another, to give her money (though of course she declined it). At last he took himself off—again reiterating his assurances, and saying that he intended to return with some ear-rings as a present; that he advised me to change my lodgings; and that he could recommend me a splendid flat which he had in his mind's eye as likely to cost me nothing. Yes, he also declared that he greatly liked me for my purity and good sense; that I must beware of dissolute young men; and that he knew Anna Thedorovna, who had charged him to inform me that she would shortly be visiting me in person. Upon that I understood all. What I did next I scarcely know, for I had never before found myself in such a position; but I believe that I broke all restraints, and made the old man feel thoroughly ashamed of himself—Thedora helping me in the task, and well-nigh turning him neck and crop out of the tenement. Neither of us doubt that this is Anna Thedorovna's work: for how otherwise could the old man have got to know about us?

Now, therefore, Makar Alexievitch, I turn to you for help. Do not, for God's sake, leave me in this plight. Borrow all the money that you can get, for I have not the wherewithal to leave these lodgings, yet cannot possibly remain in them any longer. At all events this is Thedora's advice. She and I need at least twenty-five roubles, which I will repay you out of what I earn by my work, while Thedora shall get me additional work from day to day, so that, if there be heavy interest to pay on the loan, you shall not be troubled with the extra burden. Nay, I will make over to you all that I possess if only you will continue to help me. Truly I grieve to have to trouble you when you yourself are so hardly situated, but my hopes rest upon you, and upon you alone. Good-bye, Makar Alexievitch. Think of me, and may God speed you on your errand! B. D.

August 4th.

MY BELOVED BARBARA ALEXIEVNA,—These unlooked-for blows have shaken me terribly, and these strange calamities have quite broken my spirit. Not content with trying to bring you to a bed of sickness, these lick-spittles and pestilent old men are trying to bring me to the same. And I assure you that they are succeeding—I assure you that they are. Yet I would rather die than not help you. If I cannot help you I *shall* die; but, to enable me to help you, you must flee like a bird out of the nest where these owls, these birds of prey, are seeking to peck you to death. How distressed I feel, my dearest! Yet how cruel you yourself are! Although you are enduring pain and insult, although you, little nestling, are in agony of spirit, you actually tell me that it grieves you to disturb me, and that you will work off your debt to me with the labour of your own hands! In other words, you, with your weak health, are proposing to kill yourself in order to relieve me to term of my financial embarrassments! Stop a moment, and think what you are saying. *Why* should you sew, and work, and torture your poor head with anxiety, and spoil your beautiful eyes, and ruin your health? Why, indeed? Ah, little Barbara, little Barbara! Do you not see that I shall never be any good to you, never any good to you? At all events, I myself see it. Yet I *will* help you in your distress. I *will* overcome every difficulty, I *will* get extra work to do, I *will* copy out manuscripts for authors, I *will* go to the latter and force them to employ me, I *will* so apply myself to the work that they shall see that I am a good copyist (and good copyists, I know, are always in demand). Thus there will be no need for you to exhaust your strength, nor will I allow you to do so—I will not have you carry out your disastrous intention. . . . Yes, little angel, I will certainly borrow some money. I would rather die than not do so. Merely tell me, my own darling, that I am not to shrink from heavy interest, and I will not shrink from it, I will not shrink from it—nay, I will shrink from nothing. I will ask for forty roubles, to begin with. That will not be much, will it, little Barbara? Yet will any one trust me even with that sum at the first asking? Do you think that I am capable of inspiring confidence at the first glance? Would the mere sight of my face lead any one to form of me a favourable opinion? Have I ever been able, remember you, to appear to any one in a favourable light? What think you? Personally, I see difficulties in the way, and feel sick at heart at the mere prospect. However, of those forty roubles I mean to set aside twenty-five for yourself, two for my landlady, and the remainder for my own spending. Of course, I ought to give more than two to my landlady, but you must remember my necessities, and see for yourself that that is the most that can be assigned to her. We need say no more about it. For one rouble I shall buy me a new pair of shoes, for I scarcely know whether my old ones will take me to the office to-morrow morning. Also, a new neck-scarf is indispensable, seeing that the old one has now passed its first year; but, since you have promised to make of your old apron not only a scarf, but also a shirt-front, I need think no more of the article in question. So much for shoes and scarves. Next, for buttons. You yourself will agree that I cannot do without buttons; nor is there on my garments a single hem unfrayed. I tremble when I think that some day his Excellency may perceive my untidiness, and say—well, what will he *not* say? Yet *I* shall never hear what he says, for I shall have expired where I sit—expired of mere shame at the thought of having been thus exposed. Ah, dearest! . . . Well, my various necessities will have left me three roubles to go on with. Part of this sum I shall expend upon a half-pound of tobacco—for I cannot live without tobacco, and it is nine days since I last put a pipe into my mouth. To tell the truth, I shall buy the tobacco without acquainting you with the fact, although I ought not so to do. The pity of it all is that, while you are depriving yourself of everything, I keep solacing *my*self with various amenities: which is why I am telling you this, that the pangs of conscience may not torment me. Frankly, I confess that I am in desperate straits—in such straits as I have never yet known. My landlady flouts me, and I enjoy the respect of no one; my arrears and debts are terrible; and in the office, though never have I found the place exactly a paradise, no one has a single word to say to me. Yet I hide, I carefully hide, this from every one. I would hide my person in the same way, were it not that daily I have to attend the office, where I have to be constantly on my guard against my fellows. Nevertheless, merely to be able to *confess* this to you renews my spiritual strength. We must not think of these things, Barbara, lest the thought of them break our courage. I write them down merely to warn you *not* to think of them, nor to torture yourself with bitter imaginings. Yet, my God, what is to become of us? Stay where you are until I can come to you; after which I shall not return hither, but simply disappear. Now I have finished my letter, and must go and shave myself, inasmuch as, when that is done, one always feels more decent, as well as consorts more easily with decency. God speed me! One prayer to Him, and I must be off. M. DIEVUSHKIN.

August 5th.

DEAREST MAKAR ALEXIEVITCH, — You must not despair. Away with melancholy! I am sending you thirty kopecks in silver, and regret that I cannot send you more. Buy yourself what you most need until to-morrow. I myself have almost nothing left, and what I am going to do I know not. Is it not dreadful, Makar Alexievitch? Yet do not be downcast—it is no good being that. Thedora declares that it would not be a bad thing if we were to remain in this tenement, since if we left it suspicions would arise, and our enemies might take it into their heads to look for us. On the other hand, *I* do not think it would be well for us to remain here. If I were feeling less sad I would tell you my reason.

What a strange man you are, Makar Alexievitch! You take things so much to heart that you never know what it is to be happy. I read your letters attentively, and can see from them that, though you worry and disturb yourself about me, you never give a thought to yourself. Yes, every letter tells me that you have a kind heart; but *I* tell *you* that that heart is over-kind. So I will give you a little friendly advice, Makar Alexievitch. I am full of gratitude towards you—I am indeed full for all that you have done for me, I am most sensible of your goodness; but to think that I should be forced to see that, in spite of your own troubles (of which I have been the involuntary cause), you live for me alone—you live but for *my* joys and *my* sorrows and *my* affection! If you take the affairs of another person so to heart, and suffer with her to such an extent, I do not wonder that you yourself are unhappy. To-day, when you came to see me after office-work was done, I felt afraid even to raise my eyes to yours, for you looked so pale and desperate, and your face had so fallen in. Yes, you were dreading to have to tell me of your failure to borrow money—you were dreading to have to grieve and alarm me; but when you saw that *I* came very near to smiling, the load was, I know, lifted from your heart. So do not be despondent, do not give way, but allow more rein to your better sense. I beg and implore this of you, for it will not be long before you see things take a turn for the better. You will but spoil your life if you constantly lament another person's sorrow. Good-bye, dear friend. I beseech you not to be over-anxious about me. B. D.

August 5th.

My darling little Barbara,—This is well, this is well, my angel! So you are of opinion that the fact that I have failed to obtain any money does not matter? Then I too am reassured, I too am happy on your account. Also, I am delighted to think that you are not going to desert your old friend, but intend to remain in your present lodgings. Indeed, my heart was overcharged with joy when I read in your letter those kindly words about myself, as well as a not wholly unmerited recognition of my sentiments. I say this not out of pride, but because now I know how much you love me to be thus solicitous for my feelings. How good to think that I may speak to you of them! You bid me, darling, not be faint-hearted. Indeed, there is no need for me to be so. Think, for instance, of the pair of shoes which I shall be wearing to the office to-morrow! The fact is that over-brooding proves the undoing of a man—his complete undoing. What has saved me is the fact that it is not for myself that I am grieving, that I am suffering, but for *you*. Nor would it matter to me in the least that I should have to walk through the bitter cold without an overcoat or boots—I could bear it, I could well endure it, for I am a simple man in my requirements; but the point is—what would people say, what would every envious and hostile tongue exclaim, when I was seen without an overcoat? It is for *other* folk that one wears an overcoat and boots. In any case, therefore, I should have needed boots to maintain my name and reputation; to both of which my ragged footgear would otherwise have spelt ruin. Yes, it is so, my beloved, and you may believe an old man who has had many years of experience, and knows both the world and mankind, rather than a set of scribblers and daubers.

But I have not yet told you in detail how things have gone with me to-day. During the morning I suffered as much agony of spirit as might have been experienced in a year. 'Twas like this. First of all, I went out to call upon the gentleman of whom I have spoken. I started very early, before going to the office. Rain and sleet were falling, and I hugged myself in my greatcoat as I walked along. "Lord," thought I, "pardon my offences, and send me fulfilment of all my desires;"

and as I passed a church I crossed myself, repented of my sins, and reminded myself that I was unworthy to hold communication with the Lord God. Then I retired into myself, and tried to look at nothing; and so, walking without noticing the streets, I proceeded on my way. Everything had an empty air, and every one whom I met looked careworn and preoccupied, and no wonder, for who would choose to walk abroad at such an early hour, and in such weather? Next a band of ragged workmen met me, and jostled me boorishly as they passed; upon which nervousness overtook me, and I felt uneasy, and tried hard not to think of the money that was my errand. Near the Voskresenski Bridge my feet began to ache with weariness, until I could hardly pull myself along; until presently I met with Ermolaev, a writer in our office, who, stepping aside, halted, and followed me with his eyes, as though to beg of me a glass of vodka. "Ah, friend," thought I, "go *you* to your vodka, but what have *I* to do with such stuff?" Then, sadly weary, I halted for a moment's rest, and thereafter dragged myself further on my way. Purposely I kept looking about me for something upon which to fasten my thoughts, with which to distract, to encourage myself; but there was nothing. Not a single idea could I connect with any given object, while, in addition, my appearance was so draggled that I felt utterly ashamed of it. At length I perceived from afar a gabled house that was built of yellow wood. This, I thought, must be the residence of the Monsieur Markov whom Emelia Ivanovitch had mentioned to me as ready to lend money on interest. Half unconscious of what I was doing, I asked a watchman if he could tell me to whom the house belonged; whereupon grudgingly, and as though he were vexed at something, the fellow muttered that it belonged to one Markov. Are *all* watchmen so unfeeling? Why did this one reply as he did? In any case I felt disagreeably impressed, for like always answers to like, and, no matter what position one be in, things invariably appear to correspond to it. Three times did I pass the house and walk the length of the street; until the further I walked the worse became my state of mind. " No, never, never will he lend me anything! " thought I to myself, " He does not know me, and my affairs will seem to him ridiculous, and I shall cut a sorry figure. However, let fate decide for me. Only, let Heaven send that I do not afterwards repent me, and eat out my heart with remorse! " Softly I opened the wicket-gate. Horrors! A great ragged brute of a watch-dog came flying out at me, and foaming at the mouth, and nearly jumping out his skin! Curious is it to note what little, trivial incidents will nearly send a man crazy, and strike terror to his heart, and annihilate the firm purpose with which he has armed himself. At all events, I approached the house more dead than alive, and walked straight into another catastrophe. That is to say, not noticing the slipperiness of the threshold, I stumbled against an old woman who was filling milk-jugs from a pail, and sent the milk flying in every direction! The foolish old dame gave a start and a cry, and then demanded of me whither I had been coming, and what it was I wanted; after which she rated me soundly for my awkwardness. Always have I found something of the kind befall me when engaged on errands of this nature. It seems to be my destiny invariably to run into something. Upon that the noise and the commotion brought out the mistress of the house—an old beldame of mean appearance. I addressed myself directly to her. " Does Monsieur Markov live here? " was my inquiry. " No," she replied, and then stood looking at me civilly enough. " But what want you with him? " she continued; upon which I told her about Emelia Ivanovitch and the rest of the business. As soon as I had finished she called her daughter—a barefooted girl in her teens—and told her to summon her father from upstairs. Meanwhile I was shown into a room which contained several portraits of generals on the walls and was furnished with a sofa, a large table, and a few pots of mignonette and balsam. " Shall I, or shall I not (come weal, come woe) take myself off? " was my thought as I waited there. Ah, how I longed to run away! " Yes," I continued, " I had better come again to-morrow, for the weather may then be better, and I shall not have upset the milk, and these generals will not be looking at me so fiercely." In fact, I had actually begun to move towards the door when Monsieur Markov entered—a grey-headed man with thievish eyes, and clad in a dirty dressing-gown fastened with a belt. Greetings over, I stumbled out something about Emelia Ivanovitch and forty roubles, and then came to a dead halt, for his eyes told me that my errand had been futile. "No," said he, "I have no money. Moreover, what security could you offer?" I admitted that I could offer none, but again added something about Emelia, as well as about my pressing needs. Markov heard me out, and then repeated that he had no money. "Ah," thought I, "I might have known this—I might have foreseen it!" And, to tell the truth, Barbara, I could have wished that the earth had opened under my feet, so chilled did I feel as he said what he did, so numbed did my legs grow as shivers began to run down my back. Thus I remained gazing at him while he returned my gaze with a look which said, "Well now, my friend? Why do you not go since you have no further business to do here?" Somehow I felt conscience-stricken. "How is it that you are in such need of money?" was what he appeared to be asking; whereupon I opened my mouth (anything rather than stand there to no purpose at all!) but found that he was not even listening. "I have no money," again he said, "or I would lend you some with pleasure." Several times I repeated that I myself possessed a little, and that I would repay any loan from him punctually, most punctually, and that he might charge me what interest he liked, since I would meet it without fail. Yes, at that moment I remembered our misfortunes, our necessities, and I remembered your half-rouble. "No," said he, "I can lend you nothing without security," and clinched his assurance with an oath, the robber!

How I contrived to leave the house and, passing through Viborskaia Street, to reach the Voskresenski Bridge I do not know. I only remember that I felt terribly weary, cold, and starved, and that it was ten o'clock before I reached the office. Arriving, I tried to clean myself up a little, but Sniegirev, the porter, said that it was impossible for me to do so, and that I should only spoil the brush, which belonged to the Government. Thus, my darling, do such fellows rate me lower than the mat on which they wipe their boots! What is it that will most surely break me? It is not the want of money, but the *little* worries of life—these whisperings and nods and jeers. Any day his Excellency himself may round upon me. Ah, dearest, my golden days are gone. To-day I have spent in reading your letters through; and the reading of them has made me sad. Good-bye, my own, and may the Lord watch over you! M. DIEVUSHKIN.

P.S.—To conceal my sorrow I would have written this letter half jestingly; but the faculty of jesting has not been given me. My one desire, however, is to afford you pleasure. Soon I will come and see you, dearest. Without fail I will come and see you.

August 11th.

O Barbara Alexievna, I am undone—we are both of us undone! Both of us are lost beyond recall! Everything is ruined—my reputation, my self-respect, all that I have in the world! And you as much as I. Never shall we retrieve what we have lost. *I, I* have brought you to this pass, for I have become an outcast, my darling—everywhere I am laughed at and despised. Even my landlady has taken to abusing me. To-day she overwhelmed me with shrill reproaches, and abased me to the level of a hearth-brush. And last night, when I was in Rataziaev's rooms, one of his friends began to read a scribbled note which I had written to you and then inadvertently pulled out of my pocket. O beloved, what laughter there arose at the recital! How those scoundrels mocked at and derided you and myself! I walked up to them, and accused Rataziaev of breaking faith. I said that he had played the traitor. But he only replied that *I* had been the betrayer in the case, by indulging in various amours. "You have kept them very dark though, Mr. Lovelace!" said he: and now I am known everywhere by this name of "Lovelace." They know *everything* about us, my darling, *everything*—both about you and your affairs and about myself; and when to-day I was for sending Phaldoni to the bakeshop for something or other he refused to go, saying that it was not his business. "But you *must* go," said I. "I will not," he replied. "You have not paid my mistress what you owe her, so I am not bound to run your errands." At such an insult from a raw peasant I lost my temper, and called him a fool; to which he retorted in a similar vein. Upon this I thought that he must be drunk, and told him so; whereupon he replied: "*What* say you that I am? Suppose you yourself go and sober up, for I know that the other day you went to visit a woman, and that you got drunk with her on two grivenniks." To such a pass have things come! I feel ashamed to be seen alive. I am, as it were, a man proclaimed; I am in a worse plight even than a tramp who has lost his passport. How misfortunes are heaping themselves upon me! I am lost—I am lost for ever! M. D.

August 13th.

MY BELOVED MAKAR ALEXIEVITCH,—It is true that misfortune is following upon misfortune. I myself scarcely know what to do. Yet, no matter how you may be fairing, you must not look for help from me, for only to-day I burnt my left hand with the iron! At one and the same moment I dropped the iron, made a mistake in my work, and burnt myself! So now I can work no longer. Also, these three days past Thedora has been ailing. My anxiety is becoming positive torture. Nevertheless I send you thirty kopecks—almost the last coins that I have left to me, much as I should have liked to have helped you more when you are so much in need. I feel vexed to the point of weeping. Good-bye, dear friend of mine. You will bring me much comfort if only you will come and see me to-day. B. D.

August 14th.

What is the matter with you, Makar Alexievitch? Surely you cannot fear the Lord God as you ought to do? You are not only driving me to distraction but also ruining yourself with this eternal solicitude for your reputation. You are a man of honour, nobility of character, and self-respect, as every one knows; yet at any moment you are ready to die with shame! Surely you should have more consideration for your grey hairs. No, the fear of God has departed from you. Thedora has told you that it is out of my power to render you any more help. See, therefore, to what a pass you have brought me! Probably you think it is nothing to me that you should behave so badly; probably you do not realise what you have made me suffer. I dare not set foot on the staircase here, for if I do so I am stared at, and pointed at, and spoken about in the most horrible manner. Yes, it is even said of me that I am "united to a drunkard." What a thing to hear! And whenever you are brought home drunk folk say, "They are carrying in that tchinovnik." *That* is not the proper way to make me help you. I swear that I *must* leave this place, and go and get work as a cook or a laundress. It is impossible for me to stay here. Long ago I wrote and asked you to come and see me, yet you have not come. Truly my tears and prayers must mean *nothing* to you, Makar Alexievitch! Whence, too, did you get the money for your debauchery? For the love of God be more careful of yourself, or you will be ruined. How shameful, how abominable of you! So the landlady would not admit you last night, and you spent the night on the doorstep? Oh, I know all about it. Yet if only you could have seen my agony when I heard the news! . . . Come and see me, Makar Alexievitch, and we will once more be happy together. Yes, we will read together, and talk of old times, and Thedora shall tell you of her pilgrimages in former days. For God's sake, beloved, do not ruin both yourself and me. I live for you alone; it is for your sake alone that I am still here. Be your better self once more—the self which still can remain firm in the face of misfortune. Poverty is no crime;

always remember that. After all, why should we despair? Our present difficulties will pass away, and God will right us. Only be brave. I send you two grivenniks for the purchase of some tobacco or anything else that you need; but for the love of heaven do not spend the money foolishly. Come you and see me soon; come without fail. Perhaps you may be ashamed to meet me, as you were before, but you *need* not feel like that—such shame would be misplaced. Only do you bring with you sincere repentance and trust in God, who orders all things for the best. B. D.

August 19th.

MY DEAREST BARBARA ALEXIEVNA,—Yes, I *am* ashamed to meet you, my darling—I *am* ashamed. At the same time, what is there in all this? Why should we not be cheerful again? Why should I mind the soles of my feet coming through my boots? The sole of one's foot is a mere bagatelle—it will never be anything but just a base, dirty sole. And shoes do not matter, either. The Greek sages used to walk about without them, so why should we coddle ourselves with such things? Yet why, also, should I be insulted and despised because of them? Tell Thedora that she is a rubbishy, tiresome, gabbling old woman, as well as an inexpressibly foolish one. As for my grey hairs, you are quite wrong about them, inasmuch as I am not such an old man as you think. Emelia sends you his greeting. You write that you are in great distress, and have been weeping. Well, I too am in great distress, and have been weeping. Nay, nay. I wish you the best of health and happiness, even as I am well and happy myself, so long as I may remain, my darling,—Your friend,

MAKAR DIEVUSHKIN.

August 21st.

MY DEAR AND KIND BARBARA ALEXIEVNA,—I feel that I am guilty, I feel that I have sinned against you. Yet also I feel, from what you say, that it is no use for me so to feel. Even before I had sinned I felt as I do now; but I gave way to despair, and the more so as I recognised my fault. Darling, I am not cruel or hard-hearted. To rend your little soul would be the act of a blood-thirsty tiger, whereas I have the heart of a sheep. You yourself know that I am not addicted to blood-thirstiness, and therefore that I cannot really be guilty of the fault in question, seeing that neither my mind nor my heart have participated in it. Nor can I understand wherein the guilt lies. To me it is all a mystery. When you sent me those thirty kopecks, and thereafter those two grivenniks, my heart sank within me as I looked at the poor little money. To think that though you had burnt your hand, and would soon be hungry, you could write to me that I was to buy tobacco! What was I to do? Remorselessly to rob you, an orphan, as any brigand might do? I felt greatly depressed, dearest. That is to say, persuaded that I should never do any good with my life, and that I was inferior even to the sole of my own boot, I took it into my head that it was absurd for me to aspire at all—rather, that I ought to account myself a disgrace and an abomination. Once a man has lost his self-respect, and decided to abjure his better qualities and human dignity, he falls headlong, and cannot choose but do so. It is decreed of fate, and therefore I am not guilty in this respect. That evening I went out merely to get a breath of fresh air, but one thing followed another: the weather was cold, all nature was looking mournful, and I had fallen in with Emelia. This man had spent everything that he possessed, and, at the time I met him, had not for two days tasted a crust of bread. He had tried to raise money by pawning, but what articles he had for the purpose had been refused by the pawnbrokers. It was more from sympathy for a fellow-man than from any liking for the individual that I yielded. That is how the fault arose, dearest. He spoke of you, and I mingled my tears with his. Yes, he is a man of kind, kind heart—a man of deep feeling. I often feel as he did, dearest, and, in addition, I know how beholden to you I am. As soon as ever I got to know you I began both to realise myself and to love you; for until you came into my life I had been a lonely man—I had been, as it were, asleep rather than alive. In former days my rascally colleagues used to tell me that I was unfit even to be seen; in fact they so disliked me that at length I began to dislike myself, for, being frequently told that I was stupid, I began to believe that I really was so. But the instant that *you* came into my life you lightened the dark places in it, you lightened both my heart and my soul. Gradually I gained rest of spirit, until I had come to see that I was no worse than other men, and that, though I had neither style nor brilliancy nor polish, I was still a *man* as regards my thoughts and feelings. But now, alas! pursued and scorned of fate, I have again allowed myself to abjure my own dignity. Oppressed of misfortune, I have lost my courage. Here is my confession to you, dearest. With tears I beseech you not to inquire further into the matter, for my heart is breaking, and life has grown indeed hard and bitter for me.—Beloved, I offer you my respect, and remain ever your faithful friend, MAKAR DIEVUSHKIN.

September 3rd.

The reason why I did not finish my last letter, Makar Alexievitch, was that I found it so difficult to write. There are moments when I am glad to be alone—to grieve and repine without any one to share my sorrow: and those moments are beginning to come upon me with ever-increasing frequency. Always in my reminiscences I find something which is inexplicable, yet strongly attractive—so much so that for hours together I remain insensible to my surroundings, oblivious of reality. Indeed, in my present life there is not a single impression —pleasant or the reverse—that I encounter which does not recall to my mind something of a similar nature in the past. More particularly is this the case with regard to my childhood, my golden childhood. Yet such moments always leave me depressed. They render me weak, and exhaust my powers of fancy; with the result that my health, already not good, grows steadily worse.

However, this morning it is a fine, fresh, cloudless day, such as we seldom get in autumn. The air has revived me; and I greet it with joy. Yet to think that already the fall of the year has come! How I used to love the country in autumn! Then but a child, I was yet a sensitive being who loved autumn evenings better than autumn mornings. I remember how beside our house, at the foot of a hill, there lay a large pond, and how the pond—I can see it even now!—shone with a broad, level surface that was as clear as crystal. On still evenings this pond would be at rest, and not a rustle would disturb the trees which grew on its banks and overhung the motionless expanse of water. How fresh it used to seem, yet how cold! The dew would be falling upon the turf, lights would be beginning to shine forth from the huts on the pond's margin, and the cattle would be wending their way home. Then quietly I would slip out of the house to look at my beloved pond, and forget myself in contemplation. Here and there a fisherman's bundle of brushwood would be burning at the water's edge, and sending its light far and wide over the surface. Above, the sky would be of a cold blue colour, save for a fringe of flame-coloured streaks on the horizon that kept turning ever paler and paler; and when the moon had come out there would be wafted through the limpid air the sounds of a frightened bird fluttering, of a bulrush rubbing against its fellows in the gentle breeze, and of a fish rising with a splash. Over the dark water there would gather a thin, transparent mist; and though, in the distance, night would be looming, and seemingly enveloping the entire horizon, everything closer at hand would be standing out as though shaped with a chisel—banks, boats, little islands, and all. Beside the margin a derelict barrel would be turning over and over in the water; a switch of laburnum, with yellowing leaves, would go meandering through the reeds; and a belated gull would flutter up, dive again into the cold depths, rise once more, and disappear into the mist. How I would watch and listen to these things! How strangely good they all would seem! But I was a mere infant in those days—a mere child.

Yes, truly I loved autumn-tide—the late autumn when the crops are garnered, and field work is ended, and the evening gatherings in the huts have begun, and every one is awaiting winter. Then does everything become more mysterious, the sky frowns with clouds, yellow leaves strew the paths at the edge of the naked forest, and the forest itself turns black and blue—more especially at eventide when damp fog is spreading and the trees glimmer in the depths like giants, like formless, weird phantoms. Perhaps one may be out late, and have got separated from one's companions. Oh horrors! Suddenly one starts and trembles as one seems to see a strange-looking being peering from out of the darkness of a hollow tree, while all the while the wind is moaning and rattling and howling through the forest—moaning with a hungry sound as it strips the leaves from the bare boughs, and whirls them into the air. High over the tree-tops, in a widespread, trailing, noisy crew, there fly, with resounding cries, flocks of birds which seem to darken and over-lay the very heavens. Then a strange feeling comes over one, until one seems to hear the voice of some one whispering: "Run, run, little child! Do not be out late, for this place will soon have become dreadful! Run, little child! Run!" And at the words terror will possess one's soul, and one will rush and rush until one's breath is spent—until, panting, one has reached home. At home, however, all will look bright and bustling as we children are set to shell peas or poppies, and the damp twigs crackle in the stove, and our mother comes to look fondly at our work, and our old nurse, Iliana, tells us stories of bygone days, or terrible legends concerning wizards and dead men. At the recital we little ones will press closer to one another, yet smile as we do so; when suddenly every one becomes silent. Surely somebody has knocked at the door? . . . But nay, nay; it is only the sound of Frolovna's spinning-wheel. What shouts of laughter arise! Later one will be unable to sleep for fear of the strange dreams which come to visit one; or, if one falls asleep, one will soon wake again, and, afraid to stir, lie quaking under the coverlet until dawn. And in the morning one will arise as fresh as a lark, and look at the window, and see the fields overlaid with hoar-frost, and fine icicles hanging from the naked branches, and the pond covered over with ice as thin as paper, and a white steam rising from the surface, and birds flying overhead with cheerful cries. Next, as the sun rises, he throws his glittering beams everywhere, and melts the thin, glassy ice until the whole scene has come to look bright and clear and exhilarating; and as the fire begins to crackle again in the stove we sit down to the tea-urn, while, chilled with the night cold, our black dog, Polkan, will look in at us through the window, and wag his tail with a cheerful air. Presently a peasant will pass the window in his cart — bound for the forest to cut firewood, and the whole party will feel merry and contented together. Abundant grain lies stored in the byres, and great stacks of wheat are glowing comfortably in the morning sunlight. Every one is quiet and happy, for God has blessed us with a bounteous harvest, and we know that there will be abundance of food for the wintertide. Yes, the peasant may rest assured that his family will not want for aught. Song and dance will arise o'nights from the village girls, and on festival days every one will repair to God's house to thank Him with grateful tears for what He has done. . . . Ah, a golden time was my time of childhood! . . .

Carried away by these memories, I could weep like a child. Everything, everything comes back so clearly to my recollection! The past stands out so vividly before me! Yet in the present everything looks dim and dark! How will it all end?—how? Do you know, I have a feeling, a sort of sure premonition, that I am going to die this coming autumn; for I feel terribly, oh so terribly ill! Often do I think of death, yet feel that I should not like to die here and be laid to rest in the soil of St. Petersburg. Once more I have had to take to my bed, as I did last spring, for I have never really recovered. Indeed I feel so depressed! Thedora has gone out for the day, and I am alone. For a long while past I have been afraid to be left by myself, for I keep fancying that there is some one else in the room, and that that some one is speaking to me. Especially do I fancy this when I have gone off into a reverie, and then suddenly awoken from it, and am feeling bewildered. That is why I have made this letter such a long one; for when I am writing the mood passes away. Good-bye. I have neither time nor paper left for more, and must close. Of the money which I saved to buy a new dress and hat there remains but a single rouble; but I am glad that you have been able to pay your landlady two roubles, for they will keep her tongue quiet for a time. And you must repair your wardrobe.

Good-bye once more. I am so tired! Nor can I think why I am growing so weak—why it is that even the smallest task now wearies me. Even if work should come my way, how am I to do it? That is what worries me above all things. B. D.

September 5th.

MY BELOVED BARBARA,—To-day I have undergone a variety of experiences. In the first place, my head has been aching, and towards evening I went out to get a breath of fresh air along the Fontanka Canal. The weather was dull and damp, and even by six o'clock darkness had begun to set in. True, rain was not actually falling, but only a mist like rain, while the sky was streaked with masses of trailing cloud. Crowds of people were hurrying along Naberezhnaia Street, with faces that looked strange and dejected. There were drunken peasants; snub-nosed old harridans in slippers, and bareheaded; artisans; cab-drivers; every species of beggar; boys; a locksmith's apprentice in a striped smock, with lean, emaciated features which seemed to have been washed in rancid oil; an ex-soldier who was offering penknives and copper rings for sale; and so on, and so on. It was the hour when one would expect to meet no other folk than these. And what a quantity of boats there were on the canal. It made one wonder how they could all find room there. On every bridge were old women selling damp ginger-bread or withered apples, and every woman looked as damp and dirty as her wares. In short, the Fontanka is a saddening spot for a walk, for there is wet granite under one's feet, and tall, dingy buildings on either side of one, and wet mist below and wet mist above. Yes, all was dark and gloomy there this evening.

By the time I had returned to Gorokhovaia Street darkness had fallen, and the lamps had been lit. However, I did not linger long in that particular spot, for Gorokhovaia Street is too noisy a place. But what sumptuous shops and stores it contains! Everything sparkles and glitters, and the windows are full of nothing but bright colours and materials and hats of different shapes. One might think that they were decked merely for display; but no,—people buy these things, and give them to their wives! Yes, it *is* a sumptuous place. Hordes of German hucksters are there, as well as quite respectable traders. And the quantities of carriages which pass along the street! One marvels that the pavement can support so many splendid vehicles, with windows like crystal, linings made of silk and velvet, and lacqueys dressed in epaulets and wearing swords! Into some of them I glanced, and saw that they contained ladies of various ages. Perhaps they were princesses and countesses! Probably at that hour such folk would be hastening to balls and other gatherings. In fact, it was interesting to be able to look so closely at a princess or a great lady. They were all very fine. At all events, I had never before seen such persons as I beheld in those carriages. . . . Then I thought of you. Ah, my own, my darling, it is often that I think of you and feel my heart sink. How is it that *you* are so unfortunate, Barbara? How is it that *you* are so much worse off than other people? In my eyes you are kind-hearted, beautiful, and clever: why, then, has such an evil fate fallen to your lot? How comes it that you are left desolate—you, so good a human being! while to others happiness comes without an invitation at all? Yes, I know—I know it well—that I ought not to say it, for to do so savours of free-thought; but why should that raven, Fate, croak out upon the fortunes of one person while she is yet in her mother's womb, while another person it permits to go forth in happiness from the home which has reared her? To even an idiot of an Ivanushka such happiness is sometimes granted. "You, you fool Ivanushka," says Fate, "shall succeed to your grandfather's money-bags, and eat, drink, and be merry;

whereas *you* (such and such another one) shall do no more than lick the dish, since that is all that you are good for." Yes, I know that it is wrong to hold such opinions, but involuntarily the sin of so doing grows upon one's soul. Nevertheless it is *you*, my darling, who ought to be riding in one of those carriages. Generals would have come seeking your favour, and, instead of being clad in a humble cotton dress, you would have been walking in silken and golden attire. Then you would not have been thin and wan as now, but fresh and plump and rosy-cheeked as a figure on a sugar-cake. Then should I too have been happy—happy if only I could look at your lighted windows from the street, and watch your shadow—happy if only I could think that *you* were well and happy, my sweet little bird! Yet how are things in reality? Not only have evil folk brought you to ruin, but there comes also an old rascal of a libertine to insult you! Just because he struts about in a frockcoat, and can ogle you through a gold-mounted lorgnette, the brute thinks that everything will fall into his hands—that you are bound to listen to his insulting condescension! Out upon him! But why is this? It is because you are an orphan, it is because you are unprotected, it is because you have no powerful friend to afford you the decent support which is your due. *What* do such facts matter to a man or to men to whom the insulting of an orphan is an offence allowed? Such fellows are not men at all, but mere vermin, no matter what they think themselves to be. Of that I am certain. Why, an organ-grinder whom I met in Gorokhovaia Street would inspire more respect than they do, for at least he walks about all day, and suffers hunger—at least he looks for a stray, superfluous groat to earn him subsistence, and is, therefore, a true gentleman, in that he supports himself. To beg alms he would be ashamed; and, moreover, he works for the benefit of mankind just as does a factory machine. "So far as in me lies," says he, "I will give you pleasure." True, he is a pauper, and nothing but a pauper; but at least he is an *honourable* pauper. Though tired and hungry, he still goes on working—working in his own peculiar fashion, yet still doing honest labour.

Yes, many a decent fellow whose labour may be disproportionate to its utility pulls the forelock to no one, and begs his bread of no one. I myself resemble that organ-grinder. That is to say, though not exactly he, I resemble him in this respect, that I work according to my capabilities, and so far as in me lies. More could be asked of no one; nor ought I to be adjudged to do more.

Apropos of the organ-grinder, I may tell you, dearest, that to-day I experienced a double misfortune. As I was looking at the grinder certain thoughts entered my head, and I stood wrapped in a reverie. Some cabmen also had halted at the spot, as well as a young girl, with a yet smaller girl who was dressed in rags and tatters. These people had halted there to listen to the organ-grinder, who was playing in front of some one's windows. Next I caught sight of a little urchin of about ten—a boy who would have been good-looking but for the fact that his face was pinched and sickly. Almost barefooted, and clad only in a shirt, he was standing agape to listen to the music — a pitiful childish figure. Nearer to the grinder a few more urchins were dancing, but in the case of this lad his hands and feet looked numbed, and he kept biting the end of his sleeve and shivering. Also I noticed that in his hands he had a paper of some sort. Presently a gentleman came by, and tossed the grinder a small coin, which fell straight into a box adorned with a representation of a Frenchman and some ladies. The instant he heard the rattle of the coin the boy started, looked timidly round, and evidently made up his mind that *I* had thrown the money; whereupon he ran to me, with his little hands all shaking, and said in a tremulous voice as he proffered me his paper: "Pl—please sign this." I turned over the paper, and saw that there was written on it what is usual under such circumstances. "Kind friends I am a sick mother with three hungry children. Pray help me. Though soon I shall be dead, yet, if you will not forget my little ones in this world, neither will I forget you in the world that is to come." The thing seemed clear enough; it was a matter of life and death. Yet what was *I* to give the lad? Well, I gave him nothing. But my heart ached for him. I am certain that, shivering with cold though he was, and perhaps hungry, the poor lad was not lying. No, no, he was not lying. The shameful point is that so many mothers take no care of their children, but send them out, half-clad, into the cold. Perhaps *this* lad's mother also was a feckless old woman, and devoid of character? Or perhaps she had no one to work for her, but was forced to sit with her legs crossed—a veritable invalid? Or perhaps she was just an old rogue who was in the habit of sending out pinched and hungry boys to deceive the public? What would such a boy learn from begging letters? His heart would soon be rendered callous, for, as he ran about begging, people would pass him by and give him nothing. Yes, their hearts would be as stone, and their replies rough and harsh. "Away with you!" they would say. "You are seeking but to trick us." He would hear that from every one, and his heart would grow hard, and he would shiver in vain with the cold, like some poor little fledgling that has fallen out of the nest. His hands and feet would be freezing, and his breath coming with difficulty; until, look you, he would begin to cough, and disease, like an unclean parasite, would worm its way into his breast until death itself had overtaken him—overtaken him in some fœtid corner whence there was no chance of escape. Yes, that is what his life would become. There are many such cases. Ah, Barbara, it is hard to hear "For Christ's sake!" and yet pass the suppliant by and give nothing, or say merely, "May the Lord give unto you!" Of course, *some* supplications mean nothing (for supplications differ greatly in character). Occasionally supplications are long-drawn-out, and drawling and stereotyped and mechanical—they are purely begging supplications. Requests of this kind it is less hard to refuse, for they are purely professional and of long standing. "The beggar is overdoing it," one thinks to oneself. "He knows the trick too well." But there are other supplications which voice a strange, hoarse, unaccustomed note, like that to-day when I took the poor boy's paper. He had been standing by the kerbstone without speaking to anybody; save that at last to myself he said, "For the love of Christ give me a groat!" in a voice so hoarse and broken that I started, and felt a queer sensation in my heart, although I did *not* give him a groat. Indeed, I had not a groat on me. Rich folk dislike hearing poor people complain of their poverty. "They disturb us," they say, "and are impertinent as well. Why should poverty be so impertinent? Why should its hungry moans prevent us from sleeping?" . . .

To tell you the truth, my darling, I have written the foregoing not merely to relieve my feelings, but, also, still more, to give you an example of the excellent style in which I can write. You yourself will recognise that my style was formed long ago, but of late such fits of despondency have seized upon me that my style has begun to correspond to my feelings; and though I know that such correspondence gains one little, it at least renders one a certain justice. For not unfrequently it happens that, for some reason or another, one feels abased, and inclined to value oneself at nothing, and to account oneself lower than a dishclout; but this merely arises from the fact that at the time one is feeling harassed and depressed, like the poor boy who to-day asked of me alms. Let me tell you an allegory, dearest, and do you hearken to it. Often, as I hasten to the office in the morning, I look around me at the city—I watch it awaking, getting out of bed, lighting its fires, cooking its breakfast, and becoming vocal; and at the sight I begin to feel smaller, as though some one had dealt me a rap on my inquisitive nose. Yes, at such times I slink along with a sense of utter humiliation in my heart. For one would have but to see what is passing within those great, black, grimy houses of the capital, and to penetrate within their walls, for one at once to realise what good reason there is for self-depreciation and heart-searching. Of course you will note that I am speaking figuratively rather than literally. Let us look at what is passing within those houses. In some dingy corner, perhaps, in some damp kennel which is supposed to be a room, an artisan has just awakened from sleep. All night he has dreamt—*if* such an insignificant fellow is capable of dreaming?—about the shoes which last night he mechanically cut out. He is a master-shoemaker, you see, and therefore able to think of nothing but his one subject of interest. Near by are some squalling children and a hungry wife. Nor is he the only man that has to greet the day in this fashion. Indeed, the incident would be nothing—it would not be worth writing about, save for another circumstance. In that same house *another* person—a person of great wealth—may also have been dreaming of shoes; but of shoes of a very different pattern and fashion (in a manner of speaking, if you understand my metaphor, we are all of us shoemakers). This, again, would be nothing, were it not that the rich person has no one to whisper in his ear: "Why dost thou think of such things? Why dost thou think of thyself alone, and live only for thyself—thou who art not a shoemaker? *Thy* children are not ailing. *Thy* wife is not hungry. Look around thee. Can'st thou not find a subject more fitting for thy thoughts than thy shoes?" That is what I want to say to you in allegorical language, Barbara. Maybe it savours a little of free-thought, dearest; but such ideas *will* keep arising in my mind, and finding utterance in impetuous speech. Why, therefore, should one not value oneself at a groat as one listens in fear and trembling to the roar and turmoil of the city? Maybe you think that I am exaggerating things—that this is a mere whim of mine, or that I am quoting from a book? No, no, Barbara. You may rest assured that it is not so. Exaggeration I abhor, with whims I have nothing to do, and of quotation I am guiltless.

I arrived home to-day in melancholy mood. Sitting down to the table, I had warmed myself some tea, and was about to drink a second glass of it, when there entered Gorshkov, the poor lodger. Already, this morning, I had noticed that he was hovering around the other lodgers, and also seeming to want to speak to myself. In passing I may say that his circumstances are infinitely worse than my own; for, only think of it, he has a wife and children! Indeed, if I were he, I do not know what I should do. Well, he entered my room, and bowed to me with the pus standing, as usual, in drops on his eyelashes, his feet shuffling about, and his tongue unable, at first, to articulate a word. I motioned him to a chair (it was a dilapidated one enough, but I had no other), and asked him to have a glass of tea. To this he demurred—for quite a long time he demurred, but at length he accepted the offer. Next, he was for drinking the tea without sugar, and renewed his excuses, but upon the sugar I insisted. After long resistance and many refusals he *did* consent to take some, but only the smallest possible lump; after which he assured me that his tea was perfectly sweet. To what depths of humility can poverty reduce a man! "Well, what is it, my good sir?" I inquired of him; whereupon he replied: "It is this, Makar Alexievitch. You have once before been my benefactor. Pray again show me the charity of God, and assist my unfortunate family. My wife and children have nothing to eat. To think that a father should have to say this!" I was about to speak again when he interrupted me. "You see," he continued, "I am afraid of the other lodgers here. That is to say, I am not so much afraid of, as ashamed to, address them, for they are a proud, conceited lot of men. Nor would I have troubled even you, my friend and former benefactor, were it not that I know that you yourself have experienced misfortune and are in debt: wherefore I have ventured to come and make this request of you, in that I know you not only to be kind-hearted, but also to be in need, and for that reason the more likely to sympathise with me in my distress." To this he added an apology for his awkwardness and presumption. I replied that, glad though I should have been to serve him, I had nothing, absolutely nothing, at my disposal. "Ah, Makar Alexievitch," he went on, "surely it is not much that I am asking of you? My—my wife and children are starving. C-could you not afford me just a grivennik?" At that my heart contracted, "How these people put me to shame!" thought I. But I had only twenty kopecks left, and upon them I had been counting for meeting my most pressing requirements. "No, good sir, I cannot," said I. "Well, what you will," he persisted "Perhaps ten kopecks?" Well I got out my cash-box, and gave him the twenty. It was a good deed. To think that such poverty should exist! Then I had some further talk with him. "How is it," I asked him, "that, though you are in such straits, you have hired a room at five roubles?" He replied that though, when he engaged the room six months ago, he paid three months' rent in advance, his affairs had subsequently turned out badly, and never righted themselves since. You see, Barbara, he was sued at law by a merchant who had defrauded the Treasury in the matter of a contract. When the fraud was discovered the merchant was prosecuted, but the transactions in which he had engaged involved Gorshkov, although the latter had been guilty only of negligence, want of prudence, and culpable indifference to the Treasury's interests. True, the affair had taken place some years ago, but various obstacles had since combined to thwart Gorshkov. "Of the disgrace put upon me," said he to me, "I am innocent. True, I to a certain extent disobeyed orders, but never did I commit theft or embezzlement." Nevertheless the affair lost him his character. He was dismissed the service, and though not adjudged capitally guilty, has been unable since to recover from the merchant a large sum of money which is his by right, as spared to him (Gorshkov) by the legal tribunal. True, the tribunal in question did not altogether believe in Gorshkov, but *I* do so. The matter is of a nature so complex and crooked that probably a hundred years would be insufficient to unravel it; and though it has now to a certain extent been cleared up, the merchant still holds the key to the situation. Personally I side with Gorshkov, and am very sorry for him. Though lacking a post of any kind, he still refuses to despair, though his resources are completely exhausted. Yes, it is a tangled affair, and meanwhile he must live, for, unfortunately, another child which has been born to him has entailed upon the family fresh expenses. Also, another of his children recently fell ill and died: which meant yet further expense. Lastly, not only is his wife in bad health, but he himself is suffering from a complaint of long standing. In short, he has had a very great deal to undergo. Yet he declares that daily he expects a favourable issue to his affair—that he has no doubt of it whatever. I am terribly sorry for him, and said what I could to give him comfort, for he is a man who has been much bullied and misled. He had come to me for protection from his troubles, so I did my best to soothe him. Now, good-bye, my darling. May Christ watch over you and preserve your health. Dearest one, even to think of you is like medicine to my ailing soul. Though I suffer for you, I at least suffer gladly.—Your true friend, MAKAR DIEVUSHKIN.

September 9th.

MY DEAREST BARBARA ALEXIEVNA,—I am beside myself as I take up my pen, for a most terrible thing has happened. My head is whirling round. Ah, beloved, how am I to tell you about it all? I had never foreseen what has happened. But no; I cannot say that I had *never* foreseen it, for my mind *did* get an inkling of what was coming, through my seeing something very similar to it in a dream.

I will tell you the whole story—simply, and as God may put it into my heart. To-day I went to the office as usual, and, on arrival, sat down to write. You must know that I had been engaged on the same sort of work yesterday, and that, while executing it, I had been approached by Timothei Ivanovitch with an urgent request for a particular document. "Makar Alexievitch," he had said, "pray copy this out for me. Copy it as quickly and as carefully as you can, for it will require to be signed to-day." Also let me tell you, dearest, that yesterday I had not been feeling myself, nor able to look at anything. I had been troubled with grave depression—my breast had felt chilled, and my head clouded. All the while I had been thinking of you, my darling. Well, I set to work upon the copying, and executed it cleanly and well, except for the fact that, whether the devil confused my mind, or a mysterious fate so ordained, or the occurrence was simply bound to happen, I left out a whole line of the document, and thus made nonsense of it! The work had been given me too late for signature last night, so it went before his Excellency this morning. I reached the office at my usual hour, and sat down beside Emelia Ivanovitch. Here I may remark that for a long time past I have been feeling twice as shy and diffident as I used to do; I have been finding it impossible to look people in the face. Let only a chair creak, and I become more dead than alive. To-day, therefore, I crept humbly to my seat and sat down in such a crouching posture that Efim Akimovitch (the most touchy man in the world) said to me *sotto voce:* "What on earth makes you sit like that, Makar Alexievitch?" Then he pulled such a grimace that every one near us rocked with laughter at my expense. I stopped my ears, frowned, and sat without moving, for I found this the best method of putting a stop to such merriment. All at once I heard a bustle and a commotion and the sound of some one running towards us. Did my ears deceive me? It was *I* who was being summoned in peremptory tones! My heart started to tremble within me, though I could not say why. I only know that never in my life before had it trembled as it did then. Still I clung to my chair—and at that moment was hardly myself at all. The voices were coming nearer and nearer, until they were shouting in my ear: "Dievushkin! Dievushkin! Where is Dievushkin?" Then at length I raised my eyes, and saw before me Evstafi Ivanovitch. He said to me: "Makar Alexievitch, go at once to his Excellency. You have made a mistake in a document." That was all, but it was enough, was it not? I felt dead and cold as ice—I felt absolutely deprived of the power of sensation; but I rose from my seat and went whither I had been bidden. Through one room, through two rooms, through three rooms I passed, until I was conducted into his Excellency's cabinet itself. Of my thoughts at that moment I can give no exact account. I merely saw his Excellency standing before me, with a knot of people around him. I have an idea that I did not salute him—that I forgot to do so. Indeed, so panic-stricken was I that my teeth were chattering and my knees knocking together. In the first place, I was greatly ashamed of my appearance (a glance into a mirror on the right had frightened me with the reflection of myself that it presented), and, in the second place, I had always been accustomed to comport myself as though no such person as I existed. Probably his Excellency had never before known even that I was alive. Of course, he *might* have heard, in passing, that there was a man named Dievushkin in his department; but never for a moment had he had any intercourse with me.

He began angrily: "What is this you have done, sir? Why are you not more careful? The document was wanted in a hurry, and you have gone and spoilt it. What do *you* think of it?"—the last being addressed to Evstafi Ivanovitch. More I did not hear, except for some flying exclamations of "What negligence and carelessness! How awkward this is!" and so on. I opened my mouth to say something or other; I tried to beg pardon, but could not. To attempt to leave the room I had not the hardihood. There then happened something the recollection of which causes the pen to tremble in my hand with shame. A button of mine—the devil take it!—a button of mine that was hanging by a single thread suddenly broke off, and hopped and skipped and rattled and rolled until it had reached the feet of his Excellency himself—this amid a profound general silence! *That* was what came of my intended self-justification and plea for mercy! *That* was the only answer that I had to return to my chief! The sequel I shudder to relate. At once his Excellency's attention became drawn to my figure and costume. I remembered what I had seen in the mirror, and hastened to pursue the button. Obstinacy of a sort seized upon me, and I did my best to arrest the thing, but it slipped away, and kept turning over and over, so that I could not grasp it, and made a sad spectacle of myself with my awkwardness. Then there came over me a feeling that my last remaining strength was about to leave me, and that all, all was lost—reputation, manhood, everything! In both ears I seemed to hear the voices of Theresa and Phaldoni. At length, however, I grasped the button, and, raising and straightening myself, stood humbly with clasped hands—looking a veritable fool! But no. First of all I tried to attach the button to the ragged threads, and smiled each time that it broke away from them, and smiled again. In the beginning his Excellency had turned away, but now he threw me another glance, and I heard him say to Evstafi Ivanovitch: " What on earth is the matter with the fellow? Look at the figure he cuts! Who to God is he? " Ah, beloved, only to hear that, " Who to God is he? " Truly I had made myself a marked man! In reply to his Excellency Evstafi murmured: " He is no one of any note, though his character is good. Besides, his salary is sufficient as the scale goes." " Very well, then; but help him out of his difficulties somehow," said his Excellency. " Give him a trifle of salary in advance." " It is all forestalled," was the reply. " He drew it some time ago. But his record is good. There is nothing against him." At this I felt as though I were in Hell fire. I could actually have died! " Well, well," said his Excellency, " let him copy out the document a second time. Dievushkin, come here. You are to make another copy of this paper, and to make it as quickly as possible." With that he turned to some other officials present, issued to them a few orders, and the company dispersed. No sooner had they done so than his Excellency hurriedly pulled out a pocket-book, took thence a note for a hundred roubles, and, with the words, " Take this. It is as much as I can afford. Treat it as you like," placed the money in my hand! At this, dearest, I started and trembled, for I was moved to my very soul. What next I did I hardly know, except that I know that I seized his Excellency by the hand. But he only grew very red, and then—no, I am not departing by a hair's-breadth from the truth—it is true that he took this unworthy hand in his, and shook it! Yes, he took this hand of mine in his, and shook it, as though I had been his equal, as though I had been a general like himself! " Go now," he said. " This is all that I can do for you. Make no further mistakes, and I will overlook your fault."

What I think about it is this. I beg of you and of Thedora, and had I any children I should beg of them also, to pray ever to God for his Excellency. I should say to my children: " For your father you need not pray; but for his Excellency I bid you pray until your lives shall end." Yes, dear one—I tell you this in all solemnity, so hearken well unto my words—that though, during these cruel days of our adversity, I have nearly died of distress of soul at the sight of you and your poverty, as well as at the sight of myself and my abasement and helplessness, I yet care less for the hundred roubles which his Excellency has given me than for the fact that he was good enough to take the hand of a wretched drunkard in his own and press it. By that act he restored me to myself. By that act he revived my courage, he made life for ever sweet to me. . . . Yes, sure am I that, sinner though I be before the Almighty, my prayers for the happiness and prosperity of his Excellency will yet ascend to the Heavenly Throne! . . .

But, my darling, for the moment I am terribly agitated and distraught. My heart is beating as though it would burst my breast, and all my body seems weak. . . . I send you forty-five roubles in notes. Another twenty I shall give to my landlady, and the remaining thirty-five I shall keep—twenty for new clothes and fifteen for actual living expenses. But these experiences of the morning have shaken me to the core, and I must rest a while. It is quiet, very quiet, here. My breath is coming in jerks: deep down in my breast I can hear it sobbing and trembling. . . . I will come and see you soon, but at the moment my head is aching with these various sensations. God sees all things, my darling, my priceless treasure!—Your steadfast friend,

MAKAR DIEVUSHKIN.

September 10th.

MY BELOVED MAKAR ALEXIEVITCH,—I am unspeakably rejoiced at your good fortune, and fully appreciate the kindness of your superior. Now, take a rest from your cares. Only do not *again* spend money to no advantage. Live as quietly and as frugally as possible, and from to-day begin always to set aside something, lest misfortune again overtake you. Do not, for God's sake, worry yourself: Thedora and I will get on somehow. Why have you sent me so much money? I really do not need it—what I had already would have been quite sufficient. True, I shall soon be needing further funds if I am to leave these lodgings, but Thedora is hoping before long to receive repayment of an old debt. Of course, at least *twenty* roubles will have to be set aside for indispensable requirements, but the remainder shall be returned to you. Pray take care of it, Makar Alexievitch. Now, good-bye. May your life continue peaceful, and may you preserve your health and spirits. I would have written to you at greater length had I not felt so terribly weary. Yesterday I never left my bed. I am glad that you have promised to come and see me. Yes, you *must* pay me a visit.

B. D.

September 11th.

MY DARLING BARBARA ALEXIEVNA,—I implore you not to leave me now that I am once more happy and contented. Disregard what Thedora says, and I will do anything in the world for you. I will behave myself better, even if only out of respect for his Excellency, and guard my every action. Once more we will exchange cheerful letters with one another, and make mutual confidence of our thoughts and joys and sorrows (if so be that we shall know any more sorrows?). Yes, we will live twice as happily and comfortably as of old. Also, we will exchange books. . . . Angel of my heart, a great change has taken place in my fortunes—a change very much for the better. My landlady has become more accommodating; Theresa has recovered her senses; even Phaldoni springs to do my bidding. Likewise I have made my peace with Rataziaev. He came to see me of his own accord, the moment that he heard the glad tidings. There can be no doubt that he is a good fellow, that there is no truth in the slanders that one hears of him. For one thing, I have discovered that he never had any intention of putting me and yourself into a book. This he told me himself, and then read to me his latest work. As for his calling me "Lovelace," he had intended no rudeness or indecency thereby. The term is merely one of foreign derivation, meaning a clever fellow, or, in more literary and elegant language, a gentleman with whom one must reckon. That is all;

it was a mere harmless jest, my beloved. Only ignorance made me lose my temper, and I have expressed to him my regret. . . . How beautiful is the weather to-day, my little Barbara! True, there was a slight frost in the early morning, as though scattered through a sieve, but it was nothing, and the breeze soon freshened the air. I went out to buy some shoes, and obtained a splendid pair. Then, after a stroll along the Nevski Prospect, I read *The Daily Bee*. This reminds me that I have forgotten to tell you the most important thing of all. It happened like this:—

This morning I had a talk with Emelia Ivanovitch and Aksenti Michaelovitch concerning his Excellency. Apparently I am not the only person to whom he has acted kindly and been charitable, for he is known to the whole world for his goodness of heart. In many quarters his praises are to be heard; in many quarters he has called forth tears of gratitude. Among other things he undertook the care of an orphaned girl, and married her to an official, the son of a poor widow, and found this man place in a certain chancellory, and in other ways benefited him. Well, dearest, I considered it to be my duty to add my mite by publishing abroad the story of his Excellency's gracious treatment of myself. Accordingly I related the whole occurrence to my interlocutors, and concealed not a single detail. In fact, I put my pride into my pocket—though why should I feel ashamed of having been elated by such an occurrence? "Let it only be noised afield," said I to myself, "and it will redound greatly to his Excellency's credit." So I expressed myself enthusiastically on the subject and never faltered. On the contrary, I felt proud to have such a story to tell. I referred to every one concerned (except to yourself, of course, dearest)—to my landlady, to Phaldoni, to Rataziaev, to Markov. I even mentioned the matter of my shoes! Some of those standing by laughed—in fact every one present did so, but probably it was my own figure or the incident of my shoes—more particularly the latter—that excited merriment, for I am sure it was not meant ill-naturedly. My hearers may have been young men, or well off: certainly they cannot have been laughing with evil intent at what I had said. Anything against his Excellency *cannot* have been in their thoughts. Eh, Barbara?

Even now I cannot wholly collect my faculties, so upset am I by recent events. . . . Have you any fuel to go on with, Barbara? You must not expose yourself to cold. Also, you have depressed my spirits with your fears for the future. Daily I pray to God on your behalf. Ah, *how* I pray to Him! . . . Likewise, have you any woollen stockings to wear, and warm clothes generally? Mind you, if there is anything you need, you must not hurt an old man's feelings by failing to apply to him for what you require. The bad times are gone now, and the future is looking bright and fair.

But what bad times they were, Barbara, even though they be gone, and can no longer matter! As the years pass on we shall gradually recover ourselves. How clearly I remember my youth! In those days I never had a kopeck to spare. Yet, cold and hungry though I was, I was always light-hearted. In the morning I would walk the Nevski Prospect, and meet nice-looking people, and be happy all day. Yes, it was a glorious, a glorious time! It was good to be alive, especially in St. Petersburg. Yet it is but yesterday that I was beseeching God with tears to pardon me my sins during the late sorrowful period—to pardon me my murmurings and evil thoughts and gambling and drunkenness. And you I remembered in my prayers, for you alone have encouraged and comforted me, you alone have given me advice and instruction. I shall never forget that, dearest. To-day I gave each one of your letters a kiss. . . . Good-bye, beloved. I have been told that there is going to be a sale of clothing somewhere in this neighbourhood. Once more good-bye, good-bye, my angel.—Yours in heart and soul,

MAKAR DIEVUSHKIN.

September 15th.

MY DEAREST MAKAR ALEXIEVITCH,—I am in terrible distress. I feel sure that something is about to happen. The matter, my beloved friend, is that Monsieur Bwikov is again in St. Petersburg, for Thedora has met him. He was driving along in a drozhki, but, on meeting

Thedora, he ordered the coachman to stop, sprang out, and inquired of her where she was living; but this she would not tell him. Next he said with a smile that he knew quite well who was living with her (evidently Anna Thedorovna had told him); whereupon Thedora could hold out no longer, but then and there, in the street, railed at and abused him—telling him that he was an immoral man, and the cause of all my misfortunes. To this he replied that a person who did not possess a groat must surely be rather badly off; to which Thedora retorted that I could always either live by the labour of my hands or marry—that it was not so much a question of my losing posts as of my losing my happiness, the ruin of which had led almost to my death. In reply he observed that, though I was still quite young, I seemed to have lost my wits, and that my "virtue appeared to be under a cloud" (I quote his exact words). Both I and Thedora had thought that he does not know where I live; but, last night, just as I had left the house to make a few purchases in the Gostinni Dvor, he appeared at our rooms (evidently he had not wanted to find me at home), and put many questions to Thedora concerning our way of living. Then, after inspecting my work, he wound up with: "Who is this tchinovnik friend of yours?" At the moment you happened to be passing through the courtyard, so Thedora pointed you out, and the man peered at you, and laughed. Thedora next asked him to depart—telling him that I was still ill from grief, and that it would give me great pain to see him there; to which, after a pause, he replied that he had come because he had had nothing better to do. Also, he was for giving Thedora twenty-five roubles, but, of course, she declined them. What does it all mean? Why has he paid this visit? I cannot understand his getting to know about me. I am lost in conjecture. Thedora, however, says that Aksinia, her sister-in-law (who sometimes comes to see her), is acquainted with a laundress named Nastasia, and that this woman has a cousin in the position of watchman to a department of which a certain friend of Anna Thedorovna's nephew forms one of the staff. Can it be, therefore, that an intrigue has been hatched through *this* channel? But Thedora may be entirely mistaken. We hardly know what to think. What if he should come again? The very thought terrifies me. When Thedora told me of this last night such terror seized upon me that I almost swooned away. What can the man be wanting? At all events I refuse to know such people. What have they to do with my wretched self? Ah, how I am haunted with anxiety, for every moment I keep thinking that Bwikov is at hand! *What* will become of me? *What* more has fate in store for me? For Christ's sake come and see me, Makar Alexievitch! For Christ's sake come and see me soon!

September 18th.

MY BELOVED BARBARA ALEXIEVNA,—To-day there took place in this house a most lamentable, a most mysterious, a most unlooked-for occurrence. First of all let me tell you that poor Gorshkov has been entirely absolved of guilt. The decision has been long in coming, but this morning he went to hear the final resolution read. It was entirely in his favour. Any culpability which had been imputed to him for negligence and irregularity was removed by the resolution. Likewise he was authorised to recover of the merchant a large sum of money. Thus he stands entirely justified, and has had his character cleansed from all stain. In short, he could not have wished for a more complete vindication. When he arrived home at three o'clock he was looking as white as a sheet, and his lips were quivering. Yet there was a smile on his face as he embraced his wife and children. In a body the rest of us ran to congratulate him, and he was greatly moved by the act. Bowing to us, he pressed our hands in turn. As he did so I thought, somehow, that he seemed to have grown taller and straighter, and that the pus-drops seemed to have disappeared from his eyelashes. Yet how agitated he was, poor fellow! He could not rest quietly for two minutes together, but kept picking up and then dropping whatsoever came to his hand, and bowing and smiling without intermission, and sitting down and getting up, and again sitting down, and chattering God only knows what about his honour and his good name and his little ones. How he did talk—yes, and weep too! Indeed, few of ourselves could refrain from tears; although Rataziaev remarked (probably to encourage Gorshkov) that honour mattered nothing when one had nothing to eat, and that money was the chief thing in the world, and that for it alone ought God to be thanked. Then he slapped Gorshkov on the shoulder, but I thought that Gorshkov somehow seemed hurt at this. He did not express any open displeasure, but threw Rataziaev a curious look, and removed his hand from his shoulder. *Once* upon a time he would not have acted thus; but characters differ. For example, I myself should have hesitated, at such a season of rejoicing, to seem proud, even though excessive deference and civility at such a moment might have been construed as a lapse both of moral courage and of mental vigour. However, this is none of my business. All that Gorshkov said was: " Yes, money *is* a good thing, glory be to God! " In fact, the whole time that we remained in his room he kept repeating to himself: " Glory be to God, glory be to God! " His wife ordered a richer and more delicate meal than usual, and the landlady herself cooked it, for at heart she is not a bad woman. But until the meal was served Gorshkov could not remain still. He kept entering every one's room in turn (whether invited thither or not), and, seating himself smilingly upon a chair, would sometimes say something, and sometimes not utter a word, but get up and go out again. In the naval officer's room he even took a pack of playing-cards into his hand, and was thereupon invited to make a fourth in a game; but after losing a few times, as well as making several blunders in his play, he abandoned the pursuit. " No," said he, " that is the sort of man that I am—that is all that I am good for," and departed. Next, encountering myself in the corridor, he took my hands in his, and gazed into my face with a rather curious air. Then he pressed my hands again, and moved away still smiling, smiling, but in an odd, weary sort of manner, much as a corpse might smile. Meanwhile his wife was weeping for joy, and everything in their room was decked in holiday guise. Presently dinner was served, and after they had dined Gorshkov said to his wife: "See now, dearest, I am going to rest a little while;" and with that went to bed. Presently he called his little daughter to his side, and, laying his hand upon the child's head, lay a long while looking at her. Then he turned to his wife again, and asked her: "What of Petinka? Where is our Petinka?" whereupon his wife crossed herself, and replied: "Why, our Petinka is dead!" "Yes, yes, I know—of course," said her husband. "Petinka is now in the Kingdom of Heaven." This showed his wife that her husband was not quite in his right senses—that the recent occurrence had upset him; so she said: "My dearest, you must sleep awhile." "I will do so," he replied, "— at once—I am rather——" And he turned over, and lay silent for a time. Then again he turned round, and tried to say something, but his wife could not hear what it was. "What do you say?" she inquired, but he made no reply. Then again she waited a few moments until she thought to herself, "He has gone to sleep," and departed to spend an hour with the landlady. At the end of that hour she returned—only to find that her husband had not yet awoken, but was still lying motionless. "He is sleeping very soundly," she reflected as she sat down and began to work at something or other. Since then she has told us that when half an hour or so had elapsed she fell into a reverie. What she was thinking of she cannot remember, save that she had forgotten altogether about her husband. Then she awoke with a curious sort of sensation at her heart. The first thing that struck her was the deathlike stillness of the room. Glancing at the bed, she perceived her husband to be lying in the same position as before. Thereupon she approached him, turned the coverlet back, and saw that he was stiff and cold—that he had died suddenly, as though smitten with a stroke. But of what precisely he died God only knows. The affair has so terribly impressed me that even now I cannot fully collect my thoughts. It would scarcely be believed that a human being could die so simply—and he such a poor, needy wretch, this Gorshkov! What a fate, what a fate, to be sure! His wife is plunged in tears and panic-stricken, while his little daughter has run away somewhere to hide herself. In their room, however, all is bustle and confusion, for the doctors are about to make an autopsy on the corpse. But I cannot tell you things for certain; I only know that I am most grieved, most grieved. How sad to think that one never knows what even a day, what even an hour, may bring forth! One seems to die to so little purpose! . . .—Your own

MAKAR DIEVUSHKIN.

September 19th.

MY BELOVED BARBARA ALEXIEVNA,—I hasten to let you know that Rataziaev has found me some work to do for a certain writer—the latter having submitted to him a large manuscript. Glory be to God, for this means a large amount of work to do. Yet, though the copy is wanted in haste, the original is so carelessly written that I hardly know how to set about my task. Indeed, certain parts of the manuscript are almost undecipherable. I have agreed to do the work for forty kopecks a sheet. You see, therefore (and this is my true reason for writing to you), that we shall soon be receiving money from an extraneous source. Good-bye now, as I must begin upon my labours.—Your sincere friend, MAKAR DIEVUSHKIN.

September 23rd.

MY DEAREST MAKAR ALEXIEVITCH,—I have not written to you these three days past for the reason that I have been so worried and alarmed.

Three days ago Bwikov came again to see me. At the time I was alone, for Thedora had gone out somewhere. As soon as I opened the door the sight of him so terrified me that I stood rooted to the spot, and could feel myself turning pale. Entering with his usual loud laugh, he took a chair, and sat down. For a long while I could not collect my thoughts: I just sat where I was, and went on with my work. Soon his smile faded, for my appearance seemed somehow to have struck him. You see, of late I have grown thin, and my eyes and cheeks have fallen in, and my face has become as white as a sheet; so that any one who knew me a year ago would scarcely recognise me now. After a prolonged inspection Bwikov seemed to recover his spirits, for he said something to which I duly replied. Then again he laughed. Thus he sat for a whole hour —talking to me the while, and asking me questions about one thing and another. At length, just before he rose to depart, he took me by the hand, and said (to quote his exact words): "Between ourselves, Barbara Alexievna, that kinswoman of yours and my good friend and acquaintance—I refer to Anna Thedorovna —is a very bad woman" (he also added a grosser term of opprobrium). "First of all she led your cousin astray, and then she ruined yourself. I also have behaved like a villain, but such is the way of the world." Again he laughed. Next, having remarked that, though not a master of eloquence, he had always considered that obligations of gentility obliged him to have with me a clear and outspoken explanation, he went on to say that he sought my hand in marriage; that he looked upon it as a duty to restore to me my honour; that he could offer me riches; that, after marriage, he would take me to his country seat in the Steppes, where we would hunt hares; that he intended never to visit St. Petersburg again, since everything there was horrible, and he had to entertain a worthless nephew whom he had sworn to disinherit in favour of a legal heir; and, finally, that it was to obtain such a legal heir that he was seeking my hand in marriage. Lastly he remarked that I seemed to be living in very poor circumstances (which was not surprising, said he, in view of the kennel that I inhabited); that I should die if I remained a month longer in that den; that all lodgings in St. Petersburg were detestable; and that he would be glad to know if I was in want of anything.

So thunderstruck was I with the proposal that I could only burst into tears. These tears he interpreted as a sign of gratitude, for he told me that he had always felt assured of my good sense, cleverness, and sensibility, but that hitherto he had hesitated to take this step until he should have learnt precisely how I was getting on. Next he asked me some questions about *you*; saying that he had heard of you as a man of good principle, and that since he was unwilling to remain your debtor, would a sum of five hundred roubles repay you for all you had done for me? To this I replied that your services to myself had been such as could never be requited with money; whereupon he exclaimed that I was talking rubbish and nonsense; that evidently I was still young enough to read poetry; that romances of this kind were the undoing of young girls, that books only corrupted morality, and that, for his part, he could not abide them. "You ought to live as long as *I* have done," he added, "and *then* you will see what men can be." With that he requested me to give his proposal my favourable consideration—saying that he would not like me to take such an important step unguardedly, since want of thought and impetuosity often spelt ruin to youthful inexperience, but that he hoped to receive an answer in the affirmative. "Otherwise," said he, "I shall have no choice but to marry a certain merchant's daughter in Moscow, in order that I may keep my vow to deprive my nephew of the inheritance." Then he pressed five hundred roubles into my hand—to buy myself some bon-bons, as he phrased it—and wound up by saying that in the country I should grow as fat as a doughnut or a cheese rolled in butter; that at the present moment he was extremely busy; and that, deeply engaged in business though he had been all day, he had snatched the present opportunity of paying me a visit. At length he departed. For a long time I sat plunged in reflection. Great though my distress of mind was, I soon arrived at a decision. . . . My friend, I am going to marry this man; I have no choice but to accept his proposal. If any one could save me from this squalor, and restore to me my good name, and avert from me future poverty and want and misfortune, he is the man to do it. What else have I to look for from the future? What more am I to ask of fate? Thedora declares that one need *never* lose one's happiness; but what, I ask *her*, can be called happiness under such circumstances as mine? At all events I see no other road open, dear friend. I see nothing else to be done. I have worked until I have ruined my health. I cannot go on working for ever. Shall I go out into the world? Nay; I am worn to a shadow with grief, and become good for nothing. Sickly by nature, I should merely be a burden upon other folks. Of course this marriage will not bring me paradise, but what else does there remain, my friend—what else does there remain? What other choice is left?

I had not asked your advice earlier for the reason that I wanted to think the matter over alone. However, the decision which you have just read is unalterable, and I am about to announce it to Bwikov himself, who in any case has pressed me for a speedy reply, owing to the fact (so he says) that his business will not wait nor allow him to remain here longer, and that therefore no trifle must be allowed to stand in its way. God alone knows whether I shall be happy, but my fate is in His holy, His inscrutable hand, and I have so decided. Bwikov is said to be kind hearted. He will at least respect me, and perhaps I shall be able to return that respect. What more could be looked for from such a marriage?

I have now told you all, Makar Alexievitch, and feel sure that you will understand my despondency. Do not, however, try to divert me from my intention, for all your efforts will be in vain. Think for a moment; weigh in your heart for a moment all that has led me to take this step. At first my anguish was extreme, but now I am quieter. What awaits me I know not. What must be must be, and as God may send. . . .

Bwikov has just arrived, so I am leaving this letter unfinished. Otherwise I had much else to say to you. Bwikov is even now at the door! . . .

September 23rd.

MY BELOVED BARBARA ALEXIEVNA,—I hasten to reply to you—I hasten to express to you my extreme astonishment. . . . In passing I may mention that yesterday we buried poor Gorshkov. . . . Yes, Bwikov has acted nobly, and you have no choice but to accept him. All things are in God's hands. This is so, and must always be so; and the purposes of the Divine Creator are at once good and inscrutable, as also is Fate, which is one with Him. . . . Thedora will share your happiness—for, of course, you will be happy, and free from want, darling, dearest, sweetest of angels! But why should the matter be so hurried? Oh, of course—Monsieur Bwikov's business affairs. Only a man who has no affairs to see to can afford to disregard such things. I got a glimpse of Monsieur Bwikov as he was leaving your door. He is a fine-looking man—a very fine-looking man: though that is not the point that I should most have noticed had I been quite myself at the time. . . . In future shall we be able to write letters to one another? I keep wondering and wondering what has led you to say all that you have done. To think that just when twenty pages of my copying are completed *this* has happened! . . . I suppose you will be able to make many purchases now—to buy shoes and dresses and all sorts of things? Do you remember the shops in Gorokhovaia Street of which I used to speak? . . . But no. You ought not to go out at present—you simply ought not to, and shall not. Presently you will be able to buy many, many things, and to keep a carriage. Also, at present the weather is bad. Rain is descending in pailfuls, and it is such a soaking kind of rain that—that you might catch cold from it, my darling, and the chill might go to your heart. Why should your fear of this man lead you to take such risks when all the time *I* am here to do your bidding? So Thedora declares great happiness to be awaiting you, does she? She is a gossiping old woman, and evidently desires to ruin you. Shall you be at the all-night Mass this evening, dearest? I should like to come and see you there. Yes, Bwikov spoke but the truth when he said that you are a woman of virtue, wit, and good feeling. Yet I think he would do far better to marry the merchant's daughter. What think *you* about it? Yes, 'twould be far better for him. As soon as it grows dark to-night I mean to come and sit with you for an hour. To-night twilight will close in early, so I shall soon be with you. Yes, come what may, I mean to see you for an hour. At present, I suppose, you are expecting Bwikov, but I will come as soon as he has gone. So stay at home until I have arrived, dearest.

MAKAR DIEVUSHKIN.

September 27th.

DEAR MAKAR ALEXIEVITCH,—Bwikov has just informed me that I must have at least three dozen linen blouses; so I must go at once and look for sempstresses to make two out of the three dozen, since time presses. Indeed, Monsieur Bwikov is quite angry about the fuss which these fripperies are entailing, seeing that there remain but five days before the wedding, and we are to depart on the following day. He keeps rushing about and declaring that no time ought to be wasted on trifles. I am terribly worried, and scarcely able to stand on my feet. There is so much to do, and, perhaps, so much that were better left undone! Moreover, I have no blond or other lace; so *there* is another item to be purchased, since Bwikov declares that he cannot have his bride look like a cook, but, on the contrary, she must "put the noses of the great ladies out of joint." That is his expression. I wish, therefore, that you would go to Madame Chiffon's, in Gorokhovaia Street, and ask her, in the first place, to send me some sempstresses, and, in the second place, to give herself the trouble of coming in person, as I am too ill to go out. Our new flat is very cold, and still in great disorder. Also, Bwikov has an aunt who is at her last gasp through old age, and may die before our departure. He himself, however, declares this to be nothing, and says that she will soon recover. He is not yet living with me, and I have to go running hither and thither to find him. Only Thedora is acting as my servant, together with Bwikov's valet, who oversees everything, but has been absent for the past three days. Each morning Bwikov goes to business, and loses his temper. Yesterday he even had some trouble with the police because of his thrashing the steward of these buildings. . . . I have no one to send with this letter, so I am going to post it. . . . Ah! I had almost forgotten the most important point—which is that I should like you to go and tell Madame Chiffon that I wish the blond lace to be changed in conformity with yesterday's patterns, if she will be good enough to bring with her a new assortment. Also say that I have altered my mind about the satin, which I wish to be tamboured with crochet-work; also that tambour is to be used with monograms on the various garments. Do you hear? Tambour, not smooth work. Do not forget that it is to be tambour. Another thing I had almost forgotten: which is that the lappets of the fur cloak must be raised, and the collar bound with lace. Please tell her these things, Makar Alexievitch.—Your friend, B. D.

P.S.—I am so ashamed to trouble you with my commissions! This is the third morning that you will have spent in running about for my sake. But what else am I to do? The whole place is in disorder, and I myself am ill. Do not be vexed with me, Makar Alexievitch. I am feeling so depressed! What is going to become of me, dear friend, dear, kind, old Makar Alexievitch? I dread to look forward into the future. Somehow I feel apprehensive; I am living, as it were, in a mist. Yet, for God's sake, forget none of my commissions. I am so afraid lest you should make a mistake! Remember that everything is to be tambour work, not smooth.

September 27th.

MY BELOVED BARBARA ALEXIEVNA,—I have carefully fulfilled your commissions. Madame Chiffon informs me that she herself had thought of using tambour work, as being more suitable (though I did not quite take in all she said). Also, she has informed me that, since you have given certain directions in writing, she has followed them (though again I do not clearly remember all that she said—I only remember that she said a very great deal, for she is a most tiresome old woman). These observations she will soon be repeating to you in person. For myself, I feel absolutely exhausted, and have not been to the office to-day. . . . Do not despair about the future, dearest. To save you trouble I would visit every shop in St. Petersburg. You write that you dare not look forward into the future. But by to-night, at seven o'clock, you will have learnt all, for Madame Chiffon will have arrived in person to see you. Hope on, and everything will order itself for the best. Of course I am referring only to these accursed gewgaws, to these frills and fripperies! Ah me, ah me, how glad I shall be to see you, my angel! Yes, how glad I shall be! Twice already to-day I have passed the gates of your abode. Unfortunately, this Bwikov is a man of such choler that—— Well, things are as they are.

MAKAR DIEVUSHKIN.

September 28th.

MY DEAREST MAKAR ALEXIEVITCH,—For God's sake go to the jeweller's, and tell him that, after all, he need not make the pearl and emerald ear-rings. Monsieur Bwikov says that they will cost him too much, that they will burn a veritable hole in his pocket. In fact, he has lost his temper again, and declares that he is being robbed. Yesterday he added that, had he but known, but foreseen, these expenses, he would never have married. Also, he says that, as things are, he intends only to have a plain wedding, and then to depart. "You must not look for any dancing or festivity or entertainment of guests, for our gala times are still in the air." Such were his words. God knows I do not want such things, but none the less Bwikov has forbidden them. I made him no answer on the subject, for he is a man all too easily irritated. What, what is going to become of me?

B. D.

September 28th.

MY BELOVED BARBARA ALEXIEVNA,—All is well as regards the jeweller. Unfortunately I have also to say that I myself have fallen ill, and cannot rise from bed. Just when so many things need to be done I have gone and caught a chill, the devil take it! Also I have to tell you that, to complete my misfortunes, his Excellency has been pleased to become stricter. To-day he railed at and scolded Emelia Ivanovitch until the poor fellow was quite put about. That is the sum of my news. No—there is something else concerning which I should like to write to you, but am afraid to obtrude upon your notice. I am a simple, dull fellow who writes down whatsoever first comes into his head.—Your friend,

MAKAR DIEVUSHKIN.

September 29th.

MY OWN BARBARA ALEXIEVNA,—To-day, dearest, I saw Thedora, who informed me that you are to be married to-morrow, and on the following day to go away—for which purpose Bwikov has ordered a post-chaise. . . . Well, of the incident of his Excellency I have already told you. Also I have verified the bill from the shop in Gorokhovaia Street. It is correct, but very long. Why is Monsieur Bwikov so out of humour with you? Nay, but you must be of good cheer, my darling. *I* am so, and shall always be so so long as you are happy. I should have come to the church to-morrow, but, alas! shall be prevented from doing so by the pain in my loins. Also, I would have written an account of the ceremony, but that there will be no one to report to me the details. . . . Yes, you have been a very good friend to Thedora, dearest. You have acted kindly, very kindly, towards her. For every such deed God will bless you. Good deeds never go unrewarded, nor does virtue ever fail to win the crown of divine justice, be it early or be it late. Much else should I have liked to write to you. Every hour, every minute I could occupy in writing. Indeed I could write to you for ever! Only your book, *The Stories of Bielkin*, is left to me. Do not deprive me of it, I pray you, but suffer me to keep it. It is not so much because I wish to read the book for its own sake as because winter is coming on, when the evenings will be long and dreary, and one will want to read at least *something*. Do you know, I am going to move from my present quarters into your old ones, which I intend to rent from Thedora; for I could never part with that good old woman. Moreover, she is such a splendid worker. Yesterday I inspected your empty room in detail, and inspected your embroidery-frame, with the work still hanging on it. It had been left untouched in its corner. Next I inspected the work itself, of which there still remained a few remnants, and saw that you had used one of my letters for a spool upon which to wind your thread. Also, on the table I found a scrap of paper which had written on it, "My dearest Makar Alexievitch, I hasten to——" that was all. Evidently some one had interrupted you at an interesting point. Lastly, behind a screen there was your little bed. . . . O darling of darlings!!! . . . Well, good-bye now, good-bye now, but for God's sake send me something in answer to this letter!

MAKAR DIEVUSHKIN.

September 30th.

MY BELOVED MAKAR ALEXIEVITCH,—All is over! The die is cast! What my lot may have in store I know not, but I am submissive to the will of God. To-morrow, then, we depart. For the last time I take my leave of you, my friend beyond price, my benefactor, my dear one! Do not grieve for me, but try to live happily. Think of me sometimes, and may the blessing of Almighty God light upon you! For myself, I shall often have you in remembrance, and recall you in my prayers. Thus our time together has come to an end. Little comfort in my new life shall I derive from memories of the past. The more, therefore, shall I cherish the recollection of you, and the dearer will you ever be to my heart. Here you have been my only friend; here you alone have loved me. Yes, I have seen all, I have known all—I have throughout known how well you love me. A single smile of mine, a single stroke from my pen, has been able to make you happy. . . . But now you must forget me. . . . How lonely you will be! Why should you stay here at all, kind, inestimable, but solitary, friend of mine? To your care I entrust the book, the embroidery frame, and the letter upon which I had begun. When you look upon the few words which the letter contains you will be able mentally to read in thought all that you would have liked further to hear or receive from me—all that I would so gladly have written, but can never now write. Think sometimes of your poor little Barbara who loved you so well. All your letters I have left behind me in the top drawer of Thedora's chest of drawers. . . . You write that you are ill, but Monsieur Bwikov will not let me leave the house to-day; so that I can only write to you. Also, I will write again before long. That is a promise. Yet God only knows when I shall be able to do so. . . . Now we must bid one another for ever farewell, my friend, my beloved, my own! Yes, it must be for ever! Ah, how at this moment I could embrace you! Good-bye, dear friend—good-bye, good-bye! May you ever rest well and happy! To the end I shall keep you in my prayers. How my heart is aching under its load of sorrow! . . . Monsieur Bwikov is just calling for me. . . . —Your ever loving B.

P.S.—My heart is full! It is full to bursting of tears! Sorrow has me in its grip, and is tearing me to pieces. Good-bye. My God, what grief!

Do not, do not forget your poor Barbara!

BELOVED BARBARA—MY JEWEL, MY PRICELESS ONE,—You are now almost en route, you are now just about to depart! Would that they had torn my heart out of my breast rather than have taken you away from me! How could you allow it? You weep, yet you go! And only this moment I have received from you a letter stained with your tears! It must be that you are departing unwillingly; it must be that you are being abducted against your will; it must be that you are sorry for me; it must be that—that you *love* me! . . . Yet how will it fare with you now? Your heart will soon have become chilled and sick and depressed. Grief will soon have sucked away its life; grief will soon have rent it in twain. Yes, you will die where you be, and be laid to rest in the cold, moist earth where there is no one to bewail you. Monsieur Bwikov will only be hunting hares! . . . Ah, my darling, my darling! *Why* did you come to this decision? How could you bring yourself to take such a step? What have you done, have you done, have you done? Soon they will be carrying you away to the tomb; soon your beauty will have become defiled, my angel. Ah, dearest one, you are as weak as a feather. And where have *I* been all this time? What have *I* been thinking of? I have treated you merely as a froward child whose head was aching. Fool that I was, I neither saw nor understood, I have behaved as though, right or wrong, the matter was in no way my concern. Yes, I have been running about after fripperies! . . . Ah, but I *will* leave my bed. To-morrow I *will* rise sound and well, and be once more myself. . . . Dearest, I could throw myself under the wheels of a passing vehicle rather than that you should go like this. By what right is it being done? . . . I will go with you; I will run behind your carriage if you will not take me—yes, I will run, and run so long as the power is in me, and until my breath shall have failed. Do you know whither you are going? Perhaps you will not know, and will have to ask me? Before you there lie the Steppes, my darling—only the Steppes, the naked Steppes, the Steppes that are as bare as the palm of my hand. *There* there live only heartless old women and rude peasants and drunkards. *There* the trees have already shed their leaves. *There* there abide but rain and cold. Why should you go thither? True, Monsieur Bwikov will have his diversions in that country—he will be able to hunt the hare: but what of yourself? Do you wish to become a mere estate lady? Nay; look at yourself, my seraph of heaven. Are you in any way fitted for such a rôle? How could you play it? To whom should I write letters? To whom should I send these missives? Whom should I call "my darling"? To whom should I apply that name of endearment? Where, too, could I find you? When you are gone, Barbara, I shall die—for certain I shall die, for my heart cannot bear this misery. I love you as I love the light of God; I love you as my own daughter; to you I have devoted my love in its entirety; only for you have I lived at all; only because you were near me have I worked and copied manuscripts and committed my views to paper under the guise of friendly letters. Perhaps you did not know all this, but it has been so. How, then, my beloved, could you bring yourself to leave me? Nay, you *must* not go—it is impossible, it is sheerly, it is utterly, impossible. The rain will fall upon you, and you are weak, and will catch cold. The floods will stop your carriage. No sooner will it have passed the city barriers than it will break down, purposely break down. Here, in St. Petersburg, they are bad builders of carriages. Yes, I know well these carriage-builders. They are jerry-builders who can fashion a toy, but nothing that is durable. Yes, I swear they can make nothing that is durable. . . . All that I can do is to go upon my knees before Monsieur Bwikov, and to tell him all, to tell him all. Do you also tell him all, dearest, and reason with him. Tell him that you *must* remain here, and must not go. Ah, why did he not marry that merchant's daughter in Moscow? Let him go and marry her now. She would suit him far better and for reasons which I well know. Then I could keep you. For what is he to you, this Monsieur Bwikov? Why has he suddenly become so dear to your heart? Is it because he can buy you gewgaws? What are *they?* What use are *they?* They are so much rubbish. One should consider human life rather than mere finery. Nevertheless, as soon as I have received my next instalment of salary I mean to buy you a new cloak. I mean to buy it at a shop with which I am acquainted. Only, you must wait until my next instalment is due, my angel of a Barbara. Ah, God, my God! To think that you are going away into the Steppes with Monsieur Bwikov—that you are going away never to return! . . . Nay, nay, but you *shall* write to me. You *shall* write me a letter as soon as you have started, even if it be your last letter of all, my dearest. Yet will it be your last letter? How has it come about so suddenly, so irrevocably, that this letter should be your last? Nay, nay; *I* will write, and you shall write—yes, *now,* when at length I am beginning to improve my style. Style? I do not know what I am writing. I never do know what I am writing. I could not possibly know, for I never read over what I have written, nor correct its orthography. At the present moment I am writing merely for the sake of writing, and to put as much as possible into this last letter of mine. . . .

Ah, dearest, my pet, my own darling! . . .

THE GAMBLER

THE GAMBLER

I

At length I returned from two weeks' leave of absence to find that my patrons had arrived three days ago in Roulettenberg. I received from them a welcome quite different to that which I had expected. The General eyed me coldly, greeted me in rather haughty fashion, and dismissed me to pay my respects to his sister. It was clear that from *somewhere* money had been acquired. I thought I could even detect a certain shamefacedness in the General's glance. Maria Philipovna, too, seemed distraught, and conversed with me with an air of detachment. Nevertheless, she took the money which I handed to her, counted it, and listened to what I had to tell. To luncheon there were expected that day a Monsieur Mezentsov, a French lady, and an Englishman; for, whenever money was in hand, a banquet in Muscovite style was always given. Polina Alexandrovna, on seeing me, inquired why I had been so long away. Then, without waiting for an answer, she departed. Evidently this was not mere accident, and I felt that I must throw some light upon matters. It was high time that I did so.

I was assigned a small room on the fourth floor of the hotel (for you must know that I belonged to the General's suite). So far as I could see, the party had already gained some notoriety in the place, which had come to look upon the General as a Russian nobleman of great wealth. Indeed, even before luncheon he charged me, among other things, to get two thousand-franc notes changed for him at the hotel counter, which put us in a position to be thought millionaires—at all events for a week! Later I was about to take Mischa and Nadia for a walk when a summons reached me from the staircase that I must attend the General. He began by deigning to inquire of me where I was going to take the children; and as he did so I could see that he failed to look me in the eyes. He *wanted* to do so, but each time was met by me with such a fixed, disrespectful stare that he desisted in confusion. In pompous language, however, which jumbled one sentence into another, and at length grew disconnected, he gave me to understand that I was to lead the children altogether away from the Casino, and out into the park. Finally his anger exploded, and he added sharply:

"I suppose you would like to take them to the Casino to play roulette? Well, excuse my speaking so plainly, but I know how addicted you are to gambling. Though I am not your mentor, nor wish to be, at least I have a right to require that you shall not actually *compromise* me."

"I have no money for gambling," I quietly replied.

"But you will soon be in receipt of some," retorted the General, reddening a little as he dived into his writing desk and applied himself to a memorandum book. From it he saw that he had 120 roubles of mine in his keeping.

"Let us calculate," he went on. "We must translate these roubles into thalers. Here—take 100 thalers, as a round sum. The rest will be safe in my hands."

In silence I took the money.

"You must not be offended at what I say," he continued. "You are too touchy about these things. What I have said I have said merely as a warning. To do so is no more than my right."

When returning home with the children before luncheon, I met a cavalcade of our party riding to view some ruins. Two splendid carriages, magnificently horsed, with Mlle. Blanche, Maria Philipovna, and Polina Alexandrovna in one of them, and the Frenchman, the Englishman, and the General in attendance on horseback! The passers-by stopped to stare at them, for the effect was splendid—the General could not have improved upon it. I calculated that, with the 4000 francs which I had brought with me, added to what my patrons seemed already to have acquired, the party must be in possession of at least 7000 or 8000 francs—though that would be none too much for Mlle. Blanche, who, with her mother and the Frenchman, was also lodging in our hotel. The latter gentleman was called by the lacqueys "Monsieur le Comte," and Mlle. Blanche's mother was dubbed "Madame la Comtesse." Perhaps in very truth they *were* "Comte et Comtesse."

I knew that "Monsieur le Comte" would take no notice of me when we met at dinner, as also that the General would not dream of introducing us, nor of recommending me to the "Comte." However, the latter had lived awhile in Russia, and knew that the person referred to as an "uchitel" is never looked upon as a bird of fine feather. Of course, strictly speaking, he *knew* me; but I was an uninvited guest at the luncheon—the General had forgotten to arrange otherwise, or I should have been dispatched to dine at the table d'hôte. Nevertheless I presented myself in such guise that the General looked at me with a touch of approval; and though the good Maria Philipovna was for showing me my place, the fact of my having previously met the Englishman, Mr. Astley, saved me, and thenceforward I figured as one of the company.

This strange Englishman I had met first in Prussia, where we had happened to sit *vis-à-vis* in a railway train in which I was travelling to overtake our party; while, later, I had run across him in France, and again in Switzerland—twice within the space of two weeks! To think, therefore, that I should suddenly encounter him again here, in Roulettenberg! Never in my life had I known a more retiring man, for he was shy to the pitch of imbecility, yet well aware of the fact (for he was no fool). At the same time, he was a gentle, amiable sort of an individual, and, even on our first encounter in Prussia I had contrived to draw him out, and he had told me that he had just been to the North Cape, and was now anxious to visit the fair at Nizhni Novgorod. How he had come to make the General's acquaintance I do not know, but, apparently, he was much struck with Polina. Also, he was delighted that I should sit next him at table, for he appeared to look upon me as his bosom friend.

During the meal the Frenchman was in great feather: he was discursive and pompous to every one. In Moscow too, I remembered, he had blown a great many bubbles. Interminably he discoursed on finance and Russian politics, and though, at times, the General made feints to contradict him, he did so humbly, and as though wishing not wholly to lose sight of his own dignity.

For myself, I was in a curious frame of mind. Even before luncheon was half finished I had asked myself the old, eternal question: "*Why* do I continue to dance attendance upon the General, instead of having left him and his family long ago?" Every now and then I would glance at Polina Alexandrovna, but she paid me no attention; until eventually I became so irritated that I decided to play the boor.

First of all I suddenly, and for no reason whatever, plunged loudly and gratuitously into the general conversation. Above everything I wanted to pick a quarrel with the Frenchman; and with that end in view I turned to the General, and exclaimed in an overbearing sort of way—indeed, I think that I actually interrupted him—that that summer it had been almost impossible for a Russian to dine anywhere at tables d'hôte. The General bent upon me a glance of astonishment.

"If one is a man of self-respect," I went on, "one risks abuse by so doing, and is forced to put up with insults of every kind. Both at Paris and on the Rhine—yes, and even in Switzerland—there are so many Poles, with their sympathisers, the French, at these tables d'hôte that one cannot get a word in edgeways if one happens only to be a Russian."

This I said in French. The General eyed me doubtfully, for he did not know whether to be angry or merely to feel surprised that I should so far forget myself.

"Of course, one always learns *something everywhere*," said the Frenchman in a careless, contemptuous sort of tone.

"In Paris, too, I had a dispute with a Pole," I continued, "and then with a French officer who supported him. After that a section of the Frenchmen present took my part. They did so as soon as I told them the story of how once I threatened to spit into Monsignor's coffee."

"To spit into it?" the General inquired with grave disapproval in his tone, and a stare of astonishment, while the Frenchman looked at me unbelievingly.

"Just so," I replied. "You must know that, on one occasion, when, for two days, I had felt certain that at any moment I might have to depart for Rome on business, I repaired to the Embassy of the Holy See in Paris, to have my passport visaed. There I encountered a sacristan of about fifty, and a man dry and cold of mien. After listening politely, but with great reserve, to my account of myself, this sacristan asked me to wait a little. I was in a great hurry to depart, but of course I sat down, pulled out a copy of *L'Opinion Nationale,* and fell to reading an extraordinary piece of invective against Russia which it happened to contain. As I was thus engaged I heard some one enter an adjoining room and ask for Monsignor; after which I saw the sacristan make a low bow to the visitor, and then another bow as the visitor took his leave. I ventured to remind the good man of my own business also; whereupon, with an expression of, if anything, increased dryness, he again asked me to wait. Soon a third visitor arrived who, like myself, had come on business (he was an Austrian of some sort); and as soon as ever he had stated his errand he was conducted upstairs! This made me very angry. I rose, approached the sacristan, and told him that, since Monsignor was receiving callers, his lordship might just as well finish off *my* affair as well. Upon this the sacristan shrunk back in astonishment. It simply passed his understanding that any insignificant Russian should dare to compare himself with other visitors of Monsignor's! In a tone of the utmost effrontery, as though he were delighted to have a chance of insulting me, he looked me up and down, and then said: 'Do you suppose that Monsignor is going to put aside his coffee for *you?*' But I only cried the louder: 'Let me tell you that I am going to *spit* into that coffee! Yes, and if you do not get me my passport visaed this very minute, I shall take it to Monsignor myself!"

"What? While he is engaged with a Cardinal?" screeched the sacristan, again shrinking back in horror. Then, rushing to the door, he spread out his arms as though he would rather die than let me enter.

Thereupon I declared that I was a heretic and a barbarian—"Je suis hérétique et barbare," I said—and that these archbishops and cardinals and monsignors, and the rest of them, meant nothing at all to me. In a word, I showed him that I was not going to give way. He looked at me with an air of infinite resentment. Then he snatched up my passport, and departed with it upstairs. A minute later the passport had been visaed! Here it is now, if you care to see it,"—and I pulled out the document, and exhibited the Roman visa.

"But——" the General began.

"What really saved you was the fact that you proclaimed yourself a heretic and a barbarian," remarked the Frenchman with a smile. "Cela n'était pas si bête."

"But is *that* how Russian subjects ought to be treated? Why, when they settle here they dare not utter even a word—they are ready even to deny the fact that they are Russians! At all events, at my hotel in Paris I received far more attention from the company after I had told them about the fracas with the sacristan. A fat Polish nobleman, who had been the most offensive of all who were present at the table d'hôte, at once went upstairs, while some of the Frenchmen were simply disgusted when I told them that two years ago I had encountered a man at whom, in 1812, a French 'hero' fired for the mere fun of discharging his musket. That man was then a boy of ten, and his family are still residing in Moscow."

"Impossible!" the Frenchman spluttered. "*No* French soldier would fire at a child!"

"Nevertheless the incident was as I say," I replied. "A very respected ex-captain told me the story, and I myself could see the scar left on his cheek."

The Frenchman then began chattering volubly, and the General supported him; but I recommended the former to read, for example, extracts from the memoirs of General Perovski, who, in 1812, was a prisoner in the hands of the French. Finally Maria Philipovna said something to interrupt the conversation. The General was furious with me for having started the altercation with the Frenchman. On the other hand, Mr. Astley seemed to take great pleasure in my brush with Monsieur, and, rising from the table, proposed that we should go and have a drink together. The same afternoon, at four o'clock, I went to have my customary talk with Polina Alexandrovna; and the talk soon extended to a stroll. We entered the Park, and approached the Casino, where Polina seated herself upon a bench near the fountain, and sent Nadia away to a little distance to play with some other children. Mischa also I dispatched to play by the fountain, and in this fashion we—that is to say, Polina and myself—contrived to find ourselves alone.

Of course, we began by talking on business matters. Polina seemed furious when I handed her only 700 gülden, for she had thought to receive from Paris, as the proceeds of the pledging of her diamonds, at least 2000 gülden, or even more.

"Come what may, I *must* have money," she said. "And get it somehow I will—otherwise I shall be ruined."

I asked her what had happened during my absence.

"Nothing; except that two pieces of news have reached us from St. Petersburg. In the first place, my grandmother is very ill, and unlikely to last another couple of days. We had this from Timothy Petrovitch himself, and he is a reliable person. Every moment we are expecting to receive news of the end."

"All of you are on the tiptoe of expectation?" I queried.

"Of course—all of us, and every minute of the day. For a year-and-a-half now we have been looking for this."

"Looking for it?"

"Yes, looking for it. I am not her blood relation, you know—I am merely the General's step-daughter.

Yet I am certain that the old lady has remembered me in her will."

"Yes, I believe that you *will* come in for a good deal," I said with some assurance.

"Yes, for she is fond of me. But how come you to think so?"

I answered this question with another one. "That Marquis of yours," I said, "—is *he* also familiar with your family secrets?"

"And why are you yourself so interested in them?" was her retort as she eyed me with dry grimness.

"Never mind. If I am not mistaken, the General has succeeded in borrowing money of the Marquis."

"It may be so."

"Is it likely that the Marquis would have lent the money if he had not known something or other about your grandmother? Did you notice, too, that three times during luncheon, when speaking of her, he called her 'La Baboulenka'?[1] What loving, friendly behaviour, to be sure!"

"Yes, that is true. As soon as ever he learnt that I was likely to inherit something from her he began to pay me his addresses. I thought you ought to know that."

"Then he has only just begun his courting? Why, I thought he had been doing so a long while!"

"You *know* he has not," retorted Polina angrily. "But where on earth did you pick up this Englishman?" She said this after a pause.

"I *knew* you would ask about him!" Whereupon I told her of my previous encounters with Astley while travelling.

"He is very shy," I said, "and susceptible. Also, he is in love with you."

"Yes, he *is* in love with me," she replied.

"And he is ten times richer than the Frenchman. In fact, what does the Frenchman possess? To me it seems at least doubtful that he possesses anything at all."

"Oh, no, there is no doubt about it. He does possess

[1] Dear little Grandmother.

some château or other. Last night the General told me that for certain. *Now* are you satisfied?"

"Nevertheless, in your place I should marry the Englishman."

"And why?" asked Polina.

"Because, though the Frenchman is the handsomer of the two, he is also the baser; whereas the Englishman is not only a man of honour, but ten times the wealthier of the pair."

"Yes? But then the Frenchman is a marquis, and the cleverer of the two," remarked Polina imperturbably.

"Is that so?" I repeated.

"Yes; absolutely."

Polina was not at all pleased at my questions; I could see that she was doing her best to irritate me with the brusquerie of her answers. But I took no notice of this.

"It amuses me to see you grow angry," she continued. "However, inasmuch as I allow you to indulge in these questions and conjectures, you ought to pay me something for the privilege."

"I consider that I have a perfect right to put these questions to you," was my calm retort; "for the reason that I am ready to pay for them, and also care little what becomes of me."

Polina giggled.

"Last time you told me—when on the Schlangenberg—that at a word from me you would be ready to jump down a thousand feet into the abyss. Some day I may remind you of that saying, in order to see if you will be as good as your word. Yes, you may depend upon it that I shall do so. I hate you because I have allowed you to go to such lengths, and I also hate you—and still more—because you are so necessary to me. For the time being I want you, so I must keep you."

Then she made a movement to rise. Her tone had sounded very angry. Indeed, of late her talks with me had invariably ended on a note of temper and irritation—yes, of real temper.

"May I ask you who is this Mlle. Blanche?" I inquired

(since I did not wish Polina to depart without an explanation).

"You *know* who she is—just Mlle. Blanche. Nothing further has transpired. Probably she will soon be Madame General—that is to say, if the rumours that Grandmamma is nearing her end should prove true. Mlle. Blanche, with her mother and her cousin, the Marquis, know very well that, as things now stand, we are ruined."

"And is the General at last in love?"

"That has nothing to do with it. Listen to me. Take these 700 florins, and go and play roulette with them. Win as much for me as you can, for I am badly in need of money."

So saying, she called Nadia back to her side, and entered the Casino, where she joined the rest of our party. For myself, I took, in musing astonishment, the first path to the left. Something had seemed to strike my brain when she told me to go and play roulette. Strangely enough, that something had also seemed to make me hesitate, and to set me analysing my feelings with regard to her. In fact, during the two weeks of my absence I had felt far more at my ease than I did now, on the day of my return; although, while travelling, I had moped like an imbecile, rushed about like a man in a fever, and actually beheld her in my dreams. Indeed, on one occasion (this happened in Switzerland, when I was asleep in the train) I had spoken aloud to her, and set all my fellow-travellers laughing. Again, therefore, I put to myself the question: "Do I, or do I not, love her?" and again I could return myself no answer—or, rather, for the hundredth time I told myself that I detested her. Yes, I detested her; there were moments (more especially at the close of our talks together) when I would gladly have given half my life to have strangled her! I swear that, had there, at such moments, been a sharp knife ready to my hand, I would have seized that knife with pleasure, and plunged it into her breast. Yet I also swear that if, on the Schlangenberg, she had *really* said to me, "Leap into that abyss," I should have leapt into it, and with equal pleasure. Yes, this I knew well. One way or the other, the thing must soon be ended. She, too, knew it in some curious way; the thought that I was fully conscious of her inaccessibility, and of the impossibility of my ever realising my dreams, afforded her, I am certain, the keenest possible pleasure. Otherwise, is it likely that she, the cautious and clever woman that she was, would have indulged in this familiarity and openness with me? Hitherto (I concluded) she had looked upon me in the same light that the old Empress did upon her servant—the Empress who hesitated not to unrobe herself before her slave, since she did not account a slave a man. Yes, often Polina must have taken me for something less than a man!"

Still, she had charged me with a commission—to win what I could at roulette. Yet all the time I could not help wondering *why* it was so necessary for her to win something, and what new schemes could have sprung to birth in her ever-fertile brain. A host of new and unknown factors seemed to have arisen during the last two weeks. Well, it behoved me to divine them, and to probe them, and that as soon as possible. Yet not now: at the present moment I must repair to the roulette-table.

II

I CONFESS I did not like it. Although I had made up my mind to play, I felt averse to doing so on behalf of some one else. In fact, it almost upset my balance, and I entered the gaming-rooms with an angry feeling at my heart. At first glance the scene irritated me. Never at any time have I been able to bear the flunkeyishness which one meets in the Press of the world at large, but more especially in that of Russia, where, almost every evening, journalists write on two subjects in particular—namely, on the splendour and luxury of the casinos to be found in the Rhenish towns, and on the heaps of gold which are daily to be seen lying on their tables. Those journalists are not paid for doing so: they write thus merely out of a spirit of disinterested complaisance. For there is nothing splendid about the establishments in question; and not only are there no heaps of gold to be seen lying on their tables, but also there is very little money to be seen at all. Of course, during the season, *some* madman or another may make his appearance—generally an Englishman, or an Asiatic, or a Turk—and (as had happened during the summer of which I write) win or lose a great deal; but, as regards the rest of the crowd, it plays only for petty gülden, and seldom does much wealth figure on the board. When, on the present occasion, I entered the gaming-rooms (for the first time in my life), it was several moments before I could even make up my mind to play. For one thing, the crowd oppressed me. Had I been playing for myself, I think I should have left at once, and never have embarked upon gambling at all, for I could feel my heart beginning to beat, and my heart was anything but cold-blooded. Also, I knew, I had long ago made up my mind, that never should I depart from Roulettenberg until some radical, some final, change had taken place in my fortunes. Thus it must and would be. However ridiculous it may seem to you that I was expecting to win at roulette, I look upon the generally accepted opinion concerning the folly and the grossness of hoping to win at gambling as a thing even *more* absurd. For why is gambling a whit worse than any other method of acquiring money? How, for instance, is it worse than trade? True, out of a hundred persons, only one can win; yet what business is that of yours or of mine?

At all events, I confined myself at first simply to looking on, and decided to attempt nothing serious. Indeed, I felt that, if I began to do anything at all, I should do it in an absent-minded, haphazard sort of way—of that I felt certain. Also, it behoved me to learn the game itself; since, despite a thousand descriptions of roulette which I had read with ceaseless avidity, I knew nothing of its rules, and had never even seen it played.

In the first place, everything about it seemed to me so foul—so morally mean and foul. Yet I am not speaking of the hungry, restless folk who, by scores—nay, even by hundreds—could be seen crowded around the gaming-tables. For in a desire to win quickly and to win much I can see nothing sordid; I have always applauded the opinion of a certain dead and gone, but cocksure, moralist who replied to the excuse that "one may always gamble moderately" by saying that to do so makes things worse, since, in that case, the profits too will always be moderate. Insignificant profits and sumptuous profits do not stand on the same footing. No, it is all a matter of proportion. What may seem a small sum to a Rothschild may seem a large sum to me, and it is not the fault of stakes or of winnings that everywhere men can be found winning, can be found depriving their fellows of something, just as they do at roulette. As to the question whether stakes and winnings are, in themselves, immoral is another question altogether, and I wish to express no opinion upon it. Yet the very fact that I was full of a strong desire to win caused this gambling for gain, in spite of its attendant squalor, to contain, if you will, something intimate, something sympathetic, to my eyes: for it is always pleasant to see men dispensing with ceremony, and acting naturally, and in an unbuttoned mood. . . . Yet why should I so deceive myself? I could see that the whole thing was a vain and unreasoning pursuit; and what, at the first glance, seemed to me the ugliest feature in this mob of roulette players was their respect for their occupation—the seriousness, and even the humility, with which they stood around the gaming-tables. Moreover, I had always drawn sharp distinctions between a game which is *de mauvais genre* and a game which is permissible to a decent man. In fact, there are two sorts of gaming—namely, the game of the gentleman and the game of the plebs—the game for gain, and the game of the herd. Herein, as said, I draw sharp distinctions. Yet how essentially base are the distinctions! For instance, a gentleman may stake, say, five or ten louis d'or—seldom more, unless he is a very rich man, when he may stake, say, a thousand francs; but he must do this simply for the love of the game itself—simply for sport, simply in order to observe the process of winning or of losing, and, above all things, as a man who remains quite uninterested in the possibility of his issuing a winner. If he wins, he will be at liberty, perhaps, to give vent to a laugh, or to pass a remark on the circumstance to a bystander, or to stake again, or to double his stake; but even this he must do solely out of curiosity, and for the pleasure of watching the play of chances and of calculations, and not because of any vulgar desire to win. In a word, he must look upon the gaming-table, upon roulette, and upon trente et quarante, as mere relaxations which have been arranged solely for his amusement. Of the existence of the lures and gains upon which the bank is founded and maintained he must profess to have not an inkling. Best of all, he ought to imagine his fellow-gamblers and the rest of the mob which stands trembling over a coin to be equally rich and gentlemanly with himself, and playing solely for recreation and pleasure. This complete ignorance of the realities, this innocent view of mankind, is what, in my opinion, constitutes the truly aristocratic. For instance, I have seen even fond mothers so far indulge their guileless, elegant daughters—misses of fifteen or sixteen—as to give them a few gold coins and teach them how to play; and though the young ladies may have won or have lost, they have invariably laughed, and departed as though they were well pleased. In the same way, I saw our General once approach the table in a stolid, important manner. A lacquey darted to offer him a chair, but the General did not even notice him. Slowly he took out his money bags, and slowly extracted 300 francs in gold, which he staked on the black, and won. Yet he did not take up his winnings —he left them there on the table. Again the black turned up, and again he did not gather in what he had won; and when, in the third round, the *red* turned up he lost, at a stroke, 1200 francs. Yet even then he rose with a smile, and thus preserved his reputation; yet I knew that his money bags must be chafing his heart, as well as that, had the stake been twice or thrice as much again, he would still have restrained himself from venting his disappointment. On the other hand, I saw a Frenchman first win, and then lose, 30,000 francs—cheerfully, and without a murmur. Yes; even if a gentleman should lose his whole substance, he must never give way to annoyance. Money must be so subservient to gentility as never to be worth a thought. Of course, the *supremely* aristocratic thing is to be entirely oblivious of the mire of rabble, with its setting; but sometimes a reverse course may be aristocratic—to remark, to scan, and even to gape at, the mob (for preference, through a lorgnette), even as though one were taking the crowd and its squalor for a sort of raree show which had been organised specially for a gentleman's diversion. Though one may be squeezed by the crowd, one must look as though one were fully assured of being the observer—of having neither part nor lot with the observed. At the same time, to stare fixedly about one is unbecoming; for that, again, is ungentlemanly, seeing that no spectacle is worth an open stare—there are no spectacles in the world which merit from a gentleman too pronounced an inspection. However, to me personally the scene *did* seem to be worth undisguised contemplation—more especially in view of the fact that I had come there not only to look at, but also to number myself sincerely and wholeheartedly with, the mob. As for my secret moral views, I had no room for them amongst my actual, practical opinions. Let that stand as written: I am writing only to relieve my conscience. Yet let me say also this: that from the first I have been consistent in having an intense aversion to any trial of my acts and thoughts by a moral standard. Another standard altogether has directed my life. . . .

As a matter of fact, the mob was playing in exceedingly foul fashion. Indeed, I have an idea that sheer robbery was going on around that gaming-table. The croupiers who sat at the two ends of it had not only to watch the stakes, but also to calculate the game—an immense amount of work for two men! As for the crowd itself—well, it consisted mostly of Frenchmen. Yet I was not then taking notes merely in order to be able to give you a description of roulette, but in order to get my bearings as to my behaviour when I myself should begin to play. For example, I noticed that nothing was more common than for another's hand to stretch out and grab one's winnings whenever one had won. Then there would arise a dispute, and frequently an uproar; and it would be a case of "I beg of you to prove, and to produce witnesses to the fact, that the stake is yours."

At first the proceedings were pure Greek to me. I could only divine and distinguish that stakes were hazarded on numbers, on "odd" or "even," and on colours. Polina's money I decided to risk, that evening, only to the amount of 100 gülden. The thought that I was not going to play for myself quite unnerved me. It was an unpleasant sensation, and I tried hard to banish it. I had a feeling that, once I had begun to play for Polina, I should wreck my own fortunes. Also, I wonder if any one has *ever* approached a gaming-table without falling an immediate prey to superstition? I began by pulling out fifty gülden, and staking them on "even." The wheel spun and stopped at 13. I had lost! With a feeling like a sick qualm, as though I would like to make my way out of the crowd and go home, I staked another fifty gülden—this time on the red. The red turned up. Next time I staked the 100 gülden just where they lay—and again the red turned up. Again I staked the whole sum, and again the red turned up. Clutching my 400 gulden, I placed 200 of them on twelve figures, to see what would come of it. The result was that the croupier paid me out three times my total stake! Thus from 100 gülden my store had grown to 800! Upon that such a curious, such an inexplicable, unwonted feeling overcame me that I decided to depart. Always the thought kept recurring to me that if I had been playing for myself alone I should never have had such luck. Once more I staked the whole 800 gülden on the "even." The wheel stopped at 4. I was paid out another 800 gülden, and, snatching up my pile of 1600, departed in search of Polina Alexandrovna.

I found the whole party walking in the park, and was able to get an interview with her only after supper. This time the Frenchman was absent from the meal, and the General seemed to be in a more expansive vein. Among other things he thought it necessary to remind me that he would be sorry to see me playing at the gaming-tables. In his opinion, such conduct would greatly compromise him—especially if I were to lose much. "And even if you were to *win* much I should be compromised," he added in a meaning sort of way. "Of course I have no *right* to order your actions, but you yourself will agree that——" As usual, he did not finish his sentence. I answered drily that I had very little money in my possession, and that, consequently, I was hardly in a position to indulge in any conspicuous play, even if I did gamble. At last, when ascending to my own room, I succeeded in handing Polina her winnings, and told her that, next time, I should not play for her.

"Why not?" she asked excitedly.

"Because I wish to play *for myself*," I replied with a feigned glance of astonishment. "That is my sole reason."

"Then are you so certain that your roulette-playing will get us out of our difficulties?" she inquired with a quizzical smile.

I said very seriously, "Yes;" and then added: "Possibly my certainty about winning may seem to you ridiculous; yet pray leave me in peace."

None the less she insisted that I ouglrt to go halves with her in the day's winnings, and offered me 800 gülden on condition that henceforth I gambled only on those terms; but I refused to do so, once and for all—stating, as my reason, that I found myself unable to play on behalf of any one else, "I am not unwilling so to do," I added, "but in all probability I should lose."

"Well, absurd though it be, I place great hopes on your playing of roulette," she remarked musingly, "wherefore you ought to play as my partner and on equal shares; wherefore, of course, you will do as I wish."

Then she left me without listening to any further protests on my part.

III

On the morrow she said not a word to me about gambling. In fact, she purposely avoided me, although her old manner to me had not changed: the same serene coolness was hers on meeting me—a coolness that was mingled even with a spice of contempt and dislike. In short, she was at no pains to conceal her aversion to me. That I could see plainly. Also, she did not trouble to conceal from me the fact that I was necessary to her, and that she was keeping me for some end which she had in view. Consequently there became established between us relations which, to a large extent, were incomprehensible to me, considering her general pride and aloofness. For example, although she knew that I was madly in love with her, she allowed me to speak to her of my passion (though she could not well have showed her contempt for me more than by permitting me, unhindered and unrebuked, to mention to her my love).

"You see," her attitude expressed, "how little I regard your feelings, as well as how little I care for what you say to me, or for what you feel for me." Likewise, though she spoke as before concerning her affairs, it was never with complete frankness. In her contempt for me there were refinements. Although she knew well that I was aware of a certain circumstance in her life—of something which might one day cause her trouble, she would speak to me about her affairs (whenever she had need of me for a given end) as though I were a slave or a passing acquaintance—yet tell them me only in so far as one would need to know them if one were going to be made temporary use of. Had I not known the whole chain of events, or had she not seen how much I was pained and disturbed by her teasing insistency, she would never have thought it worth while to soothe me with this frankness—even though, since she not infrequently used me to execute commissions that were not only troublesome, but risky, she ought, in my opinion, to have been frank in *any* case. But, forsooth, it was not worth her while to trouble about *my* feelings—about the fact that *I* was uneasy, and, perhaps, thrice as put about by her cares and misfortunes as she was herself!

For three weeks I had known of her intention to take to roulette. She had even warned me that she would like me to play on her behalf, since it was unbecoming for her to play in person; and from the tone of her words I had gathered that there was something on her mind besides a mere desire to win money. As if money could matter to *her!* No, she had some end in view, and there were circumstances at which I could guess, but which I did not know for certain. True, the slavery and abasement in which she held me might have given me (such things often do so) the power to question her with abrupt directness (seeing that, inasmuch as I figured in her eyes as a mere slave and nonentity, she could not very well have taken offence at any rude curiosity); but the fact was that, though she let me question her, she never returned me a single answer, and at times did not so much as notice me. That is how matters stood.

Next day there was a good deal of talk about a telegram which, four days ago, had been sent to St. Petersburg, but to which there had come no answer. The General was visibly disturbed and moody, for the matter concerned his mother. The Frenchman, too, was excited, and after dinner the whole party talked long and seriously together—the Frenchman's tone being extraordinarily presumptuous and off-hand to everybody. It almost reminded one of the proverb, "Invite a man to your table, and soon he will place his feet upon it." Even to Polina he was brusque almost to the point of rudeness. Yet still he seemed glad to join us in our walks in the Casino, or in our rides and drives about the town. I had long been aware of certain circumstances which bound the General to him; I had long been aware that in Russia they had hatched some scheme together—although I did not know whether the plot had come to anything, or whether it was still only in the stage of being talked of. Likewise I was aware, in part, of a family secret—namely, that, last year, the Frenchman had bailed the General out of debt, and given him 30,000 roubles wherewith to pay his Treasury dues on retiring from the service. And now, of course, the General was in a vice—although the chief part in the affair was being played by Mlle. Blanche. Yes, of this last I had no doubt.

But *who* was this Mlle. Blanche? It was said of her that she was a Frenchwoman of good birth who, living with her mother, possessed a colossal fortune. It was also said that she was some relation to the Marquis, but only a distant one—a cousin, or cousin-german, or something of the sort. Likewise I knew that, up to the time of my journey to Paris, she and the Frenchman had been more ceremonious towards our party—they had stood on a much more precise and delicate footing with them; but that now their acquaintanceship—their friendship, their intimacy—had taken on a much more off-hand and rough-and-ready air. Perhaps they thought that our means were too modest for them, and therefore unworthy of politeness or reticence. Also, for the last three days I had noticed certain looks which Astley had kept throwing at Mlle. Blanche and her mother; and it had occurred to me that he must have had some previous acquaintance with the pair. I had even surmised that the Frenchman too must have met Mr. Astley before. Astley was a man so shy, reserved, and taciturn in his manner that one might have looked for anything from him. At all events the Frenchman accorded him only the slightest of greetings, and scarcely even looked at him. Certainly he did not seem to be afraid of him; which was intelligible enough. But why did Mlle. Blanche also never look at the Englishman?—particularly since, *à propos* of something or another, the Marquis had declared the Englishman to be immensely and indubitably rich? Was not that a sufficient reason to make Mlle. Blanche look at the Englishman? Anyway the General seemed extremely uneasy; and one could well understand what a telegram to announce the death of his mother would mean for him!

Although I thought it probable that Polina was avoiding me for a definite reason, I adopted a cold and indifferent air; for I felt pretty certain that it would not be long before she of herself approached me. For two days, therefore, I devoted my attention to Mlle. Blanche. The poor General was in despair! To fall in love at fifty-five, and with such vehemence, is indeed a misfortune! And add to that his widowerhood, his children, his ruined property, his debts, and the woman with whom he had fallen in love! Though Mlle. Blanche was extremely good-looking, I may or may not be understood when I say that she had one of those faces which one is afraid of. At all events, I myself have always feared such women. Apparently about twenty-five years of age, she was tall and broad-shouldered, with shoulders that sloped; yet though her neck and bosom were ample in their proportions, her skin was dull yellow in colour, while her hair (which was extremely abundant — sufficient to make two coiffures) was as black as Indian ink. Add to that a pair of black eyes with yellowish whites, a proud glance, gleaming teeth, and lips which were perennially pomaded and redolent of musk. As for her dress, it was invariably rich, effective, and chic, yet in good taste. Lastly, her feet and hands were astonishing, and her voice a deep contralto. Sometimes, when she laughed, she displayed her teeth, but at ordinary times her air was taciturn and haughty—especially in the presence of Polina and Maria Philipovna. Yet she seemed to me almost destitute of education, and even of wits, though cunning and suspicious. This, apparently, was not because her life had been lacking in incident. Perhaps, if all were known, the Marquis was not her kinsman at all, nor her mother her mother; but there was evidence that in Berlin, where we had first come across the pair, they had possessed acquaintances of good standing. As for the Marquis himself, I doubt to this day if he *was* a marquis—although about the fact that he had formerly belonged to high society (for instance, in Moscow and Germany) there could be no doubt whatever. What he had formerly been in France I had not a notion. All I knew was that he was said to possess a château. During the last two weeks I had looked for much to transpire, but am still ignorant whether at that time anything decisive ever passed between Mademoiselle and the General. Everything seemed to depend upon our means—upon whether the General would be able to flourish sufficient money in her face. If ever the news should arrive that the grandmother was not dead, Mlle. Blanche, I felt sure, would disappear in a twinkling. Indeed, it surprised and amused me to observe what a passion for intrigue I was developing. But how I loathed it all! With what pleasure would I have given everybody and everything the go-by! Only —I could not leave Polina. How, then, could I show contempt for those who surrounded her? Espionage is a base thing, but—what have I to do with that?

Mr. Astley, too, I found a curious person. I was only sure that he had fallen in love with Polina. A remarkable and diverting circumstance is the amount which may lie in the mien of a shy and painfully modest man who has been touched with the divine passion—especially when he would rather sink into the earth than betray himself by a single word or look. Though Mr. Astley frequently met us when we were out walking, he would merely take off his hat and pass us by, though I knew he was dying to join us. Even when invited to do so, he would refuse. Again, in places of amusement —in the Casino, at concerts, or near the fountain—he was never far from the spot where we were sitting. In fact, *wherever* we were—in the Park, in the forest, or on the Schlangenberg—one needed but to raise one's eyes and glance around to catch sight of at least a *portion* of Mr. Astley's frame sticking out—whether on an adjacent path or behind a bush. Yet never did he lose any chance of speaking to myself; and one morning when we had met, and exchanged a couple of words, he burst out in his usual abrupt way, without saying "Good-morning."

"That Mlle. Blanche," he said. "Well, I have seen a good many women like her."

After that he was silent as he looked me meaningly in the face. What he meant I did not know, but to my glance of inquiry he returned only a dry nod, and a reiterated "It is so." Presently, however, he resumed:

"Does Mlle. Polina like flowers?"

"I really cannot say," was my reply.

"What? You cannot say?" he cried in great astonishment.

"No; I have never noticed whether she does so or not," I repeated with a smile.

"Hm! Then I have an idea in my mind," he concluded. Lastly, with a nod, he walked away with a pleased expression on his face. The conversation had been carried on in execrable French.

IV

To-DAY has been a day of folly, stupidity, and ineptness. The time is now eleven o'clock in the evening, and I am sitting in my room and thinking. It all began, this morning, with my being forced to go and play roulette for Polina Alexandrovna. When she handed me over her store of six hundred gülden I exacted two conditions—namely, that I should *not* go halves with her in her winnings, if any (that is to say, I should not take anything for myself), and that she should explain to me, that same evening, why it was so necessary for her to win, and how much was the sum which she needed. For I could not suppose that she was doing all this merely for the sake of money. Yet clearly she *did* need some money, and that as soon as possible, and for a special purpose. Well, she promised to explain matters, and I departed. There was a tremendous crowd in the gaming-rooms. What an arrogant, greedy crowd it was! I pressed forward towards the middle of the room until I had secured a seat at a croupier's elbow. Then I began to play in timid fashion; venturing only twenty or thirty gülden at a time. Meanwhile I observed and took notes. It seemed to me that calculation was superfluous, and by no means possessed of the importance which certain other players attached to it, even though they sat with ruled papers in their hands, whereon they set down the coups, calculated the chances, reckoned, staked, and—lost exactly as we more simple mortals did who played without any reckoning at all. However, I deduced from the scene one conclusion which seemed to me reliable—namely, that in the flow of fortuitous chances there is, if not a system, at all events a sort of order. This, of course, is a very strange thing. For instance, after a dozen middle figures there would always occur a dozen or so outer ones. Suppose the ball stopped twice at a dozen outer figures; it would then pass to a dozen of the first ones, and then, again, to a dozen of the middle ciphers, and fall upon them three or four times, and then revert to a dozen outers; whence, after another couple of rounds, the ball would again pass to the first figures, strike upon them once, and then return thrice to the middle series—continuing thus for an hour and a half, or two hours. One, three, two: one, three, two. It was all very curious. Again, for the whole of a day or a morning the red would alternate with the black, but almost without any order, and from moment to moment, so that scarcely two consecutive rounds would end upon either the one or the other. Yet, next day, or, perhaps, the next evening, the red alone would turn up, and attain a run of over two score, and continue so for quite a length of time—say, for a whole day. Of these circumstances the majority were pointed out to me by Mr. Astley, who stood by the gaming-table the whole morning, yet never once staked in person. For myself, I lost all that I had on me, and with great speed. To begin with, I staked two hundred gülden on "even," and won. Then I staked the same amount again, and won: and so on some two or three times. At one moment I must have had in my hands—gathered there within a space of five minutes—about 4000 gülden. That, of course, was the proper moment for me to have departed, but there arose in me a strange sensation as of a challenge to Fate—as of a wish to deal her a blow on the cheek, and to put out my tongue at her. Accordingly I set down the largest stake allowed by the rules—namely, 4000 gülden—and lost. Fired by this mishap, I pulled out all the money left to me, staked it all on the same venture, and—again lost! Then I rose from the table, feeling as though I were stupefied. What had happened to me I did not know, but before luncheon I told Polina of my losses; until which time I walked about the Park.

At luncheon I was as excited as I had been at the meal three days ago. Mlle. Blanche and the Frenchman were lunching with us, and it appeared that the former had been to the Casino that morning, and had seen my exploits there. So now she showed me more attention when talking to me; while, for his part, the Frenchman approached me, and asked outright if it had been my own money that I had lost. He appeared to be suspicious as to something being on foot between Polina and myself, but I merely fired up, and replied that the money had been all my own.

At this the General seemed extremely surprised, and asked me whence I had procured it; whereupon I replied that, though I had begun only with 100 gülden, six or seven rounds had increased my capital to 5000 or 6000 gülden, and that subsequently I had lost the whole in two rounds.

All this, of course, was plausible enough. During my recital I glanced at Polina, but nothing was to be discerned on her face. However, she had allowed me to fire up without correcting me, and from that I concluded that it was my *cue* to fire up, and to conceal the fact that I had been playing on her behalf. "At all events," I thought to myself, "she, in her turn, has promised to give me an explanation to-night, and to reveal to me something or another."

Although the General appeared to be taking stock of me, he said nothing. Yet I could see uneasiness and annoyance in his face. Perhaps his straitened circumstances made it hard for him to have to hear of piles of gold passing through the hands of an irresponsible fool like myself within the space of a quarter of an hour. Now, I have an idea that, last night, he and the Frenchman had a sharp encounter with one another. At all events they closeted themselves together, and then had a long and vehement discussion; after which the Frenchman departed in what appeared to be a passion, but returned, early this morning, to renew the combat. On hearing of my losses, however, he only remarked with a sharp, and even a malicious, air that a man ought to go more carefully. Next, for some reason or another, he added that, though a great many Russians go in for gambling, they are no good at the game.

"*I* think that roulette was devised specially for Russians," I retorted; and when the Frenchman smiled contemptuously at my reply I further remarked that I was sure I was right; also that, speaking of Russians in the capacity of gamblers, I had far more blame for them than praise—of that he could be quite sure.

"Upon what do you base your opinion?" he inquired.

"Upon the fact that to the virtues and merits of the civilised Westerner there has become historically added —though this is not his chief point—a capacity for acquiring capital; whereas not only is the Russian incapable of acquiring capital, but also he exhausts it wantonly and of sheer folly. None the less we Russians often need money; wherefore we are glad of, and greatly devoted to, a method of acquisition like roulette—whereby, in a couple of hours, one may grow rich without doing any work. This method, I repeat, has a great attraction for us, but since we play in wanton fashion, and without taking any trouble, we almost invariably lose."

"To a certain extent that is true," assented the Frenchman with a self-satisfied air.

"Oh no, it is not true," put in the General sternly. "And you," he added to me, "you ought to be ashamed of yourself for traducing your own country!"

"I beg pardon," I said. "Yet it would be difficult to say which is the worst of the two—Russian ineptitude or the German method of growing rich through honest toil."

"What an extraordinary idea," cried the General.

"And what a *Russian* idea!" added the Frenchman.

I smiled, for I was rather glad to have a quarrel with them.

"I would rather live a wandering life in tents," I cried, "than bow the knee to a German idol!"

"To *what* idol?" exclaimed the General, now seriously angry.

"To the German method of heaping up riches. I have not been here very long, but I can tell you that what I have seen and verified makes my Tartar blood boil. Good Lord! I wish for no virtues of that kind. Yesterday I went for a walk of about ten versts; and everywhere I found that things were even as we read of them in good German picture-books—that every house has its 'Vater,' who is horribly beneficent and extraordinarily honourable. So honourable is he that it is dreadful to have anything to do with him; and I cannot bear people of that sort. Each such 'Vater' has his family, and in the evenings they read improving books aloud. Over their roof-trees there murmur elms and chestnuts; the sun has sunk to his rest; a stork is roosting on the gable; and all is beautifully poetic and touching. Do not be angry, General. Let me tell you something that is even more touching than that. I can remember how, of an evening, my own father, now dead, used to sit under the lime trees in his little garden, and to read books aloud to myself and my mother. Yes, I know how things ought to be done. Yet every German family is bound to slavery and to submission to its 'Vater.' They work like oxen, and amass wealth like Jews. Suppose the 'Vater' has put by a certain number of gülden which he hands over to his eldest son, in order that the said son may acquire a trade or a small plot of land. Well, one result is to deprive the daughter of a dowry, and so leave her among the unwedded. For the same reason, the parents will have to sell the younger son into bondage or the ranks of the army, in order that he may earn more towards the family capital. Yes, such things *are* done, for I have been making inquiries on the subject. It is all done out of sheer rectitude—out of a rectitude which is magnified to the point of the younger son believing that he has been *rightly* sold, and that it is simply idyllic for the victim to rejoice when he is made over into pledge. What more have I to tell? Well, this—that matters bear just as hardly upon the eldest son. Perhaps he has his Gretchen to whom his heart is bound; but he cannot marry her, for the reason that he has not yet amassed sufficient gülden. So the pair wait on in a mood of sincere and virtuous expectation, and smilingly deposit themselves in pawn the while. Gretchen's cheeks grow sunken, and she begins to wither; until at last, after some twenty years, their substance has multiplied, and sufficient gülden have been honourably and virtuously accumulated. Then the 'Vater' blesses his forty-year-old heir and the thirty-five-year-old Gretchen with the sunken bosom and the scarlet nose; after which he bursts into tears, reads the pair a lesson on morality, and dies. In turn the eldest son becomes a virtuous 'Vater,' and the old story begins again. In fifty or sixty years' time the grandson of the original 'Vater' will have amassed a considerable sum; and that sum he will hand over to his son, and the latter to *his* son, and so on for several generations; until at length there will issue a Baron Rothschild, or a 'Hoppe and Company,' or the devil knows what! Is it not a beautiful spectacle — the spectacle of a century or two of inherited labour, patience, intellect, rectitude, character, perseverance, and calculation, with a stork sitting on the roof above it all? What is more, they think there can never be anything better than this; wherefore from *their* point of view they begin to judge the rest of the world, and to censure all who are at fault—that is to say, who are not exactly like themselves. Yes, there you have it in a nutshell. For my own part, I would rather grow fat after the Russian manner, or squander my whole substance at roulette. I have no wish to be 'Hoppe and Company' at the end of five generations. I want the money for *myself*, for in no way do I look upon my personality as necessary to, or meet to be given over to, capital. I may be wrong, but there you have it. Those are *my* views."

"How far you may be right in what you have said I do not know," remarked the General moodily; "but

I *do* know that you are becoming an insufferable *farçeur* whenever you are given the least chance."

As usual, he left his sentence unfinished. Indeed, whenever he embarked upon anything that in the least exceeded the limits of daily small-talk, he left unfinished what he was saying. The Frenchman had listened to me contemptuously, with a slight protruding of his eyes; but he could not have understood very much of my harangue. As for Polina, she had looked on with serene indifference. She seemed to have heard neither my voice nor any other during the progress of the meal.

V

YES, she had been extraordinarily meditative. Yet, on leaving the table, she immediately ordered me to accompany her for a walk. We took the children with us, and set out for the fountain in the Park.

I was in such an irritated frame of mind that in rude and abrupt fashion I blurted out a question as to " why our Marquis de Griers had ceased to accompany her for strolls, or to speak to her for days together."

" Because he is a brute," she replied in rather a curious way. It was the first time that I had heard her speak so of De Griers: consequently I was momentarily awed into silence by this expression of resentment.

" Have you noticed, too, that to-day he is by no means on good terms with the General? " I went on.

" Yes; and I suppose you want to know why," she replied with dry captiousness. " You are aware, are you not, that the General is mortgaged to the Marquis, with all his property? Consequently, if the General's mother does not die, the Frenchman will become the absolute possessor of everything which he now holds only in pledge."

" Then it is really the case that everything is mortgaged? I have heard rumours to that effect, but was unaware how far they might be true."

" Yes, they *are* true. What then? "

"Why, it will be a case of 'Farewell, Mlle. Blanche,'" I remarked; "for in such an event she would never become Madame General. Do you know, I believe the old man is so much in love with her that he will shoot himself if she should throw him over. At his age it is a dangerous thing to fall in love."

"Yes, something, I believe, *will* happen to him," assented Polina thoughtfully.

"And what a fine thing it all is!" I continued. "Could anything be more abominable than the way in which she has agreed to marry for money alone? Not one of the decencies has been observed; the whole affair has taken place without the least ceremony. And as for the grandmother, what could be more comical, yet more dastardly, than the sending of telegram after telegram to know if she is dead? What do *you* think of it, Polina Alexandrovna?"

"Yes, it is very horrible," she interrupted with a shudder. "Consequently I am the more surprised that *you* should be so cheerful. What are *you* so pleased about? About the fact that you have gone and lost my money?"

"What? The money that you gave me to lose? I told you I should never win for other people—least of all for you. I obeyed you simply because you ordered me to; but you must not blame me for the result. I warned you that no good would ever come of it. You seem much depressed at having lost your money. Why do you need it so greatly?"

"Why do *you* ask me these questions?"

"Because you promised to explain matters to me. Listen. I am certain that, as soon as ever I begin to play for myself (and I still have 120 gülden left), I shall win. You can then take of me what you require."

She made a contemptuous grimace.

"You must not be angry with me," I continued, "for making such a proposal. I am so conscious of being only a nonentity in your eyes that you need not mind accepting money from me. A gift from me could not possibly offend you. Moreover, it was I who lost your gülden."

She glanced at me, but, seeing that I was in an irritable, sarcastic mood, changed the subject.

"My affairs cannot possibly interest you," she said. "Still, if you *do* wish to know, I am in debt. I borrowed some money, and must pay it back again. I have a curious, a senseless idea that I am bound to win at the gaming-tables. Why I think so I cannot tell, but I do think so, and with some assurance. Perhaps it is because of that assurance that I now find myself without any other resource."

"Or perhaps it is because it is so *necessary* for you to win. It is like a drowning man catching at a straw. You yourself will agree that, unless he were drowning he would not mistake a straw for the trunk of a tree."

Polina looked surprised.

"What?" she said. "Do not you also hope something from it? Did you not tell me again and again, two weeks ago, that you were certain of winning at roulette if you played here? And did you not ask me not to consider you a fool for doing so? Were you joking? You cannot have been, for I remember that you spoke with a gravity which forbade the idea of your jesting."

"True," I replied gloomily. "I always felt certain that I should win. Indeed, what you say makes me ask myself—Why have my absurd, senseless losses of to-day raised a doubt in my mind? Yet I am *still* positive that, so soon as ever I begin to play for myself, I shall infallibly win."

"And why are you so certain?"

"To tell the truth, I do not know. I only know that I *must* win—that it is the one resource I have left. Yes, why do I feel so assured on the point?"

"Perhaps because one cannot help winning if one is fanatically certain of doing so."

"Yet I dare wager that you do not think me capable of serious feeling in the matter?"

"I do not care whether you are so or not," answered Polina with calm indifference. "Well, since you ask me, I *do* doubt your ability to take anything seriously. You are capable of worrying, but not deeply. You are too ill-regulated and unsettled a person for that. But why do you want money? Not a single one of the reasons which you have given can be looked upon as serious."

"By the way," I interrupted, "you say you want to pay off a debt. It must be a large one. Is it to the Frenchman?"

"What do you mean by asking all these questions? You are very clever to-day. Surely you are not drunk?"

"You know that you and I stand on no ceremony, and that sometimes I put to you very plain questions. I repeat that I am your slave—and slaves cannot be shamed or offended."

"You talk like a child. It is always possible to comport oneself with dignity. If one has a quarrel it ought to elevate rather than to degrade one."

"A maxim straight from the copybook! Suppose I *cannot* comport myself with dignity. By that I mean that, though I am a man of self-respect, I am unable to carry off a situation properly. Do you know the reason? It is because we Russians are too richly and multifariously gifted to be able at once to find the proper mode of expression. It is all a question of mode. Most of us are so bounteously endowed with intellect as to require also a spice of genius to choose the right form of behaviour. And genius is lacking in us for the reason that so little genius at all exists. It belongs only to the French—though a few other Europeans have elaborated their forms so well as to be able to figure with extreme dignity, and yet be wholly undignified persons. That is why, with us, the mode is so all-important. The Frenchman may receive an insult—a real, a venomous insult: yet he will not so much as frown. But a tweaking of the nose he cannot bear, for the reason that such an act is an infringement of the accepted, of the time-hallowed, order of decorum. That is why our good ladies are so fond of Frenchmen—the Frenchman's manners, they say, are perfect! But in my opinion there is no such thing as a Frenchman's manners. The Frenchman is only a bird—the *coq gaulois*. At the same time, as I am not a woman, I do not properly understand the question. Cocks may be excellent birds.

If I am wrong you must stop me. You ought to stop and correct me more often when I am speaking to you, for I am too apt to say everything that is in my head. You see, I have lost my manners. I agree that I have none, nor yet any dignity. I will tell you why. I set no store upon such things. Everything in me has undergone a check. You know the reason. I have not a single human thought in my head. For a long while I have been ignorant of what is going on in the world—here or in Russia. I have been to Dresden, yet am completely in the dark as to what Dresden is like. You know the cause of my obsession. I have no hope now, and am a mere cipher in your eyes; wherefore I tell you outright that wherever I go I see only you—all the rest is a matter of indifference. Why or how I have come to love you I do not know. It may be that you are not altogether fair to look upon. Do you know, I am ignorant even as to what your face is like. In all probability, too, your heart is not comely, and it is possible that your mind is wholly ignoble."

"And because you do not believe in my nobility of soul you think to purchase me with money?" she said.

"*When* have I thought to do so?" was my reply.

"You are losing the thread of the argument. If you do not wish to purchase me, at all events you wish to purchase my respect."

"Not at all. I have told you that I find it difficult to explain myself. You are hard upon me. Do not be angry at my chattering. You know why you ought not to be angry with me—that I am simply an imbecile. However, I do not mind if you *are* angry. Sitting in my room, I need but to think of you, to imagine to myself the rustle of your dress, and at once I fall almost to biting my hands. Why should you be angry with me? Because I call myself your slave? Revel, I pray you, in my slavery—revel in it. Do you know that sometimes I could kill you?—not because I do not love, or am jealous of, you, but because I feel as though I could simply devour you. You are laughing!"

"No, I am not," she retorted. "But I order you, nevertheless, to be silent."

She stopped, well nigh breathless with anger. God knows, she may not have been a beautiful woman, yet I loved to see her come to a halt like this, and was therefore the more fond of arousing her temper. Perhaps she divined this, and for that very reason gave way to rage. I said as much to her.

"What rubbish!" she cried with a shudder.

"I do not care," I continued. "Also, do you know that it is not safe for us to take walks together? Often I have a feeling that I should like to strike you, to disfigure you, to strangle you. Are you certain that it will never come to that? You are driving me to frenzy. Am I afraid of a scandal, or of your anger? Why should I fear your anger? I love without hope, and know that hereafter I shall love you a thousand times more. If ever I should kill you I should have to kill myself too. But I shall put off doing so as long as possible, for I wish to continue enjoying the unbearable pain which your coldness gives me. Do you know a very strange thing? It is that, with every day, my love for you increases—though that would seem to be almost an impossibility. Why should I not become a fatalist? Remember how, on the third day that we ascended the Schlangenberg, I was moved to whisper in your ear: 'Say but the word, and I will leap into the abyss.' Had you said it, I should have leapt. Do you not believe me?"

"What stupid rubbish!" she cried.

"I care not whether it be wise or stupid," I cried in return. "I only know that in your presence I must speak, speak, speak. Therefore I am speaking. I lose all conceit when I am with you, and everything ceases to matter."

"Why should I have wanted you to leap from the Schlangenberg?" she said drily, and (I think) with wilful offensiveness. "*That* would have been of no use to me."

"Splendid!" I shouted. "I know well that you must have used the words 'of no use' in order to crush me. *I* can see through you. 'Of no use,' did you say? Why, to give pleasure is *always* of use; and as for barbarous, unlimited power—even if it be only over a tly—why, it is a kind of luxury. Man is a despot by nature, and loves to torture. You, in particular, love to do so."

I remember that at this moment she looked at me in a peculiar way. The fact is that my face must have been expressing all the maze of senseless, gross sensations which were seething within me. To this day I can remember, word for word, the conversation as I have written it down. My eyes were suffused with blood, and the foam had caked itself on my lips. Also, on my honour I swear that, had she bidden me cast myself from the summit of the Schlangenberg, I should have done it. Yes, had she bidden me in jest, or only in contempt and with a spit in my face, I should have cast myself down.

"Oh no! Why so? I believe you," she said, but in such a manner—in the manner of which, at times, she was a mistress—and with such a note of disdain and viperish arrogance in her tone, that God knows I could have killed her.

Yes, at that moment she stood in peril. I had not lied to her about that.

"Surely you are not a coward?" suddenly she asked me.

"I do not know," I replied. "Perhaps I am, but I do not know. I have long given up thinking about such things."

"If I said to you, 'Kill that man,' would you kill him?"

"Whom?"

"Whomsoever I wish?"

"The Frenchman?"

"Do not ask me questions; return me answers. I repeat, whomsoever I wish? I desire to see if you were speaking seriously just now."

She awaited my reply with such gravity and impatience that I found the situation unpleasant.

"Do *you*, rather, tell me," I said, "what is going on here. Why do you seem half-afraid of me? I can see for myself what is wrong. You are the step-daughter of a ruined and insensate man who is smitten with love for this devil of a Blanche. And there is this Frenchman, too, with his mysterious influence over you. Yet you actually ask me such a question! If you do not tell me how things stand I shall have to put in my oar and do something. Are you ashamed to be frank with me? Are you shy of me?"

"I am not going to talk to you on that subject. I have asked you a question, and am waiting for an answer."

"Well, then—I will kill whomsoever you wish," I said. "But are you *really* going to bid me do such deeds?"

"Why should you think that I am going to let you off? I shall bid you do it, or else renounce me. Could you ever do the latter? No, you know that you couldn't. You would first kill whom I had bidden you, and then kill *me* for having dared to send you away."

Something seemed to strike upon my brain as I heard these words. Of course, at the time I took them half in jest and half as a challenge: yet she had spoken them with great seriousness. I felt thunderstruck that she should so express herself, that she should assert such a right over me, that she should assume such authority and say outright: "Either you kill whom I bid you, or I will have nothing more to do with you." Indeed, in what she had said there was something so cynical and unveiled as to pass all bounds. For how could she ever regard me as the same after the killing was done? This was more than slavery and abasement; it was sufficient to bring a man back to his right senses. Yet, despite the outrageous improbability of our conversation, my heart shook within me.

Suddenly she burst out laughing. We were seated on a bench near the spot where the children were playing—just opposite the point in the alley-way before the Casino where the carriages drew up in order to set down their occupants.

"Do you see that fat Baroness?" she cried. "It is the Baroness Burmergelm. She arrived three days ago. Just look at her husband—that tall, wizened Prussian there, with the stick in his hand. Do you remember how he stared at us the other day? Well, go to the

Baroness, take off your hat to her, and say something in French."

"Why?"

"Because you have sworn that you would leap from the Schlangenberg for my sake, and that you would kill any one whom I might bid you kill. Well, instead of such murders and tragedies, I wish only for a good laugh. Go without answering me, and let me see the Baron give you a sound thrashing with his stick."

"Then you throw me out a challenge?—you think that I will not do it?"

"Yes, I do challenge you. Go, for such is my will."

"Then I *will* go, however mad be your fancy. Only, look here: shall you not be doing the General a great disservice, as well as, through him, a great disservice to yourself? It is not about myself I am worrying; it is about you and the General. Why, for a mere fancy, should I go and insult a woman?"

"Ah! Then I can see that you are only a trifler," she said contemptuously. "Your eyes are swimming with blood—but only because you have drunk a little too much at luncheon. Do I not know that what I have asked you to do is foolish and wrong, and that the General will be angry about it? But I want to have a good laugh, all the same. I want that, and nothing else. Why should you insult a woman, indeed? Well, you will be given a sound thrashing for so doing."

I turned away, and went silently to do her bidding. Of course the thing was folly, but I could not get out of it. I remember that, as I approached the Baroness, I felt as excited as a schoolboy. I was in a frenzy, as though I were drunk.

VI

Two days have passed since that day of lunacy. What a noise and a fuss and a chattering and an uproar there was! And what a welter of unseemliness and disorder and stupidity and bad manners! And *I* the cause of it all! Yet part of the scene was also ridiculous—at all events to myself it was so. I am not quite sure what was the matter with me—whether I was merely stupefied or whether I purposely broke loose and ran amok. At times my mind seems all confused; while at other times I seem almost to be back in my childhood, at the school desk, and to have done the deed simply out of mischief.

It all came of Polina—yes, of Polina. But for her, there might never have been a fracas. Or perhaps I did the deed in a fit of despair (though it may be foolish of me to think so)? What there is so attractive about her I cannot think. Yet there *is* something attractive about her—something passing fair, it would seem. Others besides myself she has driven to distraction. She is tall and straight, and very slim. Her body looks as though it could be tied into a knot, or bent double, like a cord. The imprint of her foot is long and narrow. It is a maddening imprint—yes, simply a maddening one! And her hair has a reddish tint about it, and her eyes are like cat's eyes—though able also to glance with proud, disdainful mien. On the evening of my first arrival, four months ago, I remember that she was sitting and holding an animated conversation with De Griers in the salon. And the way in which she looked at him was such that later, when I retired to my own room upstairs, I kept fancying that she had smitten him in the face—that she had smitten him right on the cheek, so peculiar had been her look as she stood confronting him. Ever since that evening I have loved her.

But to my tale.

I stepped from the path into the carriage-way, and took my stand in the middle of it. There I awaited the Baron and the Baroness. When they were but a few paces distant from me I took off my hat, and bowed.

I remember that the Baroness was clad in a voluminous silk dress, pale grey in colour, and adorned with flounces and a crinoline and train. Also, she was short and inordinately stout, while her gross, flabby chin completely concealed her neck. Her face was purple, and the little eyes in it had an impudent, malicious expression. Yet she walked as though she were conferring a favour upon everybody by so doing. As for the Baron, he was tall, wizened, bony-faced after the German fashion, spectacled, and, apparently, about forty-five years of age. Also, he had legs which seemed to begin almost at his chest—or, rather, at his chin! Yet, for all his air of peacock-like conceit, his clothes sagged a little, and his face wore a sheepish air which might have passed for profundity.

These details I noted within a space of a few seconds.

At first my bow and the fact that I had my hat in my hand barely caught their attention. The Baron only scowled a little, and the Baroness swept straight on.

"Madame la Baronne," said I, loudly and distinctly—embroidering each word, as it were—"j'ai l'honneur d'être votre esclave."

Then I bowed again, put on my hat, and walked past the Baron with a rude smile on my face.

Polina had ordered me merely to take off my hat: the bow and the general effrontery were of my own invention. God knows what instigated me to perpetrate the outrage! In my frenzy I felt as though I were walking on air.

"Hein!" ejaculated—or, rather, growled—the Baron as he turned towards me in angry surprise.

I too turned round, and stood waiting in pseudo-courteous expectation. Yet still I wore on my face an impudent smile as I gazed at him. He seemed to hesitate, and his brows contracted to their utmost limits. Every moment his visage was growing darker. The Baroness also turned in my direction, and gazed at me in wrathful perplexity, while some of the passers-by also began to stare at us, and others of them halted outright.

"Hein!" the Baron vociferated again, with a redoubled growl and a note of growing wrath in his voice.

"Ja wohl!" I replied, still looking him in the eyes.

"Sind Sie rasend?" he exclaimed, brandishing his stick, and, apparently, beginning to feel nervous. Perhaps it was my costume which intimidated him, for I was well and fashionably dressed, after the manner of a man who belongs to indisputably good society.

"Ja wo-o-ohl!" cried I again with all my might—with a long-drawn rolling of the "ohl" sound after the fashion of the Berliners (who constantly use the phrase

"Ja wohl!" in conversation, and more or less prolong the syllable "ohl" according as they desire to express different shades of meaning or of mood).

At this the Baron and the Baroness faced sharply about, and almost fled in their alarm. Some of the bystanders gave vent to excited exclamations, and others remained staring at me in astonishment. But I do not remember the details very well.

Wheeling quietly about, I returned in the direction of Polina Alexandrovna. But when I had got within a hundred paces of her seat I saw her rise, and set out with the children towards the hotel.

At the portico I caught her up.

"I have perpetrated the—the piece of idiocy," I said as I came level with her.

"Have you? Then you can take the consequences," she replied without so much as looking at me. Then she moved towards the staircase.

I spent the rest of the evening walking in the park. Thence I passed into the forest, and walked on until I found myself in a neighbouring principality. At a wayside restaurant I partook of an omelette and some wine, and was charged for the idyllic repast a thaler and a half.

Not until eleven o'clock did I return home—to find a summons awaiting me from the General.

Our party occupied two suites in the hotel; each of which contained two rooms. The first (the larger suite) comprised a salon and a smoking-room, with, adjoining the latter, the General's study. It was here that he was awaiting me as he stood posed in a majestic attitude beside his writing-table. Lolling on a divan close by was De Griers.

"My good sir," the General began, "may I ask you what this is that you have gone and done?"

"I should be glad," I replied, "if we could come straight to the point. Probably you are referring to my encounter of to-day with a German?"

"With a German? Why, the German was the Baron Burmergelm—a most important personage! I hear that you have been rude both to him and to the Baroness?"

"No, I have not."

"But I understand that you simply terrified them, my good sir?" shouted the General.

"Not in the least," I replied. "You must know that when I was in Berlin I frequently used to hear the Berliners repeat, and repellently prolong, a certain phrase—namely, 'Ja wohl!'; and, happening to meet this couple in the carriage-drive, I found, for some reason or another, that this phrase suddenly recurred to my memory, and exercised a rousing effect upon my spirits. Moreover, on the three previous occasions that I have met the Baroness she has walked towards me as though I were a worm which could easily be crushed with the foot. Not unnaturally, I too possess a measure of self-respect; wherefore on *this* occasion I took off my hat, and said politely (yes, I assure you it was said politely): 'Madame, j'ai l'honneur d'être votre esclave.' Then the Baron turned round, and said 'Hein!'; whereupon I felt moved to ejaculate in answer 'Ja wohl!' Twice I shouted it at him—the first time in an ordinary tone, and the second time with the greatest prolonging of the words of which I was capable. That is all."

I must confess that this puerile explanation gave me great pleasure. I felt a strong desire to overlay the incident with an even added measure of grossness; so, the further I proceeded, the more did the gusto of my proceeding increase.

"You are only making fun of me!" vociferated the General as, turning to the Frenchman, he declared that my bringing about of the incident had been gratuitous. De Griers smiled contemptuously, and shrugged his shoulders.

"Do not think *that*," I put in. "It was not so at all. I grant you that my behaviour was bad—I fully confess that it was so, and make no secret of the fact. I would even go so far as to grant you that my behaviour might well be called stupid and indecent tomfoolery; but *more* than that it was not. Also, let me tell you that I am very sorry for my conduct. Yet there is one circumstance which, in my eyes, almost absolves me from regret in the matter. Of late—that is to say, for the last two or three weeks—I have been feeling not at all well. That is to say, I have been in a sick, nervous, irritable, fanciful condition, so that I have periodically lost control over myself. For instance, on more than one occasion I have tried to pick a quarrel even with Monsieur le Marquise here; and under the circumstances he had no choice but to answer me. In short, I have recently been showing signs of ill-health. Whether the Baroness Burmergelm will take this circumstance into consideration when I come to beg her pardon (for I *do* intend to make her amends) I do not know, but I doubt if she will, and the less so since, so far as I know, the circumstance is one which, of late, has begun to be abused in the legal world, in that advocates in criminal cases have taken to justifying their clients on the ground that, at the moment of the crime, they (the clients) were unconscious of what they were doing—that, in short, they were out of health. 'My client committed the murder—that is true; but he has no recollection of having committed it.' And doctors actually support these advocates by affirming that there really *is* such a malady—that there really *can* arise temporary delusions which make a man remember nothing of a given deed, or only a half or a quarter of it! But the Baron and Baroness are members of an older generation, as well as Prussian Jünkers and landowners. To them such a process in the medico-judicial world will be unknown, and therefore they are the more unlikely to accept any such explanation. What is *your* opinion about it, General?"

"Enough, sir!" he thundered with barely restrained fury. "Enough, I say! Once and for all I must endeavour to rid myself of you and your impertinence. To justify yourself in the eyes of the Baron and Baroness will be impossible. Any intercourse with you, even though it be confined to a begging of their pardons, they would look upon as a degradation. I may tell you that, on learning that you formed part of my household, the Baron approached me in the Casino, and demanded of me additional satisfaction. Do you understand, then, what it is that you have entailed upon me—upon *me*, my good sir? You have entailed upon me the fact of my being forced to sue humbly to the Baron, and to give him my word of honour that this very day you shall cease to belong to my establishment!"

"Excuse me, General," I interrupted, "but did he make an express point of it that I should 'cease to belong to your establishment,' as you call it?"

"No; I of my own initiative thought that I ought to afford him that satisfaction: and with it he was satisfied. So we must part, good sir. It is my duty to hand over to you forty gülden, three florins, as per the accompanying statement. Here is the money, and here the account, which you are at liberty to verify. Farewell. From henceforth we are strangers. From you I have never had anything but trouble and unpleasantness. I am about to call the landlord, and explain to him that from to-morrow onwards I shall no longer be responsible for your hotel expenses. Also I have the honour to remain your obedient servant."

I took the money and the account (which was indited in pencil), and, bowing low to the General, said to him very gravely:

"The matter cannot end here. I regret very much that you should have been put to unpleasantness at the Baron's hands; but the fault (pardon me) is your own. How came you to answer for me to the Baron? And what did you mean by saying that I formed part of your household? I am merely your family tutor—not a son of yours, nor yet your ward, nor a person of any kind for whose acts you need be responsible. I am a judicially competent person, a man of twenty-five years of age, a university graduate, a gentleman, and, until I met yourself, a complete stranger to you. Only my boundless respect for your merits restrains me from demanding satisfaction at your hands, as well as a further explanation as to the reasons which have led you to take it upon yourself to answer for my conduct."

So struck was he with my words that, spreading out his hands, he turned to the Frenchman, and interpreted to him that I had challenged himself (the General) to a duel. The Frenchman laughed aloud.

"Nor do I intend to let the Baron off," I continued calmly, but with not a little discomfiture at De Griers' merriment. "And since you, General, have to-day been so good as to listen to the Baron's complaints, and to enter into his concerns—since you have made yourself a participator in the affair—I have the honour to inform you that, to-morrow morning at the latest, I shall, in my own name, demand of the said Baron a formal explanation as to the reasons which have led him to disregard the fact that the matter lies between him and myself alone, and to put a slight upon me by referring it to another person, as though I were unworthy to answer for my own conduct."

Then there happened what I had foreseen. The General, on hearing of this further intended outrage, showed the white feather.

"What?" he cried. "Do you intend to go on with this damned nonsense? Do you not realise the harm that it is doing me? I beg of you not to laugh at me, sir—not to laugh at me, for we have police authorities here who, out of respect for my rank, and for that of the Baron—— In short, sir, I swear to you that I will have you arrested, and marched out of the place, to prevent any further brawling on your part. Do you understand what I say?" He was almost breathless with anger, as well as in a terrible fright.

"General," I replied with that calmness which he never could abide, "one cannot arrest a man for brawling until he has brawled. I have not so much as begun my explanations to the Baron, and you are altogether ignorant as to the form and time which my intended procedure is likely to assume. I wish but to disabuse the Baron of what is, to me, a shameful supposition—namely, that I am under the guardianship of a person who is qualified to exercise control over my freewill. It is vain for you to disturb and alarm yourself."

"For God's sake, Alexis Ivanovitch, do put an end to this senseless scheme of yours!" he muttered, but with a sudden change from a truculent tone to one of entreaty as he caught me by the hand. "Do you know what is likely to come of it? Merely further unpleasantness. You will agree with me, I am sure, that at present I ought to move with especial care—yes, with very especial care. You cannot be fully aware of how I am situated. When we leave this place I shall be ready to receive you back into my household; but for the time being I—— Well, I cannot tell you all my reasons." With that he wound up in a despairing voice: "O Alexis Ivanovitch, Alexis Ivanovitch!"

I moved towards the door—begging him to be calm, and promising that everything should be done decently and in order; whereafter I departed.

Russians, when abroad, are over-apt to play the poltroon, and to watch all their words, and to wonder what people are thinking of their conduct, or whether such and such a thing is *comme il faut*. In short, they are over-apt to cosset themselves, and to lay claim to great importance. Always they prefer the form of behaviour which has once and for all become accepted and established. This they will follow slavishly—whether in hotels, on promenades, at meetings, or when on a journey. But the General had avowed to me that, over and above such considerations as these, there were circumstances which compelled him to "move with especial care at present": and the fact had actually made him poor-spirited and a coward—had made him altogether change his tone towards me. This fact I took into my calculations, and duly noted it, for, of course, he *might* apply to the authorities to-morrow, and it behoved me to go carefully.

Yet it was not the General but Polina that I wanted to anger. She had treated me with such cruelty, and had got me into such a hole, that I felt a longing to force her to beseech me to stop. Of course, my tomfoolery might compromise her; yet certain other feelings and desires had begun to form themselves in my brain. If I was never to rank in her eyes as anything but a nonentity, it would not greatly matter if I figured as a draggle-tailed cockerel, and the Baron were to give me a good thrashing; but the fact was that I desired to have the laugh of them all, and to come out myself unscathed. Let people see what they *would* see. Let Polina, for once, have a good fright, and be forced to whistle me to heel again. But, however much she might whistle, she should see that I was at least no draggle-tailed cockerel!

. . . .

I have just received a surprising piece of news. I have just met our chambermaid on the stairs, and been informed by her that Maria Philipovna departed to-day, by the night train, to stay with a cousin at Carlsbad. What can that mean? The maid declares that Madame packed her trunks early in the day. Yet how is it that no one else seems to have been aware of the circumstance? Or is it that *I* have been the only person to be unaware of it? Also, the maid has just told me that, three days ago, Maria Philipovna had some high words with the General. I understand, then! Probably the words were concerning Mlle. Blanche. Certainly something decisive is approaching.

VII

In the morning I sent for the maitre d'hôtel, and explained to him that, in future, my bill was to be rendered to me personally. As a matter of fact, my expenses had never been so large as to alarm me, nor to lead me to quit the hotel; while, moreover, I still had 160 gülden left to me, and—in them—yes, in them, perhaps, riches awaited me. It was a curious fact, that, though I had not yet won anything at play, I nevertheless acted, thought, and felt as though I were sure, before long, to become wealthy, since I could not imagine myself otherwise.

Next I bethought me, despite the earliness of the hour, of going to see Mr. Astley, who was staying at the Hôtel de l'Angleterre (a hostelry at no great distance from our own). But suddenly De Griers entered my room. This had never before happened, for of late that gentleman and I had stood on the most strained and distant of terms—he attempting no concealment of his contempt for me (he even made an express point of showing it), and I having no reason to desire his company. In short,

I detested him. Consequently his entry at the present moment the more astounded me. At once I divined that something out of the way was on the carpet.

He entered with marked affability, and began by complimenting me on my room. Then, perceiving that I had my hat in my hands, he inquired whither I was going so early; and no sooner did he hear that I was bound for Mr. Astley's than he stopped, looked grave, and seemed plunged in thought.

He was a true Frenchman in so far as that, though he could be lively and engaging when it suited him, he became insufferably dull and wearisome as soon as ever the need for being lively and engaging had passed. Seldom is a Frenchman *naturally* civil: he is civil only as though to order and of set purpose. Also, if he thinks it incumbent upon him to be fanciful, original, and out of the way, his fancy always assumes a foolish, unnatural vein, for the reason that it is compounded of trite, hackneyed forms. In short, the natural Frenchman is a conglomeration of commonplace, petty, everyday positiveness, so that he is the most tedious person in the world. Indeed, I believe that none but greenhorns and excessively Russian people feel an attraction towards the French; for, to any man of sensibility, such a compendium of outworn forms—a compendium which is built up of drawing-room manners, expansiveness, and gaiety—becomes at once over noticeable and unbearable.

"I have come to see you on business," De Griers began in a very off-hand, yet polite, tone; "nor will I seek to conceal from you the fact that I have come in the capacity of an emissary, of an intermediary, from the General. Having small knowledge of the Russian tongue, I lost most of what was said last night; but the General has now explained matters, and I must confess that——"

"See here, Monsieur de Griers," I interrupted. "I understand that you have undertaken to act in this affair as an intermediary. Of course I am only 'un utchitel,' a tutor, and have never claimed to be an intimate of this household, nor to stand on at all familiar terms with it. Consequently I do not know the whole of its circumstances. Yet pray explain to me this: have you yourself become one of its members, seeing that you are beginning to take such a part in everything, and are now present as an intermediary?"

The Frenchman seemed not over-pleased at my question. It was one which was too outspoken for his taste—and he had no mind to be frank with me.

"I am connected with the General," he said drily, "partly through business affairs, and partly through special circumstances. My principal has sent me merely to ask you to forego your intentions of last evening. What you contemplate is, I have no doubt, very clever; yet he has charged me to represent to you that you have not the slightest chance of succeeding in your end, since not only will the Baron refuse to receive you, but also he (the Baron) has at his disposal every possible means for obviating further unpleasantness from you. Surely you can see that yourself? What, then, would be the good of going on with it all? On the other hand, the General promises that at the first favourable opportunity he will receive you back into his household, and, in the meantime, will credit you with your salary—with 'vos appointements.' Surely that will suit you, will it not?"

Very quietly I replied that he (the Frenchman) was labouring under a delusion; that perhaps, after all, I should *not* be expelled from the Baron's presence, but, on the contrary, be listened to; finally, that I should be glad if Monsieur de Griers would confess that he was now visiting me merely in order to see how far I intended to go in the affair.

"Good heavens!" cried de Griers. "Seeing that the General takes such an interest in the matter, is there anything very unnatural in his desiring also to know your plans?"

Again I began my explanations, but the Frenchman only fidgeted and rolled his head about as he listened with an expression of manifest and unconcealed irony on his face. In short, he adopted a supercilious attitude. For my own part, I endeavoured to pretend that I took the affair very seriously. I declared that, since the Baron had gone and complained of me to the General, as though I were a mere servant of the General's, he had, in the first place, lost me my post, and, in the second place, treated me like a person to whom, as to one not qualified to answer for himself, it was not even worth while to speak. Naturally, I said, I felt insulted at this. Yet, comprehending, as I did, differences of years, of social status, and so forth (here I could scarcely help smiling), I was not anxious to bring about further scenes by going personally to demand or to request satisfaction of the Baron. All that I felt was that I had a right to go in person and beg the Baron's and the Baroness's pardon—the more so since, of late, I had been feeling unwell and unstrung, and had been in a fanciful condition. And so forth, and so forth. Yet (I continued) the Baron's offensive behaviour to me of yesterday (that is to say, the fact of his referring the matter to the General) as well as his insistence that the General should deprive me of my post, had placed me in such a position that I could not well express my regret to him (the Baron) and to his good lady, for the reason that in all probability both he and the Baroness, with the world at large, would imagine that I was doing so merely because I hoped, by my action, to recover my post. Hence I found myself forced to request the Baron to express to me *his own* regrets, as well as to express them in the most unqualified manner—to say, in fact, that he had never had any wish to insult me. After the Baron had done *that*, I should, for my part, at once feel free to express to him, whole-heartedly and without reserve, my own regrets. "In short," I declared in conclusion, "my one desire is that the Baron may make it possible for me to adopt the latter course."

"Oh fie! What refinements and subtleties!" exclaimed De Griers. "Besides, what have you to express regret for? Confess, Monsieur, Monsieur—pardon me, but I have forgotten your name—confess, I say, that all this is merely a plan to annoy the General? Or perhaps you have some other and special end in view? Eh?"

"In return you must pardon *me*, mon cher Marquis, and tell me what *you* have to do with it."

"The General——"

"But what of the General? Last night he said that, for some reason or another, it behoved him to 'move with especial care at present;' wherefore he was feeling nervous. But I did not understand the reference."

"Yes, there *do* exist special reasons for his doing so," assented De Griers in a conciliatory tone, yet with rising anger. "You are acquainted with Mlle. de Cominges, are you not?"

"Mlle. Blanche, you mean?"

"Yes, Mlle. Blanche de Cominges. Doubtless you know also that the General is in love with this young lady, and may even be about to marry her before he leaves here? Imagine, therefore, what any scene or scandal would entail upon him!"

"I cannot see that the marriage scheme need be affected by scenes or scandals."

"Mais le Baron est si irascible—un caractère prussien, vous savez! Enfin il fera une querelle d'Allemand."

"I do not care," I replied, "seeing that I no longer belong to his household" (of set purpose I was trying to talk as senselessly as possible). "But is it quite settled that Mlle. is to marry the General? What are they waiting for? Why should they conceal such a matter—at all events from ourselves, the General's own party?"

"I cannot tell you. The marriage is not yet a settled affair, for they are awaiting news from Russia. The General has business transactions to arrange."

"Ah! Connected, doubtless, with madame his mother?"

De Griers shot at me a glance of hatred.

"To cut things short," he interrupted, "I have complete confidence in your native politeness, as well as in your tact and good sense. I feel sure that you will do what I suggest, even if it is only for the sake of this family which has received you as a kinsman into its bosom and has always loved and respected you."

"Be so good as to observe," I remarked, "that the same family has just *expelled* me from its bosom. All that you are saying you are saying but for show; but when people have just said to you, 'Of course we do not wish to turn you out, yet, for the sake of appearances, you must *permit* yourself to be turned out,' nothing can matter very much."

"Very well, then," he said, in a sterner and more arrogant tone. "Seeing that my solicitations have had no effect upon you, it is my duty to mention that other measures will be taken. There exist here police, you must remember, and this very day they shall send you packing. Que diable! To think of a blanc bec like yourself challenging a person like the Baron to a duel! Do you suppose that you will be *allowed* to do such things? Just try doing them, and see if any one will be afraid of you! The reason why I have asked you to desist is that I can see that your conduct is causing the General annoyance. Do you believe that the Baron could not tell his lacquey simply to put you out of doors?"

"Nevertheless I should not *go* out of doors," I retorted with absolute calm. "You are labouring under a delusion, Monsieur de Griers. The thing will be done in far better trim than you imagine. I was just about to start for Mr. Astley's, to ask him to be my intermediary—in other words, my second. He has a strong liking for me, and I do not think that he will refuse. He will go and see the Baron on my behalf, and the Baron will certainly not decline to receive him. Although I am only a tutor—a kind of subaltern, Mr. Astley is known to all men as the nephew of a real English lord, the Lord Piebroch, as well as a lord in his own right. Yes, you may be pretty sure that the Baron will be civil to Mr. Astley, and listen to him. Or, should he decline to do so, Mr. Astley will take the refusal as a personal affront to himself (for you know how persistent the English are?) and thereupon introduce to the Baron a friend of his own (and he has many friends in a good position). That being so, picture to yourself the issue of the affair—an affair which will not quite end as you think it will."

This caused the Frenchman to bethink him of playing the coward. "Really things may be as this fellow says," he evidently thought. "Really he *might* be able to engineer another scene."

"Once more I beg of you to let the matter drop," he continued in a tone that was now entirely conciliatory. "One would think that it actually *pleased* you to have scenes! Indeed, it is a brawl rather than genuine satisfaction that you are seeking. I have said that the affair may prove to be diverting, and even clever, and that possibly you may attain something by it; yet none the less I tell you" (he said this only because he saw me rise and reach for my hat) "that I have come hither also to hand you these few words from a certain person. Read them, please, for I must take her back an answer."

So saying, he took from his pocket a small, compact, wafer-sealed note, and handed it to me. In Polina's handwriting I read:

"I hear that you are thinking of going on with this affair. You have lost your temper now, and are beginning to play the fool! Certain circumstances, however, I may explain to you later. Pray cease from your folly, and put a check upon yourself. For folly it all is. I have need of you, and, moreover, you have promised to obey me. Remember the Schlangenberg. I ask you to be obedient. If necessary, I shall even *bid* you be obedient.—Your own POLINA.

"*P.S.*—If so be that you still bear a grudge against me for what happened last night, pray forgive me."

Everything, to my eyes, seemed to change as I read these words. My lips grew pale, and I began to tremble. Meanwhile the cursed Frenchman was eyeing me discreetly and askance, as though he wished to avoid witnessing my confusion. It would have been better if he had laughed outright.

"Very well," I said, "you can tell Mlle. not to disturb herself. But," I added sharply, "I would also ask you why you have been so long in handing me this note? Instead of chattering about trifles, you ought to have delivered me the missive at once—if you have really come commissioned as you say."

"Well, pardon some natural haste on my part, for the situation is so strange. I wished first to gain some personal knowledge of your intentions; and, moreover, I did not know the contents of the note, and thought that it could be given you at any time."

"I understand," I replied. "So you were ordered to hand me the note only in the last resort, and if you could not otherwise appease me? Is it not so? Speak out, Monsieur de Griers."

"Perhaps," said he, assuming a look of great forbearance, but gazing at me in a meaning way.

I reached for my hat; whereupon he nodded, and went out. Yet on his lips I fancied that I could see a mocking smile. How could it have been otherwise?

"You and I are to have a reckoning later, Master Frenchman," I muttered as I descended the stairs. "Yes, we will measure our strength together." Yet my thoughts were all in confusion, for again something seemed to have struck me dizzy. Presently the air revived me a little, and, a couple of minutes later, my brain had sufficiently cleared to enable two ideas in particular to stand out in it. Firstly, I asked myself, which of the absurd, boyish, and extravagant threats which I had uttered at random last night had made everybody so alarmed? Secondly, what was the influence which this Frenchman appeared to exercise over Polina? He had but to give the word, and at once she did as he desired—at once she wrote me a note to beg of me to forbear! Of course, the relations between the pair had, from the first, been a riddle to me—they had been so ever since I had first made their acquaintance, but of late I had remarked in her a strong aversion for—even a contempt for—him, while, for his part, he had scarcely even looked at her, but had behaved towards her always in the most churlish fashion. Yes, I had noted that. Also, Polina herself had mentioned to me her dislike for him, and delivered herself of some remarkable confessions on the subject. Hence he must have got her into his power somehow—somehow he must be holding her as in a vice.

VIII

All at once, on the Promenade, as it was called—that is to say, in the Chestnut Avenue—I came face to face with my Englishman.

"I was just coming to see you," he said; "and you appear to be out on a similar errand. So you have parted with your employers?"

"How do you know that?" I asked in astonishment. "Is *every one* aware of the fact?"

"By no means. Not every one would consider such a fact to be of moment. Indeed, I have never heard any one speak of it."

"Then how come you to know it?"

"Because I have had occasion to do so. Whither are you bound? I like you, and was therefore coming to pay you a visit."

"What a splendid fellow you are, Mr. Astley!" I cried, though still wondering how he had come by his knowledge. "And since I have not yet had my coffee, and you have, in all probability, scarcely tasted yours, let us adjourn to the Casino Café, where we can sit and smoke and have a talk."

The café in question was only a hundred paces away; so when coffee had been brought we seated ourselves, and I lit a cigarette. Astley was no smoker, but, taking a seat by my side, he prepared himself to listen.

"I do not intend to go away," was my first remark. "I intend, on the contrary, to remain here."

"That I never doubted," he answered good-humouredly.

It is a curious fact that, on my way to see him, I had never even thought of telling him of my love for Polina. In fact, I had purposely meant to avoid any mention of the subject. Nor, during our stay in the place, had I ever made aught but the scantiest reference to it. You see, not only was Astley a man of great reserve, but also from the first I had perceived that Polina had made a great impression upon him, although he never spoke of her. But now, strangely enough, he had no sooner seated himself and bent his steely gaze upon me, than, for some reason or another, I felt moved to tell him everything—to speak to him of my love in all its phases. For an hour and a half did I discourse on the subject, and found it a pleasure to do so, even though this was the first occasion on which I had referred to the matter. Indeed, when, at certain moments, I perceived that my more ardent passages confused him, I purposely increased my ardour of narration. Yet one thing I regret: and that is that I made references to the Frenchman which were a little over-personal.

Mr. Astley sat without moving as he listened to me. Not a word nor a sound of any kind did he utter as he stared into my eyes. Suddenly, however, on my mentioning the Frenchman, he interrupted me, and inquired sternly whether I did right to speak of an extraneous matter (he had always been a strange man in his mode of propounding questions).

"No, I fear not," I replied.

"And concerning this Marquis and Mlle. Polina you know nothing beyond surmise?"

Again I was surprised that such a categorical question should come from such a reserved individual.

"No, I know nothing *for certain* about them," was my reply. "No—nothing."

"Then you have done very wrong to speak of them to me, or even to imagine things about them."

"Quite so, quite so," I interrupted in some astonishment. "I admit that. Yet that is not the question." Whereupon I related to him in detail the incident of two days ago. I spoke of Polina's outburst, of my encounter with the Baron, of my dismissal, of the General's extraordinary pusillanimity, and of the call which De Griers had that morning paid me. In conclusion, I showed Astley the note which I had lately received.

"What do you make of it?" I asked. "When I met you I was just coming to ask you your opinion. For myself, I could have killed this Frenchman, and am not sure that I shall not do so even yet."

"I feel the same about it," said Mr. Astley. "As

for Mlle. Polina—well, you yourself know that, if necessity drives, one enters into relation with people whom one simply detests. Even between this couple there may be something which, though unknown to you, depends upon extraneous circumstances. For my own part, I think that you may reassure yourself—or at all events partially. And as for Mlle. Polina's proceedings of two days ago, they were, of course, strange; not because she can have meant to get rid of you, or to earn for you a thrashing from the Baron's cudgel (which, for some curious reason, he did not use, although he had it ready in his hands), but because such proceedings on the part of such—well, of such a refined lady as Mlle. Polina are, to say the least of it, unbecoming. But she cannot have guessed that you would carry out her absurd wish to the letter?"

"Do you know what?" suddenly I cried as I fixed Mr. Astley with my gaze. "I believe that you have already heard the story from some one—very possibly from Mlle. Polina herself?"

In return he gave me an astonished stare.

"Your eyes look very fiery," he said with a return of his former calm, "and in them I can read suspicion. Now, you have no right whatever to be suspicious. It is not a right which I can for a moment recognise, and I absolutely refuse to answer your questions."

"Enough! You need say no more," I cried with a strange emotion at my heart, yet not altogether understanding what had aroused that emotion in my breast. Indeed, when, where, and how could Polina have chosen Astley to be one of her confidants? Of late I had come rather to overlook him in this connection, even though Polina had always been a riddle to me—so much so that now, when I had just permitted myself to tell my friend of my infatuation in all its aspects, I had found myself struck, during the very telling, with the fact that in my relations with her I could specify nothing that was explicit, nothing that was positive. On the contrary, my relations had been purely fantastic, strange, and unreal; they had been unlike anything else that I could think of.

"Very well, very well," I replied with a warmth equal to Astley's own. "Then I stand confounded, and have no further opinions to offer. But you are a good fellow, and I am glad to know what you think about it all, even though I do not need your advice."

Then, after a pause, I resumed:

"For instance, what reason should you assign for the General taking fright in this way? Why should my stupid clowning have led the world to elevate it into a serious incident? Even De Griers has found it necessary to put in his oar (and he only interferes on the most important occasions), and to visit me, and to address to me the most earnest supplications. Yes, *he*, De Griers, has actually been playing the suppliant to *me!* And, mark you, although he came to me as early as nine o'clock, he had ready-prepared in his hand Mlle. Polina's note. When, I would ask, was that note written? Mlle. Polina must have been aroused from sleep for the express purpose of writing it. At all events the circumstance shows that she is an absolute slave to the Frenchman, since she actually begs my pardon in the note—actually begs my pardon! Yet what is her personal concern in the matter? Why is she interested in it at all? Why, too, is the whole party so afraid of this precious Baron? And what sort of a business do you call it for the General to be going to marry Mlle. Blanche de Cominges? He told me last night that, because of the circumstance, he must 'move with especial care at present.' What is your opinion of it all? Your look convinces me that you know more about it than I do."

Mr. Astley smiled and nodded.

"Yes, I think I *do* know more about it than you do," he assented. "The affair centres around this Mlle. Blanche. Of that I feel certain."

"And what of Mlle. Blanche?" I cried impatiently (for in me there had dawned a sudden hope that this would enable me to discover something about Polina).

"Well, my belief is that at the present moment Mlle. Blanche has, in very truth, a special reason for wishing to avoid any trouble with the Baron and the Baroness.

It might lead not only to some unpleasantness, but even to a scandal."

"Oh, oh!"

"Also I may tell you tnat Mlle. Blanche has been in Roulettenberg before, for she was staying here three seasons ago. I myself was in the place at the time, and in those days Mlle. Blanche was not known as Mlle. de Cominges, nor was her mother, the Widow de Cominges, even in existence. In any case no one ever mentioned the latter. De Griers, too, had not materialised, and I am convinced that not only do the parties stand in no relation to one another, but also they have not long enjoyed one another's acquaintance. Likewise the *Marquisate* de Griers is of recent creation. Of that I have reason to be sure, owing to a certain circumstance. Even the name De Griers itself may be taken to be a new invention, seeing that I have a friend who once met the said 'Marquis' under a different name altogether."

"Yet he possesses a good circle of friends?"

"Possibly. Mlle. Blanche also may possess that. Yet it is not three years since she received from the local police, at the instance of the Baroness, an invitation to leave the town. And she left it."

"But why?"

"Well, I must tell you that she first appeared here in company with an Italian—a prince of some sort, a man who bore an historic name (Barberini or something of the kind). The fellow was simply a mass of rings and diamonds — real diamonds, too — and the couple used to drive out in a marvellous carriage. At first Mlle. Blanche played trente et quarante with fair success, but, later, her luck took a marked change for the worse. I distinctly remember that in a single evening she lost an enormous sum. But worse was to ensue, for one fine morning her prince disappeared—horses, carriage, and all. Also, the hotel bill which he left unpaid was enormous. Upon this Mlle. Zelma (the name which she assumed after figuring as Madame Barberini) was in despair. She shrieked and howled all over the hotel, and even tore her clothes in her frenzy. In the hotel there was staying also a Polish count (you must know that *all* travelling Poles are counts!), and the spectacle of Mlle. Zelma tearing her clothes and, catlike, scratching her face with her beautiful, scented nails produced upon him a strong impression. So the pair had a talk together, and by luncheon time she was consoled. Indeed, that evening the couple entered the Casino arm in arm — Mlle. Zelma laughing loudly, according to her custom, and showing even more expansiveness in her manners than she had before shown. For instance, she thrust her way into the file of women roulette-players in the exact fashion of those ladies who, to clear a space for themselves at the tables, push their fellow-players roughly aside. Doubtless you have noticed them?"

"Yes, certainly."

"Well, they are not worth noticing. To the annoyance of the decent public they are allowed to remain here—at all events such of them as daily change 4000 franc notes at the tables (though, as soon as ever these women cease to do so, they receive an invitation to depart). However, Mlle. Zelma continued to change notes of this kind, but her play grew more and more unsuccessful, despite the fact that such ladies' luck is frequently good, for they have a surprising amount of cash at their disposal. Suddenly the Count too disappeared, even as the Prince had done, and that same evening Mlle. Zelma was forced to appear in the Casino alone. On this occasion no one offered her a greeting. Two days later she had come to the end of her resources; whereupon, after staking and losing her last louis d'or, she chanced to look around her, and saw standing by her side the Baron Burmergelm, who had been eyeing her with fixed disapproval. To his distaste, however, Mlle. paid no attention, but, turning to him with her well-known smile, requested him to stake, on her behalf, ten louis on the red. Later that evening a complaint from the Baroness led the authorities to request Mlle. not to re-enter the Casino. If you feel in any way surprised that I should know these petty and unedifying details, the reason is that I had them from a relative of mine who, later that evening, drove Mlle. Zelma in his carriage from Roulettenberg to Spa. Now, mark you, Mlle. wants to become Madame General, in order that, in future, she may be spared the receipt of such invitations from Casino authorities as she received three years ago. At present she is not playing; but that is only because, according to the signs, she is lending money to other players. Yes, that is a much more paying game. I even suspect that the unfortunate General is himself in her debt, as well as, perhaps, also De Griers. Or it may be that the latter has entered into a partnership with her. Consequently you yourself will see that, until the marriage shall have been consummated, Mlle. would scarcely like to have the attention of the Baron and the Baroness drawn to herself. In short, to any one in her position, a scandal would be most detrimental. You form a member of the ménage of these people; wherefore any act of yours might cause such a scandal—and the more so since daily she appears in public arm in arm with the General or with Mlle. Polina. *Now* do you understand?"

"No, I do not!" I shouted as I banged my fist down upon the table—banged it with such violence that a frightened waiter came running towards us. "Tell me, Mr. Astley, why, if you knew this history all along, and, consequently, always knew who this Mlle. Blanche is, you never warned either myself or the General, nor, most of all, Mlle. Polina (who is accustomed to appear in the Casino—in public everywhere—with Mlle. Blanche)? How could you do it?"

"It would have done no good to warn you," he replied quietly, "for the reason that you could have effected nothing. Against what was I to warn you? As likely as not, the General knows more about Mlle. Blanche even than I do; yet the unhappy man still walks about with her and Mlle. Polina. Only yesterday I saw this Frenchwoman riding, splendidly mounted, with De Griers, while the General was careering in their wake on a roan horse. He had said, that morning, that his legs were hurting him, yet his riding-seat was easy enough. As he passed I looked at him, and the thought occurred to me that he was a man lost for ever.

However, it is no affair of mine, for I have only recently had the happiness to make Mlle. Polina's acquaintance. Also"—he added this as an afterthought—"I have already told you that I do not recognise your right to ask me certain questions, however sincere be my liking for you."

"Enough," I said, rising. "To me it is as clear as day that Mlle. Polina knows all about this Mlle. Blanche, but cannot bring herself to part with her Frenchman; wherefore she consents also to be seen in public with Mlle. Blanche. You may be sure that nothing else would ever have induced her either to walk about with this Frenchwoman or to send me a note not to touch the Baron. Yes, it is *there* that the influence lies before which everything in the world must bow! Yet she herself it was who launched me at the Baron! The devil take it, but I was left no choice in the matter."

"You forget, in the first place, that this Mlle. de Cominges is the General's inamorata, and, in the second place, that Mlle. Polina, the General's step-daughter, has a younger brother and sister who, though they are the General's own children, are completely neglected by this madman, and robbed as well."

"Yes, yes; that is so. For me to go and desert the children now would mean their total abandonment; whereas, if I remain, I should be able to defend their interests, and, perhaps, to save a moiety of their property. Yes, yes; that is quite true. And yet, and yet—Oh, I can well understand why they are all so interested in the General's mother!"

"In whom?" asked Mr. Astley.

"In the old woman of Moscow who declines to die, yet concerning whom they are for ever expecting telegrams to notify the fact of her death."

"Ah, then of course their interests centre around her. It is a question of succession. Let that but be settled, and the General will marry, Mlle. Polina will be set free, and De Griers——"

"Yes, and De Griers?"

"Will be repaid his money, which is what he is now waiting for."

"What? You think that he is waiting for *that?*"

"I know of nothing else," asserted Mr. Astley doggedly.

"But, I do, I do!" I shouted in my fury. "He is waiting also for the old woman's will, for the reason that it awards Mlle. Polina a dowry. As soon as ever the money is received, she will throw herself upon the Frenchman's neck. All women are like that. Even the proudest of them become abject slaves where marriage is concerned. What Polina is good for is to fall head over ears in love. That is *my* opinion. Look at her—especially when she is sitting alone, and plunged in thought. All this was pre-ordained and foretold, and is accursed. Polina could perpetrate any mad act. She—she—But who called me by name?" I broke off. "Who is shouting for me? I heard some one calling in Russian, 'Alexis Ivanovitch!' It was a woman's voice. Listen!"

At the moment we were approaching my hotel. We had left the café long ago, without even noticing that we had done so.

"Yes, I *did* hear a woman's voice calling, but whose I do not know. The some one was calling you in Russian. Ah! *Now* I can see whence the cries come. They come from that lady there—the one who is sitting on the settee, the one who has just been escorted to the verandah by a crowd of lacqueys. Behind her see that pile of luggage! She must have arrived by train."

"But why should she be calling *me?* Hear her calling again! See! She is beckoning to us!"

"Yes, so she is," assented Mr. Astley.

"Alexis Ivanovitch, Alexis Ivanovitch! Good heavens, what a stupid fellow!" came in a despairing wail from the verandah.

We had almost reached the portico, and I was just setting foot upon the space before it, when my hands fell to my sides in limp astonishment, and my feet glued themselves to the pavement!

IX

For on the topmost tier of the hotel verandah, after being carried up the steps in an armchair amid a bevy of footmen, maid-servants, and other menials of the hotel, headed by the landlord (that functionary had actually run out to meet a visitor who arrived with so much stir and din, attended by her own retinue, and accompanied by so great a pile of trunks and portmanteaux)—on the topmost tier of the verandah, I say, there was sitting—*the Grandmother!* Yes, it was *she*—rich, and imposing, and seventy-five years of age—Antonida Vassilievna Tarassevitcha, landowner and *grande dame* of Moscow—the "La Baboulenka" who had caused so many telegrams to be sent off and received—who had been dying, yet not dying—who had, in her own person, descended upon us even as snow might fall from the clouds! Though unable to walk, she had arrived borne aloft in an armchair (her mode of conveyance for the last five years), yet as brisk, aggressive, self-satisfied, bolt-upright, loudly imperious, and generally abusive as ever. In fact, she looked exactly as she had done on the only two occasions when I had seen her since my appointment to the General's household. Naturally enough, I stood petrified with astonishment. She had sighted me a hundred paces off! Even while she was being carried along in her chair she had recognised me, and called me by name and surname (which, as usual, after hearing once, she had remembered ever afterwards).

"And this is the woman whom they had thought to see in her grave after making her will!" I thought to myself. "Yet she will outlive us, and every one else in the hotel. Good Lord! what is going to become of us now? What on earth is to happen to the General? She will turn the place upside down!"

"My good sir," the old woman continued in a stentorian voice, "what are you standing *there* for, with your eyes almost falling out of your head? Cannot you come and say how-do-you-do? Are you too proud to shake hands? Or do you not recognise me? Here, Potapitch!" she cried to an old servant who, dressed in a frock coat and white waistcoat, had a bald, red head (he was the chamberlain who always accompanied her on her journeys). "Just think! Alexis Ivanovitch does not recognise me! They have buried me for good and all! Yes, and after sending hosts of telegrams to know if I were dead or not! Yes, yes, I have heard the whole story. I am very much alive, though, as you may see."

"Pardon me, Antonida Vassilievna," I replied good humouredly as I recovered my presence of mind. "*I* have no reason to wish you ill. I am merely rather astonished to see you. Why should I not be so, seeing how unexpected——"

"*Why* should you be astonished? I just got into my chair, and came. Things are quiet enough in the train, for there is no one there to chatter. Have you been out for a walk?"

"Yes. I have just been to the Casino."

"Oh? Well, it is quite nice here," she went on as she looked about her. "The place seems comfortable, and all the trees are out. I like it very well. Are your people at home? Is the General, for instance, indoors?"

"Yes; and probably all of them."

"Do they observe the convenances, and keep up appearances? Such things always give one tone. I have heard that they are keeping a carriage, even as Russian gentlefolks ought to do. When abroad, our Russian people always cut a dash. Is Prascovia here too?"

"Yes. Polina Alexandrovna is here."

"And the Frenchwoman? However, I will go and look for them myself. Tell me the nearest way to their rooms. Do *you* like being here?"

"Yes, I thank you, Antonida Vassilievna."

"And you, Potapitch, go you and tell that fool of a landlord to reserve me a suitable suite of rooms. They must be handsomely decorated, and not too high up. Have my luggage taken up to them. But what are you tumbling over yourselves for? Why are you all tearing about? What scullions these fellows are!—Who is that with you?" she added to myself.

"A Mr. Astley," I replied.

"And who is Mr. Astley?"

"A fellow-traveller, and my very good friend, as well as an acquaintance of the General's."

"Oh, an Englishman? Then that is why he stared at me without even opening his lips. However, I like Englishmen. Now, take me upstairs, direct to their rooms. Where are they lodging?"

Madame was lifted up in her chair by the lacqueys, and I preceded her up the grand staircase. Our progress was exceedingly effective, for every one whom we met stopped to stare at the cortège. It happened that the hotel had the reputation of being the best, the most expensive, and the most aristocratic in all the spa, and at every turn on the staircase or in the corridors we encountered fine ladies and important-looking Englishmen—more than one of whom hastened downstairs to inquire of the awestruck landlord who the newcomer was. To all such questions he returned the same answer—namely, that the old lady was an influential foreigner, a Russian, a Countess, and a *grande dame*, and that she had taken the suite which, during the previous week, had been tenanted by the Grande Duchesse de N. Meanwhile the cause of the sensation—the Grandmother—was being borne aloft in her armchair. Every person whom she met she scanned with an inquisitive eye, after first of all interrogating me about him or her at the top of her voice. She was stout of figure, and, though she could not leave her chair, one felt, the moment that one first looked at her, that she was also tall of stature. Yet her back was as straight as a board, and never did she lean back in her seat. Also, her large grey head, with its keen, rugged features, remained always erect as she glanced about her in an imperious, challenging sort of way, with looks and gestures that clearly were unstudied. Though she had reached her seventy-sixth year, her face was still fresh, and her teeth had not decayed. Lastly, she was dressed, in a black silk gown and white mobcap.

"She interests me tremendously," whispered Mr. Astley as, still smoking, he walked by my side. Meanwhile I was reflecting that probably the old lady knew all about the telegrams, and even about De Griers, though little or nothing about Mlle. Blanche. I said as much to Mr. Astley.

But what a frail creature is man! No sooner was my first surprise abated than I found myself rejoicing in the shock which we were about to administer to the General. So much did the thought inspire me that I marched ahead in the gayest of fashions.

Our party was lodging on the third floor. Without knocking at the door, or in any way announcing our presence, I threw open the portals, and the Grandmother was borne through them in triumph. As though of set purpose, the whole party chanced at that moment to be assembled in the General's study. The time was eleven o'clock, and it seemed that an outing of some sort (at which a portion of the party were to drive in carriages, and others to ride on horseback, accompanied by one or two extraneous acquaintances) was being planned. The General was present, and also Polina, the children, the latter's nurses, De Griers, Mlle. Blanche (attired in a riding-habit), her mother, the young Prince, and a learned German whom I beheld for the first time. Into the midst of this assembly the lacqueys conveyed Madame in her chair, and set her down within three paces of the General! Good heavens! Never shall I forget the spectacle which ensued! Just before our entry the General had been holding forth to the company, with De Griers in support of him. I may also mention that, for the last two or three days, Mlle. Blanche and De Griers had been making a great deal of the young Prince, under the very nose of the poor General. In short, the company, though decorous and conventional, was in a gay, familiar mood. But no sooner did the Grandmother appear than the General stopped dead in the middle of a word, and, with jaw dropping, stared hard at the old lady—his eyes almost starting out of his head, and his expression as spellbound as though he had just seen a basilisk. In return the

Grandmother stared at him silently and without moving—though with a look of mingled challenge, triumph, and ridicule in her eyes. For ten seconds did the pair remain thus eyeing one another, amid the profound silence of the company; and even De Griers sat petrified—an extraordinary look of uneasiness dawning on his face. As for Mlle. Blanche, she too stared wildly at the Grandmother, with eyebrows raised and her lips parted; while the Prince and the German savant contemplated the tableau in profound amazement. Only Polina looked anything but perplexed or surprised. Presently, however, she too turned as white as a sheet, and then reddened to her temples. Truly the Grandmother's arrival seemed to be a catastrophe for everybody! For my own part, I stood looking from the Grandmother to the company, and back again, while Mr. Astley, as usual, remained in the background, and gazed calmly and decorously at the scene.

"Well, here I am—and instead of a telegram, too!" the Grandmother at last ejaculated, to dissipate the silence. "What? You were not expecting me?"

"Antonida Vassilievna! O my dearest mother! But how on earth did you, did you——?" The mutterings of the unhappy General died away.

I verily believe that if the Grandmother had held her tongue a few seconds longer she would have had a stroke.

"How on earth did I *what?*" she exclaimed. "Why, I just got into the train and came here. What else is the railway meant for? But you thought that I had turned up my toes and left my property to the lot of you. Oh, I know *all* about the telegrams which you have been dispatching. They must have cost you a pretty sum, I should think, for telegrams are not sent from abroad for nothing. Well, I picked up my heels, and came here. Who is this Frenchman? Monsieur de Griers, I suppose?"

"Oui, madame," assented De Griers. "Et, croyez, je suis si enchanté! Votre santé—c'est un miracle de vous voir ici. Une surprise charmante!"

"Just so. 'Charmante!' I happen to know you

as a mountebank, and therefore trust you no more than *this*." She indicated her little finger. "And who is *that?*" she went on, turning towards Mlle. Blanche. Evidently the Frenchwoman looked so becoming in her riding-habit, with her whip in her hand, that she had made an impression upon the old lady. "Who is that woman there?"

"Mlle. de Cominges," I said. "And this is her mother, Madame de Cominges. They also are staying in the hotel.

"Is the daughter married?" asked the old lady, without the least semblance of ceremony.

"No," I replied as respectfully as possible, but under my breath.

"Is she good company?"

I failed to understand the question.

"I mean, is she or is she not a bore? Can she speak Russian? When this De Griers was in Moscow he soon learnt to make himself understood."

I explained to the old lady that Mlle. Blanche had never visited Russia.

"Bonjour, then," said Madame, with sudden brusquerie.

"Bonjour, madame," replied Mlle. Blanche with an elegant, ceremonious bow as, under cover of an unwonted modesty, she endeavoured to express, both in face and figure, her extreme surprise at such strange behaviour on the part of the Grandmother.

"How the woman sticks out her eyes at me! How she mows and minces!" was the Grandmother's comment. Then she turned suddenly to the General, and continued: "I have taken up my abode here, so am going to be your next-door neighbour. Are you glad to hear that, or are you not?"

"My dear mother, believe me when I say that I am sincerely delighted," returned the General, who had now, to a certain extent, recovered his senses; and inasmuch as, when occasion arose, he could speak with fluency, gravity, and a certain effect, he set himself to be expansive in his remarks, and went on: "We have been so dismayed and upset by the news of your indisposition! We had received such hopeless telegrams about you! Then suddenly——"

"Fibs, fibs!" interrupted the Grandmother.

"How on earth, too, did you come to decide upon the journey?" continued the General, with raised voice as he hurried to overlook the old lady's last remark. "Surely, at your age, and in your present state of health, the thing is so unexpected that our surprise is at least intelligible. However, I am glad to see you (as indeed, are we all"—he said this with a dignified, yet conciliatory, smile), "and will use my best endeavours to render your stay here as pleasant as possible."

"Enough! All this is empty chatter. You are talking the usual nonsense. I shall know quite well how to spend my time. How did I come to undertake the journey, you ask? Well, is there anything so very surprising about it? It was done quite simply. What is every one going into ecstasies about?—How do you do, Prascovia? What are *you* doing here?"

"And how are *you*, Grandmother?" replied Polina, as she approached the old lady. "Were you long on the journey?"

"The most sensible question that I have yet been asked! Well, you shall hear for yourself how it all happened. I lay and lay, and was doctored and doctored; until at last I drove the physicians from me, and called in an apothecary from Nicolai who had cured an old woman of a malady similar to my own—cured her merely with a little hayseed. Well, he did me a great deal of good, for on the third day I broke into a sweat, and was able to leave my bed. Then my German doctors held another consultation, put on their spectacles, and told me that if I would go abroad, and take a course of the waters, the indisposition would finally pass away. 'Why should it not?' I thought to myself. So I had things got ready, and on the following day—a Friday—set out for here. I occupied a special compartment in the train, and wherever I had to change I found at the station bearers who were ready to carry me for a few coppers. You have nice quarters here," she went on as she glanced around the room. "But where on earth did you get the money for them, my good sir? I thought that everything of yours had been mortgaged? This Frenchman alone must be your creditor for a good deal. Oh, I know all about it, all about it."

"I—I am surprised at you, my dearest mother," said the General in some confusion. "I — I am greatly surprised. But I do not need any extraneous control of my finances. Moreover, my expenses do not exceed my income, and we——"

"They do not exceed it? Fie! Why, you are robbing your children of their last kopeck—you, their guardian!"

"After this," said the General, completely taken aback, "—after what you have just said, I do not know whether——"

"You do not know *what?* By heavens, are you *never* going to drop that roulette of yours? Are you going to whistle all your property away?"

This made such an impression upon the General that he almost choked with fury.

"Roulette, indeed? *I* play roulette? Really, in view of my position—— Recollect what you are saying, my dearest mother. You must still be unwell."

"Rubbish, rubbish!" she retorted. "The truth is that you *cannot* be got away from that roulette. You are simply telling lies. This very day I mean to go and see for myself what roulette is like. Prascovia, tell me what there is to be seen here; and do you, Alexis Ivanovitch, show me everything; and do you, Potapitch, make me a list of excursions. What *is* there to be seen?" again she inquired of Polina.

"There is a ruined castle, and the Schlangenberg."

"The Schlangenberg? What is it? A forest?"

"No, a mountain on the summit of which there is a place fenced off. From it you can get a most beautiful view."

"Could a chair be carried up that mountain of yours?"

"Doubtless we could find bearers for the purpose," I interposed.

At this moment Theodosia, the nursemaid, approached the old lady with the General's children.

" No, I *don't* want to see them," said the Grandmother. " I hate kissing children, for their noses are always wet. How are you getting on, Theodosia ? "

" I am very well, thank you, Madame," replied the nursemaid. " And how is your ladyship? We have been feeling so anxious about you ! "

" Yes, I know, you simple soul.—But who are those other guests ? " the old lady continued, turning again to Polina. " For instance, who is that old rascal in the spectacles ? "

" Prince Nilski, Grandmamma," whispered Polina.

" Oh, a Russian ? Why, I had no idea that he could understand me ! Surely he did not hear what I said? As for Mr. Astley, I have seen him already, and I see that he is here again. How do you do ? " she added to the gentleman in question.

Mr. Astley bowed in silence

" Have you *nothing* to say to me ? " the old lady went on. " Say something, for goodness' sake ! Translate to him, Polina."

Polina did so.

" I have only to say," replied Mr. Astley gravely, but also with alacrity, " that I am indeed glad to see you in such good health." This was interpreted to the Grandmother, and she seemed much gratified.

" How well English people know how to answer one ! " she remarked. " That is why I like them so much better than French. Come here," she added to Mr. Astley. " I will try not to bore you too much. Polina, translate to him that I am staying in rooms on a lower floor. Yes, on a lower floor," she repeated to Astley, pointing downwards with her finger.

Astley looked pleased at receiving the invitation.

Next the old lady scanned Polina from head to foot with minute attention.

" I could almost have liked you, Prascovia," suddenly she remarked, " for you are a nice girl—the best of the lot. You have some character about you. I too have character. Turn round. Surely that is not false hair that you are wearing ? "

" No, Grandmamma. It is my own."

" Well, well. I do not like the stupid fashions of to-day. You are very good looking. I should have fallen in love with you if I had been a man. Why do you not get married? It is time now that I was going. I want to walk, yet I always have to ride. Are you still in a bad temper? " she added to the General.

" No, indeed," rejoined the now mollified General. " I quite understand that at your time of life——"

" Cette vieille est tombée en enfance," De Griers whispered to me.

" But I want to look round a little," the old lady added to the General. " Will you lend me Alexis Ivanovitch for the purpose? "

" As much as you like. But I myself—yes, and Polina and Monsieur de Griers too—we all of us hope to have the pleasure of escorting you."

" Mais, madame, cela sera un plaisir," De Griers commented with a bewitching smile.

" 'Plaisir' indeed! Why, I look upon you as a perfect fool, monsieur." Then she remarked to the General: " I am not going to let *you* have any of my money. I must be off to my rooms now, to see what they are like. Afterwards we will look round a little. Lift me up."

Again the Grandmother was borne aloft, and carried down the staircase amid a perfect bevy of followers—the General walking as though he had been hit over the head with a cudgel, and De Griers seeming to be plunged in thought. Endeavouring to be left behind, Mlle. Blanche next thought better of it, and followed the rest, with, in her wake, the Prince. Only the German savant and Madame de Cominges did not leave the General's apartments.

X

At spas—and, probably, all over Europe—hotel landlords and managers are guided in their allotment of rooms to visitors, not so much by the wishes and requirements of those visitors, as by their personal estimate of the same. It may also be said that these landlords and managers seldom make a mistake. To the Grandmother, however, our landlord, for some reason or another, allotted such a sumptuous suite that he fairly overreached himself; for he assigned her a suite consisting of four magnificently appointed rooms, with bathroom, servants' quarters, a separate room for her maid, and so on. In fact, during the previous week the suite had been occupied by no less a personage than a Grand Duchess: which circumstance was duly explained to the new occupant, as an excuse for raising the price of these apartments. The Grandmother had herself carried —or, rather, wheeled—through each room in turn, in order that she might subject the whole to a close and attentive scrutiny, while the landlord—an elderly, bald-headed man—walked respectfully by her side.

What every one took the Grandmother to be I do not know, but it appeared, at least, that she was accounted a person not only of great importance, but also, and still more, of great wealth; and without delay they entered her in the hotel register as "Madame la générale, princesse de Tarassevitcheva," although she had never been a princess in her life. Her retinue, her reserved compartment in the train, her pile of unnecessary trunks, portmanteaux, and strong-boxes, all helped to increase her prestige; while her wheeled chair, her sharp tone and voice, her eccentric questions (put with an air of the most overbearing and unbridled imperiousness), her whole figure—upright, rugged, and commanding as it was—completed the general awe in which she was held. As she inspected her new abode she ordered her chair to be stopped at intervals in order that, with finger extended towards some article of furniture, she might ply the respectfully smiling, yet secretly apprehensive, landlord with unexpected questions. She addressed them to him in French, although her pronunciation of the language was so bad that sometimes I had to translate them. For the most part, the landlord's answers were unsatisfactory, and failed to please her; nor were the questions themselves of a practical nature, but related, generally, to God knows what.

For instance, on one occasion she halted before a picture which, a poor copy of a well-known original, had a mythological subject.

"Of whom is this a portrait?" she inquired.

The landlord explained that it was probably that of a countess.

"But how know you that?" the old lady retorted. "You live here, yet you cannot say for certain! And why is the picture there at all? And why do its eyes look so crooked?"

To all these questions the landlord could return no satisfactory reply, despite his floundering endeavours.

"The blockhead!" exclaimed the Grandmother in Russian.

Then she proceeded on her way—only to repeat the same story in front of a Saxon statuette which she had sighted from afar, and had commanded, for some reason or another, to be brought to her. Finally she inquired of the landlord what was the value of the carpet in her bedroom, as well as where the said carpet had been manufactured; but the landlord could do no more than promise to make inquiries.

"What donkeys these people are!" she commented. Next, she turned her attention to the bed.

"What a huge counterpane!" she exclaimed. "Turn it back, please." The lacqueys did so.

"Further yet, further yet," the old lady cried. "Turn it *right* back. Also, take off those pillows and bolsters, and lift up the feather bed."

The bed was opened for her inspection.

"Mercifully it contains no bugs," she remarked. "Pull off the whole thing, and then put on my own pillows and sheets. The place is too luxurious for an old woman like myself. It is too large for any one person. Alexis Ivanovitch, come and see me whenever you are not teaching your pupils."

"After to-morrow I shall no longer be in the General's service," I replied, "but merely living in the hotel on my own account."

"Why so?"

"Because, the other day, there arrived from Berlin

a German and his wife—persons of some importance; and it chanced that, when taking a walk, I spoke to them in German without having properly compassed the Berlin accent."

"Indeed?"

"Yes: and this action on my part the Baron held to be an insult, and complained about it to the General, who yesterday dismissed me from his employ."

"But I suppose you must have threatened that precious Baron, or something of the kind? However, even if you did so, it was a matter of no moment."

"No, I did not. The Baron was the aggressor by raising his stick at me."

Upon that the Grandmother turned sharply to the General.

"What? You permitted yourself to treat your tutor thus, you nincompop, and to dismiss him from his post? You are a blockhead—an utter blockhead! I can see that clearly."

"Do not alarm yourself, my dear mother," the General replied with a lofty air—an air in which there was also a tinge of familiarity. "I am quite capable of managing my own affairs. Moreover, Alexis Ivanovitch has not given you a true account of the matter."

"What did you do next?" The old lady inquired of me.

"I wanted to challenge the Baron to a duel," I replied as modestly as possible; "but the General protested against my doing so."

"And *why* did you so protest?" she inquired of the General. Then she turned to the landlord, and questioned him as to whether *he* would not have fought a duel, if challenged. "For," she added, "I can see no difference between you and the Baron; nor can I bear that German visage of yours." Upon this the landlord bowed and departed, though he could not have understood the Grandmother's compliment.

"Pardon me, Madame," the General continued with a sneer; "but are duels really feasible?"

"Why not? All men are crowing cocks, and that is why they quarrel. *You*, though, I perceive, are a blockhead—a man who does not even know how to carry his breeding. Lift me up. Potapitch, see to it that you always have *two* bearers ready. Go and arrange for their hire. But we shall not require more than two, for I shall need only to be carried upstairs. On the level or in the street I can be *wheeled* along. Go and tell them that, and pay them in advance, so that they may show me some respect. You too, Potapitch, are always to come with me, and *you*, Alexis Ivanovitch, are to point out to me this Baron as we go along, in order that I may get a squint at the precious 'Von.' And where is that roulette played?"

I explained to her that the game was carried on in the salons of the Casino; whereupon there ensued a string of questions as to whether there were many such salons, whether many people played in them, whether those people played a whole day at a time, and whether the game was managed according to fixed rules. At length I thought it best to say that the most advisable course would be for her to go and see it for herself, since a mere description of it would be a difficult matter.

"Then take me straight there," she said; "and do you walk on in front of me, Alexis Ivanovitch."

"What, mother? Before you have so much as rested from your journey?" the General inquired with some solicitude. Also, for some reason which I could not divine, he seemed to be growing nervous; and, indeed, the whole party was evincing signs of confusion, and exchanging glances with one another. Probably they were thinking that it would be a ticklish—even an embarrassing—business to accompany the Grandmother to the Casino, where, very likely, she would perpetrate further eccentricities, and in public too! Yet on their own initiative they had offered to escort her!

"Why should I rest?" she retorted. "I am not tired, for I have been sitting still these past five days. Let us see what your medicinal springs and waters are like, and where they are situated. What, too, about that, that—what did you call it, Prascovia?—oh, about that mountain top?"

" Yes, we are going to see it, Grandmamma."

" Very well. Is there anything else for me to see here? "

" Yes; quite a number of things," Polina forced herself to say.

" Martha, *you* must come with me as well," went on the old lady to her maid.

" No, no, mother! " ejaculated the General. " Really she cannot come. They would not admit even Potapitch to the Casino."

" Rubbish! Because she is my servant, is that a reason for turning her out? Why, she is only a human being like the rest of us; and as she has been travelling for a week she might like to look about her. With whom else could she go out but myself? She would never dare to show her nose in the street alone."

" But, mother——"

" Are you ashamed to be seen with me? Stop at home, then, and you will be asked no questions. A pretty General *you* are, to be sure! I am a general's widow myself. But, after all, why should I drag the whole party with me? I will go and see the sights with only Alexis Ivanovitch as my escort."

De Griers strongly insisted that *every one* ought to accompany her. Indeed, he launched out into a perfect shower of charming phrases concerning the pleasure of acting as her cicerone, and so forth. Every one was touched with his words.

" Mais elle est tombée en enfance," he added aside to the General. " Seule, elle fera des bêtises." More than this I could not overhear, but he seemed to have got some plan in his mind, or even to be feeling a slight return of his hopes.

The distance to the Casino was about half a verst, and our route led us through the Chestnut Avenue until we reached the square directly fronting the building. The General, I could see, was a trifle reassured by the fact that, though our progress was distinctly eccentric in its nature, it was, at least, correct and orderly. As a matter of fact, the spectacle of a person who is unable to walk is not anything to excite surprise at a spa. Yet it was clear that the General had a great fear of the Casino itself: for why should a person who had lost the use of her limbs—more especially an old woman—be going to rooms which were set apart only for roulette? On either side of the wheeled chair walked Polina and Mlle. Blanche—the latter smiling, modestly jesting, and, in short, making herself so agreeable to the Grandmother that in the end the old lady relented towards her. On the other side of the chair Polina had to answer an endless flow of petty questions —such as "Who was it passed just now?" "Who is that coming along?" "Is the town a large one?" "Are the public gardens extensive?" "What sort of trees are those?" "What is the name of those hills?" "Do I see eagles flying yonder?" "What is that absurd-looking building?" and so forth. Meanwhile Astley whispered to me, as he walked by my side, that he looked for much to happen that morning. Behind the old lady's chair marched Potapitch and Martha—Potapitch in his frockcoat and white waistcoat, with a cloak over all, and the forty-year-old and rosy, but slightly grey-headed, Martha in a mobcap, cotton dress, and squeaking shoes. Frequently the old lady would twist herself round to converse with these servants. As for De Griers, he spoke as though he had made up his mind to do something (though it is also possible that he spoke in this manner merely in order to hearten the General, with whom he appeared to have held a conference). But, alas, the Grandmother had uttered the fatal words, "I am not going to give you any of my money;" and though De Griers might regard these words lightly, the General knew his mother better. Also, I noticed that De Griers and Mlle. Blanche were still exchanging looks; while of the Prince and the German savant I lost sight at the end of the Avenue, where they had turned back and left us.

Into the Casino we marched in triumph. At once, both in the person of the commissionaire and in the persons of the footmen, there sprang to life the same reverence as had arisen in the lacqueys of the hotel. Yet it was not without some curiosity that they eyed us.

Without loss of time the Grandmother gave orders that she should be wheeled through every room in the establishment; of which apartments she praised a few, while to others she remained indifferent. Concerning everything, however, she asked questions. Finally we reached the gaming-salons, where a lacquey who was acting as guard over the doors flung them open as though he were a man possessed.

The Grandmother's entry into the roulette-salon produced a profound impression upon the public. Around the tables, and at the further end of the room, where the trente-et-quarante table was set out, there may have been gathered from 150 to 200 gamblers, ranged in several rows. Those who had succeeded in pushing their way to the tables were standing with their feet firmly planted, in order to avoid having to give up their places until they should have finished their game (since merely to stand looking on — thus occupying a gambler's place for nothing—was not permitted). True, chairs were provided around the tables, but few players made use of them—more especially if there was a large attendance of the general public; since to stand allowed of a closer approach, and therefore of greater facilities for calculation and staking. Behind the foremost row were herded a second and a third row of people awaiting their turn; but sometimes their impatience led these people to stretch a hand through the first row, in order to deposit their stakes. Even third-row individuals would dart forward to stake; whence seldom did more than five or ten minutes pass without a scene over disputed money arising at one or another end of the table. On the other hand, the police of the Casino were an able body of men; and though to escape the crush was an impossibility, however much one might wish it, the eight croupiers apportioned to each table kept an eye upon the stakes, performed the necessary reckoning, and decided disputes as they arose. In the last resort they always called in the Casino police, and the disputes would immediately come to an end. Policemen were stationed about the Casino in ordinary costume, and mingled with the spectators so as to make it impossible to recognise them. In particular they kept a look-out for pickpockets and swindlers, who simply swarmed in the roulette salons, and reaped a rich harvest. Indeed, in every direction money was being filched from pockets or purses—though, of course, if the attempt miscarried, a great uproar ensued. One had only to approach a roulette table, and begin to play, and then openly grab some one else's winnings, for a din to be raised, and the thief to start vociferating that the stake was *his;* and if the coup had been carried out with sufficient skill, and the witnesses wavered at all in their testimony, the thief would as likely as not succeed in getting away with the money, provided that the sum was not a large one—not large enough to have attracted the attention of the croupiers or some fellow-player. Moreover, if it were a stake of insignificant size, its true owner would sometimes decline to continue the dispute, rather than become involved in a scandal. Conversely, if the thief was detected he was ignominiously expelled the building.

Upon all this the Grandmother gazed with open-eyed curiosity; and, on some thieves happening to be turned out of the place, she was delighted. Trente-et-quarante interested her but little; she preferred roulette, with its ever-revolving wheel. At length she expressed a wish to view the game closer; whereupon in some mysterious manner the lacqueys and other officious agents (especially one or two ruined Poles of the kind who keep offering their services to successful gamblers and foreigners in general) at once found and cleared a space for the old lady among the crush, at the very centre of one of the tables, and next to the chief croupier; after which they wheeled her chair thither. Upon this a number of visitors who were not playing, but only looking on (particularly some Englishmen with their families), pressed closer forward towards the table, in order to watch the old lady from among the ranks of the gamblers. Many a lorgnette I saw turned in her direction, and the croupiers' hopes rose high that such an eccentric player was about to provide them with something out of the common. An old lady of seventy-five years who, though unable to walk, desired to play was not an everyday phenomenon. I too pressed forward towards the table, and ranged myself by the Grandmother's side; while Martha and Potapitch remained somewhere in the background among the crowd, and the General, Polina, and De Griers, with Mlle. Blanche, also remained hidden among the spectators.

At first the old lady did no more than watch the gamblers, and ply me, in a half-whisper, with sharp-spoken questions as to who was so-and-so. Especially did her favour light upon a very young man who was plunging heavily, and had won (so it was whispered) as much as 40,000 francs, which were lying before him on the table in a heap of gold and bank-notes. His eyes kept flashing, and his hands shaking; yet all the while he staked without any sort of calculation—just what came to his hand, as he kept winning and winning, and raking and raking in his gains. Around him lacqueys fussed—placing chairs just behind where he was standing, and clearing the spectators from his vicinity, so that he should have more room, and not be crowded—the whole done, of course, in expectation of a generous largesse. From time to time other gamblers would hand him part of their winnings—being glad to let him stake for them as much as his hand could grasp; while beside him stood a Pole in a state of violent, but respectful, agitation, who, also in expectation of a generous largesse, kept whispering to him at intervals (probably telling him what to stake, and advising and directing his play). Yet never once did the player throw him a glance as he staked and staked, and raked in his winnings. Evidently the player in question was dead to all besides.

For a few minutes the Grandmother watched him.

"Go and tell him," suddenly she exclaimed with a nudge at my elbow, "—go and tell him to stop, and to take his money with him, and go home. Presently he will be losing—yes, losing everything that he has now won." She seemed almost breathless with excitement.

" Where is Potapitch? " she continued. " Send Potapitch to speak to him. No; *you* must tell him, *you* must tell him,"—here she nudged me again—" for I have not the least notion where Potapitch is. Sortez, sortez," she shouted to the young man, until I leant over in her direction and whispered in her ear that no shouting was allowed, nor even loud speaking, since to do so disturbed the calculations of the players, and might lead to our being ejected.

" How provoking! " she retorted. " Then the young man is done for! I suppose he *wishes* to be ruined. Yet I could not bear to see him have to return it all. What a fool the fellow is! "—and the old lady turned sharply away.

On the left, among the players at the other half of the table, a young lady was playing, with, beside her, a dwarf. Who the dwarf may have been—whether a relative or a person whom she took with her to act as a foil—I do not know; but I had noticed her there on previous occasions, since, every day, she entered the Casino at one o'clock precisely, and departed at two—thus playing for exactly one hour. Being well-known to the attendants, she always had a seat provided for her; and, taking some gold and a few thousand-franc notes out of her pocket—would begin quietly, coldly, and after much calculation, to stake, and mark down the figures in pencil on a paper, as though striving to work out a system according to which, at given moments, the odds might group themselves. Always she staked large coins, and either lost or won one, two, or three thousand francs a day, but not more; after which she would depart. The Grandmother took a long look at her.

" *That* woman is not losing," she said. " To whom does she belong? Do you know her? Who is she? "

" She is, I believe, a Frenchwoman," I replied.

" Ah! A bird of passage, evidently. Besides, I can see that she has her shoes polished. Now, explain to me the meaning of each round in the game, and the way in which one ought to stake."

Upon this I set myself to explain the meaning of all the combinations—of " rouge et noir," of " pair et impair," of "manque et passe," with, lastly, the different values in the system of numbers. The Grandmother listened attentively, took notes, put questions in various forms, and laid the whole thing to heart. Indeed, since an example of each system of stakes kept constantly occurring, a great deal of information could be assimilated with ease and celerity. The Grandmother was vastly pleased.

"But what is zero?" she inquired. "Just now I heard the flaxen-haired croupier call out 'zero!' And why does he keep raking in all the money that is on the table? To think that he should grab the whole pile for himself! What does zero mean?"

"Zero is what the bank takes for itself. If the wheel stops at that figure, everything lying on the table becomes the absolute property of the bank. Also, whenever the wheel has begun to turn, the bank ceases to pay out anything."

"Then I should receive nothing if I were staking?"

"No; unless by any chance you had *purposely* staked on zero; in which case you would receive thirty-five times the value of your stake."

"Why thirty-five times, when zero so often turns up? And if so, why do not more of these fools stake upon it?"

"Because the number of chances against its occurrence is thirty-six."

"Rubbish! Potapitch, Potapitch! Come here, and I will give you some money." The old lady took out of her pocket a tightly-clasped purse, and extracted from its depths a ten-gülden piece. "Go at once, and stake that upon zero."

"But, Madame, zero has only this moment turned up," I remonstrated; "wherefore it may not do so again for ever so long. Wait a little, and you may then have a better chance."

"Rubbish! Stake, please."

"Pardon me, but zero might not turn up again until, say, to-night, even though you had staked thousands upon it. It often happens so."

"Rubbish, rubbish! Who fears the wolf should

never enter the forest. What? We have lost? Then stake again."

A second ten-gülden piece did we lose, and then I put down a third. The Grandmother could scarcely remain seated in her chair, so intent was she upon the little ball as it leapt through the notches of the ever-revolving wheel. However, the third ten-gülden piece followed the first two. Upon this the Grandmother went perfectly crazy. She could no longer sit still, and actually struck the table with her fist when the croupier cried out, "Trente-six," instead of the desiderated zero.

"To listen to him!" fumed the old lady. "When will that accursed zero ever turn up? I cannot breathe until I see it. I believe that that infernal croupier is *purposely* keeping it from turning up. Alexis Ivanovitch, stake *two* golden pieces this time. The moment we cease to stake, that cursed zero will come turning up, and we shall get nothing."

"My good Madame——"

"Stake, stake! It is not *your* money."

Accordingly I staked two ten-gülden pieces. The ball went hopping round the wheel until it began to settle through the notches. Meanwhile the Grandmother sat as though petrified, with my hand convulsively clutched in hers.

"Zero!" called the croupier.

"There! You see, you see!" cried the old lady, as she turned and faced me, wreathed in smiles. "I told you so! It was the Lord God himself who suggested to me to stake those two coins. Now, how much ought I to receive? Why do they not pay it out to me? Potapitch! Martha! Where are they? What has become of our party? Potapitch, Potapitch!"

"Presently, Madame," I whispered. "Potapitch is outside, and they would decline to admit him to these rooms. See! You are being paid out your money. Pray take it." The croupiers were making up a heavy packet of coins, sealed in blue paper, and containing fifty ten-gülden pieces, together with an unsealed packet containing another twenty. I handed the whole to the old lady in a money-shovel.

" Faites le jeu, messieurs! Faites le jeu, messieurs! Rien ne va plus," proclaimed the croupier as once more he invited the company to stake, and prepared to turn the wheel.

" We shall be too late! He is going to spin again! Stake, stake!" The Grandmother was in a perfect fever. " Do not hang back! Be quick!" She seemed almost beside herself, and nudged me as hard as she could.

" Upon what shall I stake, Madame?"

" Upon zero, upon zero! Again upon zero! Stake as much as ever you can. How much have we got? Seventy ten-gülden pieces? We shall not miss them, so stake twenty pieces at a time."

" Think a moment, Madame. Sometimes zero does not turn up for two hundred rounds in succession. I assure you that you may lose all your capital."

" You are wrong—utterly wrong. Stake, I tell you! What a chattering tongue you have! I know perfectly well what I am doing." The old lady was shaking with excitement.

" But the rules do not allow of more than 120 gülden being staked upon zero at a time."

" How 'do not allow'? Surely you are wrong? Monsieur, monsieur——" here she nudged the croupier who was sitting on her left, and preparing to spin—" combien zero? Douze? Douze?"

I hastened to translate.

" Oui, Madame," was the croupier's polite reply. " No single stake must exceed four thousand florins. That is the regulation."

" Then there is nothing else for it. We must risk 120 gülden."

" Le jeu est fait!" the croupier called. The wheel revolved, and stopped at thirty. We had lost!

" Again, again, again! Stake again!" shouted the old lady. Without attempting to oppose her further, but merely shrugging my shoulders, I placed twelve more ten-gülden pieces upon the table. The wheel whirled around and around, with the Grandmother simply quaking as she watched its revolutions.

"Does she again think that zero is going to be the winning coup?" thought I as I stared at her in astonishment. Yet an absolute assurance of winning was shining on her face; she looked perfectly convinced that zero was about to be called again. At length the ball dropped off into one of the notches.

"Zero!" cried the croupier.

"Ah!!!" screamed the old lady as she turned to me in a whirl of triumph.

I myself was at heart a gambler. At that moment I became acutely conscious both of that fact and of the fact that my hands and knees were shaking, and that the blood was beating in my brain. Of course this was a rare occasion—an occasion on which zero had turned up no less than three times within a dozen rounds; yet in such an event there was nothing so very surprising, seeing that, only three days ago, I myself had been a witness to zero turning up *three times in succession,* so that one of the players who was recording the coups on paper was moved to remark that for several days past zero had never turned up at all!

With the Grandmother, as with any one who has won a very large sum, the management settled up with great attention and respect, since she was fortunate to have to receive no less than 4200 gülden. Of these gülden the odd 200 were paid her in gold, and the remainder in bank notes.

This time the old lady did not call for Potapitch; for that she was too preoccupied. Though not outwardly shaken by the event (indeed, she seemed perfectly calm), she was trembling inwardly from head to foot. At length, completely absorbed in the game, she burst out:

"Alexis Ivanovitch, did not the croupier just say that 4000 florins were the most that could be staked at any one time? Well, take these 4000, and stake them upon the red."

To oppose her was useless. Once more the wheel revolved.

"Rouge!" proclaimed the croupier.

Again 4000 florins—in all 8000!

"Give me them," commanded the Grandmother, "and stake the other 4000 upon the red again."

I did so.

"Rouge!" proclaimed the croupier.

"Twelve thousand!" cried the old lady. "Hand me the whole lot. Put the gold into this purse here, and count the bank notes. Enough! Let us go home. Wheel my chair away."

XI

THE chair, with the old lady beaming in it, was wheeled away towards the doors at the further end of the salon, while our party hastened to crowd around her, and to offer her their congratulations. In fact, eccentric as was her conduct, it was also overshadowed by her triumph; with the result that the General no longer feared to be publicly compromised by being seen with such a strange woman, but, smiling in a condescending, cheerfully familiar way, as though he were soothing a child, he offered his greetings to the old lady. At the same time, both he and the rest of the spectators were visibly impressed. Everywhere people kept pointing to the Grandmother, and talking about her. Many people even walked beside her chair, in order to view her the better, while, at a little distance, Astley was carrying on a conversation on the subject with two English acquaintances of his. De Griers was simply overflowing with smiles and compliments, and a number of fine ladies were staring at the Grandmother as though she had been something curious.

"Quelle victoire!" exclaimed De Griers.

"Mais, Madame, c'était du feu!" added Mlle. Blanche with an elusive smile.

"Yes, I have won twelve thousand florins," replied the old lady. "And then there is all this gold. With it the total ought to come to nearly thirteen thousand. How much is that in Russian money? Six thousand roubles, I think?"

However, I calculated that the sum would exceed

seven thousand roubles—or, at the present rate of exchange, even eight thousand.

"Eight thousand roubles! What a splendid thing! And to think of you simpletons sitting there and doing nothing! Potapitch! Martha! See what I have won!"

"How *did* you do it, Madame?" Martha exclaimed ecstatically. "Eight thousand roubles!"

"And I am going to give you fifty gülden apiece. There they are."

Potapitch and Martha rushed towards her to kiss her hand.

"And to each bearer also I will give a ten-gülden piece. Let them have it out of the gold, Alexis Ivanovitch. But why is this footman bowing to me, and that other man as well? Are they congratulating me? Well, let them have ten gülden apiece."

"Madame la princesse—Un pauvre expatrié—Malheur continuel—Les princes russes sont si généreux!" said a man who for some time past had been hanging around the old lady's chair—a personage who, dressed in a shabby frockcoat and coloured waistcoat, kept taking off his cap, and smiling pathetically.

"Give him ten gülden," said the Grandmother. "No, give him twenty. Now, enough of that, or I shall never get done with you all. Take a moment's rest, and then carry me away. Prascovia, I mean to buy a new dress for you to-morrow. Yes, and for you too, Mlle. Blanche. Please translate, Prascovia."

"Merci, Madame," replied Mlle. Blanche gratefully as she twisted her face into the mocking smile which usually she kept only for the benefit of De Griers and the General. The latter looked confused, and seemed greatly relieved when we reached the Avenue.

"How surprised Theodosia too will be!" went on the Grandmother (thinking of the General's nursemaid). "She, like yourselves, shall have the price of a new gown. Here, Alexis Ivanovitch! Give that beggar something" (a crooked-backed ragamuffin had approached to stare at us).

"But perhaps he is *not* a beggar—only a rascal," I replied.

"Never mind, never mind. Give him a gülden."

I approached the beggar in question, and handed him the coin. Looking at me in great astonishment, he silently accepted the gülden, while from his person there proceeded a strong smell of liquor.

"Have you never tried your luck, Alexis Ivanovitch?"

"No, Madame."

"Yet just now I could see that you were burning to do so?"

"I *do* mean to try my luck presently."

"Then stake everything upon zero. You have seen how it ought to be done? How much capital do you possess?"

"Two hundred gülden, Madame."

"Not very much. See here; I will lend you five hundred if you wish. Take this purse of mine." With that she added sharply to the General: "But *you* need not expect to receive any."

This seemed to upset him, but he said nothing, and De Griers contented himself by scowling.

"Que diable!" he whispered to the General. "C'est une terrible vieille."

"Look! Another beggar, another beggar!" exclaimed the grandmother. "Alexis Ivanovitch, go and give him a gülden."

As she spoke I saw approaching us a greyheaded old man with a wooden leg—a man who was dressed in a blue frockcoat and carrying a staff. He looked like an old soldier. As soon as I tendered him the coin he fell back a step or two, and eyed me threateningly.

"Was ist der Teufel!" he cried, and appended thereto a round dozen of oaths.

"The man is a perfect fool!" exclaimed the Grandmother, waving her hand. "Move on now, for I am simply famished. When we have lunched we will return to that place."

"What?" cried I. "You are going to play *again?*"

"What else do you suppose?" she retorted. "Are you going only to sit here, and grow sour, and let me look at you?"

"Madame," said De Griers confidentially, "les

chances peuvent tourner. Une seule mauvaise chance, et vous perdrez tout—surtout avec votre jeu. C'était terrible!"

"Oui; vous perdrez absolument," put in Mlle. Blanche.

"What has that got to do with *you?*" retorted the old lady. "It is not *your* money that I am going to lose; it is my own. And where is that Mr. Astley of yours?" she added to myself.

"He stayed behind in the Casino."

"What a pity! He is such a nice sort of man!"

Arriving home, and meeting the landlord on the staircase, the Grandmother called him to her side, and boasted to him of her winnings—thereafter doing the same to Theodosia, and conferring upon her thirty gülden; after which she bid her serve luncheon. The meal over, Theodosia and Martha broke into a joint flood of ecstasy.

"I was watching you all the time, Madame," quavered Martha, "and I asked Potapitch what mistress was trying to do. And, my word! the heaps and *heaps* of money that were lying upon the table! Never in my life have I seen so much money. And there were gentlefolk around it, and other gentlefolk sitting down. So I asked Potapitch where all these gentry had come from; for, thought I, maybe the Holy Mother of God will help our mistress among them. Yes, I prayed for you, Madame, and my heart died within me, so that I kept trembling and trembling. The Lord be with her, I thought to myself; and in answer to my prayer He has now sent you what He has done! Even yet I tremble—I tremble to think of it all."

"Alexis Ivanovitch," said the old lady, "after luncheon,—that is to say, about four o'clock—get ready to go out with me again. But in the meanwhile, good-bye. Do not forget to call a doctor, for I must take the waters. Now go and get rested a little."

I left the Grandmother's presence in a state of bewilderment. Vainly I endeavoured to imagine what would become of our party, or what turn the affair would next take. I could perceive that none of the party had yet recovered their presence of mind—least of all the General. The factor of the Grandmother's appearance in place of the hourly expected telegram to announce her death (with, of course, resultant legacies) had so upset the whole scheme of intentions and projects that it was with a decided feeling of apprehension and growing paralysis that the conspirators viewed any future performances of the old lady at roulette. Yet this second factor was not quite so important as the first, since, though the Grandmother had twice declared that she did not intend to give the General any money, that declaration was not a complete ground for the abandonment of hope. Certainly De Griers, who, with the General, was up to the neck in the affair, had not wholly lost courage; and I felt sure that Mlle. Blanche also—Mlle. Blanche who was not only as deeply involved as the other two, but also expectant of becoming Madame General and an important legatee—would not lightly surrender the position, but would use her every resource of coquetry upon the old lady, in order to afford a contrast to the impetuous Polina, who was difficult to understand, and lacked the art of pleasing. Yet now, when the Grandmother had just performed an astonishing feat at roulette; now, when the old lady's personality had been so clearly and typically revealed as that of a rugged, arrogant woman who was "tombée en enfance"; now, when everything appeared to be lost,—why, now the Grandmother was as merry as a child which plays with thistle-down. "Good Lord!" I thought with, may God forgive me, a most malicious smile, "every ten-gülden piece which the Grandmother staked must have raised a blister on the General's heart, and maddened De Griers, and driven Mlle. de Cominges almost to frenzy with the sight of this spoon dangling before her lips." Another factor is the circumstance that even when, overjoyed at winning, the Grandmother was distributing alms right and left, and taking every one to be a beggar, she again snapped out to the General that he was not going to be allowed any of her money: which meant that the old lady had quite made up her mind on the point, and was sure of it. Yes, danger loomed ahead.

All these thoughts passed through my mind during the few moments that, having left the old lady's rooms,

I was ascending to my own room on the top storey. What most struck me was the fact that, though I had divined the chief, the stoutest, threads which united the various actors in the drama, I had, until now, been ignorant of the methods and secrets of the game. For Polina had never been completely open with me. Although, on occasions, it had happened that involuntarily, as it were, she had revealed to me something of her heart, I had noticed that in most cases—in fact, nearly always—she had either laughed away these revelations, or grown confused, or purposely imparted to them a false guise. Yes, she must have concealed a great deal from me. But I had a presentiment that now the end of this strained and mysterious situation was approaching. Another stroke, and all would be finished and exposed. Of my own fortunes, interested though I was in the affair, I took no account. I was in the strange position of possessing but two hundred gülden, of being at a loose end, of lacking both a post, the means of subsistence, a shred of hope, and any plans for the future, yet of caring nothing for these things. Had not my mind been so full of Polina, I should have given myself up to the comical piquancy of the impending dénouement, and laughed my fill at it. But the thought of Polina was torture to me. That her fate was settled I already had an inkling; yet *that* was not the thought which was giving me so much uneasiness. What I really wished for was to penetrate her secrets. I wanted her to come to me and say, "I love you;" and if she would not so come, or if to hope that she would ever do so was an unthinkable absurdity—why, then there was nothing else for me to want. Even now I do not know what I am wanting. I feel like a man who has lost his way. I yearn but to be in her presence, and within the circle of her light and splendour—to be there now, and for ever, and for the whole of my life. More I do not know. How can I ever bring myself to leave her?

On reaching the third storey of the hotel I experienced a shock. I was just passing the General's suite when something caused me to look round. Out of a door about twenty paces away there was coming Polina!

She hesitated for a moment on seeing me, and then beckoned me to her.

"Polina Alexandrovna!"

"Hush! Not so loud."

"Something startled me just now," I whispered, "and I looked round, and saw you. Some electrical influence seems to emanate from your form."

"Take this letter," she went on with a frown (probably she had not even heard my words, she was so preoccupied), "and hand it personally to Mr. Astley. Go as quickly as ever you can, please. No answer will be required. He himself——" She did not finish her sentence.

"To Mr. Astley?" I asked, in some astonishment.

But she had vanished again.

Aha! So the two were carrying on a correspondence! However, I set off to search for Astley—first at his hotel, and then at the Casino, where I went the round of the salons in vain. At length, vexed, and almost in despair, I was on my way home when I ran across him among a troop of English ladies and gentlemen who had been out for a ride. Beckoning to him to stop, I handed him the letter. We had barely time even to look at one another, but I suspected that it was of set purpose that he restarted his horse so quickly.

Was jealousy, then, gnawing at me? At all events, I felt exceedingly depressed, despite the fact that I had no desire to ascertain what the correspondence was about. To think that *he* should be her confidant! "My friend, mine own familiar friend!" passed through my mind. Yet *was* there any love in the matter? "Of course not," reason whispered to me. But reason goes for little on such occasions. I felt that the matter must be cleared up, for it was becoming unpleasantly complex.

I had scarcely set foot in the hotel when the commissionaire and the landlord (the latter issuing from his room for the purpose) alike informed me that I was being searched for high and low—that three separate messages to ascertain my whereabouts had come down from the General. When I entered his study I was feeling anything but kindly disposed. I found there the General himself, De Griers, and Mlle. Blanche, but not Mlle.'s mother, who was a person whom her reputed daughter used only for show purposes, since in all matters of business the daughter fended for herself, and it is unlikely that the mother knew anything about them.

Some very heated discussion was in progress, and meanwhile the door of the study was open—an unprecedented circumstance. As I approached the portals I could hear loud voices raised, for mingled with the pert, venomous accents of De Griers were Mlle. Blanche's excited, impudently abusive tongue and the General's plaintive wail as, apparently, he sought to justify himself in something. But on my appearance every one stopped speaking, and tried to put a better face upon matters. De Griers smoothed his hair, and twisted his angry face into a smile—into the mean, studiedly polite French smile which I so detested; while the downcast, perplexed General assumed an air of dignity—though only in a mechanical way. On the other hand, Mlle. Blanche did not trouble to conceal the wrath that was sparkling in her countenance, but bent her gaze upon me with an air of impatient expectancy. I may remark that hitherto she had treated me with absolute superciliousness, and, so far from answering my salutations, had always ignored them.

"Alexis Ivanovitch," began the General in a tone of affectionate upbraiding, "may I say to you that I find it strange, exceedingly strange, that—— In short, your conduct towards myself and my family—— In a word, your—er—extremely——"

"Eh! Ce n'est pas ça," interrupted De Griers in a tone of impatience and contempt (evidently he was the ruling spirit of the conclave). "Mon cher monsieur, notre général se trompe. What he means to say is that he warns you—he begs of you most earnestly—not to ruin him. I use the expression because——"

"Why? Why?" I interjected.

"Because you have taken upon yourself to act as guide to this, to this—how shall I express it?—to this old lady, à cette pauvre terrible vieille. But she will only gamble away all that she has—gamble it away like thistledown. You yourself have seen her play. Once she has acquired the taste for gambling, she will never leave the roulette-table, but, of sheer perversity and temper, will stake her all, and lose it. In cases such as hers a gambler can never be torn away from the game; and then—and then——"

"And then," asseverated the General, "you will have ruined my whole family. I and my family are her heirs, for she has no nearer relatives than ourselves. I tell you frankly that my affairs are in great—very great disorder; how much they are so you yourself are partially aware. If she should lose a large sum, or, may be, her whole fortune, what will become of us—of my children" (here the General exchanged a glance with De Griers) "or of me?" (here he looked at Mlle. Blanche, who turned her head contemptuously away). "Alexis Ivanovitch, I beg of you to save us."

"Tell me, General, how am I to do so? On what footing do I stand here?"

"Refuse to take her about. Simply leave her alone."

"But she would soon find some one else to take my place?"

"Ce n'est pas ça, ce n'est pas ça," again interrupted De Griers. "Que diable! Do not leave her alone so much as advise her, persuade her, draw her away. In any case do not let her gamble; find her some counter-attraction."

"And how am I to do that? If only *you* would undertake the task, Monsieur de Griers!" I said this last as innocently as possible, but at once saw a rapid glance of excited interrogation pass from Mlle. Blanche to De Griers, while in the face of the latter also there gleamed something which he could not repress.

"Well, at the present moment she would refuse to accept my services," said he with a gesture. "But if, later——"

Here he gave Mlle. Blanche another glance which was full of meaning; whereupon she advanced towards me with a bewitching smile, and seized and pressed my hands. Devil take it, but how that devilish visage of hers could change! At the present moment it was a visage full of supplication, and as gentle in its expression as that of a smiling, roguish infant. Stealthily she drew me apart from the rest, as though the more completely to separate me from them; and though no harm came of her doing so—for it was merely a stupid manœuvre, and no more—I found the situation very unpleasant.

The General hastened to lend her his support.

"Alexis Ivanovitch," he began, "pray pardon me for having said what I did just now—for having said more than I meant to do. I beg and beseech you, I kiss the hem of your garment, as our Russian saying has it, for you, and only you, can save us. I and Mlle. de Cominges, we all of us beg of you—— But you understand, do you not? Surely you understand?" and with his eyes he indicated Mlle. Blanche. Truly he was cutting a pitiful figure!

At this moment three low, respectful knocks sounded at the door; which, on being opened, revealed a chambermaid, with Potapitch behind her—come from the Grandmother to request that I should attend her in her rooms. "She is in a bad humour," added Potapitch.

The time was half-past three.

"My mistress was unable to sleep," explained Potapitch; "so, after tossing about for a while, she suddenly rose, called for her chair, and sent me to look for you. She is now in the verandah."

"Quelle mégère!" exclaimed De Griers.

True enough, I found Madame in the hotel verandah—much put about at my delay, for she had been unable to contain herself until four o'clock.

"Lift me up," she cried to the bearers, and once more we set out for the roulette-salons.

XII

THE Grandmother was in an impatient, irritable frame of mind. Without doubt the roulette had turned her head, for she appeared to be indifferent to everything else, and, in general, seemed much distraught. For instance, she asked me no questions about objects *en route*, except that, when a sumptuous barouche passed us and raised a cloud of dust, she lifted her hand for a moment, and inquired, " What was that? " Yet even then she did not appear to hear my reply, although at times her abstraction was interrupted by sallies and fits of sharp, impatient fidgeting. Again, when I pointed out to her the Baron and Baroness Burmergelm walking to the Casino, she merely looked at them in an absent-minded sort of way, and said with complete indifference, " Ah! " Then, turning sharply to Potapitch and Martha, who were walking behind us, she rapped out:

" Why have *you* attached yourselves to the party? We are not going to take *you* with us every time. Go home at once." Then, when the servants had pulled hasty bows and departed, she added to me: " *You* are all the escort I need."

At the Casino the Grandmother seemed to be expected, for no time was lost in procuring her her former place beside the croupier. It is my opinion that though croupiers seem such ordinary, humdrum officials—men who care nothing whether the bank wins or loses—they are, in reality, anything but indifferent to the bank's losing, and are given instructions to attract players, and to keep a watch over the bank's interests; as also that for such services these officials are awarded prizes and premiums. At all events, the croupiers of Roulettenberg seemed to look upon the Grandmother as their lawful prey: whereafter there befell what our party had foretold.

It happened thus.

As soon as ever we arrived the Grandmother ordered me to stake twelve ten-gülden pieces in succession upon zero. Once, twice, and thrice I did so, yet zero never turned up.

" Stake again," said the old lady with an impatient nudge of my elbow, and I obeyed.

" How many times have we lost? " she inquired—actually grinding her teeth in her excitement.

" We have lost 144 ten-gülden pieces," I replied. " I tell you, Madame, that zero may not turn up until nightfall."

"Never mind," she interrupted. "Keep on staking upon zero, and also stake a thousand gülden upon rouge. Here is a bank-note with which to do so.

The red turned up, but zero missed again, and we only got our thousand gülden back.

"But you see, you see!" whispered the old lady. "We have now recovered almost all that we staked. Try zero again. Let us do so another ten times, and then leave off."

By the fifth round, however, the Grandmother was weary of the scheme.

"To the devil with that zero!" she exclaimed. "Stake four thousand gülden upon the red."

"But, Madame, that will be so much to venture!" I remonstrated. "Suppose the red should *not* turn up?" The Grandmother almost struck me in her excitement. Her agitation was rapidly making her quarrelsome. Consequently, there was nothing for it but to stake the whole four thousand gülden as she had directed.

The wheel revolved while the Grandmother sat as bolt upright, and with as proud and quiet a mien, as though she had not the least doubt of winning.

"Zero!" cried the croupier.

At first the old lady failed to understand the situation; but as soon as she saw the croupier raking in her four thousand gülden, together with everything else that happened to be lying on the table, and recognised that the zero which had been so long turning up, and on which we had lost nearly two hundred ten-gülden pieces, had at length, as though of set purpose, made a sudden reappearance—why, the poor old lady fell to cursing it, and to throwing herself about, and wailing and gesticulating at the company at large. Indeed, some people in our vicinity actually burst out laughing.

"To think that that accursed zero should have turned up *now!*" she sobbed. "The accursed, accursed thing! And it is all *your* fault," she added, rounding upon me in a frenzy. "It was *you* who persuaded me to cease staking upon it."

"But, Madame, I only explained the game to you.

How am *I* to answer for every mischance which may occur in it?"

"You and your mischances!" she whispered threateningly. "Go! Away at once!"

"Farewell, then, Madame." And I turned to depart.

"No; stay," she put in hastily. "Where are you going to? Why should you leave me? You fool! No, no; stay here. It is *I* who was the fool. Tell me what I ought to do."

"I cannot take it upon myself to advise you, for you will only blame me if I do so. Play at your own discretion. Say exactly what you wish staked, and I will stake it."

"Very well. Stake another four thousand gülden upon the red. Take this banknote to do it with. I have still got twenty thousand roubles in actual cash."

"But," I whispered, "such a quantity of money——"

"Never mind. I cannot rest until I have won back my losses. Stake!"

I staked, and we lost.

"Stake again, stake again — eight thousand at a stroke!"

"I cannot, Madame. The largest stake allowed is four thousand gülden."

"Well, then; stake four thousand."

This time we won, and the Grandmother recovered herself a little.

"You see, you see!" she exclaimed as she nudged me. "Stake another four thousand."

I did so, and lost. Again, and yet again, we lost.

"Madame, your twelve thousand gülden are now gone," at length I reported.

"I see they are," she replied with, as it were, the calmness of despair. "I see they are," she muttered again as she gazed straight in front of her, like a person lost in thought. "Ah well, I do not mean to rest until I have staked another four thousand."

"But you have no money with which to do it, Madame. In this satchel I can see only a few five per cent. bonds and some transfers—no actual cash."

"And in the purse?"

"A mere trifle."

" But there is a money-changer's office here, is there not? They told me I should be able to get any sort of paper security changed? "

" Quite so; to any amount you please. But you will lose on the transaction what would frighten even a Jew."

" Rubbish! I am *determined* to retrieve my losses. Take me away, and call those fools of bearers."

I wheeled the chair out of the throng, and, the bearers making their appearance, we left the Casino.

" Hurry, hurry! " commanded the Grandmother. " Show me the nearest way to the money-changer's. Is it far? "

" A couple of steps, Madame."

At the turning from the square into the Avenue we came face to face with the whole of our party—the General, De Griers, Mlle. Blanche, and her mother. Only Polina and Mr. Astley were absent.

" Well, well, well! " exclaimed the Grandmother. " But we have no time to stop. What do you want? I can't talk to you here."

I dropped behind a little, and immediately was pounced upon by De Griers.

" She has lost this morning's winnings," I whispered, " and also twelve thousand gülden of her original money. At the present moment we are going to get some bonds changed."

De Griers stamped his foot with vexation, and hastened to communicate the tidings to the General. Meanwhile we continued to wheel the old lady along.

" Stop her, stop her," whispered the General in consternation.

" You had better try and stop her yourself," I returned—also in a whisper.

" My good mother," he said as he approached her, "—my good mother, pray let, let—"(his voice was beginning to tremble and sink) "—let us hire a carriage, and go for a drive. Near here there is an enchanting view to be obtained. We—we—we were just coming to invite you to go and see it."

" Begone with you and your views! " said the Grandmother angrily as she waved him away.

"And there are trees there, and we could have tea under them," continued the General — now in utter despair.

"Nous boirons du lait, sur l'herbe fraiche," added De Griers with the snarl almost of a wild beast.

"Du lait, de l'herbe fraiche"—the idyll, the ideal of the Parisian bourgeois—his whole outlook upon "la nature et la verité"!

"Have done with you and your milk!" cried the old lady. "Go and stuff *yourself* as much as you like, but *my* stomach simply recoils from the idea. What are you stopping for? I have nothing to say to you."

"Here we are, Madame," I announced. "Here is the money-changer's office."

I entered to get the securities changed, while the Grandmother remained outside in the porch, and the rest waited at a little distance, in doubt as to their best course of action. At length the old lady turned such an angry stare upon them that they departed along the road towards the Casino.

The process of changing involved complicated calculations which soon necessitated my return to the Grandmother for instructions.

"The thieves!" she exclaimed as she clapped her hands together. "Never mind, though. Get the documents cashed.—No; send the banker out to me," she added as an afterthought.

"Would one of the clerks do, Madame?"

"Yes, one of the clerks. The thieves!"

The clerk consented to come out when he perceived that he was being asked for by an old lady who was too infirm to walk; after which the Grandmother began to upbraid him at length, and with great vehemence, for his alleged usuriousness, and to bargain with him in a mixture of Russian, French, and German—I acting as interpreter. Meanwhile the grave-faced official eyed us both, and silently nodded his head. At the Grandmother, in particular, he gazed with a curiosity which almost bordered upon rudeness. At length, too, he smiled.

"Pray recollect yourself!" cried the old lady. "And

may my money choke you! Alexis Ivanovitch, tell him that we can easily repair to some one else."

"The clerk says that others will give you even less than he."

Of what the ultimate calculations consisted I do not exactly remember, but at all events they were alarming. Receiving twelve thousand florins in gold, I took also the statement of accounts, and carried it out to the Grandmother.

"Well, well," she said, "I am no accountant. Let us hurry away, hurry away." And she waved the paper aside.

"Neither upon that accursed zero, however, nor upon that equally accursed red do I mean to stake a cent," I muttered to myself as I entered the Casino.

This time I did all I could to persuade the old lady to stake as little as possible—saying that a turn would come in the chances when she would be at liberty to stake more. But she was so impatient that, though at first she agreed to do as I suggested, nothing could stop her when once she had begun. By way of prelude she won stakes of a hundred and two hundred gülden.

"There you are!" she said as she nudged me. "See what we have won! Surely it would be worth our while to stake four thousand instead of a hundred, for we might win another four thousand, and then——! Oh, it was *your* fault before—all your fault."

I felt greatly put out as I watched her play, but I decided to hold my tongue, and to give her no more advice.

Suddenly De Griers appeared on the scene. It seemed that all this while he and his companions had been standing beside us—though I noticed that Mlle. Blanche had withdrawn a little from the rest, and was engaged in flirting with the Prince. Clearly the General was greatly put out at this. Indeed, he was in a perfect agony of vexation. But Mlle. was careful never to look his way, though he did his best to attract her notice. Poor General! By turns his face blanched and reddened, and he was trembling to such an extent that he could scarcely follow the old lady's play. At length Mlle. and the Prince took their departure, and the General followed them.

"Madame, Madame," sounded the honeyed accents of De Griers as he leant over to whisper in the Grandmother's ear. "That stake will never win. No, no, it is impossible," he added in Russian with a writhe. "No, no!"

"But why not?" asked the Grandmother, turning round. "Show me what I ought to do."

Instantly De Griers burst into a babble of French as he advised, jumped about, declared that such and such chances ought to be waited for, and started to make calculations of figures. All this he addressed to me in my capacity as translator—tapping the table the while with his finger, and pointing hither and thither. At length he seized a pencil, and began to reckon sums on paper until he had exhausted the Grandmother's patience.

"Away with you!" she interrupted. "You talk sheer nonsense, for, though you keep on saying 'Madame, Madame,' you haven't the least notion what ought to be done. Away with you, I say!"

"Mais, Madame," cooed De Griers—and straightway started afresh with his fussy instructions.

"Stake just *once* as he advises," the Grandmother said to me, "and then we shall see what we *shall* see. Of course, his stake *might* win."

As a matter of fact, De Grier's one object was to distract the old lady from staking large sums; wherefore he now suggested to her that she should stake upon certain numbers, singly and in groups. Consequently, in accordance with his instructions I staked a ten-gülden piece upon several odd numbers in the first twenty, and five ten-gülden pieces upon certain groups of numbers—groups of from twelve to eighteen, and from eighteen to twenty-four. The total staked amounted to 160 gülden.

The wheel revolved. "Zero!" cried the croupier.

We had lost it all!

"The fool!" cried the old lady as she turned upon De Griers. "You infernal Frenchman, to think that *you* should advise! Away with you! Though you fuss and fuss, you don't even know what you're talking about."

Deeply offended, De Griers shrugged his shoulders, favoured the Grandmother with a look of contempt, and departed. For some time past he had been feeling ashamed of being seen in such company, and this had proved the last straw.

An hour later we had lost everything in hand.

"Home!" cried the Grandmother.

Not until we had turned into the Avenue did she utter a word; but from that point onwards, until we arrived at the hotel, she kept venting exclamations of "What a fool I am! What a silly old fool I am, to be sure!"

Arrived at the hotel, she called for tea, and then gave orders for her luggage to be packed.

"We are off again," she announced.

"But whither, Madame?" inquired Martha.

"What business is that of *yours?* Let the cricket stick to its hearth.[1] Potapitch, have everything packed, for we are returning to Moscow at once. I have fooled away fifteen thousand roubles."

"Fifteen thousand roubles, good mistress? My God!" And Potapitch spat upon his hands—probably to show that he was ready to serve her in any way he could.

"Now then, you fool! At once you begin with your weeping and wailing! Be quiet, and pack. Also, run downstairs, and get my hotel bill."

"The next train leaves at 9.30, Madame," I interposed, with a view to checking her agitation.

"And what is the time now?"

"Half-past eight."

"How vexing! But never mind. Alexis Ivanovitch, I have not a kopeck left; I have but these two bank notes. Please run to the office and get them changed. Otherwise I shall have nothing to travel with."

Departing on her errand, I returned half an hour later to find the whole party gathered in her rooms. It appeared that the news of her impending departure for Moscow had thrown the conspirators into consternation even greater than her losses had done. For, said they, even if her departure should save her fortune, what will

[1] The Russian form of "Mind your own business."

become of the General later? And who is to repay De Griers? Clearly Mlle. Blanche would never consent to wait until the Grandmother was dead, but would at once elope with the Prince or some one else. So they had all gathered together—endeavouring to calm and dissuade the Grandmother. Only Polina was absent. For her part the Grandmother had nothing for the party but abuse.

"Away with you, you rascals!" she was shouting. "What have my affairs to do with you? Why, in particular, do *you*"—here she indicated De Griers—"come sneaking here with your goat's beard? And what do *you*"—here she turned to Mlle. Blanche—"want of me? What are *you* finicking for?"

"Diantre!" muttered Mlle. under her breath, but her eyes were flashing. Then all at once she burst into a laugh, and left the room—crying to the General as she did so: "Elle vivra cent ans!"

"So you have been counting upon my death, have you?" fumed the old lady. "Away with you! Clear them out of the room, Alexis Ivanovitch. What business is it of *theirs?* It is not *their* money that I have been squandering, but my own."

The General shrugged his shoulders, bowed, and withdrew, with De Griers behind him.

"Call Prascovia," commanded the Grandmother, and in five minutes Martha reappeared with Polina, who had been sitting with the children in her own room (having purposely determined not to leave it that day). Her face looked grave and careworn.

"Prascovia," began the Grandmother, "is what I have just heard through a side wind true—namely, that this fool of a stepfather of yours is going to marry that silly whirligig of a Frenchwoman — that actress, or something worse? Tell me, is it true?"

"I do not know *for certain*, Grandmamma," replied Polina; "but from Mlle. Blanche's account (for she does not appear to think it necessary to conceal anything) I conclude that——"

"You need not say any more," interrupted the Grandmother energetically. "I understand the situation. I always thought we should get something like this from him, for I always looked upon him as a futile, frivolous fellow who gave himself unconscionable airs on the fact of his being a general (though he only became one because he retired as a colonel). Yes, I know *all* about the sending of the telegrams to inquire whether 'the old woman is likely to turn up her toes soon.' Ah, they were looking for the legacies! Without money that wretched woman (what is her name?—Oh, De Cominges) would never dream of accepting the General and his false teeth—no, not even for him to be her lacquey—since she herself, they say, possesses a pile of money, and lends it on interest, and makes a good thing out of it. However, it is not *you*, Prascovia, that I am blaming: it was not *you* who sent those telegrams. Nor, for that matter, do I wish to recall old scores. True, I know that you are a vixen by nature—that you are a wasp which will sting one if one touches it; yet my heart is sore for you, for I loved your mother, Katerina. Now, will you leave everything here, and come away with me? Otherwise I do not know what is to become of you, and it is not right that you should continue living with these people. Nay," she interposed, the moment that Polina attempted to speak, "I have not yet finished. I ask of you nothing in return. My house in Moscow is, as you know, large enough for a palace, and you could occupy a whole floor of it if you liked, and keep away from me for weeks together. Will you come with me, or will you not?"

"First of all, let me ask of *you*," replied Polina, "whether you are intending to depart at once?"

"What? You suppose me to be jesting? I have said that I am going, and I *am* going. To-day I have squandered fifteen thousand roubles at that accursed roulette of yours, and though, five years ago, I promised the people of a certain suburb of Moscow to build them a stone church in place of a wooden one, I have been fooling away my money here! However, I am going back now to build my church."

"But what about the waters, Grandmamma? Surely you came here to take the waters?"

"You and your waters! Do not anger me, Prascovia. Surely you are trying to? Say, then: will you, or will you not, come with me?"

"Grandmamma," Polina replied with deep feeling, "I am very, very grateful to you for the shelter which you have so kindly offered me. Also, to a certain extent you have guessed my position aright, and I am beholden to you to such an extent that it may be that I *will* come and live with you, and that very soon; yet there are important reasons why—why I cannot make up my mind just yet. If you would let me have, say, a couple of weeks to decide in——?"

"You mean that you are *not* coming?"

"I mean only that I cannot come just yet. At all events, I could not well leave my little brother and sister here, since—since—if I were to leave them, they would be abandoned altogether. But if, Grandmamma, you would take the little ones *and* myself, then, of course, I could come with you, and would do all I could to serve you" (this she said with great earnestness). "Only, without the little ones I *cannot* come."

"Do not make a fuss" (as a matter of fact, Polina never at any time either fussed or wept). "The Great Foster-Father [1] can find for all his chicks a place. You are not coming without the children? But see here, Prascovia. I wish you well, and nothing but well: yet I have divined the reason why you will not come. Yes, I know all, Prascovia. That Frenchman will never bring you good of any sort."

Polina coloured hotly, and even I started. "For," thought I to myself, "every one seems to know about that affair. Or perhaps I am the only one who does *not* know about it?

"Now, now! Do not frown," continued the Grandmother. "But I do not intend to slur things over. You will take care that no harm befalls you, will you not? For you are a girl of sense, and I am sorry for you—I regard you in a different light to the rest of them. And now, please, leave me. Good-bye."

[1] Translated literally—The Great Poulterer.

"But let me stay with you a little longer," said Polina.

"No," replied the other; "you need not. Do not bother me, for you and all of them have tired me out."

Yet when Polina tried to kiss the Grandmother's hand, the old lady withdrew it, and herself kissed the girl on the cheek. As she passed me, Polina gave me a momentary glance, and then as swiftly averted her eyes.

"And good-bye to you, also, Alexis Ivanovitch. The train starts in an hour's time, and I think that you must be weary of me. Take these five hundred gülden for yourself."

"I thank you humbly, Madame, but I am ashamed to——"

"Come, come!" cried the Grandmother so energetically, and with such an air of menace, that I did not dare refuse the money further.

"If, when in Moscow, you have no place where you can lay your head," she added, "come and see me, and I will give you a recommendation. Now, Potapitch, get things ready."

I ascended to my room, and lay down upon the bed. A whole hour I must have lain thus, with my head resting upon my hand. So the crisis had come! I needed time for its consideration. To-morrow I would have a talk with Polina. Ah! The Frenchman! So it *was* true? But how could it be so? Polina and De Griers! What a combination!

No, it was too improbable. Suddenly I leapt up with the idea of seeking Astley and forcing him to speak. There could be no doubt that he knew more than I did. Astley? Well, he was another problem for me to solve.

Suddenly there came a knock at the door, and I opened it to find Potapitch awaiting me.

"Sir," he said, "my mistress is asking for you."

"Indeed? But she is just departing, is she not? The train leaves in ten minutes' time."

"She is uneasy, sir; she cannot rest. Come quickly, sir; do not delay."

I ran downstairs at once. The Grandmother was just being carried out of her rooms into the corridor. In her hands she held a roll of bank-notes.

"Alexis Ivanovitch," she cried, "walk on ahead, and we will set out again."

"But whither, Madame?"

"I cannot rest until I have retrieved my losses. March on ahead, and ask me no questions. Play continues until midnight, does it not?"

For a moment I stood stupefied—stood deep in thought; but it was not long before I had made up my mind.

"With your leave, Madame," I said, "I will not go with you."

"And why not? What do you mean? Is *every one* here a stupid-good-for-nothing?"

"Pardon me, but I have nothing to reproach myself with. I merely will not go. I merely intend neither to witness nor to join in your play. I also beg to return you your five hundred gülden. Farewell."

Laying the money upon a little table which the Grandmother's chair happened to be passing, I bowed and withdrew.

"What folly!" the Grandmother shouted after me. "Very well, then. Do not come, and I will find my way alone. Potapitch, *you* must come with me. Lift up the chair, and carry me along."

I failed to find Mr. Astley, and returned home. It was now growing late—it was past midnight, but I subsequently learnt from Potapitch how the Grandmother's day had ended. She had lost all the money which, earlier in the day, I had got for her paper securities—a sum amounting to about ten thousand roubles. This she did under the direction of the Pole whom, that afternoon, she had dowered with two ten-gülden pieces. But before his arrival on the scene she had commanded Potapitch to stake for her; until at length she had told him also to go about his business. Upon that the Pole had leapt into the breach. Not only did it happen that he knew the Russian language, but also he could speak a mixture of three different dialects, so that the pair were able to understand one another. Yet the old lady never ceased to abuse him, despite his deferential manner, and to compare him unfavourably with myself (so, at all events, Potapitch declared). "*You,*" the old chamberlain said to me, " treated her as a gentleman should, but he—he robbed her right and left, as I could see with my own eyes. Twice she caught him at it, and rated him soundly. On one occasion she even pulled his hair, so that the bystanders burst out laughing. Yet she lost everything, sir—that is to say, she lost all that you had changed for her. Then we brought her home, and, after asking for some water and saying her prayers, she went to bed. So worn out was she that she fell asleep at once. May God send her dreams of angels! And *this* is all that foreign travel has done for us! Oh, my own Moscow! For what have we not at home there, in Moscow? Such a garden and flowers as you could never see here, and fresh air and apple-trees coming into blossom, and a beautiful view to look upon. Ah, but what must she do but go travelling abroad? Alack, alack!"

XIII

ALMOST a month has passed since I last touched these notes—notes which I began under the influence of impressions at once poignant and disordered. The crisis which I then felt to be approaching has now arrived, but in a form a hundred times more extensive and unexpected than I had looked for. To me it all seems strange, uncouth, and tragic. Certain occurrences have befallen me which border upon the marvellous. At all events, that is how I view them. I view them so in one regard at least. I refer to the whirlpool of events in which, at the time, I was revolving. But the most curious feature of all is my relation to those events, for hitherto I had never clearly understood myself. Yet now the actual crisis has passed away like a dream. Even my passion for Polina is dead. *Was* it ever so strong and genuine as I thought? If so, what has become of it now? At times I fancy that I must be mad; that somewhere I am sitting in a madhouse; that these events have merely *seemed* to happen; that still they merely *seem* to be happening.

I have been arranging and re-perusing my notes (perhaps for the purpose of convincing myself that I am not in a madhouse). At present I am lonely and alone. Autumn is coming—already it is mellowing the leaves; and as I sit brooding in this melancholy little town (and how melancholy the little towns of Germany can be!), I find myself taking no thought for the future, but living under the influence of passing moods, and of my recollections of the tempest which recently drew me into its vortex, and then cast me out again. At times I seem still to be caught within that vortex. At times the tempest seems once more to be gathering, and, as it passes overhead, to be wrapping me in its folds, until I have lost my sense of order and reality, and continue whirling and whirling and whirling around.

Yet it may be that I shall be able to stop myself from revolving if once I can succeed in rendering myself an exact account of what has happened within the month just past. Somehow I feel drawn towards the pen; on many and many an evening I have had nothing else in the world to do. But, curiously enough, of late I have taken to amusing myself with the works of M. Paul de Kock, which I read in German translations obtained from a wretched local library. These works I cannot abide, yet I read them, and find myself marvelling that I should be doing so. Somehow I seem to be afraid of any *serious* book—afraid of permitting any *serious* preoccupation to break the spell of the passing moment. So dear to me is the formless dream of which I have spoken, so dear to me are the impressions which it has left behind it, that I fear to touch the vision with anything new, lest it should dissolve in smoke. But *is* it so dear to me? Yes, it *is* dear to me, and will ever be fresh in my recollections—even forty years hence. . . .

So let me write of it, but only partially, and in a more abridged form than my full impressions might warrant.

First of all, let me conclude the history of the Grandmother. Next day she lost every gülden that she possessed. Things were bound to happen so, for persons of her type who have once entered upon that road descend it with ever-increasing rapidity, even as a sledge descends a toboggan-slide. All day until eight o'clock that evening did she play; and though I personally did not witness her exploits, I learnt of them later through report.

All that day Potapitch remained in attendance upon her; but the Poles who directed her play she changed more than once. As a beginning she dismissed her Pole of the previous day—the Pole whose hair she had pulled—and took to herself another one; but the latter proved worse even than the former, and incurred dismissal in favour of the first Pole, who, during the time of his unemployment, had nevertheless hovered around the Grandmother's chair, and from time to time obtruded his head over her shoulder. At length the old lady became desperate, for the second Pole, when dismissed, imitated his predecessor by declining to go away; with the result that one Pole remained standing on the right of the victim, and the other on her left; from which vantage points the pair quarrelled, abused each other concerning the stakes and rounds, and exchanged the epithet "laidak"[1] and other Polish terms of endearment. Finally they effected a mutual reconciliation, and, tossing the money about anyhow, played simply at random. Once more quarrelling, each of them staked money on his own side of the Grandmother's chair (for instance, the one Pole staked upon the red, and the other one upon the black), until they had so confused and browbeaten the old lady that, nearly weeping, she was forced to appeal to the head croupier for protection, and to have the two Poles expelled. No time was lost in this being done, despite the rascals' cries and protestations that the old lady was in their debt, that she had cheated them, and that her general behaviour had been mean and dishonourable. The same evening the unfortunate Potapitch related the story to me with tears—

[1] Rascal.

complaining that the two men had filled their pockets with money (he himself had seen them do it) which had been shamelessly pilfered from his mistress. For instance one Pole demanded of the Grandmother fifty gülden for his trouble, and then staked the money by the side of her stake. She happened to win; whereupon he cried out that the winning stake was his, and hers the loser. As soon as the two Poles had been expelled, Potapitch left the room, and reported to the authorities that the men's pockets were full of gold; and, on the Grandmother also requesting the head croupier to look into the affair, the police made their appearance, and, despite the protests of the Poles (who, indeed, had been caught redhanded), their pockets were turned inside out, and the contents handed over to the Grandmother. In fact, in view of the circumstance that she lost all day, the croupiers and other authorities of the Casino showed her every attention; and on her fame spreading through the town, visitors of every nationality—even the most knowing of them, the most distinguished—crowded to get a glimpse of "la vieille comtesse russe, tombée en enfance," who had lost "so many millions."

Yet with the money which the authorities restored to her from the pockets of the Poles the Grandmother effected very, very little, for there soon arrived to take his countrymen's place a third Pole—a man who could speak Russian fluently, was dressed like a gentleman (albeit in lacqueyish fashion), and sported a huge moustache. Though polite enough to the old lady, he took a high hand with the bystanders. In short, he offered himself less as a servant than as an *entertainer*. After each round he would turn to the old lady, and swear terrible oaths to the effect that he was a "Polish gentleman of honour" who would scorn to take a kopeck of her money; and though he repeated these oaths so often that at length she grew alarmed, he had her play in hand, and began to win on her behalf; wherefore she felt that she could not well get rid of him. An hour later the two Poles who, earlier in the day, had been expelled from the Casino made a reappearance behind the old lady's chair, and renewed their offers of service—even if it were only to be sent on messages; but from Potapitch I subsequently had it that between these rascals and the said "gentleman of honour" there passed a wink, as well as that the latter put something into their hands. Next, since the Grandmother had not yet lunched—she had scarcely for a moment left her chair—one of the two Poles ran to the restaurant of the Casino, and brought her thence a cup of soup, and afterwards some tea. In fact, *both* the Poles hastened to perform this office. Finally, towards the close of the day, when it was clear that the Grandmother was about to play her last bank-note, there could be seen standing behind her chair no fewer than six natives of Poland—persons who, as yet, had been neither audible nor visible; and as soon as ever the old lady played the note in question, they took no further notice of her, but pushed their way past her chair to the table, seized the money, and staked it—shouting and disputing the while, and arguing with the "gentleman of honour" (who also had forgotten the Grandmother's existence), as though he were their equal. Even when the Grandmother had lost her all, and was returning (about eight o'clock) to the hotel, some three or four Poles could not bring themselves to leave her, but went on running beside her chair and volubly protesting that the Grandmother had cheated them, and that she ought to be made to surrender what was not her own. Thus the party arrived at the hotel; whence, presently, the gang of rascals was ejected neck and crop.

According to Potapitch's calculations, the Grandmother lost, that day, a total of ninety thousand roubles, in addition to the money which she had lost the day before. Every paper security which she had brought with her—five per cent. bonds, internal loan scrip, and what not—she had changed into cash. Also, I could not but marvel at the way in which, for seven or eight hours at a stretch, she sat in that chair of hers, almost never leaving the table. Again, Potapitch told me that there were three occasions on which she really began to win; but that, led on by false hopes, she was unable to tear herself away at the right moment. Every gambler knows how a person may sit a day and a night at cards without ever casting a glance to right or to left.

Meanwhile, that day, some other very important events were passing in our hotel. As early as eleven o'clock—that is to say, before the Grandmother had quitted her rooms—the General and De Griers decided upon their last stroke. In other words, on learning that the old lady had changed her mind about departing, and was bent on setting out for the Casino again, the whole of our gang (Polina only excepted) proceeded *en masse* to her rooms, for the purpose of finally and frankly treating with her. But the General, quaking and greatly apprehensive as to his possible future, overdid things. After half an hour's prayers and entreaties, coupled with a full confession of his debts, and even of his passion for Mlle. Blanche (yes, he had quite lost his head), he suddenly adopted a tone of menace, and started to rage at the old lady—exclaiming that she was sullying the family honour, that she was making a public scandal of herself, and that she was smirching the fair name of Russia. The upshot was that the Grandmother turned him out of the room with her stick (it was a real stick, too!). Later in the morning he held several consultations with De Griers—the question which occupied him being: Is it in any way possible to make use of the police—to tell them that "this respected, but unfortunate, old lady has gone out of her mind, and is squandering her last kopeck," or something of the kind? In short, is it in any way possible to engineer a species of supervision over, or of restraint upon, the old lady? De Griers, however, shrugged his shoulders at this, and laughed in the General's face, while the old warrior went on chattering volubly, and running up and down his study. Finally De Griers waved his hand, and disappeared from view; and by evening it became known that he had left the hotel, after holding a very secret and important conference with Mlle. Blanche. As for the latter, from early morning she had taken decisive measures, by completely excluding the General from her presence, and bestowing upon him not a glance. Indeed, even when the General pursued her to the Casino, and met her walking arm in arm with the Prince, he (the General) received from her and her mother not the slightest recognition. Nor did the Prince himself bow. The rest of the day Mlle. spent in probing the Prince, and trying to make him declare himself; but in this she made a woeful mistake. The little incident occurred in the evening. Suddenly Mlle. Blanche realised that the Prince had not even a copper to his name, but, on the contrary, was minded to borrow of her money wherewith to play at roulette. In high displeasure she drove him from her presence, and shut herself up in her room.

The same morning I went to see—or, rather, to look for—Mr. Astley, but was unsuccessful in my quest. Neither in his rooms nor in the Casino nor in the Park was he to be found; nor did he, that day, lunch at his hotel as usual. However, at about five o'clock I caught sight of him walking from the railway station to the Hotel d'Angleterre. He seemed to be in a great hurry and much preoccupied, though in his face I could discern no actual traces of worry or perturbation. He held out to me a friendly hand, with his usual ejaculation of "Ah!" but did not check his stride. I turned and walked beside him, but found, somehow, that his answers forbade any putting of definite questions. Moreover, I felt reluctant to speak to him of Polina; nor, for his part, did he ask me any questions concerning her, although, on my telling him of the Grandmother's exploits, he listened attentively and gravely, and then shrugged his shoulders.

"She is gambling away everything that she has," I remarked.

"Indeed? She arrived at the Casino even before I had taken my departure by train, so I knew she had been playing. If I should have time I will go to the Casino to-night, and take a look at her. The thing interests me."

"Where have you been to-day?" I asked—surprised at myself for having, as yet, omitted to put to him that question.

"To Frankfort."

"On business?"

"On business."

What more was there to be asked after that? I accompanied him until, as we drew level with the Hotel des Quatre Saisons, he suddenly nodded to me and disappeared. For myself, I returned home, and came to the conclusion that, even had I met him at *two* o'clock in the afternoon, I should have learnt no more from him than I had done at five o'clock, for the reason that I had no definite question to ask. It was bound to have been so. For me to formulate the query which I really wished to put was a simple impossibility.

Polina spent the whole of that day either in walking about the park with the nurse and children or in sitting in her own room. For a long while past she had avoided the General and had scarcely had a word to say to him (scarcely a word, I mean, on any *serious* topic). Yes, that I had noticed. Still, even though I was aware of the position in which the General was placed, it had never occurred to me that he would have any reason to avoid *her*, or to trouble her with family explanations. Indeed, when I was returning to the hotel after my conversation with Astley, and chanced to meet Polina and the children, I could see that her face was as calm as though the family disturbances had never touched her. To my salute she responded with a slight bow, and I retired to my room in a very bad humour.

Of course, since the affair with the Burmergelms I had exchanged not a word with Polina, nor had with her any kind of intercourse. Yet I had been at my wits' end, for, as time went on, there was arising in me an ever-seething dissatisfaction. Even if she did not love me she ought not to have trampled upon my feelings, nor to have accepted my confessions with such contempt, seeing that she must have been aware that I loved her (of her own accord she had allowed me to tell her as much). Of course the situation between us had arisen in a curious manner. About two months ago I had noticed that she had a desire to make me her friend, her confidant—that she was making trial of me for the purpose; but for some reason or another the desired result had never come about, and we had fallen into the present strange relations, which had led me to address her as I had done. At the same time, if my love was distasteful to her, why had she not *forbidden* me to speak of it to her?

But she had not so forbidden me. On the contrary, there had been occasions when she had even *invited* me to speak. Of course, this might have been done out of sheer wantonness, for I well knew—I had remarked it only too often!—that, after listening to what I had to say, and angering me almost beyond endurance, she loved suddenly to torture me with some fresh outburst of contempt and aloofness. Yet she must have known that I could not live without her. Three days had elapsed since the affair with the Baron, and I could bear the severance no longer. When, that afternoon, I met her near the Casino, my heart almost made me faint, it beat so violently. She too could not live without me, for had she not said that she had *need* of me? Or had that too been spoken in jest?

That she had a secret of some kind there could be no doubt. What she had said to the Grandmother had stabbed me to the heart. On a thousand occasions I had challenged her to be open with me, nor could she have been ignorant that I was ready to give my very life for her. Yet always she had kept me at a distance with that contemptuous air of hers; or else she had demanded of me, in lieu of the life which I offered to lay at her feet, such escapades as I had perpetrated with the Baron. Ah, was it not torture to me, all this? For could it be that her whole world was bound up with the Frenchman? What, too, about Mr. Astley? The affair was inexplicable throughout. My God, what distress it caused me!

Arrived home, I, in a fit of frenzy, indited the following:

"Polina Alexandrovna, I can see that there is approaching us an exposure which will involve you too. For the last time I ask of you—have you, or have you not, any need of my life? If you have, then make such dispositions as you wish, and I shall always be discoverable in my room if required. If you have need of my life, write or send for me."

I sealed the letter, and dispatched it by the hand of a corridor lacquey, with orders to hand it to the addressee in person. Though I expected no answer, scarcely three minutes had elapsed before the lacquey returned with " the compliments of a certain person."

Next, about seven o'clock, I was sent for by the General. I found him in his study, apparently preparing to go out again, for his hat and stick were lying on the sofa. When I entered he was standing in the middle of the room—his feet wide apart, and his head bent down. Also, he appeared to be talking to himself. But as soon as ever he saw me at the door he came towards me in such a curious manner that involuntarily I retreated a step, and was for leaving the room; whereupon he seized me by both hands, and, drawing me towards the sofa, and seating himself thereon, he forced me to sit down on a chair opposite him. Then, without letting go of my hands, he exclaimed with quivering lips and a sparkle of tears on his eyelashes:

" Oh, Alexis Ivanovitch! Save me, save me! Have some mercy upon me! "

For a long time I could not make out what he meant, although he kept talking and talking, and constantly repeating to himself, " Have mercy, mercy! " At length, however, I divined that he was expecting me to give him something in the nature of advice—or, rather, that, deserted by every one, and overwhelmed with grief and apprehension, he had bethought himself of my existence, and sent for me to relieve his feelings by talking and talking and talking.

In fact, he was in such a confused and despondent state of mind that, clasping his hands together, he actually went down upon his knees and begged me to go to Mlle. Blanche, and beseech and advise her to return to him, and to accept him in marriage."

" But, General," I exclaimed, " possibly Mlle. Blanche has scarcely even remarked my existence? What could *I* do with her? "

It was in vain that I protested, for he could understand nothing that was said to him. Next he started talking about the Grandmother, but always in a disconnected sort of fashion—his one thought being to send for the police.

"In Russia," said he, suddenly boiling over with indignation, "or in any well-ordered State where there exists a government, old women like my mother are placed under proper guardianship. Yes, my good sir," he went on, relapsing into a scolding tone as he leapt to his feet and started to pace the room, "do you not know this" (he seemed to be addressing some imaginary auditor in the corner) "—do you not know this, that in Russia old women like her are subjected to restraint, the devil take them?" Again he threw himself down upon the sofa.

A minute later, though sobbing and almost breathless, he managed to gasp out that Mlle. Blanche had refused to marry him, for the reason that the Grandmother had turned up in place of a telegram, and it was therefore clear that he had no inheritance to look for. Evidently he supposed that I had hitherto been in entire ignorance of all this. Again, when I referred to De Griers, the General made a gesture of despair. "He has gone away," he said, "and everything which I possess is mortgaged to him. I stand stripped to my skin. Even of the money which you brought me from Paris I know not if seven hundred francs be left. Of course that sum will do to go on with, but, as regards the future, I know nothing, I know nothing."

"Then how will you pay your hotel bill?" I cried in consternation. "And what shall you do afterwards?"

He looked at me vaguely, but it was clear that he had not understood—perhaps had not even heard—my questions. Then I tried to get him to speak of Polina and the children, but he only returned brief answers of "Yes, yes," and again started to maunder about the Prince, and the likelihood of the latter marrying Mlle. Blanche. "What on earth am I to do?" he concluded. "What on earth am I to do? Is not this ingratitude? Is it not sheer ingratitude?" And he burst into tears.

Nothing could be done with such a man. Yet to leave him alone was dangerous, for something might happen to him. I withdrew from his rooms for a little while, but warned the nursemaid to keep an eye upon him, as well as exchanged a word with the corridor lacquey (a very talkative fellow), who likewise promised to remain on the look-out.

Hardly had I left the General when Potapitch approached me with a summons from the Grandmother. It was now eight o'clock, and she had returned from the Casino after finally losing all that she possessed. I found her sitting in her chair—much distressed and evidently fatigued. Presently Martha brought her up a cup of tea, and forced her to drink it; yet even then I could detect in the old lady's tone and manner a great change.

"Good evening, Alexis Ivanovitch," she said slowly, with her head drooping. "Pardon me for disturbing you again. Yes, you must pardon an old, old woman like myself, for I have left behind me all that I possess —nearly a hundred thousand roubles! You did quite right in declining to come with me this evening. Now I am without money—without a single groat. But I must not delay a moment; I must leave by the 9.30 train. I have sent for that English friend of yours, and am going to beg of him three thousand francs for a week. Please try and persuade him to think nothing of it, nor yet to refuse me, for I am still a rich woman who possesses three villages and a couple of mansions. Yes, the money shall be found, for I have not yet squandered *everything*. I tell you this in order that he may have no doubts about—— Ah, but here he is! Clearly he is a good fellow."

True enough, Astley had come hot-foot on receiving the Grandmother's appeal. Scarcely stopping even to reflect, and with scarcely a word, he counted out the three thousand francs under a note of hand which she duly signed. Then, his business done, he bowed, and lost no time in taking his departure.

"You too leave me, Alexis Ivanovitch," said the Grandmother. "All my bones are aching, and I still have an hour in which to rest. Do not be hard upon me, old fool that I am. Never again shall I blame young people for being frivolous. I should think it wrong even to blame that unhappy General of yours. Nevertheless I do not mean to let him have any of my money (which is all that he desires), for the reason that I look upon him as a perfect blockhead, and consider myself, simpleton though I be, at least wiser than *he* is. How surely does God visit old age, and punish it for its presumption! Well, good-bye. Martha, come and lift me up."

However, I had a mind to see the old lady off; and, moreover, I was in an expectant frame of mind—somehow I kept thinking that *something* was going to happen; wherefore I could not rest quietly in my room, but stepped out into the corridor, and then into the Chestnut Avenue for a few minutes' stroll. My letter to Polina had been clear and firm, and the present crisis, I felt sure, would prove final. I had heard of De Griers' departure, and, however much Polina might reject me as a *friend*, she might not reject me altogether as a *servant*. She would need me to fetch and carry for her, and I was ready to do so. How could it have been otherwise?

Towards the hour of the train's departure I hastened to the station, and put the Grandmother into her compartment—she and her party occupying a reserved family saloon.

"Thanks for your disinterested assistance," she said at parting. "Oh, and please remind Prascovia of what I said to her last night. I expect soon to see her."

Then I returned home. As I was passing the door of the General's suite, I met the nursemaid, and inquired after her master. "There is nothing new to report, sir," she replied quietly. Nevertheless I decided to enter, and was just doing so when I halted thunderstruck on the threshold. For before me I beheld the General and Mlle. Blanche — laughing gaily at one another! while beside them, on the sofa, there was seated her mother. Clearly the General was almost out of his mind with joy, for he was talking all sorts of nonsense, and bubbling over with a long-drawn, nervous laugh—a laugh which twisted his face into innumerable wrinkles, and caused his eyes almost to disappear.

Afterwards I learnt from Mlle. Blanche herself that, after dismissing the Prince and hearing of the General's tears, she bethought her of going to comfort the old man, and had just arrived for the purpose when I entered. Fortunately the poor General did not know that his fate had been decided—that Mlle. had long ago packed her trunks in readiness for the first morning train to Paris!

Hesitating a moment on the threshold I changed my mind as to entering, and departed unnoticed. Ascending to my own room, and opening the door, I perceived in the semi-darkness a figure seated on a chair in the corner by the window. The figure did not rise when I entered, so I approached it swiftly, peered at it closely, and felt my heart almost stop beating. The figure was Polina!

XIV

The shock made me utter an exclamation.

"What is the matter? What is the matter?" she asked in a strange voice. She was looking pale, and her eyes were dim.

"What is the matter?" I re-echoed. "Why, the fact that you are *here!*"

"If I am here, I have come with all that I have to bring," she said. "Such has always been my way, as you shall presently see. Please light a candle."

I did so; whereupon she rose, approached the table, and laid upon it an open letter.

"Read it," she added.

"It is De Griers' handwriting!" I cried as I seized the document. My hands were so tremulous that the lines on the pages danced before my eyes. Although, at this distance of time, I have forgotten the exact phraseology of the missive, I append, if not the precise words, at all events the general sense.

"Mademoiselle," the document ran, "certain untoward circumstances compel me to depart in haste. Of course, you have of yourself remarked that hitherto

I have always refrained from having any final explanation with you, for the reason that I could not well state the whole circumstances; and now to my difficulties the advent of the aged Grandmother, coupled with her subsequent proceedings, has put the final touch. Also, the involved state of my affairs forbids me to write with any finality concerning those hopes of ultimate bliss upon which, for a long while past, I have permitted myself to feed. I regret the past, but at the same time hope that in my conduct you have never been able to detect anything that was unworthy of a gentleman and a man of honour. Having lost, however, almost the whole of my money in debts incurred by your stepfather, I find myself driven to the necessity of saving the remainder; wherefore I have instructed certain friends of mine in St. Petersburg to arrange for the sale of all the property which has been mortgaged to myself. At the same time, knowing that, in addition, your frivolous stepfather has squandered money which is exclusively yours, I have decided to absolve him from a certain moiety of the mortgages on his property, in order that you may be in a position to recover of him what you have lost, by suing him in legal fashion. I trust, therefore, that, as matters now stand, this action of mine may bring you some advantage. I trust also that this same action leaves me in the position of having fulfilled every obligation which is incumbent upon a man of honour and refinement. Rest assured that your memory will for ever remain graven in my heart."

"All this is clear enough," I commented. "Surely you did not expect aught else from him?" Somehow I was feeling annoyed.

"I expected nothing at all from him," she replied—quietly enough, to all outward seeming, yet with a note of irritation in her tone. "Long ago I made up my mind on the subject, for I could read his thoughts, and knew what he was thinking. He thought that possibly I should sue him—that one day I might become a nuisance." Here Polina halted for a moment, and stood biting her lips. "So of set purpose I redoubled my contemptuous treatment of him, and waited to see what he would do. If a telegram to say that we had become legatees had arrived from St. Petersburg, I should have flung at him a quittance for my foolish stepfather's debts, and then dismissed him. For a long time I have hated him. Even in earlier days he was not a man; and now!—— Oh, how gladly I could throw those fifty thousand roubles in his face, and spit in it, and then rub the spittle in!"

"But the document returning the fifty-thousand-rouble mortgage—has the General got it? If so, possess yourself of it, and send it to De Griers."

"No, no; the General has not got it."

"Just as I expected! Well, what is the General going to do?" Then an idea suddenly occurred to me. "What about the Grandmother?" I asked.

Polina looked at me with impatience and bewilderment.

"What makes you speak of *her?*" was her irritable inquiry. "I cannot go and live with her. Nor," she added hotly, "will I go down upon my knees to *any one*."

"Why should you?" I cried. "Yet to think that you should have loved De Griers! The villain, the villain! But I will kill him in a duel. Where is he now?"

"In Frankfort, where he will be staying for the next three days."

"Well, bid me do so, and I will go to him by the first train to-morrow," I exclaimed with enthusiasm.

She smiled.

"If you were to do that," she said, "he would merely tell you to be so good as first to return him the fifty thousand francs. What, then, would be the use of having a quarrel with him? You talk sheer nonsense."

I ground my teeth.

"The question," I went on, "is how to raise the fifty thousand francs. We cannot expect to find them lying about on the floor. Listen. What of Mr. Astley?" Even as I spoke a new and strange idea formed itself in my brain.

Her eyes flashed fire.

"What? *You yourself* wish me to leave you for him?"

she cried with a scornful look and a proud smile. Never before had she addressed me thus.

Then her head must have turned dizzy with emotion, for suddenly she seated herself upon the sofa, as though she were powerless any longer to stand.

A flash of lightning seemed to strike me as I stood there. I could scarcely believe my eyes or my ears. She *did* love me, then! It *was* to me, and not to Mr. Astley, that she had turned! Although she, an unprotected girl, had come to me in my room—in an hotel room—and had probably compromised herself thereby, I had not understood!

Then a second mad idea flashed into my brain.

"Polina," I said, "give me but an hour. Wait here just one hour until I return. Yes, you *must* do so. Do you not see what I mean? Just stay here for that time."

And I rushed from the room without so much as answering her look of inquiry. She called something after me, but I did not return.

Sometimes it happens that the most insane thought, the most impossible conception, will become so fixed in one's head that at length one believes the thought or the conception to be reality. Moreover, if with the thought or the conception there is combined a strong, a passionate, desire, one will come to look upon the said thought or conception as something fated, inevitable, and foreordained—something bound to happen. Whether by this there is connoted something in the nature of a combination of presentiments, or a great effort of will, or a self-annulment of one's true expectations, and so on, I do not know; but at all events that night saw happen to me (a night which I shall never forget) something in the nature of the miraculous. Although the occurrence can easily be explained by arithmetic, I still believe it to have been a miracle. Yet why did this conviction take such a hold upon me at the time, and remain with me ever since? Previously I had thought of the idea, not as an occurrence which was ever likely to come about, but as something which *never* could come about.

The time was a quarter past eleven o'clock when I

entered the Casino in such a state of hope (though, at the same time, of agitation) as I had never before experienced. In the gaming-rooms there were still a large number of people, but not half as many as had been present in the morning.

At eleven o'clock there usually remained behind only the real, the desperate gamblers—persons for whom, at spas, there existed nothing beyond roulette, and who went thither for that alone. These gamesters took little note of what was going on around them, and were interested in none of the appurtenances of the season, but played from morning till night, and would have been ready to play through the night until dawn had that been possible. As it was, they used to disperse unwillingly when, at midnight, roulette came to an end. Likewise, as soon as ever roulette was drawing to a close and the head croupier had called "Les trois derniers coups," most of them were ready to stake on the last three rounds all that they had in their pockets—and, for the most part, lost it. For my own part I proceeded towards the table at which the Grandmother had lately sat; and since the crowd around it was not very large, I soon obtained standing room among the ring of gamblers, while directly in front of me, on the green cloth, I saw marked the word "Passe."

"Passe" was a row of numbers from 19 to 36 inclusive; while a row of numbers from 1 to 18 inclusive was known as "Manque." But what had that to do with me? I had not noticed—I had not so much as heard—the numbers upon which the previous coup had fallen, and so took no bearings when I began to play, as, in my place, any *systematic* gambler would have done. No, I merely extended my stock of twenty ten-gülden pieces, and threw them down upon the space "Passe" which happened to be confronting me.

"Vingt-deux!" called the croupier.

I had won! I staked upon the same again—both my original stake and my winnings.

"Trente-et-un!" called the croupier.

Again I had won, and was now in possession of eighty ten-gülden pieces. Next I moved the whole eighty on to twelve middle numbers (a stake which, if successful, would bring me in a triple profit, but also involved a risk of two chances to one). The wheel revolved, and stopped at twenty-four. Upon this I was paid out notes and gold until I had by my side a total sum of two thousand gülden.

It was as in a fever that I moved the pile, *en bloc*, on to the red. Then suddenly I came to myself (though that was the only time during the evening's play when fear cast its cold spell over me, and showed itself in a trembling of the hands and knees). For with horror I had realised that I *must* win, and that upon that stake there depended all my life.

"Rouge!" called the croupier. I drew a long breath, and hot shivers went coursing over my body. I was paid out my winnings in bank-notes—amounting, of course, to a total of four thousand florins, eight hundred gülden (I could still calculate the amounts).

After that, I remember, I again staked two thousand florins upon twelve middle numbers, and lost. Again I staked the whole of my gold, with eight hundred gülden in notes, and lost. Then madness seemed to come upon me, and seizing my last two thousand florins, I staked them upon twelve of the first numbers—wholly by chance, and at random, and without any sort of reckoning. Upon my doing so there followed a moment of suspense only comparable to that which Madame Blanchard must have experienced when, in Paris, she was descending earthwards from a balloon.

"Quatre!" called the croupier.

Once more, with the addition of my original stake I was in possession of six thousand florins! Once more I looked around me like a conqueror—once more I feared nothing as I threw down four thousand of these florins upon the black. The croupiers glanced around them, and exchanged a few words; the bystanders murmured expectantly.

The black turned up. After that I do not exactly remember either my calculations or the order of my stakings. I only remember that, as in a dream, I won in one round sixteen thousand florins; that in the three following rounds I lost twelve thousand; that I moved the remainder (four thousand) on to "Passe" (though quite unconscious of what I was doing—I was merely waiting, as it were, mechanically, and without reflection, for something), and won; and that, finally, four times in succession I lost. Yes, I can remember raking in money by thousands—but most frequently on the twelve middle numbers, to which I constantly adhered, and which kept appearing in a sort of regular order—first, three or four times running, and then, after an interval of a couple of rounds, in another break of three or four appearances. Sometimes, this astonishing regularity manifested itself in patches; a thing to upset all the calculations of note-taking gamblers who play with a pencil and a memorandum-book in their hands. Fortune perpetrates some terrible jests at roulette!

Since my entry not more than half an hour could have elapsed. Suddenly a croupier informed me that I had won thirty thousand florins, as well as that, since the latter was the limit for which, at any one time, the bank could make itself responsible, roulette at that table must close for the night. Accordingly I caught up my pile of gold, stuffed it into my pocket, and, grasping my sheaf of bank-notes, moved to the table in an adjoining salon, where a second game of roulette was in progress. The crowd followed me in a body, and cleared a place for me at the table; after which I proceeded to stake as before—that is to say, at random and without calculating. What saved me from ruin I do not know.

Of course there were times when fragmentary reckonings *did* come flashing into my brain. For instance, there were times when I attached myself for a while to certain figures and coups—though always leaving them again before long, without knowing what I was doing. In fact, I cannot have been in possession of all my faculties, for I can remember the croupiers correcting my play more than once, owing to my having made mistakes of the gravest order. My brows were damp with sweat, and my hands were shaking. Also, Poles came around me to proffer their services, but I heeded none of them. Nor did my luck fail me now. Suddenly there arose around me a loud din of talking and laughter. "Bravo, bravo!" was the general shout, and some people even clapped their hands. I had raked in thirty thousand florins, and again the bank had had to close for the night!

"Go away now, go away now," a voice whispered to me on my right. The person who had spoken to me was a certain Jew of Frankfurt—a man who had been standing beside me the whole while, and occasionally helping me in my play.

"Yes, for God's sake go," whispered a second voice in my left ear. Glancing around, I perceived that the second voice had come from a modestly, plainly dressed lady of rather less than thirty—a woman whose face, though pale and sickly-looking, bore also very evident traces of former beauty. At the moment I was stuffing the crumpled bank-notes into my pockets, and collecting all the gold that was left on the table. Seizing up my last note for five hundred gülden, I contrived to insinuate it, unperceived, into the hand of the pale lady. An overpowering impulse had made me do so, and I remember how her thin little fingers pressed mine in token of her lively gratitude. The whole affair was the work of a moment.

Then, collecting my belongings, I crossed to where trente et quarante was being played—a game which could boast of a more aristocratic public, and was played with cards instead of with a wheel. At this diversion the bank made itself responsible for a hundred thousand thalers as the limit, but the highest stake allowable was, as in roulette, four thousand florins. Although I knew nothing of the game—although I scarcely knew the stakes, except those on black and red—I joined the ring of players, while the rest of the crowd massed itself around me. At this distance of time I cannot remember whether I ever gave a thought to Polina; I seemed only to be conscious of a vague pleasure in seizing and raking in the bank-notes which kept massing themselves in a pile before me.

But, as ever, fortune seemed to be at my back. As though of set purpose, there came to my aid a circumstance which not infrequently repeats itself in gaming. The circumstance is that not infrequently luck attaches itself to, say, the red, and does not leave it for a space of, say, ten, or even fifteen, rounds in succession. Three days ago I had heard that, during the previous week, there had been a run of twenty-two coups on the red —an occurrence never before known at roulette, so that men spoke of it with astonishment. Naturally enough, many deserted the red after a dozen rounds, and practically no one could now be found to stake upon it. Yet upon the black also—the antithesis of the red—no experienced gambler would stake anything, for the reason that every practised player knows the meaning of "capricious fortune." That is to say, after the sixteenth (or so) success of the red, one would think that the seventeenth coup would inevitably fall upon the black; wherefore novices would be apt to back the latter in the seventeenth round, and even to double or treble their stakes upon it—only, in the end, to lose.

Yet some whim or other led me, on remarking that the red had come up consecutively for seven times, to attach myself to that colour. Probably this was mostly due to self-conceit, for I wanted to astonish the bystanders with the riskiness of my play. Also, I remember that—oh, strange sensation!—I suddenly, and without any challenge from my own presumption, became obsessed with a *desire* to take risks. If the spirit has passed through a great many sensations, possibly it can no longer be sated with them, but grows more excited, and demands more sensations, and stronger and stronger ones, until at length it falls exhausted. Certainly, if the rules of the game had permitted even of my staking fifty thousand florins at a time, I should have staked them. All of a sudden I heard exclamations arising that the whole thing was a marvel, since the red was turning up for the fourteenth time!

"Monsieur a gagné cent mille florins," a voice exclaimed beside me.

I awoke to my senses. What? I had won a hundred thousand florins? If so, what more did I need to win? I grasped the bank-notes, stuffed them into my pockets.

raked in the gold without counting it, and started to leave the Casino. As I passed through the salons people smiled to see my bulging pockets and unsteady gait, for the weight which I was carrying must have amounted to half a pood! Several hands I saw stretched out in my direction, and as I passed I filled them with all the money that I could grasp in my own. At length two Jews stopped me near the exit.

"You are a bold young fellow," one said; "but mind you depart early to-morrow—as early as you can, for if you do not you will lose everything that you have won."

But I did not heed them. The Avenue was so dark that it was barely possible to distinguish one's hand before one's face, while the distance to the hotel was half a verst or so; but I feared neither pickpockets nor highwaymen. Indeed, never since my boyhood have I done that. Also, I cannot remember what I thought about on the way. I only felt a sort of fearful pleasure—the pleasure of success, of conquest, of power (how can I best express it?). Likewise, before me there flitted the image of Polina; and I kept remembering, and reminding myself, that it was to *her* I was going, that it was in *her* presence I should soon be standing, that it was *she* to whom I should soon be able to relate and show everything. Scarcely once did I recall what she had lately said to me, or the reason why I had left her, or all those varied sensations which I had been experiencing a bare hour and a half ago. No, those sensations seemed to be things of the past, to be things which had righted themselves and grown old, to be things concerning which we needed to trouble ourselves no longer, since, for us, life was about to begin anew. Yet I had just reached the end of the Avenue when there *did* come upon me a fear of being robbed or murdered. With each step the fear increased until, in my terror, I almost started to run. Suddenly, as I issued from the Avenue, there burst upon me the lights of the hotel, sparkling with a myriad lamps! Yes, thanks be to God, I had reached home!

Running up to my room, I flung open the door of it.

Polina was still on the sofa, with a lighted candle in front of her, and her hands clasped. As I entered she stared at me in astonishment (for, at the moment, I must have presented a strange spectacle). All I did, however, was to halt before her, and fling upon the table my burden of wealth.

XV

I REMEMBER, too, how, without moving from her place, or changing her attitude, she gazed into my face.

"I have won two hundred thousand francs!" cried I as I pulled out my last sheaf of bank-notes. The pile of paper currency occupied the whole table. I could not withdraw my eyes from it. Consequently, for a moment or two Polina escaped my mind. Then I set myself to arrange the pile in order, and to sort the notes, and to mass the gold in a separate heap. That done, I left everything where it lay, and proceeded to pace the room with rapid strides as I lost myself in thought. Then I darted to the table once more, and began to re-count the money; until all of a sudden, as though I had remembered something, I rushed to the door, and closed and double-locked it. Finally I came to a meditative halt before my little trunk.

"Shall I put the money there until to-morrow?" I asked, turning sharply round to Polina as the recollection of her returned to me.

She was still in her old place—still making not a sound. Yet her eyes had followed every one of my movements. Somehow in her face there was a strange expression—an expression which I did not like. I think that I shall not be wrong if I say that it indicated sheer hatred.

Impulsively I approached her.

"Polina," I said, "here are twenty-five thousand florins—fifty thousand francs, or more. Take them, and to-morrow throw them in De Griers' face."

She returned no answer.

"Or, if you should prefer," I continued, "let me take

them to him myself to-morrow—yes, early to-morrow morning. Shall I?"

Then all at once she burst out laughing, and laughed for a long while. With astonishment and a feeling of offence I gazed at her. Her laughter was too like the derisive merriment which she had so often indulged in of late—merriment which had broken forth always at the time of my most passionate explanations. At length she ceased, and frowned at me from under her eyebrows.

"I am *not* going to take your money," she said contemptuously.

"Why not?" I cried. "Why not, Polina?"

"Because I am not in the habit of receiving money for nothing."

"But I am offering it to you as a *friend*. In the same way I would offer you my very life."

Upon this she threw me a long, questioning glance, as though she were seeking to probe me to the depths.

"You are giving too much for me," she remarked with a smile. "The beloved of De Griers is not worth fifty thousand francs."

"Oh Polina, how can you speak so?" I exclaimed reproachfully. "Am *I* De Griers?"

"You?" she cried with her eyes suddenly flashing. "Why, I *hate* you! Yes, yes, I *hate* you! I love you no more than I do De Griers."

Then she buried her face in her hands, and relapsed into hysterics. I darted to her side. Somehow I had an intuition of something having happened to her which had nothing to do with myself. She was like a person temporarily insane.

"Buy me, would you, would you? Would you buy me for fifty thousand francs as De Griers did?" she gasped between her convulsive sobs.

I clasped her in my arms, kissed her hands and feet, and fell upon my knees before her.

Presently the hysterical fit passed away, and, laying her hands upon my shoulders, she gazed for a while into my face, as though trying to read it. Something I said to her, but it was clear that she did not hear it. Her face looked so dark and despondent that I began to fear for her reason. At length she drew me towards herself—a trustful smile playing over her features; and then, as suddenly, she pushed me away again as she eyed me dimly.

Finally she threw herself upon me in an embrace.

"You love me?" she said. "*Do* you?—you who were willing even to quarrel with the Baron at my bidding?"

Then she laughed—laughed as though something dear, but laughable, had recurred to her memory. Yes, she laughed and wept at the same time. What was I to do? I was like a man in a fever. I remember that she began to say something to me—though *what* I do not know, since she spoke with a feverish lisp, as though she were trying to tell me something very quickly. At intervals, too, she would break off into the smile which I was beginning to dread. "No, no!" she kept repeating. "*You* are my dear one; *you* are the man I trust." Again she laid her hands upon my shoulders, and again she gazed at me as she reiterated: "You love me, you love me? Will you *always* love me?" I could not take my eyes off her. Never before had I seen her in this mood of humility and affection. True, the mood was the outcome of hysteria; but—! All of a sudden she noticed my ardent gaze, and smiled slightly. The next moment, for no apparent reason, she began to talk of Astley.

She continued talking and talking about him, but I could not make out all she said—more particularly when she was endeavouring to tell me of something or other which had happened recently. On the whole, she appeared to be laughing at Astley, for she kept repeating that he was waiting for her, and did I know whether, even at that moment, he was not standing beneath the window? "Yes, yes, he is there," she said. "Open the window, and see if he is not." She pushed me in that direction; yet no sooner did I make a movement to obey her behest than she burst into laughter, and I remained beside her, and she embraced me.

"Shall we go away to-morrow?" presently she asked, as though some disturbing thought had recurred to her recollection. "How would it be if we were to try and overtake Grandmamma? I think we should do so at Berlin. And what think you she would have to say to us when we caught her up, and her eyes first lit upon us? What, too, about Mr. Astley? *He* would not leap from the Schlangenberg for my sake! No! Of that I am *very* sure!"—and she laughed. "Do you know where he is going next year? He says he intends to go to the North Pole for scientific investigations, and has invited me to go with him! Ha, ha, ha! He also says that we Russians know nothing, can do nothing, without European help. But he is a good fellow all the same. For instance, he does not blame the General in the matter, but declares that Mlle. Blanche—that love—— But no; I do not know, I do not know." She stopped suddenly, as though she had said her say, and were feeling bewildered. "What poor creatures these people are. How sorry I am for them, and for Grandmamma! But when are you going to kill De Griers? Surely you do not intend actually to murder him? You fool! Do you suppose that I should *allow* you to fight De Griers? Nor shall you kill the Baron." Here she burst out laughing. "How absurd you looked when you were talking to the Burmergelms! I was watching you all the time—watching you from where I was sitting. And how unwilling you were to go when I sent you! Oh, how I laughed and laughed!"

Then she kissed and embraced me again; again she pressed her face to mine with tender passion. Yet I neither saw nor heard her, for my head was in a whirl. . . .

It must have been about seven o'clock in the morning when I awoke. Daylight had come, and Polina was sitting by my side—a strange expression on her face, as though she had seen a vision and were unable to collect her thoughts. She too had just awoken, and was now staring at the money on the table. My head ached; it felt heavy. I attempted to take Polina's hand, but she pushed me from her, and leapt from the sofa. The dawn was full of mist, for rain had fallen, yet she moved to the window, opened it, and, leaning her elbows upon the window-sill, thrust out her head and shoulders to take the air. In this position did she remain for several minutes, without ever looking round at me, or listening to what I was saying. Into my head there came the uneasy thought: What is to happen now? How is it all to end? Suddenly Polina rose from the window, approached the table, and, looking at me with an expression of infinite aversion, said with lips which quivered with anger:

"Well? Are you going to hand me over my fifty thousand francs?"

"Polina, you say that *again, again?*" I exclaimed.

"You have changed your mind, then? Ha, ha, ha! You are sorry you ever promised them?"

On the table where, the previous night, I had counted the money there still was lying the packet of twenty-five thousand florins. I handed it to her.

"The francs are mine, then, are they? They are mine?" she inquired viciously as she balanced the money in her hands.

"Yes; they have *always* been yours," I said.

"Then *take* your fifty thousand francs!" and she hurled them full in my face. The packet burst as she did so, and the floor became strewed with bank-notes. The instant that the deed was done she rushed from the room.

At that moment she cannot have been in her right mind: yet what was the cause of her temporary aberration I cannot say. For a month past she had been unwell. Yet what had brought about this *present* condition of mind—above all things, this outburst? Had it come of wounded pride? Had it come of despair over her decision to come to me? Had it come of the fact that, presuming too much on my good fortune, I had seemed to be intending to desert her (even as De Griers had done) when once I had given her the fifty thousand francs? But, on my honour, I had never cherished any such intention. What was at fault, I think, was her own pride, which kept urging her not to trust me, but, rather, to insult me—even though she had not realised the fact. In her eyes I corresponded to De Griers, and therefore had been condemned for a fault not wholly my own. Her mood, of late, had been a sort of delirium, a sort of lightheadedness—that I knew full well; yet never had I sufficiently taken it into consideration. Perhaps she would not pardon me now? Ah, but this was *the present.* What about the future? Her delirium and sickness were not likely to make her forget what she had done in bringing me De Griers' letter. No, she must have known what she was doing when she brought it.

Somehow I contrived to stuff the pile of notes and gold under the bed, to cover them over, and then to leave the room some ten minutes after Polina. I felt sure that she had returned to her own room; wherefore I intended quietly to follow her, and to ask the nursemaid who opened the door how her mistress was. Judge, therefore, of my surprise when, meeting the domestic on the stairs, she informed me that Polina had not yet returned, and that she (the domestic) was at that moment on her way to my room in quest of her!

"Mlle. left me but ten minutes ago," I said. "What can have become of her?"

The nursemaid looked at me reproachfully.

Already sundry rumours were flying about the hotel. Both in the office of the commissionaire and in that of the landlord it was whispered that, at seven o'clock that morning, the Fraülein had left the hotel, and set off, despite the rain, in the direction of the Hôtel d'Angleterre. From words and hints let fall I could see that the fact of Polina having spent the night in my room was now public property. Also, sundry rumours were circulating concerning the General's family affairs. It was known that last night he had gone out of his mind, and paraded the hotel in tears; also, that the old lady who had arrived was his mother, and that she had come from Russia on purpose to forbid her son's marriage with Mlle. de Cominges, as well as to cut him out of her will if he should disobey her; also that, because he had disobeyed her, she had squandered all her money at roulette, in order to have nothing more to leave to him. "Oh, these Russians!" exclaimed the landlord, with an angry toss of the head; while the bystanders laughed and the clerk betook himself to his accounts. Also, every one had learnt about my winnings; Karl, the corridor lacquey, was the first to congratulate me. But with these folk I had nothing to do. My business was to set off at full speed to the Hotel d'Angleterre.

As yet it was early for Mr. Astley to receive visitors; but as soon as he learnt that it was *I* who had arrived, he came out into the corridor to meet me, and stood looking at me in silence with his steel-grey eyes as he waited to hear what I had to say. I inquired after Polina.

"She is ill," he replied, still looking at me with his direct, unwavering glance.

"And she is in your rooms?"

"Yes, she is in my rooms."

"Then you are minded to keep her there?"

"Yes, I am minded to keep her there."

"But, Mr. Astley, that will raise a scandal. It ought not to be allowed. Besides, she is very ill. Perhaps you had not remarked that?"

"Yes, I have. It was *I* who told *you* about it. Had she not been ill, she would not have gone and spent the night with you."

"Then you know all about it?"

"Yes; for last night she was to have accompanied me to the house of a relative of mine. Unfortunately, being ill, she made a mistake, and went to your rooms instead."

"Indeed? Then I wish you joy, Mr. Astley. Apropos, you have reminded me of something. Were you beneath my window last night? Every moment Mlle. Polina kept telling me to open the window and see if you were there; after which she always smiled."

"Indeed? No, I was *not* there; but I *was* waiting in the corridor, and walking about the hotel."

"She ought to see a doctor, you know, Mr. Astley."

"Yes, she ought. I have sent for one, and, if she dies, I shall hold you responsible."

This surprised me.

"Pardon me," I replied, "but what do you mean?"

"Never mind. Tell me if it is true that, last night, you won two hundred thousand thalers?"

"No; I won a hundred thousand florins."

"Good heavens! Then I suppose you will be off to Paris this morning?"

"Why?"

"Because all Russians who have grown rich go to Paris," explained Astley, as though he had read the fact in a book.

"But what could I do in Paris in summer time?—I *love* her, Mr. Astley! Surely you know that?"

"Indeed? I am sure that you do *not*. Moreover, if you were to stay here, you would lose everything that you possess, and have nothing left with which to pay your expenses in Paris. Well, good-bye now. I feel sure that to-day will see you gone from here."

"Good-bye. But I am *not* going to Paris. Likewise —pardon me—what is to become of this family? I mean that the affair of the General and Mlle. Polina will soon be all over the town."

"I daresay; yet I hardly suppose that that will break the General's heart. Moreover, Mlle. Polina has a perfect right to live where she chooses. In short, we may say that, as a family, this family has ceased to exist."

I departed, and found myself smiling at the Englishman's strange assurance that I should soon be leaving for Paris, "I suppose he means to shoot me in a duel, should Polina die. Yes, that is what he intends to do." Now, although I was honestly sorry for Polina, it is a fact that, from the moment when, the previous night, I had approached the gaming-table, and begun to rake in the packets of bank-notes, my love for her had entered upon a new plane. Yes, I can say that now; although, at the time, I was barely conscious of it. Was I, then, at heart a gambler? Did I, after all, love Polina not so *very* much? No, no! As God is my witness, I loved her! Even when I was returning home from Mr. Astley's my suffering was genuine, and my self-reproach sincere. But presently I was to go through an exceedingly strange and ugly experience.

I was proceeding to the General's rooms when I heard a door near me open, and a voice call me by name. It was Mlle.'s mother, the Widow de Cominges, who was inviting me, in her daughter's name, to enter.

I did so; whereupon I heard a laugh and a little cry proceed from the bedroom (the pair occupied a suite of two apartments), where Mlle. Blanche was just arising.

" Ah, c'est lui! Viens, donc, bête! Is it true that you have won a mountain of gold and silver? J'aimerais mieux l'or."

" Yes," I replied with a smile.

" How much? "

" A hundred thousand florins."

" Bibi, comme tu es bête! Come in here, for I can't hear you where you are now. Nous ferons bombance, n'est-ce pas? "

Entering her room, I found her lolling under a pink satin coverlet, and revealing a pair of swarthy, wonderfully healthy shoulders—shoulders such as one sees in dreams—shoulders covered over with a white cambric nightgown which, trimmed with lace, stood out, in striking relief, against the darkness of her skin.

" Mon fils, as-tu du cœur? " she cried when she saw me, and then giggled. Her laugh had always been a very cheerful one, and at times it even sounded sincere.

" Tout autre——" I began, paraphrasing Corneille.

" See here," she prattled on. " Please search for my stockings, and help me to dress. Aussi, si tu n'es pas trop bête, je te prends à Paris. I am just off, let me tell you."

" This moment? "

" In half an hour."

True enough, everything stood ready-packed—trunks, portmanteaux, and all. Coffee had long been served.

" Eh bien, tu verras Paris. Dis donc, qu'est-ce que c'est qu'un ' utchitel '? Tu étais bien bête quand tu étais 'utchitel.' Where are my stockings? Please help me to dress."

And she lifted up a really ravishing foot—small, swarthy, and not misshapen like the majority of feet which look dainty only in bottines. I laughed, and started to draw on to the foot a silk stocking, while Mlle. Blanche sat on the edge of the bed, and chattered.

"Eh bien, que feras-tu si je te prends avec moi? First of all I must have fifty thousand francs, and you shall give them to me at Frankfurt. Then we will go on to Paris, where we will live together, et je te ferai voir des étoiles en plein jour. Yes, you shall see such women as your eyes have never lit upon."

"Stop a moment. If I were to give you those fifty thousand francs, what should I have left for myself?"

"Another hundred thousand francs, please to remember. Besides, I could live with you in your rooms for a month, or even for two, or even for longer. But it would not take us more than two months to get through fifty thousand francs; for, look you, je suis bonne enfante, et tu verras des étoiles, you may be sure."

"What? You mean to say that we should spend the whole in two months?"

"Certainly. Does that surprise you very much? Ah, vil esclave! Why, one month of that life would be better than all your previous existence. One month—et après, le déluge! Mais tu ne peux comprendre. Va! Away, away! You are not worth it.—Ah, que fais-tu?"

For, while drawing on the other stocking, I had felt constrained to kiss her. Immediately she shrunk back, kicked me in the face with her toes, and turned me neck and crop out of the room.

"Eh bien, mon 'utchitel'," she called after me, "je t'attends, si tu veux. I start in a quarter of an hour's time."

I returned to my own room with my head in a whirl. It was not *my* fault that Pólina had thrown a packet in my face, and preferred Mr. Astley to myself. A few bank-notes were still fluttering about the floor, and I picked them up. At that moment the door opened, and the landlord appeared—a person who, until now, had never bestowed upon me so much as a glance. He had come to know if I would prefer to move to a lower floor—to a suite which had just been tenanted by Count V.

For a moment I reflected.

"No!" I shouted. "My account, please, for in ten minutes I shall be gone."

"To Paris, to Paris!" I added to myself. "Every man of birth must make her acquaintance."

Within a quarter of an hour all three of us were seated in a family compartment—Mlle. Blanche, the Widow de Cominges, and myself. Mlle. kept laughing hysterically as she looked at me, and Madame re-echoed her; but *I* did not feel so cheerful. My life had broken in two, and yesterday had infected me with a habit of staking my all upon a card. Although it might be that I had failed to win my stake, that I had lost my senses, that I desired nothing better, I felt that the scene was to be changed only *for a time*. "Within a month from now," I kept thinking to myself, "I shall be back again in Roulettenberg; and *then* I mean to have it out with you, Mr. Astley!" Yes, as now I look back at things, I remember that I felt greatly depressed, despite the absurd gigglings of the egregious Blanche.

"What is the matter with you? How dull you are!" she cried at length as she interrupted her laughter to take me seriously to task.

"Come, come! We are going to spend your two hundred thousand francs for you, et tu seras heureux comme un petit roi. I myself will tie your tie for you, and introduce you to Hortense. And when we have spent your money you shall return here, and break the bank again. What did those two Jews tell you?—that the thing most needed is daring, and that you possess it. Consequently this is not the first time that you will be hurrying to Paris with money in your pocket. Quant à moi, je veux cinquante mille francs de rente, et alors——"

"But what about the General?" I interrupted.

"The General? You know well enough that at about this hour every day he goes to buy me a bouquet. On this occasion I took care to tell him that he must hunt for the choicest of flowers; and when he returns home the poor fellow will find the bird flown! Possibly he may take wing in pursuit—ha, ha, ha! And if so, I shall not be sorry, for he could be useful to me in Paris, and Mr. Astley will pay his debts here."

In this manner did I depart for the Gay City.

XVI

Of Paris what am I to say? The whole proceeding was a delirium, a madness. I spent a little over three weeks there, and, during that time, saw my hundred thousand francs come to an end. I speak only of the *one* hundred thousand francs, for the other hundred thousand I gave to Mlle. Blanche in pure cash. That is to say, I handed her fifty thousand francs at Frankfurt, and, three days later (in Paris), advanced her another fifty thousand on note of hand. Nevertheless a week had not elapsed before she came to me for more money. " Et les cent mille francs qui nous restent," she added, " tu les mangeras avec moi, mon utchitel." Yes, she always called me her " utchitel." A person more economical, grasping, and mean than Mlle. Blanche one could not imagine. But this was only as regards *her own* money. *My* hundred thousand francs (as she explained to me later) she needed to set up her establishment in Paris, " so that once and for all I may be on a decent footing, and proof against any stones which may be thrown at me—at all events for a long time to come." Nevertheless I saw nothing of those hundred thousand francs, for my own purse (which she inspected daily) never managed to amass in it more than a hundred francs at a time; and generally the sum did not reach even that figure.

" What do *you* want with money? " she would say to me with air of absolute simplicity; and I never disputed the point. Nevertheless, though she fitted out her flat very badly with the money, the fact did not prevent her from saying when, later, she was showing me over the rooms of her new abode: " See what care and taste can do with the most wretched of means! " However, her " wretchedness " had cost fifty thousand francs, while with the remaining fifty thousand she purchased a carriage and horses. Also, we gave a couple of balls—evening parties attended by Hortense and Lisette and Cléopatre, who were women remarkable both for the number of their liaisons and (though only in some cases) for their good looks. At these reunions

I had to play the part of host—to meet and entertain fat mercantile parvenus who were impossible by reason of their rudeness and braggadocio, colonels of various kinds, hungry authors, and journalistic hacks: all of whom disported themselves in fashionable tailcoats and pale yellow gloves, and displayed such an aggregate of conceit and gasconade as would be unthinkable even in St. Petersburg—which is saying a great deal! They used to try to make fun of me, but I would console myself by drinking champagne, and then lolling in a retiring-room. Nevertheless I found it deadly work. " C'est un utchitel," Blanche would say of me, " qui a gagné deux cent mille francs, and but for me, would have had not a notion how to spend them. Presently he will have to return to his tutoring. Does any one know of a vacant post? You know, one *must* do something for him." I had the more frequent recourse to champagne in that I constantly felt depressed and bored, owing to the fact that I was living in the most bourgeois commercial milieu imaginable—a milieu wherein every sou was counted and grudged. Indeed, two weeks had not elapsed before I perceived that Blanche had no real affection for me, even though she dressed me in elegant clothes, and herself tied my tie each day. In short, she utterly despised me. But that caused me no concern. Blasé and inert, I spent my evenings generally at the Château des Fleurs, where I would get fuddled and then dance the cancan (which, in that establishment, was a very indecent performance) with éclat. At length the time came when Blanche had drained my purse dry. She had conceived an idea that, during the term of our residence together, it would be well if I were always to walk behind her with a paper and pencil, in order to jot down exactly what she spent, and what she had saved—what she was paying out, and what she was laying by. Well, of course I could not fail to be aware that this would entail a battle over every ten francs; so, although for every possible objection that I might make she had prepared a suitable answer, she soon saw that I made no objections, and therefore had to start disputes herself. That is to say, she would burst out into tirades which were met only with silence as I lolled on a sofa and stared fixedly at the ceiling. This greatly surprised her. At first she imagined that it was due merely to the fact that I was a fool, " un utchitel "; wherefore she would break off her harangue in the belief that, being too stupid to understand, I was a hopeless case. Then she would leave the room, but return, ten minutes later, to resume the contest. This continued throughout her squandering of my money—a squandering altogether out of proportion to our means. An example is the way in which she changed her first pair of horses for a pair which cost sixteen thousand francs.

" Bibi," she said on the latter occasion as she approached me, " surely you are not angry? "

" No-o-o: I am merely tired," was my reply as I pushed her from me. This seemed to her so curious that straightway she seated herself by my side.

" You see," she went on, " I decided to spend so much upon these horses only because I can easily sell them again. They would go at any time for *twenty* thousand francs."

" Yes, yes. They are splendid horses, and you have got a splendid turn-out. I am quite content. Let me hear no more of the matter."

" Then you are not angry? "

" No. Why should I be? You are wise to provide yourself with what you need, for it will all come in handy in the future. Yes, I quite see the necessity of your establishing yourself on a good basis, for without it you will never earn your million. My hundred thousand francs I look upon merely as a beginning—as a mere drop in the bucket."

Blanche, who had by no means expected such declarations from me, but, rather, an uproar and protests, was rather taken aback.

" Well, well, what a man you are! " she exclaimed. " Mais tu as l'esprit pour comprendre. Sais-tu, mon garçon, although you are a tutor, you ought to have been born a prince. Are you not sorry that your money should be going so quickly? "

" No. The quicker it goes the better."

"Mais—sais-tu—mais dis donc, are you *really* rich? Mais sais-tu, you have too much contempt for money. Qu'est-ce que tu feras après, dis donc?"

"Après, I shall go to Homburg, and win another hundred thousand francs."

"Oui, oui, c'est ça, c'est magnifique! Ah, I *know* you will win them, and bring them to me when you have done so. Dis donc—you will end by making me love you. Since you are what you are, I mean to love you all the time, and never to be unfaithful to you. You see, I have not loved you before parce que je croyais que tu n'es qu'un utchitel (quelque chose comme un lacquais, n'est-ce pas?) Yet all the time I have been true to you, parce que je suis bonne fille."

"You lie!" I interrupted. "Did I not see you, the other day, with Albert—with that black-jowled officer?"

"Oh, oh! Mais tu es——"

"Yes, you are lying right enough. But what makes you suppose that I should be angry? Rubbish! Il faut que jeunesse se passe. Even if that officer were here *now*, I should refrain from putting him out of the room if I thought you really cared for him. Only, mind you, do not give him any of my money. You hear?"

"You say, do you, that you would not be angry? Mais tu es un vrai philosophe, sais-tu? Oui, un vrai philosophe! Eh bien, je t'aimerai, je t'aimerai. Tu verras—tu seras content."

True enough, from that time onward she seemed to attach herself only to me, and in this manner we spent our last ten days together. The promised "étoiles" I did not see, but in other respects she, to a certain extent, kept her word. Moreover, she introduced me to Hortense, who was a remarkable woman in her way, and known among us as Thérèse Philosophe.

But I need not enlarge further, for to do so would require a story to itself, and entail a colouring which I am loth to impart to the present narrative. The point is that with all my faculties I desired the episode to come to an end as speedily as possible. Unfortunately, our hundred thousand francs lasted us, as I have said, for very nearly a month—which greatly surprised me.

At all events Blanche bought herself articles to the tune of eighty thousand francs, and the rest sufficed just to meet our expenses of living. Towards the close of the affair Blanche grew almost frank with me (at least, she scarcely lied to me at all)—declaring, amongst other things, that none of the debts which she had been obliged to incur were going to fall upon my head. "I have purposely refrained from making you responsible for my bills or borrowings," she said, "for the reason that I am sorry for you. Any other woman in my place would have done so, and have let you go to prison. See, then, how much I love you, and how goodhearted I am! Think, too, what this accursed marriage with the General is going to cost me!"

True enough, the marriage took place. It did so at the close of her and my month together, and I am bound to suppose that it was upon the ceremony that the last remnants of my money were spent. With it the episode—that is to say, my sojourn with the Frenchwoman—came to an end, and I formally retired from the scene.

It happened thus. A week after we had taken up our abode in Paris there arrived thither the General. He came straight to see us, and thenceforward lived with us practically as our guest, though he had a flat of his own as well. Blanche met him with merry badinage and laughter, and even threw her arms around him. In fact, she managed it so that he had to follow everywhere in her train—whether when promenading on the Boulevards, or when driving, or when going to the theatre, or when paying calls; and this use which she made of him quite satisfied the General. Still of imposing appearance and presence, as well as of fair height, he had a dyed moustache and whiskers (he had formerly been in the cuirassiers), and a handsome, though a somewhat wrinkled, face. Also, his manners were excellent, and he could carry a frockcoat well—the more so since, in Paris, he took to wearing his orders. To promenade the Boulevards with such a man was not only a thing possible, but also, so to speak, a thing advisable; and with this programme the good, but foolish, General had not a fault to find. The truth is that he had never counted upon this programme when he came to Paris to seek us out. On that occasion he had made his appearance nearly shaking with terror, for he had supposed that Blanche would at once raise an outcry, and have him put from the door; wherefore he was the more enraptured at the turn that things had taken, and spent the month in a state of senseless ecstasy. Already I had learnt that, after our unexpected departure from Roulettenberg, he had had a sort of a fit—that he had fallen into a swoon, and spent a week in a species of garrulous delirium. Doctors had been summoned to him, but he had broken away from them, and suddenly taken train to Paris. Of course Blanche's reception of him had acted as the best of all possible cures, but for long enough he carried the marks of his affliction, despite his present condition of rapture and delight. To think clearly, or even to engage in any serious conversation, had now become impossible for him; he could only ejaculate after each word " Hm! " and then nod his head in confirmation. Sometimes, also, he would laugh, but only in a nervous, hysterical sort of a fashion; while at other times he would sit for hours looking as black as night, with his heavy eyebrows knitted. Of much that went on he remained wholly oblivious, for he grew extremely absent-minded, and took to talking to himself. Only Blanche could awake him to any semblance of life. His fits of depression and moodiness in corners always meant either that he had not seen her for some while, or that she had gone out without taking him with her, or that she had omitted to caress him before departing. When in this condition he would refuse to say what he wanted; nor had he the least idea that he was thus sulking and moping. Next, after remaining in this condition for an hour or two (this I remarked on two occasions when Blanche had gone out for the day—probably to see Albert), he would begin to look about him, and to grow uneasy, and to hurry about with an air as though he had suddenly remembered something, and must try and find it; after which, not perceiving the object of his search, nor succeeding in recalling what that object had been, he would as suddenly relapse into oblivion, and continue so until the reappearance of Blanche—merry, wanton, half-dressed, and laughing her strident laugh as she approached to pet him, and even to kiss him (though the latter reward he seldom received). Once he was so overjoyed at her doing so that he burst into tears. Even I myself was surprised.

From the first moment of his arrival in Paris Blanche set herself to plead with me on his behalf; and at such times she even rose to heights of eloquence—saying that it was for *me* she had abandoned him, though she had almost become his betrothed and promised to become so; that it was for *her* sake he had deserted his family; that, having been in his service, I ought to remember the fact, and to feel ashamed. To all this I would say nothing, however much she chattered on; until at length I would burst out laughing, and the incident would come to an end (at first, as I have said, she had thought me a fool, but since she had come to deem me a man of sense and sensibility). In short, I had the happiness of calling her better nature into play; for though, at first, I had not deemed her so, she was, in reality, a kind-hearted woman—after her own fashion. "You are good and clever," she said to me towards the finish, "and my one regret is that you are also so wrong-headed. You will *never* be a rich man!" "Un vrai Russe—un Kalmuk" she usually called me.

Several times she sent me to give the General an airing in the streets, even as she might have done with a lacquey and her spaniel; but I preferred to take him to the theatre, to the Bal Mabille, and to restaurants. For this purpose she usually allowed me some money, though the General had a little of his own, and enjoyed taking out his purse before strangers. Once I had to use actual force to prevent him from buying a phaeton at a price of seven hundred francs, after a vehicle had caught his fancy in the Palais Royal as seeming to be a desirable present for Blanche. What could *she* have done with a seven-hundred-franc phaeton?—and the General possessed in the world but a thousand francs!

The origin even of those francs I could never determine, but imagined them to have emanated from Mr. Astley—the more so since the latter had paid the family's hotel bill. As for what view the General took of myself, I think that he never divined the footing on which I stood with Blanche. True, he had heard, in a dim sort of way, that I had won a good deal of money; but more probably he supposed me to be acting as secretary—or even as a kind of servant—to his inamorata. At all events he continued to address me in his old haughty style, as my superior. At times he even took it upon himself to scold me. One morning, in particular, he started to sneer at me over our matutinal coffee. Though not a man prone to take offence, he suddenly, and for some reason of which to this day I am ignorant, fell out with me. Of course even he himself did not know the reason. To put things shortly, he began a speech which had neither beginning nor ending, and cried out, à bâtons rompus, that I was a boy whom he would soon put to rights—and so forth, and so forth. Yet no one could understand what he was saying, and at length Blanche exploded in a burst of laughter. Finally something appeased him, and he was taken out for his walk. More than once, however, I noticed that his depression was growing upon him; that he seemed to be feeling the want of somebody or something; that, despite Blanche's presence, he was missing some person in particular. Twice, on these occasions, did he plunge into a conversation with me, though he could not make himself intelligible, and only went on rambling about the service, his late wife, his home, and his property. Every now and then, also, some particular word would please him; whereupon he would repeat it a hundred times in the day—even though the word happened to express neither his thoughts nor his feelings. Again, I would try to get him to talk about his children, but always he cut me short in his old snappish way, and passed to another subject. "Yes, yes—my children," was all that I could extract from him. "Yes, you are right in what you have said about them." Only once did he disclose his real feelings. That was when we were taking him to the theatre, and suddenly he exclaimed: "My unfortunate children! Yes, sir, they *are* unfortunate children." Once, too, when I chanced to mention Polina, he grew quite bitter against her. "She is an ungrateful woman!" he exclaimed. "She is a bad and ungrateful woman! She has broken up a family. If there were laws here, I would have her impaled. Yes, I would." As for De Griers, the General would not have his name mentioned. "He has ruined me," he would say. "He has robbed me, and cut my throat. For two years he was a perfect nightmare to me. For months at a time he never left me in my dreams. Do not speak of him again."

It was now clear to me that Blanche and he were on the point of coming to terms: yet, true to my usual custom, I said nothing. At length Blanche took the initiative in explaining matters. She did so a week before we parted.

"Il a de la chance," she prattled; "for the Grandmother is now *really* ill, and therefore bound to die. Mr. Astley has just sent a telegram to say so, and you will agree with me that the General is likely to be her heir. Even if he should not be so, he will not come amiss, since, in the first place, he has his pension, and, in the second place, he will be content to live in a back room; whereas *I* shall be Madame General, and get into a good circle of society" (she was always thinking of this) "and become a Russian châtelaine. Yes, I shall have a mansion of my own, and peasants, and a million of money at my back."

"But, suppose he should prove jealous? He might demand all sorts of things, you know. Do you follow me?"

"Oh, dear no! How ridiculous that would be of him! Besides, I have taken measures to prevent it. You need not be alarmed. That is to say, I have induced him to sign notes of hand in Albert's name. Consequently, at any time I could get him punished. Isn't he ridiculous?"

"Very well, then. Marry him."

And, in truth, she did so—though the marriage was a family one only, and involved no pomp or ceremony.

In fact, she invited to the nuptials none but Albert and a few other friends. Hortense, Cléopatre, and the rest she kept firmly at a distance. As for the bridegroom, he took a great interest in his new position. Blanche herself tied his tie, and Blanche herself pomaded him: with the result that, in his frockcoat and white waistcoat, he looked quite comme il faut.

"Il est, pourtant, *très* comme il faut," Blanche remarked when she issued from his room, as though the idea that he was "*très* comme il faut" had impressed even her. For myself, I had so little knowledge of the minor details of the affair, and took part in it so much as a supine spectator, that I have forgotten most of what passed on this occasion. I only remember that Blanche and the Widow figured at it, not as "de Cominges," but as "du Placet." Why they had hitherto been "de Cominges" I do not know: I only know that this entirely satisfied the General—that he liked the name "du Placet" even better than he had liked the name "de Cominges." On the morning of the wedding he paced the salon in his gala attire, and kept repeating to himself with an air of great gravity and importance: "Mlle. Blanche du Placet! Mlle. Blanche du Placet, du Placet!" He beamed with satisfaction as he did so. Both in the church and at the wedding breakfast he remained, not only pleased and contented, but even proud. She too underwent a change, for now she assumed an air of added dignity.

"I must behave altogether differently," she confided to me with a serious air. "Yet, mark you, there is a tiresome circumstance of which I had never before thought—which is, how best to pronounce my new family name. Zagorianski, Zagozianski, Madame la Générale de Sago, Madame la Générale de Fourteen Consonants—oh, these infernal Russian names! The *last* of them would be the best to use, don't you think?"

At length the time had come for us to part, and Blanche, the egregious Blanche, shed real tears as she took her leave of me. "Tu étais bon enfant," she said with a sob. "Je te croyais bête, et tu en avais l'air, but it suited you." Then, having given me a final handshake, she exclaimed, "Attends!"; whereafter, running into her boudoir, she brought me thence two thousand-franc notes. I could scarcely believe my eyes! "They may come in handy for you," she explained; "for, though you are a very learned tutor, you are a very stupid man. More than two thousand francs, however, I am not going to give you, for the reason that, if I did so, you would gamble them all away. Now good-bye. Nous serons toujours bons amis, and if you win again, do not fail to come to me, et tu seras heureux."

I myself had still five hundred francs left, as well as a watch worth a thousand francs, a few diamond studs, and so on. Consequently, I could subsist for quite a length of time without particularly bestirring myself. Purposely I have taken up my abode where I am now—partly to pull myself together, and partly to wait for Mr. Astley, who, I have learnt, will soon be here for a day or so on business. Yes, I know that, and then—and then I shall go to Homburg. But to Roulettenberg I shall not go until next year, for they say it is bad to try one's luck twice in succession at a table. Moreover, Homburg is where the *best* play is carried on.

XVII

It is a year and eight months since I last looked at these notes of mine. I do so now only because, being overwhelmed with depression, I wish to distract my mind by reading them through at random. I left them off at the point where I was just going to Homburg. My God, with what a light heart (comparatively speaking) did I write the concluding lines!—though, it may be, not so much with a light heart as with a measure of self-confidence and unquenchable hope. At that time had I any doubts of myself? Yet behold me now. Scarcely a year and a half have passed, yet I am in a worse position than the meanest beggar. But what *is* a beggar? A fig for beggary! I have ruined myself—that is all. Nor is there anything with which I can compare myself; there is no moral which it would be of any use for you to read to me. At the present moment nothing could well be more incongruous than a moral. Oh, you self-satisfied persons who, in your unctuous pride, are for ever ready to mouth your maxims—if only you knew how fully I myself comprehend the sordidness of my present state, you would not trouble to wag your tongues at me! What could you say to me that I do not already know? Well, wherein lies my difficulty? It lies in the fact that by a single turn of a roulette wheel everything, for me, has become changed. Yet, had things befallen otherwise, these moralists would have been among the first (yes, I feel persuaded of it) to approach me with friendly jests and congratulations. Yes, they would never have turned from me as they are doing now! A fig for all of them! What am I? I am zero—nothing. What shall I be to-morrow? I may be risen from the dead, and have begun life anew. For still I may discover the man in myself, if only my manhood has not become utterly shattered.

I went, I say, to Homburg, but afterwards went also to Roulettenberg, as well as to Spa and Baden; in which latter place, for a time, I acted as valet to a certain rascal of a Privy Councillor, by name Heintze, who until lately was also my master here. Yes, for five months I lived my life with lacqueys! That was just after I had come out of Roulettenberg prison, where I had lain for a small debt which I owed. Out of that prison I was bailed by—by whom? By Mr. Astley? By Polina? I do not know. At all events the debt was paid to the tune of two hundred thalers, and I sallied forth a free man. But what was I to do with myself? In my dilemma I had recourse to this Heintze, who was a young scapegrace, and the sort of man who could speak and write three languages. At first I acted as his secretary, at a salary of thirty gülden a month, but afterwards I became his lacquey, for the reason that he could not afford to keep a secretary—only an unpaid servant. I had nothing else to turn to, so I remained with him, and allowed myself to become his flunkey. But by stinting myself in meat and drink I saved, during my five months of service, some seventy gülden; and one evening, when we were at Baden, I told him that I wished to resign my post, and then hastened to betake myself to roulette. Oh, how my heart beat as I did so! No, it was not the money that I valued: what I wanted was to make all this mob of Heintzes, hotel proprietors, and fine ladies of Baden talk about me, recount my story, wonder at me, extol my doings, and worship my winnings. True, these were childish fancies and aspirations, but who knows but that I might meet Polina, and be able to tell her everything, and see her look of surprise at the fact that I had overcome so many adverse strokes of fortune. No, I had no desire for money for its own sake, for I was perfectly well aware that I should only squander it upon some new Blanche, and spend another three weeks in Paris after buying a pair of horses which had cost sixteen thousand francs. No, I never believed myself to be a hoarder; in fact, I knew only too well that I was a spendthrift. And already, with a sort of fear, a sort of sinking, in my heart, I could hear the cries of the croupiers—"Trente et un, rouge, impair et passe," "Quarte, noir, pair et manque"! How greedily I gazed upon the gaming-table, with its scattered louis d'or, ten-gülden pieces, and thalers; upon the streams of gold as they issued from the croupier's hands, and piled themselves up into heaps of gold scintillating as fire; upon the ell-long rolls of silver lying around the croupier. Even at a distance of two rooms I could hear the chink of that money—so much so that I nearly fell into convulsions.

Ah, the evening when I took those seventy gülden to the gaming table was a memorable one for me. I began by staking ten gülden upon passe. For passe I had always had a sort of predilection, yet I lost my stake upon it. This left me with sixty gülden in silver. After a moment's thought I selected zero—beginning by staking five gülden at a time. Twice I lost, but the third round suddenly brought up the desired coup. I could almost have died with joy as I received my one hundred and seventy-five gülden. Indeed, I have been less pleased when, in former times, I have won a hundred thousand gülden. Losing no time, I staked another hundred gülden upon the red, and won; two hundred upon the red, and won; four hundred upon the black, and won; eight hundred upon manque, and won. Thus, with the addition of the remainder of my original capital, I found myself possessed, within five minutes, of seventeen hundred gülden! Ah, at such moments one forgets both oneself and one's former failures! This I had gained by risking my very life. I had dared so to risk, and, behold, again I was a member of mankind!

I went and hired a room, I shut myself up in it, and sat counting my money until three o'clock in the morning. To think that when I awoke on the morrow, I was no lacquey! I decided to leave at once for Homburg. There I should neither have to serve as a footman nor to lie in prison. Half an hour before starting I went and ventured a couple of stakes—no more; with the result that, in all, I lost fifteen hundred florins. Nevertheless I proceeded to Homburg, and have now been there for a month.

Of course I am living in constant trepidation—playing for the smallest of stakes, and always looking out for something—calculating, standing whole days by the gaming-tables to watch the play—even seeing that play in my dreams—yet seeming, the while, to be in some way stiffening, to be growing caked, as it were, in mire. But I must conclude my notes, which I finish under the impression of a recent encounter with Mr. Astley. I had not seen him since we parted at Roulettenberg, and now we met quite by accident. At the time I was walking in the public gardens, and meditating upon the fact that not only had I still some fifty gülden in my possession, but also I had fully paid up my hotel bill three days ago. Consequently I was in a position to try my luck again at roulette; and if I won anything I should be able to continue my play, whereas, if I lost what I now possessed, I should once more have to accept a lacquey's place, provided that, in the alternative, I failed to discover a Russian family which stood in need of a tutor.

Plunged in these reflections, I started on my daily walk through the Park and forest towards a neighbouring principality. Sometimes, on such occasions, I spent four hours on the way, and would return to Homburg tired and hungry; but on this particular occasion I had scarcely left the gardens for the Park when I caught sight of Astley, seated on a bench. As soon as he perceived me, he called me by name, and I went and sat down beside him; but on noticing that he seemed a little stiff in his manner, I hastened to moderate the expression of joy which the sight of him had called forth.

"*You* here?" he said. "Well, I had an idea that I should meet you. Do not trouble to tell me anything, for I know all—yes, all. In fact, your whole life during the past twenty months lies within my knowledge."

"How closely you watch the doings of your old friends!" I replied. "That does you infinite credit. But stop a moment. You have reminded me of something. Was it you who bailed me out of Roulettenberg prison when I was lying there for a debt of two hundred gülden? *Some one* did so."

"Oh dear no!—though I knew all the time that you were lying there."

"Perhaps you could tell me who *did* bail me out?"

"No; I am afraid I could not."

"What a strange thing! For I know no Russians at all here, so it cannot have been a Russian who befriended me. In Russia we Orthodox folk *do* go bail for one another, but in this case I thought it must have been done by some English stranger who was not conversant with the ways of the country."

Mr. Astley seemed to listen to me with a sort of surprise. Evidently he had expected to see me looking more crushed and broken than I was.

"Well," he said—not very pleasantly, "I am none the less glad to find that you retain your old independence of spirit, as well as your buoyancy."

"Which means that you are vexed at not having found me more abased and humiliated than I am?" I retorted with a smile.

Astley was not quick to understand this, but presently did so and laughed.

"Your remarks please me as they always did," he continued. "In those words I see the clever, triumphant, and, above all things, cynical friend of former days. Only Russians have the faculty of combining within themselves so many opposite qualities. Yes, most men love to see their best friend in abasement; for generally it is on such abasement that friendship is founded. All thinking persons know that ancient truth. Yet, on the present occasion, I assure you, I am sincerely glad to see that you are *not* cast down. Tell me, are you never going to give up gambling?"

"Damn the gambling! Yes, I should certainly have given it up, were it not that——"

"That you are losing? I thought so. You need not tell me any more. I know how things stand, for you have said that last in despair, and therefore truthfully. Have you no other employment than gambling?"

"No; none whatever."

Astley gave me a searching glance. At that time it was ages since I had last looked at a paper or turned the pages of a book.

"You are growing blasé," he said. "You have not only renounced life, with its interests and social ties—the duties of a citizen and a man; you have not only renounced the friends whom I know you to have had, and every aim in life but that of winning money; but you have also renounced your memory. Though I can remember you in the strong, ardent period of your life, I feel persuaded that you have now forgotten every better feeling of that period—that your present dreams and aspirations of subsistence do not rise above pair, impair, rouge, noir, the twelve middle numbers, and so forth."

"Enough, Mr. Astley!" I cried with some irritation—almost in anger. "Kindly do not recall to me any more recollections, for I can remember things for myself. Only for a time have I put them out of my head. Only until I shall have rehabilitated myself am I keeping my memory dulled. When that hour shall come you will see me arise from the dead."

"Then you will have to be here another ten years," he replied "Should I then be alive, I will remind you—here, on this very bench—of what I have just said. In fact, I will bet you a wager that I shall do so."

"Say no more," I interrupted impatiently. "And to show you that I have not wholly forgotten the past, may I enquire where Mlle. Polina is? If it was not you who bailed me out of prison, it must have been she. Yet never have I heard a word concerning her."

"No, I do not think it was she. At the present moment she is in Switzerland, and you will do me a favour by ceasing to ask me these questions about her." Astley said this with a firm, and even an angry, air.

"Which means that she has dealt you a serious wound?" I burst out with an involuntary sneer.

"Mlle. Polina," he continued, "is the best of all possible living beings; but I repeat that I shall thank you to cease questioning me about her. You never really knew her, and her name on your lips is an offence to my moral feeling."

"Indeed? On what subject, then, have I a better right to speak to you than on this? With it are bound up all your recollections and mine. However, do not be alarmed: I have no wish to probe too far into your private, your secret affairs. My interest in Mlle. Polina does not extend beyond her outward circumstances and surroundings. About them you could tell me in two words."

"Well, on condition that the matter shall end there, I will tell you that for a long time Mlle. Polina was ill, and still is so. My mother and sister entertained her for a while at their home in the north of England, and thereafter Mlle. Polina's grandmother (you remember the mad old woman?) died, and left Mlle. Polina a personal legacy of seven thousand pounds sterling. That was about six months ago, and now Mlle. is travelling with my sister's family—my sister having since married. Mlle.'s little brother and sister also benefited by the Grandmother's will, and are now being educated in London. As for the General, he died in Paris last month, of a stroke. Mlle. Blanche did well by him, for she succeeded in having transferred to herself all that he received from the Grandmother. That, I think, concludes all that I have to tell."

"And De Griers? Is he too travelling in Switzerland?"

"No; nor do I know where he is. Also I warn you once more that you had better avoid such hints and ignoble suppositions; otherwise you will assuredly have to reckon with me."

"What? In spite of our old friendship?"

"Yes, in spite of our old friendship."

"Then I beg your pardon a thousand times, Mr. Astley. I meant nothing offensive to Mlle. Polina, for I have nothing of which to accuse her. Moreover, the question of there being anything between this Frenchman and this Russian lady is not one which you and I need discuss, nor even attempt to understand."

"If," replied Astley, "you do not care to hear their names coupled together, may I ask you what you mean by the expressions 'this Frenchman,' 'this Russian lady,' and 'there being anything between them'? Why do you call them so particularly a 'Frenchman' and a 'Russian lady'?"

"Ah, I see you are interested, Mr. Astley. But it is a long, long story, and calls for a lengthy preface. At the same time, the question is an important one, however ridiculous it may seem at the first glance. A Frenchman, Mr. Astley, is merely a fine figure of a man. With this you, as a Britisher, may not agree. With it I also, as a Russian, may not agree—out of envy. Yet possibly our good ladies are of another opinion. For instance, one may look upon Raçine as a broken-down, hobbledehoy, perfumed individual—one may even be unable to read him; and I too may think him the same, as well as, in some respects, a subject for ridicule. Yet about him, Mr. Astley, there is a certain charm, and, above all things, he is a great poet—though one might like to deny it. Yes, the Frenchman, the Parisian, as a national figure, was in process of developing into a figure of elegance before we Russians had even ceased to be bears. The Revolution bequeathed to the French nobility its heritage, and now every whipper-snapper of a Parisian may possess manners, methods of expression, and even thoughts that are above reproach in form, while all the time he himself may share in that form neither in initiative nor in intellect nor in soul—his manners, and the rest, having come to him through inheritance. Yes, taken by himself, the Frenchman is frequently a fool of fools and a villain of villains. Per contra, there is no one in the world more worthy of confidence and respect than this young Russian lady. De Griers might so mask his face and play a part as easily to overcome her heart, for he has an imposing figure, Mr. Astley, and this young lady might easily take that figure for his real self—for the natural form of his heart and soul instead of the mere cloak with which heredity has dowered him. And even though it may offend you, I feel bound to say that the majority also of English people are uncouth and unrefined, whereas we Russian folk can recognise beauty wherever we see it, and are always eager to cultivate the same. But to distinguish beauty of soul and personal originality there is needed far more independence and freedom than is possessed by our women, especially by our younger ladies. At all events they need more *experience*. For instance, this Mlle. Polina—pardon me, but the name has passed my lips, and I cannot well recall it—is taking a very long time to make up her mind to prefer you to Monsieur de Griers. She may respect you, she may become your friend, she may open out her heart to you; yet over that heart there will be reigning that loathsome villain, that mean and petty usurer, De Griers. This will be due to obstinacy and self-love—to the fact that De Griers once appeared to her in the transfigured guise of a marquis, of a disenchanted and ruined liberal who was doing his best to help her family and the frivolous old General; and although these transactions of his have since been exposed, you will find that the exposure has made no impression upon her mind. Only give her the De Griers of former days, and she will ask of you no more. The more she may detest the present De Griers, the more will she lament the De Griers of the past—even though the latter never existed but in her own imagination. You are a sugar refiner, Mr. Astley, are you not?"

"Yes, I belong to the well-known firm of Lovell and Co."

"Then see here. On the one hand, you are a sugar refiner, while, on the other hand, you are an Apollo Belvedere. But the two characters do not mix with one another. I, again, am not even a sugar refiner; I am a mere roulette gambler who has also served as a lacquey. Of this fact Mlle. Polina is probably well aware, since she appears to have an excellent force of police at her disposal."

"You are saying this because you are feeling bitter," said Astley with cold indifference. "Yet there is not the least originality in your words."

"I agree. But therein lies the horror of it all—that, however mean and farcical my accusations may be, they are none the less *true*. But I am only wasting words."

"Yes, you are, for you are only talking nonsense!" exclaimed my companion—his voice now trembling and his eyes flashing fire. "Are you aware," he continued, "that, wretched, ignoble, petty, unfortunate man though you are, it was at *her* request I came to Homburg, in order to see you, and to have a long, serious talk with you, and to report to her your feelings and thoughts and hopes—yes, and your recollections of her, too?"

"Indeed? Is that really so?" I cried—the tears beginning to well from my eyes. Never before had this happened.

"Yes, poor unfortunate," continued Astley. "She *did* love you: and I may tell you this now for the reason that now you are utterly lost. Even if I were also to tell you that she still loves you, you would none the less have to remain where you are. Yes, you have ruined yourself beyond redemption. Once upon a time you had a certain amount of talent, and you were of a lively disposition, and your good looks were not to be despised. You might even have been useful to your country, which needs men like you. Yet you remained here, and your life is now over. I am not blaming you for this: in my view all Russians resemble you, or are inclined to do so. If it is not roulette, then it is something else. The exceptions are very rare. Nor are you the first to learn what a taskmaster is yours. For roulette is not exclusively a Russian game. Hitherto you have honourably preferred to serve as a lacquey rather than to act as a thief; but what the future may have in store for you I tremble to think. Now good-bye. You are in want of money, I suppose? Then take these ten louis d'or. More I shall not give you, for you would only gamble it away. Take care of these coins, and farewell. Once more, *take care* of them."

"No, Mr. Astley. After all that has been said I——"

"*Take care* of them!" repeated my friend. "I am certain you are still a gentleman, and therefore I give you the money as one gentleman may give money to another. Also, if I could be certain that you would leave both Homburg and the gaming-tables, and return to your own country, I would give you a thousand pounds down to start life afresh; but I give you ten louis d'or instead of a thousand pounds for the reason that at the present time a thousand pounds and ten louis d'or will be all the same to you—you will lose the one as readily as you will the other. Take the money, therefore, and good-bye."

"Yes, I *will* take it if at the same time you will embrace me."

"With pleasure."

So we parted—on terms of sincere affection.

. . . .

But he was wrong. If *I* was hard and undiscerning as regards Polina and De Griers, *he* was hard and undiscerning as regards Russian people generally. Of myself I say nothing. Yet—yet words are only words. I need to *act*. Above all things I need to think of Switzerland. To-morrow, to-morrow—— Ah, but if only I could set things right to-morrow, and be born again, and rise again from the dead! But no—I cannot. Yet I must show her what I can do. Even if she should do no more than learn that I can still play the man, it would be worth it. To-dav it is too late, but *to-morrow*.

Yet I have a presentiment that things can never be otherwise. I have got fifteen louis d'or in my possession, although I began with fifteen gülden. If I were to play carefully at the start—— But no, no! Surely I am not such a fool as that? Yet *why* should I not rise from the dead? I should require at first but to go cautiously and patiently and the rest would follow. I should require but to put a check upon my nature for one hour, and my fortunes would be changed entirely. Yes, my nature is my weak point. I have only to remember what happened to me some months ago at Roulettenberg, before my final ruin. What a notable instance that was of my capacity for resolution! On the occasion in question I had lost everything—everything; yet, just as I was leaving the Casino, I heard another gülden give a rattle in my pocket! "Perhaps I shall need it for a meal," I thought to myself; but a hundred paces further on, I changed my mind, and returned. That gülden I staked upon manque—and there *is* something in the feeling that, though one is alone, and in a foreign land, and far from one's own home and friends, and ignorant of whence one's next meal is to come, one is nevertheless staking one's very last coin! Well, I won the stake, and in twenty minutes had left the Casino with a hundred and seventy gülden in my pocket! That is a fact, and it shows what a last remaining gülden can do. . . . But what if my heart had failed me, or I had shrunk from making up my mind? . . .

No; to-morrow all shall be ended!